DIAMONDS IN AUSCHWITZ

⭒ *a novel* ⭒

MEG HAMAND

RIVER GROVE
BOOKS

This is a work of fiction. Although most of the characters, organizations, and events portrayed in the novel are based on actual historical counterparts, the dialogue and thoughts of these characters are products of the author's imagination.

Published by River Grove Books
Austin, TX
www.rivergrovebooks.com

Copyright © 2025 Meg's Writing Co.

All rights reserved.

Thank you for purchasing an authorized edition of this book and for complying with copyright law. No part of this book may be reproduced, stored in a retrieval system, or transmitted by any means, electronic, mechanical, photocopying, recording, or otherwise, without written permission from the copyright holder.

Distributed by River Grove Books

Design and composition by Greenleaf Book Group and Mimi Bark
Cover design by Greenleaf Book Group and Mimi Bark
Cover image used under license from ©Shutterstock.com/mapman

Publisher's Cataloging-in-Publication data is available.

Print ISBN: 978-1-63299-916-0

eBook ISBN: 978-1-63299-917-7

First Edition

For Luci, my life

Chapter 1

RACHAEL

Rachael dug her hands into the mud and pushed herself onto her heels, preparing to stand up. She was slow in getting to her feet. The slick mud pooled around her fingers, sinking under her fingernails, into the cuts and peeling blisters of her overworked hands. She was not expecting anything but the slime of the dirt—wet from rain, blood, tears, and any other sort of fluid that could excrete from a human in complete terror—but as she tried to connect with the firm earth, she felt something small and solid press into her palm. Without thinking, living on instinct like she had for the last few months, she closed her fist around the object and stood up. It was just in time; she could see a surly female guard readying her fist for a blow. She reminded Rachael of a foothold trap, arm pulled back, ready to strike with a quick snap at the slightest sign of weakness, disobedience, or hesitation. Anywhere else in the world, the sight might have been comical. In this world, there were no reasons for laughter.

Rachael followed orders, but the guard brought down her fist anyway, striking Rachael hard on the head. She saw black spots and felt her body sway. Her mind told her to fall, to stay in the mud, to end it all finally, but her feet did otherwise. They kept her standing and even took steps away from the guard and toward her destination.

The whole time, she kept hold of the solid object from the mud. Whatever it was dug into her hand with a sharp edge, but she welcomed this pain. It took her mind off of the ringing in her ears and the splitting headache that was rapidly descending upon her.

For months, she had been in pain. Or was it for years? It was one pain after another. Since the war, her heart was a dull ache that continued to beat only on impulse. If grief could stop a heart, she was sure hers would have stopped a hundred times over since the Germans invaded. Grief had replaced the marrow of her bones, pumping through her veins in place of blood. It was in her lungs, making it impossible to breathe a full breath. It filled her mouth, overflowed from her eyes, seeped out of her pores. Yet here she was, somehow alive, working to be set free—if one believed the words that hung over the entry gate—in this prison they called Auschwitz.

Since coming to this place, everything hurt—her feet from the shoes and endless work, her back from the wooden plank that served as a bed, her chest from breathing in the smoke and ashes, her toes and hands from the cold, and any other part of her body that the guards deemed worthy of a beating.

This, though—this pain from whatever she held in her hand—was brought on by her own actions. She squeezed hard and felt it cut into her skin. She loosened her grip and the pain eased. She was in control. She decided when the pain came and when it left. Just to confirm it was true, she squeezed the object again. The pain opened her eyes just a little more.

When she was given the coarse potato sack of a dress after first stepping into Auschwitz, a woman in her barracks told her she was lucky—her dress had a pocket. She had bitten her tongue in rage at those words. After just minutes in this place, she knew she would never again call herself lucky. The God of Abraham himself could part the double barbed wire fence like the Red Sea and she could skip out of this living hell, but she still would never consider herself lucky. She knew even then what kind of place she had entered, one where the measuring stick of good fortune was a single pocket in a dress. *What was the point*, Rachael thought, *when you had nothing to put into it?* But as Rachael slipped the hard, cutting object into her pocket, she thought maybe she could see the woman's point.

When the rock dropped into the bottom of her pocket, she felt the dress tug down just a fraction. She still did not dare look at what she had picked up, but with more energy than she had felt in months, she started toward the large pile of suitcases, clothing, and other odd possessions the guards had piled up from the newest arrivals.

Rachael's job was sorting through the belongings of newly arrived prisoners as they were dropped off at the concentration camp by the trainload. She would find small books with notes in the margin and dog-eared pages, and precious jewelry—probably gifts from husbands and dearly departed grandparents. She would sort through garments of all shapes and sizes and occasions, one day finding a silk evening gown and the next a soldier's coat from the Great War. She would tally up small pieces of gold, which took her two days to realize were fillings pulled from people's mouths. If she had any curiosity left, combing through the large stack in front of her would have been intriguing. Each day, she would find an array of items, each one carefully chosen by someone who had then been forced to relinquish it. These possessions were the final treasures taken by the Nazis, who had already taken everything else.

As Rachael sorted through the large pile, her mind slowly focused as the throbbing in her head subsided. She was used to completing this task without thinking. It was best not to think. She knew she could have a worse job—cleaning out the one broken latrine for every barrack, moving large rocks onto the beds of trucks with no assistance but the crack of the whip to speed up progress, or gathering the bodies from their bunks. This job was relaxing compared to those, as long as she didn't think about the owners of these mismatched possessions.

When she started to think too much, she would picture a fog rolling over her surroundings. As a girl, she loved looking out the small window of her family's kitchen and observing the cold fog that layered the ground. It was white and clean and softened the sharp images of the world around her, and she could pretend that just paces away from where she stood, the world was different than what she truly knew it to be. When the world around her in Auschwitz started to come into focus, she would imagine that early morning fog and let the white wipe away the pain that was trying to peek through.

Today, though, every movement clinked the small stone against her leg. Each time it touched her, she was brought back to the present. It was curiosity, she finally decided. A terrible curiosity that kept bringing her back. The monotony was what allowed her to make up the fog. But with this hidden treasure in her pocket, the day was no longer mundane. The stone was like an alarm clock, waking her up out of a dreamless sleep far too early. For that, she cursed it.

She stopped herself short of thinking that she was thankful today was a train station day. *Never be thankful for anything in Auschwitz*, she reminded herself. At least the day after new prisoners arrived, she could be kept busy and away from other locations. On a bad day, she would be assigned to sift through articles at the sanitation station. The items she sorted there were nothing but scraps of clothing, bits of string that had been treasured, maybe a stray crumb or two—the meager possessions of someone who just hours ago had existed and now no longer did.

She regretted picking up the rock. She could list a hundred reasons why it was a terrible idea to hold on to anything, even a worthless rock. She could not think of one reason to keep it. She glanced over her shoulder quickly, searching for the surly guard. The Nazi was walking between two other prisoners, both loading food taken from newly arrived prisoners into boxes that would find their way to the Nazi barracks. Rachael, still bent over the pile of clothing she was meant to move onto a wagon, slid her hand into her pocket, grasping the nuisance within. She was going to drop it back into the mud and be done with the whole experience.

"What have you got there?"

Rachael jumped at the voice, dropping the stone back into her pocket. She did not make eye contact with the other prisoner who was now looking intently at Rachael.

"You have something in your pocket." The woman pointed to Rachael's dress.

Rachael turned her back on the woman, hoping she would be offended enough by Rachael's rudeness to stop talking, but not so offended as to report her to a guard.

The woman moved closer under the guise of helping to move the clothing into the waiting wagon. "I saw you put something in your pocket," she hissed. Rachael could tell she was the type of woman whom hardship had made equally hard. "Share it with me, or I'll tell that guard over there." She motioned her head slightly toward the guard who had already delighted in hitting Rachael today.

Rachael had seen enough of the other workers take lashes from the bullwhip favored by many of the guards for even looking at an item for too long, let alone trying to take possession of it. Even if the item was just a worthless rock, a guard would not take that into consideration before striking her.

Without saying a word, Rachael reached back into her pocket. In a flash, she grabbed the rock, revealed it to the woman next to her, and slipped it back into her pocket.

"It's a rock?" the woman said. She seemed appalled that Rachael would risk stealing something so worthless. Rachael just shrugged. The woman rolled her eyes, dropped the load of coats she had in her arms, and walked away.

With no one watching now, Rachael could drop the rock and walk away. Instead, she put her head down and went back to work.

It was not until later, after a meager meal of watery soup with what she was told was parsnips and once Rachael was lying on her back on the thin wooden board that constituted her bed, that she dared reach into her pocket again. The setting sun threw rays of gray through the open window near her bunk. It was enough light to keep her eyes from closing in a restless sleep, but not much to properly examine the object. When she reached for the stone, she felt bits of dried dirt scatter inside her pocket as they broke off piece by piece from the treasure.

She glanced around the dark bunk. Women were shuffling into the barracks, heads down, feet dragging. Rachael didn't need to see them clearly to know the state of her fellow prisoners. She could hear it in their slow movements, their groans as they climbed onto their bunks, the sniffles of suppressed cries and coughs of the truly ill. She could smell it on them—the filth of their clothes and the sickness of their bodies.

"*Erev tov.*" Rachael shoved her hand, clenched in a fist around the stone, back into her pocket. The woman who slept in the bunk beneath Rachael offered her the Yiddish greeting. Rachael murmured the greeting back. This woman slept only meters away from Rachael, yet she did not know her name.

A different woman might talk in hushed whispers to her bunkmates after a long day. Rachael knew her job of going through the stolen possessions was especially fraught with gossip potential. She could share with this woman what she saw, lamenting person after person who had been separated from their prized objects. But as a general rule, she did not speak to her bunkmates. Dead people did not speak. She and everyone surrounding her were dead people, just waiting to die.

As her bunkmate settled into the bed below, Rachael reached back into her pocket. She scoffed at herself. She had wanted to lose her mind—to lose all sense of who she was, who she had been, to permanently live in the delirious and pain-free fog. For the first time, she hoped it might actually be happening. Why else would she clutch at a sharp rock in the midst of a mudhole, steal it at the literal risk of her life and allow it to haunt her the whole day? Now here she was, like a child hiding a contraband toy, uncovering it in the fading light of day. She'd half decided already to toss the silly thing away, but as she pulled it from her pocket, she saw the light reflect quickly, forming a rainbow prism on her drab dress.

It was like a flash of lightning in the midnight sky. Her life had been dark for months, but that strike of brightness blinded her. She was unable to see anything else. If she thought she had been awake from it tapping on her leg all day, now she was truly alert. She sat up as straight as she could on her top bunk, her head just brushing the ceiling.

She could see it now. It was a ring. It was still hidden behind dried mud, but the face of the square diamond was peeking out from the dirt, shining among the filth. Rachael used part of her broken thumbnail to start chipping away the rest of the muck, slowly uncovering a European cut diamond, bordered by smaller diamonds and intricate scrollwork. Rachael's breath caught as she continued to dig out the treasure. She discovered triangular-shaped sapphires on the corners of the ring, reminding her with far too much clarity of her children.

The shock of it caused her to drop the ring on her bed. She glanced around the barrack to see if everyone had noticed this momentous event. Surely, it was not just she who was changed by this discovery. But no one else even glanced her way. Two women in the bunks next to her were sharing names of some of the new transports; the woman below her was already snoring softly.

Rachael looked again at the ring. Was it just another trick of the devil's or the Germans'? Some cruel torture to make sure she was not only suffering terribly in body but in mind as well? Life worked in complicated ways just to torment her. And here, with this buried treasure, it had done it again. She had been proud of herself for the walls she had forcibly erected in her heart. She did not think of them—of her children—anymore. But the ring recalled them to the forefront of her mind.

It was their eyes. The brown of the mud, the blue of the sapphires, the glow of the diamond—they all worked together to conjure in her mind three pairs of perfect, innocent eyes.

In the waning light of day, Rachael was forced to see them, though their images were blurred, like a pencil outline. The soft brown of the mud looked like Catarina's wide, brown eyes, silently taking in the world. The sparkling of the sapphires was the baby's eyes, still the perfect blue of a child who hadn't seen enough of life yet to decide what color eyes to display. And the diamond, reflecting the muted grays and browns and whites around her, looked so much like Radek's eyes that Rachael's breath caught in her throat. It had been so long since she had seen them. She thought she wouldn't recognize those eyes anymore.

She picked up the ring, dirt still caked in its crevices. She sat up as much as the low ceiling would allow, studying each facet. Her children would have loved finding this treasure. Radek's entrepreneurial brain would have calculated its worth. Catarina would have been struck silent by its beauty. She would have held her hand open, eyes hopeful to possess such a treasure. And the baby—he would have laughed at the pretty, sparkly thing. She would have dangled it in front of his eyes and watched them light up to match the glow of the diamond.

She should put it back in the ground. Rachael could think of so many reasons to do so—it was dangerous, probably punishable by a severe beating, if not death, to be found with such an item. She had no reason to keep it. It was no good to her in Auschwitz, where she couldn't even sell it or trade it for anything. Most of all, it woke her up. She had spent every minute in this place trying to stay numb. This ring took all that away. She was no longer sleepwalking. Wasn't that the only hope she had remaining—to sleepwalk through this hell of a life?

Even so, her hands continued to clean the dirt from the intricate scrollwork and from around the set stones of the ring. She stopped before it was completely clean though, saving some of the soft brown of Catarina's eyes.

Chapter 2

SAMUAL

His mind was full of Hanna when the sparkle from the Celetna Street shop window caught his attention. The sun was struggling to penetrate the shop canopy and shine past the black shadow of the hanging Swastika flag. The bold colors of the flag clashed—*as Hanna would say*, he thought with a smile—against the mint green and gold of the buildings. Samual's unartistic eye never noticed such things until he met Hanna six months ago.

But now, that same unartistic eye was dazzled by the ring in the window of the small jewelry shop, nestled snuggly between the bakery and the Gentile bank. The muted people on the streets of Prague dodged eye contact and looked at their feet when passing the soldiers with sharply shined boots and even sharper tempers, but the ring dared to glow brightly. It dared to catch Samual's eye, and it dared to pull his future into focus.

It was obvious that Hanna needed that ring. And he needed to be the one to present it to her.

It reminded him of his grandmother's ring. As her favorite grandson, he had been sure he would inherit the heirloom when he finally found the right girl. The right Jewish girl. His mother and grandmother—really his whole family—would be pleased when he introduced them to Hanna. It wouldn't be enough to earn back the ring, though. He knew there was no going back when he converted. But maybe Hanna could help pave his way back into his family's good graces.

Not that their opinion was of much importance to him. He made that abundantly clear when he left home and replaced his Tanakh with the gospel of Jesus Christ. He didn't need his grandmother's ring to give to Hanna or to pass on to their children. This ring would be his new legacy. Together, he and Hanna would start their own traditions.

He noticed her immediately when he sat down at the outdoor café in Old City Square in the late summer of 1940. He was certain every man, young and old, noticed her. Of course, they did—her glossy brown hair pulled into a knot at the nape of her neck, a few stray hairs falling carelessly around her face, her brown eyes glowing with joy at the simple act of being alive and working at that café. He was also certain that she noticed the attention too.

He knew he shouldn't be attracted to her. She was everything he did not want. He knew it to the depths of his soul when he heard her flirt in Yiddish with a patron at the neighboring table.

But he also felt a pang of jealousy when she innocently called the elderly man *"neshama shelí"*—a familiar endearment meaning "my soul." He didn't mean for it to happen, but he wanted her to call him that, even in teasing.

He would have stayed committed to his resolve to ignore her, but then she almost burnt him with coffee. She had been flitting from table to table, effortlessly and gracefully, when she carelessly dripped across his table, spotting his tan trousers with hot coffee. In that moment, he felt more irritation than attraction.

"So sorry," she said in a tone that implied she was no such thing. "I was distracted."

He finally looked up. She was pointing to the Baroque steeples of the Church of Our Lady before Tyn.

"Doesn't it look like the sun has set Mary on fire? Like the sun is punishing the Gentiles for what they're letting happen to this city and its people?"

She was distracted by the city. His city.

He looked at the steeples. He, too, was easily distracted by the architecture of the city, but he had never looked at the church in that way. She was right. The midday sun was shining so brightly on the golden image of the Virgin Mary that it reflected back like a fiery furnace. So fierce was the glow that it was hard to look into the sky, even to see the dark steeples of Adam and Eve.

Samual couldn't begrudge anyone who found beauty in his city. He glanced up from his book to the apologizing girl. It was her eyes that convinced him that this girl—no matter her religion—was worth a second look. After a year and a half of occupation, Samual was used to the eyes of Prague's citizens, especially the Jewish ones. Though Prague, thus far, had been spared air strikes and bombings, its people walked around with the shell-shocked eyes.

But Hanna . . . Hanna was awake. Every feature of her face was alive—her eyes, her rosy cheeks, her lips with a playful smile starting to form at the edges. Samual wouldn't call her blind to the horrors around her. She saw the city as it was—both its beauty and its tragedy, its resistance and its submission.

The look was fleeting, and Samual was sure she barely noted the man whose pants she had nearly ruined. But he noticed her, and there was no going back.

It took three more visits to the café before he summoned the courage to ask her out for a walk after her shift of pouring coffee and delivering pastries.

He shook his head, pushing away the fond memories of those first meetings at the café. As much as he was drawn to her, he could not have imagined at that time that he would be standing outside a jeweler's shop, imagining their future together.

This ring was the first step.

Samual didn't believe in destiny, but seeing the ring, he saw their future as clearly as any of the paintings Hanna admired. Like a crystal ball reflecting a clear image of what will be. He saw her saying yes to his proposal. He saw the ring on her finger. He saw the veil and the wedding and their first house on the edge of the Jewish Quarter. He saw the buildings he would design and the pictures she would paint. He saw the children running through the kitchen stealing tastes from the pot on the stove.

But most clearly, he saw his city in the ring. Their city.

The closer he looked at it through the window, the more he saw Prague. The diamond was round and painstakingly hand cut. Though everything worked against it, it still caught the shine from the afternoon sun, reflecting it in prisms around its velvet shelf. The ring was all edges and angles, intricate scrollwork and two triangular-cut sapphires bordering each side.

In it, he saw the different angles of the Tyn church, its sharp steeples and straight corners. He saw the colors of Old City Square—the silvers and coppers and blues. He saw the intricate details of the shop sidings in the silver band of the ring.

He walked into the store without hesitation despite the handwritten sign on the front door declaring "Aryans Only." With his sandy blond hair and light eyes, he didn't concern himself with such signs. The shopkeeper would deal with him, especially when he showed his wallet.

The Germans had taken over the city in March of 1939, but Samual's life wasn't much disrupted. He followed the curfew. He knew Hanna avoided shops with such signs as these. And he had seen his friend David lose job after job. But his position as an architect remained firm and fruitful. His talents were needed. He was respectful to all the authorities, though he hated diverting his eyes and saluting the SS soldiers as they swaggered through the streets.

Even with the occupation, he had no regrets about leaving Hamburg. As soon as he was old enough, he had packed up his favorite books and two extra suits and walked out of his family's house. After traveling from city to city—with an extended stop in Berlin—he arrived in Prague.

It was on a whim that he stepped off the train into this ancient city of Czechoslovakia. But at first sight of the melting pot of building styles—Baroque, Gothic, and his favorite, Art Nouveau—he knew he had found his home. He felt like he could finally breathe—and he hadn't even realized he'd been holding his breath for the last twenty-one years of his life.

He did return to Hamburg once or twice over the last seven years, but never with any intention to stay. Prague was his home now. And soon he would make Hanna his wife and build a permanent life here.

He walked into the shop, and as he expected, the owner didn't mention his sign. Samual knew it was partly because the shop owner probably never wanted to hang it to begin with, and partly because Samual hardly looked like the Jews who populated a good portion of the city. Growing up, he considered his light hair and light eyes an oddity. He didn't fit in with the other boys in the synagogue. He didn't look like his brother and cousins. But as the Germans started to infiltrate more and more of the city, he was happy to hide behind his Aryan looks.

Samual knew the shrewd shop owner didn't care where the money came from—Jew and Gentile money spent the same. And selling jewelry in an occupied city could not be a lucrative business these days.

"Lovely day," the owner commented to Samual as he wiped down the glass enclosing other items of jewelry—necklaces, studded earrings, dainty bracelets. "What brings you in here, *Herr*?"

"You have some lovely window displays," Samual said, trying to effect an air of casualness. He walked slowly around the shop, looking at the items. None struck him like the ring in the window. He was trying to suppress his excitement but also to see if the shop owner was going to ask for his identification papers. The man just spread his hands in a gesture inviting him to look around the store.

"Are you shopping for anything in particular?" he asked. "Or anyone in particular?" He smiled knowingly.

From the corner of his eye, Samual noticed a flutter. It was the edge of a dress in the doorway separating the storefront from the back office. A moment later, a woman—the shop owner's wife, Samual assumed—poked her head through the doorway. She must have decided it was safe to see the new customer.

Samual did not blame her curiosity or caution. He doubted that many people frequented a jewelry store these days, except maybe the soldiers. In the beginning of the occupation, the German soldiers were good customers. But these days, Samual knew, they often paid for goods with a punch to the stomach rather than any currency.

"I noticed a ring in the window," Samual said when he had made his way around the entire store. "A diamond one with sapphires. How much for that?"

The shop owner's wife audibly sighed.

"Pardon me," Samual said, feeling his heart drop. "It is already sold?"

"No, no," the owner said quickly. "Not sold, Herr. My wife just loves that ring. I'm sure she's sad to see it leave our shop window. But that, of course"—he looked pointedly at his wife—"is what the display is for. To sell."

"*Wunderbar*," Samual said, still trying to disguise his excitement.

He and the shop owner halfheartedly haggled over the price—the shop owner was clearly willing to take less since he knew any sale was better than no sale at all. As they talked, the shop owner's wife took the ring from the window, placed it in a small black box, and wrapped it like a truly hidden treasure in plain brown paper tied with a small piece of string. Samual did not fault her for the look of sadness she had on her face.

The shop owner, though, glowed. Samual made a note to pass by this store in a few months to see if it still survived or if it, with its sweet owners and sparkling gems, was just one more casualty of this war that had found its way to Prague. He felt pride as he left the store with his treasure, not only in the purchase he made for Hanna, but also in the small part he played in keeping the lives of these people together for just a little bit longer.

"Zeigen sie mir ihre papiere!"

Samual paused in mid-thought. His heart stuttered but he forced his hands to remain steady.

"Of course, my papers," he said, in perfect German, causing the soldier to raise his eyebrows just a fraction. The soldier peered at Samual more closely.

Samual had never seen naked meanness in his life—until the Germans occupied the city. He thought he had been bullied in school, but he did not know true bullying until he first encountered a Nazi. Between his appearance and his perfect German accent, he was rarely given any trouble by the Nazis patrolling the streets, but he quickly saw that this soldier was not to be stopped by something as small as innocence. As much as he hated it, Samual lowered his head as a sign of subservience and respect. He handed over his papers.

The Nazi held the papers for a long time, without looking down. He was appraising Samual instead. Samual kept his eyes on the soldier's shining black boots, noting how the sun reflected off of them. To stop himself from looking the soldier directly in the eye or calling the Nazi "*skopcak*"—which would earn him a knock in the mouth with the soldier's Luger or a night in a jail cell outside of town where no one could hear his cries—Samual imagined the effort it must take the soldier to shine his shoes to such a gleam. He busied his mind with the image of the Nazi sweating over the toes of his shoes, of getting a cuff on the ears by his superior for a scuff.

More than anything, Samual needed to make sure the soldier did not search him and find the ring tucked inside his coat pocket. His mastery of the language and blond hair could only get him so far. If the soldier gave his papers more than a cursory glance, the stigma of his past religion would be hard to explain. Samual knew that this Nazi—as they all did—thought Jews no more than swine, rats, a poison to the human race.

He felt the burn of the Nazi's gaze on his lowered head. Unable to take the silence any longer, Samual looked up at the soldier. He offered a small smile and quickly lowered his gaze once more. The soldier grunted. Samual took it as a sound of approval. He looked up once more, with more confidence this time. The soldier slammed Samual's identification papers into his chest with a curt nod.

"Stay out of my way next time," he said. He gave a quick Nazi salute, turned on the heel of his shiny boot, and walked away down the street.

Chapter 3

RACHAEL

Rachael had never had problems sleeping before the war. Alexey would tease that she slept like a corpse—on her back, hands folded neatly on her stomach, not moving an inch. She thought her peaceful nights were a reward for long days of work. "If you did all the cooking and cleaning and caring for the children," she teased, "I could sleep more restlessly." Sleep came to her easily, like wading into warm water. Each step into the tide of slumber relaxed her muscles, starting with her feet, gliding over her legs, warming up her body, and finally lulling her mind.

These days, unconsciousness still came easily, a reward for a life harder than she could have ever imagined. But it was no longer the full night's rest of pre-war times. Instead of the gradual flow of slumber, it hit her like a flood—pinning her to the bed, weighing down her limbs. She never dreamt before except maybe soft images and the essence of moods. Here, though, Rachael dreamt every night. Though her body screamed for rest, she fought to keep her eyes open as long as possible. She never won. And when she awoke in the morning, there was no relief of rest, just the depressing notion of starting another day and another night of the same torment.

On this night, Rachael placed the ring on her middle finger and twirled it in easy circles as she willed herself to fall into a numbing sleep. Her mind was restless though, thinking of this treasure she had stumbled upon. It was clearly the engagement ring of some poor soul who found herself joining the rest of the dead in Auschwitz. It could not have been easy to hold on to the ring all these years. Why someone would go to such lengths was unfathomable to her. Surely, the woman was convinced she had achieved something—keeping that ring off the ugly finger of a German soldier's lover, perhaps. But to what end? What did she prove? What did she gain? Absolutely nothing, because the Nazis did not even feel the sting of this miniscule defeat. This woman's energies could have been better spent on something that mattered—feeding her children, keeping others safe. But those efforts resulted in nothing as well.

Rachael had grown up in Prague, spent her entire life there. That was exactly how she wanted it—even before the Germans came, she was doing as she had always dreamt of. She had two lively and loving children. Her husband worked hard and still came home with smiles and kisses for all of them. She stayed home, caring for the household, as she had always wanted. Still, there were notes of discontent. She wanted a bigger house, with more of a yard for the children. She worried about the group of boys that Radek gravitated toward after school, not convinced they were the right influence for her impressionable child. She wanted music lessons for Catarina, who was always singing nonsense songs in her sweet, soprano voice. Maybe there was a future in music for her.

Those concerns and wants seemed so silly now. How could she bicker with Alexey over trivial matters like a patch of grass or purchasing a piano for their toddler when war and death and the destruction of everything they knew was just around the corner? She lived her life in the comfort and safety of the Jewish Quarter, never worrying about what happened outside of those blocks, in the rest of the world. When Alexey came home on that early spring day with the news that Adolf Hitler now controlled Czechoslovakia, Rachael looked at him and said, "Who?"

Usually, her husband would tease her good naturedly about her ignorance of worldly affairs. She would retort with a flip of her hair that she was singularly devoted to the care of his children, to which he would reply with a kiss on her forehead.

But on that March day, Alexey had no humor in him. "Don't be funny with me," he scolded. Rachael's temper would normally flare up like a firework at being chastised like one of the children, but the look on Alexey's face stopped her from starting an argument. His eyes, the tight line of his mouth, the sag of defeat in his shoulders all showed his feelings. She saw anger and worry, but mostly, fear.

Rachael would like to go back in time and shake the shoulders of the naïve woman that she was—shake them until her head bobbed back and forth. Truly, if she was to go back in time to perform an act of violence, she'd go all the way back to the birth of the devil himself, this Fuhrer, and smother him with a feather pillow. Years ago, Rachael would have been shocked that such a thought could even cross her mind, but as she lay on her bunk praying for any dreams but those of her children, she allowed this thought to give her the slightest bit of pleasure.

Like any good Jewish girl, Rachael had been resigned to her mother arranging her marriage. She knew her parents' happiness was independent of marital bliss, so she worried little about the man she would eventually marry. Her mother was gifted, as many Jewish mothers were, and found her a perfect match. Rachael was prepared to find all her fulfillment in children, and even before the war put all the wonderful things in her life into perspective, she knew how blessed she was to have Alexey. From the beginning, he had been kind and generous. He was gentle and tolerant. But when she thought of him in her sleep, it was his laugh that haunted her.

She had been considered funny back in those days. She was wry and sarcastic and quick with a sharp wit. Her brothers and her father despised that flaw in her character, but Alexey was amused, if not proud of her humor. He would watch her with bemusement, waiting in thinly veiled anticipation of the words that would next leave her mouth. When she made him laugh, the sound would echo throughout the entire house, and Rachael could never help but feel a true sense of accomplishment.

Rachael thought she loved Alexey more than humans were meant to love one another. And she thought her heart was filled beyond measure when she first felt the flutter of kicks in her womb. But when her son was born, when that messy little being came out of her womb and into the world, she realized she had been blissfully ignorant about the definition of true love.

It was not easy, his birth. Rachael had never known terror as she did when Radek was born not breathing. He was a fighter, though, and she knew that about him from the first minutes of his life. His fighting spirit had not changed in the thirteen years she had him with her.

Though she knew many women would curse their lot in life, having only one child, Rachael was never unhappy with it. For ten years, she was sure Radek was the only baby she would carry, in her womb and in her arms. Yet she was content. He was the son to envy—beautiful and tall, polite and calm, but with that same determination that saved his life on the day he was born.

It was him she dreamed of that night, still wearing the ring loosely around her finger. In this dream, that fighting spirit killed him rather than saved him.

The dream blurred that evening. The edges of her vision became tainted with red, and she felt the burning of the terror reach her feet, then her legs, then her stomach, as she ran from room to room, over and over, yelling Radek's name louder and louder.

She felt a cold hand grip her shoulder, waking her from the nightmare.

"Shhh," a voice whispered. "You're fine. You're just fine."

Rachael was swept out of the dreamworld into this real nightmare. She was still on her hard bunk with the thin straw padding poking into her back like little needles. The woman from the bunk below held on to Rachael's shoulder, gently shaking her and making soft clucking sounds with her tongue.

"You cried in your sleep," the woman said.

"Doesn't everyone?" Rachael said back. She knew the words came out short and sharp, but the nightmare had exhausted her, making it impossible to have the energy for manners.

"True." The woman attempted a small smile. "You more than others, though, I think."

Rachael rolled onto her side, away from the woman and away from her touch.

"I know you don't like to talk," the woman whispered into the darkness, "but maybe that is what you need."

"It isn't," Rachael said, without turning to face her neighbor. What she needed was her children with her, Radek especially.

The Nazis had come to Prague in the spring of 1939. Radek, only thirteen, but with the height and thoughts of one much older, was frustrated with the passivity that met their entrance. There was no fight to stop them, only a subdued parade where German natives cheered and German soldiers marched in with straight faces and cold eyes. Rachael's plan to survive the war was easy: do not hassle the soldiers and they wouldn't hassle her. She preached to her children the importance of keeping their heads down, staying out of the way of the Nazis, and surviving the coming days in such a way.

Catarina listened. Only three years old that spring, she clung to her mother's skirt with one fist and held a small, stuffed duck in the other. With her large brown eyes, she saw all that occurred around her—the slow closing of the stores available for their weekly shopping, the shrinking portions of meat on their dinner table, but most of all, the increasing anger of her big brother, whom she idolized.

Rachael tricked herself into thinking Radek listened, that he walked home from school while looking only at his worn leather shoes and that he pursed his lips together tightly to prevent any sharp words from escaping. Lying on the rough boards in Auschwitz, though, Rachael could see that it was nothing more than a mother's willing blindness. Radek was never meant to be happy with a life of indifference.

She had come home later than usual that night, Catarina trailing like a soft, humming shadow behind her. As the supply of food grew shorter, the queues grew longer. "Food is scarce," she had told Alexey that morning before she left, "but rumors are abundant. If only we could dine on rumors." This particular day, as she waited in line, there was more chatter than before—everything from Nazis tearing people out of their beds at night and executing them in the street to the closure of all Jewish schools across occupied Czechoslovakia. When details turned too gruesome, Rachael had chatted aimlessly with Catarina, hoping to distract the small child. But like a sponge, the girl was still able to absorb everything around her.

Up until that day, Rachael had dismissed most of the rumors—there was simply no use in worrying. Either it would happen, or, most likely, it would not. Such violence and hatred and cruelty were unfathomable to her.

Her ears did perk up at the mention of arrests made that afternoon. The women in front of her in the line whispered about it as they waited for their ration of potatoes. Their voices were soft, and in her experience, the quieter the words spoken, the more truth backed them. They spoke of teenage boys rounded up in the northside of the Jewish Quarter—beaten with butts of rifles and arrested like street criminals. Their crime was vague—something like inciting public disorder or disrespecting German officials. Their fates were a mystery.

She and Catarina entered a cold, dark house. There were no lights to brighten up the winter evening, no sight of Radek at the kitchen table completing his schoolwork and complaining about his empty stomach.

Panic licked at Rachael's heels like a fire as she calmly went from the kitchen to the sitting room to Radek's small bedroom in the back of the house. She forced her voice to stay neutral as she called his name. She would not allow the flames of hysteria to burn her. She went back room to room. She reminded herself of how Radek would sometimes tuck his long limbs into a corner with a comic book, oblivious to the world around him. He had not gotten a new comic book in months, but maybe he had some good fortune today.

On that terrible night, Rachael remembered when she finally broke down and let the burn of terror take over her body. She had forced herself to walk, though her legs wanted to carry her faster than they ever had, to the neighbors' homes, to inquire softly and with deliberated slowness if Radek had happened to leave a message for her. Forcing further calmness on her body, she stood like a statue at the front room window until Alexey came home from work. Catarina hovered nearby, singing softly in her small child's voice to her stuffed duck. She cuddled the toy and instinctively knew when to transfer those hugs to her mother.

Rachael waited at the kitchen table with her hands in her lap. She watched the minute hand of the clock over the sitting room fireplace tick away the last half hour to curfew. She thought her heart would just stop beating when the hour hand reached that dreaded mark and her son was still not home.

In her dream, the clock had burst into flames when the hour of curfew hit. But in her memory, that moment was marked by complete silence. Like a canary in the coal mine, Rachael's little songbird had gone silent. She looked over at her small daughter and saw that Catarina was quietly crying, small tears coming out of her big brown eyes like the first drops before a tempest. It was then that the flames engulfed Rachael completely. She became a woman on fire.

There was no relief or escape in knowing the fate of her son. In fact, knowing would be worse, Rachael thought. Now she did not even hope. On that terrible night, as she paced the floor, biting her nails until they bled and her fingertips throbbed, she still harbored a small spark of hope. She guarded that spark like it was the last light in the world.

It burned like a dying ember until the day she entered Auschwitz. Radek was in a work camp, she had been told. She even received a letter—just one—that said he was well and working his way to freedom. Then he would come home to his family and his mother's arms. She sent letter after letter, but no reply. He was busy, she told herself. He was working hard so he could come home sooner. When she had the means, she sent small packages—neatly darned socks, a bite of chocolate she had saved from their first Christmas without him, pencil drawings from the sister who missed him more than her words would say.

The burning ember was smothered to a cold, black nothing when she looked around the barracks in Auschwitz, a place that promised freedom through work. She listened to the women asleep in the bunks surrounding her. They were not working their way to freedom. They were simply existing until death finally came for them. If she had any remaining hope of where Radek was, she need only look around her. In the creeping light of early dawn, women slept on wooden planks with scraps of cloth for blankets, widowed and childless, most of them sick in heart and body. She could hear the whimpers of bad dreams, the coughs of consumptive lungs, and the muffled sobs.

Her son was no longer of this world, and most likely had not been for years. Staring at the wooden planks above her head, where cracks showed the start of another gray day, she could see Radek's true end: shot in the back of the head after digging his own mass grave only kilometers outside of Prague on that first night of his disappearance; maybe a brutal death at the hands of a Nazi beast with a whip, who did not think Radek was carrying enough weight, working fast enough, completing enough of some meaningless task; or possibly, the slow death of one who works too hard and is fed too little, becoming weaker and weaker until one day he was unable to raise his head off of the makeshift pillow and he succumbed to a sleep that would never end.

Chapter 4

SAMUAL

Samual was confident in his decision to propose to Hanna, but like all young bachelors, he dreaded what came next: telling his bachelor friends. As they all reclined in their favorite dingy pub overlooking the Vltava River, Samual could hear his friends' words even before they spoke them.

"You bought a ring? A diamond ring?" David asked as he sat up straight, elbows on the bar table, his smudged glasses slipping down his nose. "That's crazy. You're going to marry some girl—"

"Hanna's not 'some girl,'" Samual interrupted with a snap to his voice.

David nodded his acquiescence; his brown hair, needing a trim, fell into his eyes. "You're going to marry Hanna and start a new life in the middle of a war? War. Samual."

"Who cares about the war?" Werner said the last word as if it was part of a fairy tale. Unlike David's lanky locks, Werner's hair was short, combed severely to the side, in the style popular with the thousands of soldiers invading the streets of Prague. "Why get married at all?" He took a long drink of his watered-down coffee, making a face that clearly said he wished it were a beer. "Look around you, Samual. Hanna's great, don't mistake me. But there are so many girls in the world. In Prague. Why rush?"

Samual smiled to himself. These words from a man who was not far away from buying his own engagement ring.

"I don't want any other girl," he said simply. "And as for the war . . ." He looked at David, who slouched back into his chair. Samual shrugged as if that was the answer to all David's concerns. "Look at me." Samual gestured to his face, his light hair. He winked. Both of his friends rolled their eyes. "I speak perfect German. Obviously. I've converted to the faith of the Fuhrer." At the mention of Adolf Hitler, Samual smiled to show his sarcasm, and David's amused expression darkened. "I can even recite the Lord's Prayer and at least half a dozen of Luther's theses. Can you do that, Werner?"

His fellow German friend laughed.

"What if you are conscripted?" Werner asked. "What happens to your young, beautiful wife then?" He waggled his blond eyebrows at Samual.

"True," Samual acknowledged. "But the Germans have been in Prague for almost two years, and no one's made a move to transport me to the front lines."

"You're a Jew. If they send you somewhere, I assure you, it won't be the front lines," David said with no humor in his voice.

Samual ignored his friend. His father was a Jew; he was not. At least, he was not anymore. "I'm an architect. I can easily persuade the Nazis to put me in a planning office with a pencil and a drafting table rather than on a battlefield with a gun and bayonet."

"Like anyone would trust you with a gun," Werner said before taking another drink of coffee and making the same face as before. Samual was tempted to remove the cup from Werner's reach as a kindness.

"You keep forgetting the most important part," David said. He sat up again. His dark eyes widened. "You. Are. A. Jew."

Samual shook his head.

"Yes, this place, this city"—David motioned to the river and town outside the pub window—"used to be a sanctuary for the Jews. Now, it's one of Dante's seven circles of hell."

Maybe David was being dramatic, but he wasn't completely wrong. Hanna said it well a few nights ago, comparing the people to frogs in a kettle. "The water's being slowly heated," she had said. "The people don't even realize they're boiling."

As much as he would like to ignore the suffering of the Jews, he had to admit that he saw it. He knew he would never forget that cold morning in March. He expected to wake up to the bustling sounds of Prague as he did every morning, but it had all suddenly disappeared. There was no happy ring in the street. There was not even the sound of alarm, confusion, disarray, or fear, as Samual would have thought.

The night before, he had been a free man in a free city, enjoying a brew with his friends after a long, productive day at a job he found meaningful. The next morning, he was a branded man in an occupied city, where the people were, at best, indifferent to his fate. That was the part he could never understand, maybe never forgive: the city's indifference. On that morning in March, there was no fight. No resistance. No protestations.

Just silence.

Ever since Germany had been given Sudetenland by the British, the citizens of Prague had hoped that Hitler's greed was satiated. But they remained always distrustful; the Czech borders became heavily guarded by soldiers. Their favorite saying rang through the entire country: "We shall not surrender a centimeter of Czech soil."

And yes, it was true that they didn't surrender a centimeter—they gave up the entire country with the swipe of a pen.

As far as Samual could tell on those first few days, very few people seemed to care.

Samual had watched from a street corner, his back pressed against the wall, his face covered in the shadow of the storefront awnings, when the Nazis goose-stepped through the streets. He could hear the cheers from German university students at the city's entrance—they celebrated the arrival of their countrymen. They were the only ones making much noise. The Nazis were eerily silent, the synchronized clip of their boots the only sound. The soldiers' eyes stared straight ahead, expressionless. They reminded Samual less of human beings and more of wind-up toys.

A few women on the street waved supporting flags. A woman in a fashionable jacket and a black wool hat with a silver brooch shed tears of happiness. She alternated between using her white handkerchief to dab the tears daintily from the corner of her eyes and waving it to the soldiers as they marched past. She smiled through her tears at Samual.

"The Germans," she said dreamily. "They are here to liberate Prague." She waited expectantly for Samual to agree with her, but he said nothing. He wanted to ask her from whose tyranny they were liberating the city, but he knew that question wouldn't be well received, so he only nodded vaguely in response.

"I still don't understand it," David continued. Werner groaned and rolled his eyes. He looked around the pub, possibly for a distraction, possibly to make sure David's often-repeated rant was not overheard.

"How can our president just sign over the people of Czechoslovakia? Just give away its history, its culture, its cities in one evening? And the people do nothing!" David slammed his fist down, and the bartender glanced toward their table. "Are they that scared? That cowardly?"

Samual shrugged. "Or that complacent?"

Samual had lived in Prague for seven years. While he was not affected much by the changes made by the Nazis, he still hated seeing what was happening to the city as a whole. He was from Germany, but he considered himself a man of Prague more than anything else. The city spoke to him. It filled his heart with something even Hanna couldn't touch.

Now the people from his home country were slowly tearing it apart. He knew, from the horror stories of other occupied states, that the people of Prague should consider themselves lucky.

"I just miss the nightlife," Werner said. Samual could see he was trying to defuse David's temper, bring him away from the edge of the cliff. "What grown men are given a curfew?" He laughed. Samual joined in, though he did not think it particularly funny.

He hated the sight of Prague at night during the curfew. Prague had been a place of activity and color. Color from its diverse people, from the dresses and ties those people wore, from the copper and pastel roofs and the setting sun as it reflected on the statues and mosaics. But during curfew, it was quiet and black—black like the Nazi symbol that had started showing up in shop windows and hanging from balconies.

Looking back, Samual realized he could mark the changes in the city by the changing faces of his favorite café, Seidling, on Celetna Street. First it advertised—to Samual's great relief when everything else seemed to be turning black—in the *Jewish News* that it still welcomed Jews to its tables. Not long after, though, a sign with thick, black letters went up in the window stating that the café was "Aryan Owned." Samual didn't blame the sweet couple who owned the restaurant. Without that sign, the German soldiers would never set their inky boots inside, and since the soldiers were the only ones guaranteed to have money, a business without such a sign would not be around for long.

But as the pressure increased, Seidling continued to change. A year after the Nazis took control of the city, Samual, with a large J stamped on his identification papers and a memorized Lutheran prayer, found himself sipping his coffee in the café's non-Aryan section. He forced himself to sit there, though his prideful heart cried out for him to leave that place of humiliation. The Jews were being treated like disease-infected animals, unfit to mingle with the Gentile people of the city.

Now, eighteen months into the occupation, many places were completely closed to him. Even the kind couple who owned Seidling moved to the other side of the street when passing Samual. These were the same people who helped him celebrate his twenty-fourth birthday at their best table with his friends only a few years before. Now, they refused to meet his eyes. Whether that was out of disgust for him or shame for themselves, he didn't know, nor did he think it mattered. But not being allowed to enter his favorite restaurant and enjoy his favorite cup of coffee was not worth mentioning in the long list of hardships and suffering the Jewish people were feeling all across the city. This Samual knew.

David was not to be placated. "Curfew?" He leaned closer to Werner and whispered the word with rage. "You're worried about a curfew when the Nazis are taking everything from us? I lost my job. The day they marched into the city, I was marched out of my office." He snapped his fingers in Werner's face. "Just like that. Like the crack of a whip. The shot of a gun. They are here, and I was sent home."

Werner did not react to David's speech, but Samual knew he felt sympathy for his friend. David had been a promising young lawyer working on Na Prikope in Old Town. Since losing his job, he had found no replacement work—not as a lawyer, not as a janitor, not as anything. He lived on the goodness of his people, who offered to share their meager dinners, their threadbare scraps, and anything else he might need to get by.

Samual had been lucky. He stayed out of sight of the Germans, and they were not looking closely at him. His manager knew nothing of his heritage until the J was stamped on his identification papers. Then he'd simply shrugged his shoulders and still expected Samual to show up for work every morning. Indifference or resistance to the Nazi orders, Samual did not know. But he was grateful for his work. It allowed him to escape into the essence of the city still. By working on the designs of the buildings in New Town, he felt connected to Prague. He was a doctor, tending to the inner workings and heartbeat of the city. He was a priest, caring for its soul and afterlife. Hanna said he was an artist, creating and coloring a legacy. Samual just knew he was happy when working at his drafting table, envisioning the next steps in the city's development, even though he felt like that progress was stalled under Nazi rule. The buildings he loved and helped design were the foundation of the city, but its people were the lifeblood. And more than half of them were suffering, while the other looked on and did nothing. Since the occupation, life for the Gentiles took on a gray regularity. For the Jews, it was full of fear and uncertainty for their futures.

Samual placed a reassuring hand on David's arm. "So, I suppose what you're saying is that you won't be buying an engagement ring as nice as this one for some time?" He held his breath, unsure if his friend was going to explode or relax. Werner reached again for his coffee, but Samual placed his hand on top of the mug, stopping him. David looked to Samual, then to Werner. He let out a small laugh and sat back into his seat, tilting two legs of the chair off the floor.

"If I had a girl like Hanna, I would find a way to get a ring like that. She's a good one." Samual breathed out a sigh of relief. "I'll never understand what she sees in you."

Chapter 5

RACHAEL

She opened her eyes to a gray morning before the early shout for roll call. Her unrested eyes absorbed the dim light shining through the glassless windows and the chinks in the barrack's wood plank walls. Along with the bland colors of the dawn, Rachael was immediately aware of the ring around her middle finger. Her hand was cramped and sore as she stretched her fingers gingerly. Apparently, in her sleep, she had made a fist.

It was beyond silly to attempt to keep this ring. In the light of day, she knew that. If a guard caught even a glimmer from the European cut diamond, she would be facing, at best, the fists of many guards intent on making her target practice. At worst, she would simply be shot.

"Did you get any rest last night?" The woman from the bunk below her stood to look into Rachael's bed.

"Is there any rest to be had here?" Rachael asked. She swung her feet around, rudely pushing the woman out of her way.

"You're not particularly friendly, are you?" The bunkmate seemed oddly unperturbed by Rachael's cool attitude.

For the first time, Rachael looked this woman in the eyes. "Why be friendly? Why speak to you? Why get to know you?" Rachael struggled down from her bed to the floor. She stood face to face with her bunkmate now. "I'm already dead. You are already dead. What more is there to say?"

The woman nodded, as if she understood. "Then why don't you do it? If you're so miserable because you lost your husband or your parents or your children or whomever—"

"All of them," Rachael said without any emotion in her voice.

The woman ignored the interruption. "Then go to the fence. Just do it."

It wasn't as if Rachael hadn't considered it. When she first arrived and realized her fate—and especially the fate of her children, whom she was never to see again in this world—death seemed like the best next step. The women of the camp called it "going to the fence." The fence was tall, barbed, and electrified. She had seen it many times before—desperate women walked slowly or ran quickly to the fence. They were dead within seconds, either gunned down by the guards in the watchtowers or electrocuted by the strong current that sparked from the fence.

Instead of the kindness the bunkmate usually showed Rachael, she turned. "Sure, going to the fence would be painful. Imagine that electricity . . . "

Rachael preferred this cruelness over her bunkmate's usual forced friendliness—finally, they were being truthful with one another. "Unless the sniper gets me first," she said. The woman coughed out a laugh.

"True, but there has to be some small satisfaction in letting the fence do it and cheating the Germans of one more notch on their belt."

Rachael shrugged. "But there would also be some satisfaction in making them waste bullets on me." She moved past the woman, starting out into the cold morning.

Rachael had never been able to do it though, just as today, she was unable to do anything but hide the ring in her small dress pocket. She knew she would die in this camp. There had never been any hope that her fate would be otherwise. She knew all of her children—Radek, Catarina, and her sweet baby—were dead.

"You know," the woman called after her, "if you end your life now, who would remember you? Who would remember your family?"

Rachael did not turn around or acknowledge the woman's words. But she heard them and all they implied. If no one was left to remember her husband, her children, did they ever even exist?

Standing in line during the morning roll call, Rachael was aware of the ring that nudged against her body as she swayed in the wind. Her body, worn down by lack of food and hard work, held no resistance to the cold wind that blew through camp, stirring up the light mist that floated down carelessly from the sky. The wind pierced her like a knife as it blew through her threadbare dress, and the drops of moisture stung her bare skin like tiny pinpricks. She focused on standing straight, unmoving, unfeeling in line.

This morning was looking to be one of those endless roll calls. The night had been long and cold. The temperature seemed to have moved from suffocating summer heat to bone-chilling winter cold in a matter of days. Her barrack had an iron stove in a far corner, but it was sporadically lit. And even if it was, the minimal heat only warmed those bunks closest to it. The gaps between boards, the lack of winter clothes or blankets, made such cold nights deadly. Rachael watched the guards walk up and down the rows of women—as carelessly and slowly as the fog working its way to the ground—counting and recounting. Numbers from the list of prisoners were not matching the skeletons standing in line.

In her old life, Rachael would have rolled her eyes, heaved a heavy sigh, and said something witty and wicked about the delay. In this life, she focused all her energy on wobbling as little as possible.

A few people down from her, Rachael saw a woman start to sway too much. She took a step forward to steady herself. In her daze, she overcorrected and stumbled even further. No one around her reached out to steady her balance. Her legs gave out. First her knees hit the frozen ground, then her face.

"What have we here?" a guard called out as she walked toward the fallen woman. "A rat too lazy to even stand?" The guard kicked the woman in the stomach. She cried out and tried to scramble back to her feet. Before she could make it, the guard began striking her with the end of her rifle. Appearing out of thin air like a nightmare, two more guards joined in the beating. They beat her with their rifles until she stopped crying out.

As Rachael willed her limbs to remain stationary despite the horror she just witnessed, her eyes skimmed the line of prisoners standing painfully at attention ahead of her, head after shorn head looking down at their often shoeless feet in defeat. But what was this—a gap in the line of lowered heads? Then a small arm and leg poked out—an anxious sort of fidgeting—and she saw there was no gap, but a person who stood there, easily two heads shorter than her companions.

It was a child. By Rachael's estimation of the small body, she was perhaps six or seven. But with malnutrition and torture and rampant diseases, the figure could just be a very small and emaciated full-grown woman. It was the movements that gave away her young age. She moved with the impatience of a child forced to stand in line for a long period of time. Whether in a cozy and encouraging classroom or in the freezing prison yard of Auschwitz, a child still felt the same jittery unease of stillness, itching to move, to play, to be free.

It was a shock to Rachael's nerves to see this child. She had not seen one in the camp before, to her memory. She was willing to admit to herself that, until yesterday afternoon, she wasn't sure that she had really seen any of her surroundings. There could have been other children there, blending in quietly with the mass of inhumanity that encompassed Rachael's endless days. This child, though, caught her eye.

The girl had longer hair than the women around her. It was light and limp brown and hung in jagged edges around her ears. It looked like the girl had tried to take children's scissors with their dull edges and emulate Dorothy Parker's popular flapper girl bob. Rachael knew the truth though—a merciless Nazi soldier had grabbed fistfuls of the child's hair, pulling hard, ignoring her cries of pain, and used a dull blade to saw through what were probably once beautiful locks. If the child was particularly unlucky or too loud with her shrieks of terror, the soldier would have placed that same blade under her throat and whispered vicious threats into the child's ear. It would not matter if she didn't speak German, the cold edge of the knife and the menace in the soldier's voice would inspire the intended fear.

The child's longer hair led Rachael to believe the girl had been a prisoner of this camp for some time. But the dress she wore said otherwise; it looked newly cleaned. It was clearly meant for an adult and made of the same rough fabric many of the women wore. On the small child, the short sleeves hung down past her elbows. The hem fell to her ankles. There was a strip of fabric, printed in green and red plaid, that had been torn off another garment and used as a makeshift belt. It was cinched tight around the tiny waist, leaving the rest of the dress baggy. The child looked like she could pull her arms in and cocoon herself inside like a turtle retreating into the safety of its shell.

In another place, she would have looked comical. She would have looked like Catarina, Rachael thought, when she played dress up in old, unused house dresses, the length of them dragging across the floor like a bridal train. Catarina would beg to wear the patent leather pumps Rachael put on for synagogue or special outings. And she would hold her arm out for the pearl bracelet that Alexey had gifted her on their tenth wedding anniversary.

Rachael watched in irritation as the girl continued to fidget, swiveling her head around on the boney shoulders that poked through the fabric of her dress. Rachael wanted to nudge her or pinch her or whisper for her to stop. Roll call was one of the most torturous parts of life in the prison camp. The exertion of standing perfectly still in the cold for hours on end when one was as weary as the women of Auschwitz was horrible, but it was the terror of those hours that truly haunted a person. Rachael never knew when roll call was really a selection, where the guards culled the weak and sick from the rest of the group and marched them off, never to be seen again. Rachael never knew when a guard would walk up to her or one of the other prisoners and commence with a beating. Fidgeting was certainly going to bring attention, and attention from the guards was the last thing anyone wanted in Auschwitz.

She did not dare call out to the girl, but she was equally irritated that the women on either side of the child did nothing to still her. Though she should be looking ahead and holding her breath, Rachael found herself watching the child with something nearing interest.

It wasn't just nerves making the girl bounce and look around. She was watching the precipitation float lazily to the ground. When the girl turned her head, Rachael saw her profile and noticed a small smile playing on the edge of her lips.

When was the last time she had seen anyone smile? Rachael felt her jaw go slack as she watched the small figure turn her face up to the sky and quickly stick her tongue out to catch a raindrop. She must be very new to the prison yard, Rachael thought, to still have her childlike wonder and innocence intact. Catarina, possibly the same age as this girl, lost that part of herself years ago. That was what happened when a child lived through war, when she saw her brother disappear and her father die, when she was moved out of her home and starved and frightened every minute of the day. When Radek was taken, Catarina stopped singing. When they lost Alexey, she stopped even humming. When they were moved away from everything she had ever known, she stopped talking almost completely.

Yet here, in the worst place on earth, Rachael watched a child catch raindrops on her tongue. It made Rachael furious. Furious with the girl for being alive, while her children were all gone; furious with the Nazi soldiers for stealing that wonder from Catarina; furious at herself for being powerless to prevent it.

Who was this child?

It was nothing short of a miracle that Rachael made it through the three-hour roll call without any guards noticing hers or the child's distraction. When they were finally allowed to resume their day, Rachael decided to stay as far away from this girl as possible. She was clearly trouble, in so many ways. A child did not belong in Auschwitz, and it was just a matter of time before the guards rectified the situation. Rachael did not want to be anywhere near the girl when they did.

It being Sunday, Rachael had a long day ahead of her. Her body needed whatever rest this day was meant to provide, but her mind almost preferred the days full of work. She went through the motions of bathing—which was nothing more than a bucket of cold water and her own hands to scrub halfheartedly at the dirt-crusted parts of her body. With her hands still wet and trembling with the cold, she walked out into the prison yard to escape the stale and acrid air of the barracks.

She walked the path between her barracks and the neighboring buildings, some also made of wooden planks and other older ones made of brick. Most of Rachael's view was taken up by manmade—German made—structures: the barracks, storage buildings that held the plunder that she sorted through every day, the tall double fence. As she walked, she sometimes could catch a glimpse of green between buildings, just the hint of shrubs and trees that had been planted to hide them—the large structures where the dead bodies smoked and floated up to the heavens, not as spirits at peace but as bits of gray ash. Rachael refused to let herself look for the small semblance of nature. She would have appreciated such landscaping, but now she saw it as just another trick of the Nazis.

As Rachael neared the end of her allowed walk, she noticed a strange woman at the edge of the prison grounds. She stood in front of the fence, staring, motionless, expressionless. Rachael, at first, did not give her much heed. It was not unusual to see that hopeless gaze fall beyond the walls of the prison, out to the distance, back home or anywhere else besides here. Upon second look, Rachael assumed the woman was contemplating whether to go to the fence. But as Rachael studied the woman, she realized suicide was not on her mind. The woman wasn't staring at the great beyond or looking to kill herself; she was looking toward the men's camp. Rachael shook her head—the woman was obviously searching for a glimpse of her man.

Rachael thought she might be new. The woman still stood tall—shoulders back, head held high. The hopelessness of their circumstances had not beaten her into submission yet. All the women wore the same shaved head and matching clothes—a burlap dress, buttoned down the front. There were no sizes, so this woman's dress hung loosely off her thin frame—she wouldn't last long on the meager meals. The only thing the differentiated this dress from many of the others was the number stitched on the outside.

Rachael had never given much thought to her hair even before the war. She always pulled it away from her face, in a bun or with barrettes if she wanted to drag out a compliment from her husband. Hair was a nuisance more than anything else. But now, without it, she realized how much it made up a part of her face. She had not seen her own reflection since coming to Auschwitz, but she saw mirror images of herself all around: dark bruises under eyes that bulged out of a thin face; teeth yellowing and decaying from lack of hygiene and proper diet; hair mostly gone but growing back in wiry patches over a bumpy skull. This woman's head was freshly shaved. There was no hint of the locks that must have flowed just days before, but Rachael imagined her with brown, glossy hair. Maybe curls falling out of a careless knot on the nape of her neck. This woman had probably been born beautiful and took it for granted.

Now she was like everyone else.

"You won't see them until evening," Rachael finally said. She broke her own rule of not speaking to the other prisoners, but this woman showed no signs of leaving the fence, ever.

"I'll wait," she said.

Rachael tried again. "Do you know which building he is in? Sometimes you can pass a message if you know." She paused. "I've never tried, but that is what other women have done."

The woman shook her head. "I don't know."

"When is the last time you saw him?"

"When we got off the train." The woman finally turned her head to look at Rachael. "I don't even know if he went to the left or to the right. I went to the left."

Rachael nodded. She didn't know if there was any use in saying it. It did not matter which direction he went. They all would face the same fate soon enough.

"What happened to the ones who went to the right?" the woman asked.

Rachael tilted her head at the woman. "You know what happened to them."

The woman shook her head, refusing to believe.

"You need me to say it?" Rachael waited. The woman turned back to the fence. "Fine. I will say it. They were killed. All of them. Shot, maybe. Gassed, probably. Dead either way."

Rachael turned to leave, thinking this was why she did not talk to the others.

"They can't kill all of us," the woman called out after her.

"Look around," Rachael said. "They already have."

Rachael left the woman standing by the fence, feeling nothing but unreasonable anger. *Crazy, hopeful woman,* she thought. Hope was a disease that seeped into your bones and could kill you faster than the Nazis. The day she set foot in this prison yard was the day she let go of the last shred of hope for Radek. She had watched the members of her family disappear one after another. Thinking that Radek, or anyone, could survive this was the most painful way a person could die. This woman did not know that yet.

What did the woman say? They can't kill us all? Of course the Nazis could kill everyone. Rachael replayed the conversation again. She had said, *"They can't kill all of us,"* she corrected in her mind. That was nothing but semantics. Rachael had reached the barracks and stopped before entering.

They can't kill all of us, she thought again. They can kill us, but if something remains, they haven't killed all of us. She thought of her family—Alexey, Radek, Catarina, the sweet baby. They were dead, gone, nothing left. But that wasn't completely true. She was still here, and she remembered them. She remembered everything—the tone of Alexey's voice when he teased her, Radek's laugh when he played with Catarina, her daughter's understanding eyes that took in everything around her, the way her baby's fingers wrapped around her own. If she lived and remembered them, were they completely gone? She had just been waiting to die so she could join them. But if she lived, they continued on. If she died, there would be nothing left of them. As if they had never lived at all.

She looked back around the prison yard. She could still see the woman staring through the fence. She saw the other despairing faces milling aimlessly around the camp. She saw the overflowing barracks, the smoke billowing into the gray sky from the chimneys of the crematorium, the hateful guards laughing and smoking in corners around the yard. Still, for the first time since losing hold of Catarina's hand, Rachael felt that monster called hope creep into her heart. She tried to push it down. Hope was like the fragrance from freshly picked flowers—sweet and uplifting when fresh, but decaying overnight.

Then she saw the child. The same girl from roll call earlier that morning. The child was playing, just as she had been in line. From the glimpses of her face earlier, Rachael had guessed this girl was the same age as Catarina, but upon further inspection, Rachael placed her closer to age nine or ten. She could have been older, Rachael guessed, as children did not grow in places like these as they should. They were flowers without fertile soil and brightening sunshine. Most withered and died quickly.

Yet, this girl was playing. Rachael found her between two barracks, fairly safe from the view of the guards for the moment. The girl touched one wall on the nearest barracks with the palm of her hand. Then, she pushed off the wall and attempted to jump to the wall of the neighboring building. She stretched her skinny legs as far as they would reach, opposite arm reaching out for the wall. She did not reach with one leap and was forced to take a small bunny hop to place her palm on the other barrack. She turned around and played the game again, this time with a small grunt of exertion as she pushed off toward the original building. Still, she did not reach it in one leap. Watching her zigzag between the barracks in this manner, Rachael felt a mix of emotions—irritation to see this troublesome child again, interest in the game the girl created in her head, and, surprisingly, a small bit of joy watching the girl smile.

When the child reached the end of the buildings, she looked up, finding Rachael watching her. Her face lit up like she had known Rachael her entire life and they were finally reunited. The girl ran toward her. Rachael quickly wiped any trace of smile from her face and folded her hands over her chest.

"Did you see?" the girl asked. "I almost made it in one jump!"

Rachael shrugged her response and turned to walk away. The girl followed.

"Can you do it in one jump?" she asked. "I bet you can. Let's try!" She tugged on Rachael's sleeve, and Rachael jerked away from the girl's touch. When was the last time someone touched her, besides a strike from a guard? She stopped and stared at the girl, appalled by her audacity. The child seemed not to notice.

"You try it."

"No."

"Do you want to play something else?"

"No."

"I can show you mirrors. I love looking in the mirrors and seeing the pretty sky in them. Want to come?" The girl resumed tugging on Rachael's sleeve again. Rachael felt the part of a weary mother, burdened with the never-ending energy of a small child. When was the last time she had felt like a mother?

"No."

Dejection finally registered on the girl's features. She sighed and turned to walk back to her game of leaps and bounds.

Rachael did not have time to think before she spoke. If she had thought about it, she would have stopped herself. But instead, she said, "But . . ."

The girl turned with expectant eyes.

"But, I have something I can show you."

Chapter 6

SAMUAL

He had spent an unreasonable amount of time trying to solve the problem of carrying the ring. He knew it was time wasted, but yet, he couldn't bring himself to make a decision.

This was the night he was to propose to Hanna. He felt confident that he had planned it down to the last detail—dinner, a walk along the flowered path on Paris Street, then the speech where he declared his undying love. But the final detail of how to carry the ring, that seemed impossible to solve.

He started with the ring tucked safely in its black velvet box, in the pocket of his suit jacket. He was comforted when he felt the firm square bounce against his chest as he moved around his flat—double checking his reflection in the mirror and straightening his tie. But he convinced himself that Hanna would spot the box immediately as she opened the door to welcome him into her arms. And if she didn't see it right away, he feared she would feel it when he brought her in for a tight embrace. Then all his rehearsal would be for naught.

He took the ring out of its nest and placed it directly into his trouser pocket. When looking in the mirror, there was no giveaway as to what precious cargo he was carrying. But Samual could no longer feel the security of the box, and even when walking around the flat, he found himself putting his hand in his pocket. While Hanna would no longer be able to the see the outline of the box in his coat, he was sure the action would arouse her suspicion.

In the end, he put the ring—unguarded by its box—in his trouser pocket and willed himself to not reach for it every five minutes in a panic. Then he headed to Hanna's flat on the edge of Josefov, the Jewish Quarter.

She was waiting for him on the cobblestone road, lounging against the bronze-colored, stone wall of her new building. She never complained of the move; it wasn't in her nature, Samual knew, to bemoan things out of her control. She also wasn't one to be disturbed by unexpected changes in her life. Sometimes, with a smile, he thought she would have made a very happy Romani—though, these days, their plight was not much happier or safer than that of the Jews.

She had been forced out of her beloved apartment and into a woman's boarding house in Josefov. Then, just recently, she was moved into this apartment near the Spanish Synagogue. She considered herself lucky to leave the boarding house, with its community washroom for thirty young women. Samual appreciated Hanna's new building for its Baroque architecture. But he knew it wasn't easy for her to share the three-bedroom home with two other families. She told him once, "I'm lucky to have this apartment. It's much closer to the café. And it's nice to have the other families around." She smiled at the time, but her eyes looked wistful. "I know my old place was small. But it was mine."

Any concerns she might have had about her new living arrangements were clearly not on her mind as Samual strolled up to her on that April evening. She smiled brightly as she saw him nearing, her hair so glossy and dark that Samual was sure he could see the reflection of the city sky in it. An emerald-green dress fell to her knees, with a matching wool coat and small hat pinned on the top of her head. She held her black gloves, running them through her fingers mindlessly as he came closer. She tilted her head to him, allowing him a chaste peck on her cheek. Then she grinned mischievously and gave him a firm kiss on his lips.

"Ready for a night on the town?" he asked, offering his arm.

She looped her arm though his and squeezed his forearm gently. "Always."

Samual led her slowly through the Jewish Quarter, through Old Town, to the Vltava River. He had picked out a small restaurant near the Josef Manes monument with a view of the river. Though it also displayed the "Aryans Only" sign on the front windows, it was a small place whose owners usually seemed sympathetic to the plight of the Jew in Prague. But Samual had no intention of revealing Hanna's religion—if he could help it.

He felt her slow down as she walked beside him and recognized where he was taking her. "Not there, dear," she said softly. "I don't want a scene tonight."

"No scene," he whispered in her ear, patting her arm in reassurance. "Just hold your head up high and walk in with confidence. We belong here."

"I completely agree," she said. "But we aren't the ones making the rules these days."

He patted her arm again. "Have no fear, my love."

Samual gave the young girl at the hostess stand his most charming smile. Hanna told him once that he looked like that American star, Gary Cooper, when he brought out his best smile. He hoped this waitress was a Gary Cooper fan.

"A table for two. With a view of the river." He tried to dazzle her with his grin again. "*Plez.*"

She smiled at him shyly and started to turn to lead them toward the patio overlooking the water. But she looked again at Hanna.

Hanna was holding tightly to Samual's hand, trying to hide behind him slightly. She stared at the floor as though trying to discern the pattern of the wooden boards.

"Papers?" the waitress said flatly.

"Papers?" Samual asked. He squeezed Hanna's hand and tried to lead her to stand next to him.

"Papers."

"Do we really need those?" He tried boring his eyes into the waitress. He wanted to tell her with his stare everything she needed to know to seat them: He was German and a Christian. Hanna was perfect and worthy to sit in any restaurant she chose. And tonight was going to be one of the most special moments of their lives.

But the waitress couldn't read any of that. "We don't serve Jews." She pointed to the sign in the window.

"Miss . . ." he started persuasively. But Hanna dropped his hand, making him lose his thought.

"We understand," she told the waitress. She had stopped staring at the floor and now looked the young girl directly in the eyes. She smiled warmly and sincerely.

The waitress lost her cold edge. "I'm sorry," she told Hanna. Now the girl was the one to drop her eyes. "But it's the rules here."

"Of course, dear," Hanna said graciously. "Sam, darling, it's not fair to ask her to seat us. She could lose her job by even having us in this entryway."

"But, Hanna . . ."

Her glance at Samual made him stop midsentence again. She looked at the girl patiently, waiting for her to meet her gaze again. When the girl finally looked up, Hanna smiled gently and walked out of the restaurant—with her head held high and the confidence of someone who belonged there.

Samual followed after her.

After walking in silence for half a block along the river, he grabbed her hand and urged her to stop. "Hanna," he started, hoping to apologize. Once again, she was right about how the people of this city were going to treat her. He kept thinking that the situation wasn't as bad as it was—that their last encounter was a fluke, that the citizens of Prague weren't falling for the Nazi lies about Jews and Communists and any other outspoken or undesirable person. Hanna saw the truth in their situation, but he kept denying it.

"You're right, Samual," she said simply. "It's not fair, but that's how it is."

He marveled at her kindness. "It's not fair. And it's not right," he said, suddenly furious, not just because his perfect, romantic spot for a marriage proposal was ruined but because he lived in a world where Hanna could be treated in such a way. "It's not right that the Nazis have everyone believing such filth. And it's not right that the people just go along with it!"

She looked at him with interest. "Let me get this straight. You're angry with your native countrymen for their actions. And you're angry with your adopted fellow citizens for their inaction. All because of the treatment of an ethnic group you are a part of but you don't associate with?"

Samual paused. "Yes?" Hanna's eyes were glittering with amusement. "I'm a complicated fellow."

Then she laughed. Her laughter rang through the silent street like the first notes of Mozart's *Symphony in D*. Without thinking, Samual kissed her in the middle of the city.

Hanna loved walking along the river, especially as the sun was setting on the city. Samual had made this promenade with her many times, and he always looked forward to it. They crossed the Charles Bridge, slowing as they passed their favorite statues—Francis of Assisi accompanied by his two angels for Hanna, and the Madonna and Saint Bernard for Samual, though Hanna despised that one, calling it a pyramid of infant heads.

"I never appreciated this view until you brought me here," Samual said.

"You never walked the Charles Bridge?" she teased. "You really need me in your life, don't you?"

He laughed. "Very true. No, I walked the bridge, I just never looked up to see where I was going."

"Many people live their entire lives that way," Hanna mused. "But you miss so much. Look at this." She threw her arms wide and gestured to the city. "It's a sea of stone. Every rooftop and building is a unique seashell with all its different shapes and colors."

"That's why I love it here," Samual said. "Every building is special."

"Like the people."

"Yes, like the people."

They looked out over the water in a comfortable silence, both enjoying the view and the company and not feeling the need to fill the space with empty words. Hanna stared contentedly at the ballet of swans floating down the river and waddling along the shore into the park grounds.

"Don't you just love the swans?" Hanna said softly, breaking her reverie.

"Love the swans? No, my dear, I cannot say I love the swans. I think only visitors to the city love the swans, and that's because they have not been here long enough to know any better."

She playfully bumped shoulders with him. "Don't say that," she scolded. "Swans are magnificent creatures."

"I think you mean pesky creatures."

"I mean what I said," she said sternly. "Just look at them. They spend their days in the water, in the mud, in the grass, yet they are pristinely white. You don't find that impressive?"

Samual looked for the first time with real interest at the swans. "No," he said after a moment of thought. "I don't find that impressive." He laughed.

"For someone who can't even keep his shirt white at a café, you certainly should," she said. They both laughed.

As Samual and Hanna continued their stroll across the bridge, chatting quietly, he forgot his nerves from earlier in the evening. It wasn't until he leaned over the wall of the Charles Bridge and felt the diamond softly press into his leg that he remembered the precious stone he carried.

With the restaurant turning them away, he floundered as to how to get the evening back on track. He had planned a romantic dinner, with their favorite view of the city and the river, with a champagne toast and his rehearsed speech. He had practiced it so much in the last few days that he had been confident he could get through the words without pause. Now, though, without the comfort of the restaurant atmosphere, without the distraction of the bubbly champagne and the glass to hold steadily, calming his nerves, he couldn't remember even the first line of his proposal.

They had lapsed back into their comfortable, serene silence as they walked off the bridge and toward Old Town, and he ran through alternatives to his plan. He could take her back to the café where they first met, though since she spent all of her work days there, she might be disappointed with that destination. He couldn't think of a restaurant between the bridge and Hanna's apartment that would allow Jews, so he had to abandon the idea of a dinner. He could stop her in the street right this instant and just ask her—no rehearsed speech, no intimate atmosphere, just simple and honest words. But looking at Hanna's beautiful profile illuminated by the evening glow, he felt that inadequate.

He wanted this night, this question, this moment in their history to be special. He wanted Hanna to boast to her friends about how he asked her to be his wife. He wanted to tell his son one day, helping to prepare the boy for his own proposal to the woman he loved. Stopping in the middle of the street did not seem right.

So they continued to stroll through Prague—aimless but content.

As they wandered the city, hand in hand, they found themselves walking up to Old Town Hall. Samual loved it for its collection of smaller structures, working together to create one complex and yet unique building that embodied the essence of the city. He sighed thinking about the mosaics on the first floor that had been white-washed a few months ago. He knew it was to save them from the Nazis, but he was still saddened by the thought, especially his favorites of Princess Libuse, who, according to Czech folklore, founded Prague after a vision of a city whose glory would touch the stars.

"Isn't it beautiful?" Hanna said, breaking him from his daydreaming. She squeezed his hand, glancing quickly to him then back to the old building.

"Yes," he replied, "it's one of the best buildings in the city. See the Gothic moldings on this side of the hall?" He pointed to the ancient portal on the building's west wall. "That's the only part—"

She squeezed his hand again to interrupt him. "Of the original structure."

He laughed. She'd heard him talk of it before. This was not their first stroll around the city.

"Do you think we can sneak in and see the mosaics?"

"The mosaics?" he said. "You must be joking. They've ruined them."

Hanna shrugged.

"You haven't been in there lately," he said, breaking the sad news to her. "They painted over the mosaics months ago. No more mythical creatures. No more Czech history."

Hanna shrugged again. "I've seen it."

"You've seen it? I know. I know. You're going to say that the whitewash can be removed some day, that they are protecting them." Samual sighed.

"That's not what I was going to say," she said. Samual turned his stare from the building to her. The sun had fallen below the city horizon, but he could still make out her face clearly by the light of the streetlamps. She looked intently at the old building, made up of smaller and different pieces—so much like the mosaics inside—until they created one perfect picture.

"I like white," she said.

"You like the innocence of white?" he teased. "White swans? White paintings?"

She squeezed his hand again and cocked an eyebrow. "You know I'm not that concerned with innocence." She smiled at him with a sideways glance.

He laughed.

"White isn't always about purity and innocence," she continued. "Sometimes, it's about the absence of anything else. There's a difference between innocence and lacking flaws. White can represent no sin, but also no heartbreak, no unhappiness, no . . ." She looked up at him and laughed with embarrassment. "I'm rambling."

"No," he encouraged her, entranced.

"It's just . . ." she started again. "It's just that when I see white, I see a blank canvas. I see a new beginning. I see a world where anything is possible. I loved the mosaics. But that was the past. That was before everything that is happening now. When they whitewashed them, I was relieved." She sighed. "We can make our own new beginning now. We can become anything we want to be. We can put up a new Czech history on those walls."

"But what if it's not a new Czech history?" Samual asked. "What if it's a Nazi history?"

"This is the question you ask?" she laughed, the teasing coming back into her voice. "You, my German friend, who thinks the Nazis won't truly hurt the Jews?"

Samual didn't answer but turned back toward Old Town Square. He didn't need to voice his doubts.

Hanna sighed, becoming serious again. "Yes, that's possible. Probably more than possible. But I have to believe. I have to believe in the strength of good people, in the power of art and beauty." She paused. "And in love. If we don't believe in those things, we are lost." Her voice sounded stronger. "So I believe that soon those walls will be painted again with all those things. And they will be even more beautiful than they were before."

His speech, his well-crafted plans, his romantic intentions all vanished when she turned to face him. Her words, her beauty, the perfection of the moment—it all spoke to him. He knew this was the time—not a moment he could have planned and forced to appear perfect. This was a real, true, honest moment. His heart started beating violently. He was sure Hanna must be able to hear it. He felt a lump rise in his throat.

With trembling hands, he reached for the diamond in his pocket. He knelt one knee on the cobblestone sidewalk. Hanna's face slowly registered shock as he pulled out the ring. His hands shook so violently and sweated so profusely that he felt his grip on the delicate ring slip. It tumbled to the sidewalk with a soft clink.

The diamond caught the light of the streetlamp and sparkled for a second as he retrieved it, embarrassed, and held it up to her. Her eyes moved from his face to the ring, and he watched with satisfaction as her mouth opened in awe.

"I can't remember the speech I was going to say," he said. "Something about how much I love you and how I want to spend my life with you."

"I bet it was a good speech," she whispered.

"Very good," he agreed. "But all I can think about right now is that I believe in us. And I want to start a new mosaic with you."

She smiled and looked into his eyes.

"Will you marry me?"

Chapter 7

RACHAEL

Rachael could not believe what she had said, or what she had done. She hadn't stopped to think about it, think through the consequences. Something in her simply would not allow the child to look so dejected. It was the same reflex that made her grip Catarina's hand when they approached a street crossing or hug the baby even tighter to her chest when she saw a German soldier approaching. It was a motherly and protective instinct, one she thought had died long ago.

There was no taking back her words. They were out of her mouth, and the girl's eyes were alight. Rachael felt her stomach churn because that look of wonder reminded her so painfully of Catarina's large eyes before her brother was taken. Those eyes had seen only adventures and miracles and magic. Though this naivety and hope would surely be the death of this child, Rachael impulsively wanted to keep it alive just a little longer.

So she quickly grabbed the girl's hand and pulled her into the deathly quiet barracks. She spoke to the girl in a whisper, though the women lying on the bunks couldn't hear her even if she shouted. Anyone still in this airless barrack was either dead or would be by morning, when whatever family or friends remained dragged their bodies out to roll call to keep the numbers accurate.

"What I'm going to show you is a *secret*," Rachael whispered into the child's ear. The girl's eyes widened at the word. "You can't tell anyone," Rachael said, stretching out the last word. The girl nodded solemnly.

Rachael slowly and dramatically put her hand into her pocket and grasped the ring in her fist. When she opened up her hand in front of the girl's face, she uncurled one finger at a time. She found herself enjoying the suspense as much as the child.

There was a small gasp. Then Rachael felt the girl's hands grip her own arms. The child was mesmerized by the ring. In the dark of the barracks, with no electricity and no candles, the ring still found the smallest source of light and refracted rainbows onto Rachael's palm. Slowly, as if she might scare it away, the girl touched the spots on Rachael's palm where the diamond created specks of blue, purple, yellow, and green. She giggled when the rainbow illuminated her own fingers.

"So pretty," she murmured. The girl bounced on her toes, but she kept her voice low, aware of the special secret Rachael was sharing with her. "Where did you get it?"

"It's buried treasure," Rachael said. "I found it."

"Can I . . ." The child looked up expectantly at Rachael but stopped herself. Clearly, holding such a precious thing was unfathomable to her. Rachael felt a flash of anger—anger that a child would think even holding a diamond engagement ring was such a privilege that she would have no right to it. Then she felt the flash turn into a wave that washed over her whole body, because the child was correct. She did not have a right to see this ring, to be mesmerized by its beauty. Rachael's own daughter had been refused the right to live. Who was this girl, trying to take the one special thing left in Rachael's life?

She quickly closed her fist around the ring and shoved it back in her pocket. The movement was so sudden that the girl jumped back in surprise. Then she giggled.

"Maybe . . . " she said shyly, "maybe I can see it again sometime?" Her eyes looked hopefully at Rachael. The last time she had seen eyes look at her with such trust was the last time she had seen Catarina. The grief became physical at that moment. Rachael pushed the girl aside with her arm, ran out of the barracks, and retched along the outside wall.

Her mind had blocked the entire experience of the train ride from the ghetto to Auschwitz. She had no specific recollection of it, besides the feel of Catarina's small hand in her own—the small hand that got colder and colder and the grip that became weaker and weaker as time stretched on.

Her daughter had always been brave—frail but brave. As a happy toddler, she sang through the house, crawling onto furniture and into small spaces. Heights and tight corners, loud noises or dark nights, none seemed to frighten her. As she lost one family member after another, the child became quieter but still fearless. Her round eyes took it all in with curiosity and seriousness, but she never looked away. Rachael worried about what such horrific sights would do to her developing child's mind, but when each day was a struggle for survival, she had to focus on what they would do to her child's body.

Rachael had always been struck by Catarina's resiliency. The child retreated further into herself with every terrible thing that befell them, but she remained strong. Increasingly silent, but still strong. Her courage and resolve endured when Rachael's had long ago failed them both—until they arrived in Auschwitz.

Seeing the small girl brought the events of her arrival into sudden clarity. After the trauma of leaving the ghetto and riding the train, smashed between hundreds of miserable strangers, Rachael finally awoke from her stupor as the train pulled into the camp. She had no idea where they were. The only word spoken about their destination was "East." East, for years, had meant nothing good. But what really awaited them in this place, further east than Rachael had ever thought to go, was a hell she could never have imagined.

The metal door rolled open with violence. Inside the train car had been near black since they boarded days earlier, so the Jews were immediately blinded by the white sunlight streaming through the door. There was no time for their eyes to adjust. Soldiers started grabbing prisoners—by the shirt, by the arm, by the hair—and pulling them onto the platform. Those who fell were attacked by dogs, snapping, snarling, drawing blood. Rachael's first real thought since boarding the train was a ludicrous one: if she ever survived this place, she would never again have a dog.

Rachael and Catarina were far enough inside the train car that she was able to assess the situation before a Nazi soldier yanked her roughly to the ground. She gripped Catarina's hand like her life depended on it. As they jumped off the train, Rachael could feel her small daughter start to shake.

They were shoved through the crowd. With the hundreds of heads around her, Rachael could not see their destination. It mattered not, she realized. She held Catarina's hand so tightly, she was sure it was hurting the child. Instead of loosening her grip, Rachael used her free hand to clutch Catarina's forearm as well. They would not be separated. No matter what. She would not lose her daughter.

They shuffled forward, seeing only the frightened people around them, hearing only the savage barks of the dogs and the shouted orders from the soldiers. Rachael focused solely on staying on her feet, for anyone who fell was instantly set upon. Many did not rise again. Those who did were bloody and had a dazed, empty look in their eyes.

Finally, Rachael saw the sea of people start to disburse into different lines. She pushed her daughter behind her, still shaking like an autumn leaf. She felt Catarina bury her face in the back of her dress. She tried to whisper comforting words to her child, but nothing could be heard over the screams of the tortured. Instead, she squeezed Catarina's hand, pulsing like the blood that was pumping through her temples. She prayed the girl could gain just a little strength from the pressing presence of her mother's hand.

More stuttering steps and Rachael saw the women were being herded into one line, men into another. She struggled through the crowd into the queue. It crossed her mind only for an instant to make a run for it. It seemed foolish to allow the Germans to push her into this obvious prison and death camp, but it was nothing less than suicidal to try to escape. Missteps from confused people were punished with a burst of gunfire into any meaty part of their body—she would only make it a dozen steps before she and Catarina would duck low under a shower of bullets. So she pulled her daughter into the line behind her, with her head down and her lips mouthing prayers to God to save them.

The screams started to thin as the line slowly made its way to a table. Behind the wooden table sat a man with glasses and an eerily pleasant smile. He seemed to be dividing the women into smaller groups. He wordlessly looked over each woman and sent them to his right or to his left. Rachael watched the man—he was not leering at the women like most soldiers she had encountered. She wanted to feel encouraged by that, but nothing around her would allow her to relax for even a second. This man's friendly gaze was even more unsettling than the others' obviously cruel glares.

There were only three women between Rachael and the man with glasses when she felt Catarina's knees give way. The girl had kept her head buried in Rachael's back as they moved slowly through the crowd and down the line. She had tried to block out the nightmare that was unfolding around her, but as they neared the front of the line, her courage failed her. Rachael quickly pulled Catarina back to her feet. She saw a Nazi notice them and start to stalk their way.

"It is fine, my love," she whispered desperately. "We are almost done. It's almost over. Stay brave just a little longer."

Catarina's large brown eyes flooded over with tears. She shook her head back and forth and continued to shake violently. Rachael tugged her forward as the line continued to move. She tried to gently push her daughter in front of her. "Momma is right here," she whispered. "I'm right behind you."

The soldier was only steps behind them, already raising his gun to take aim. Rachael squeezed her daughter quickly. "No fear, my sweet girl." She kissed her daughter's head. "I'll go first. You'll see—all will be well."

Rachael stepped in front of Catarina. The seated man, his smile gone, barely raised his eyes from the table to glance at her. He tilted his head to the left. Rachael understood and walked in that direction. After half a dozen steps, she turned to see her daughter follow. Instead, she saw her daughter being shoved roughly by the soldier in the other direction.

Rachael made to follow Catarina, but a soldier grabbed her arm and continued to force her down the line. Rachael fought him, but the strength that tales had promised would come to a frantic mother did not magically appear. She could not lift a boulder off her child and she could not fight this Nazi to reach her. The soldier delivered a blow from the butt of his rifle into her stomach. Her breath rushed out of her with the enormous force. She had no air to breathe, no strength to fight, and no voice to cry out to her daughter. She lay on the ground. Her mouth had dirt in it and her tears rapidly turned the soil smeared on her face into a soft mud.

She felt a cold metal force dig into the back of her head. "Get up," a menacing voice said in German. The voice was quiet, a contrast to the barks and shouts all around her. It was like a bucket of cold water—shocking, and it made her tremble all over. The gun barrel pushed hard, forcing her face into the dirt. Later, when Rachael would think of this moment, she knew she should have stayed down. She should have let that soldier pull the trigger, spill her blood and brains into the mud made by her tears. But that monster called hope made her get up, shakily, to her feet. Her head continued to swivel, looking for a glimpse of Catarina, but her feet numbly moved her forward.

Her eyes blurred with tears and every breath causing a shooting pain, she blindly followed the woman in front of her, staring only at her feet. One foot moved forward, then the other. Rachael imagined her daughter, her only remaining child, doing the same in a line on the other side of the camp. Though instead of numb with worry, Catarina would be trembling head to toe with terror. Rachael imagined her daughter's fearful face—those eyes taking in the scared women and children around her. Rachael sent all the strength she had left to her daughter in her thoughts. If she concentrated, maybe she could make Catarina feel the warmth of her love, like rays of sunshine warming her bare arms, and the child would stop shaking until they were reunited.

The line of women took her into a room full of tables. There were guards—both male and female—as well as others whom Rachael could only assume were prisoners. Neither had any compassion or kind words for the confused and terrified women. Orders were shouted telling them what to do, but Rachael could not focus on the words, so she let herself be pushed from behind to the first long table.

The woman in front of Rachael did not appear to understand German. She kept shaking her head frantically as the SS guard shouted at her. Finally, the guard grabbed the woman by the shirt collar and, with his large, calloused hands, ripped it apart until it fell down around the woman's shoulders. She shrieked and tried to cover herself. Rachael finally looked past this woman to the others in the room. Most were modestly undressing, trying to keep on their underclothes or hide their most private parts. The guards in this room did not leer like the ones outside. They looked at the women like they were garbage, not worth a second look. She was no longer a woman, or even a human being, to these soldiers. How terrified Catarina must be at this moment, being forced to undress among so many strangers! She was determined to get through this as quickly as possible so she could find Catarina and comfort her.

Numbly, she took off the dress that had seen so much heartbreak in the ghetto and on the train ride to this place. She felt no regret in shedding this garment. Maybe she could leave the bad memories hanging on a hook here in this brick building, too.

When she was completely naked, Rachael was shaved. She never knew true humiliation until she allowed all the hair from her body to be removed by a ruthless female guard with a dull razor. Rachael also never knew how well she could compartmentalize the horror around her. She stared straight ahead to the plain brick wall and repeated in her mind: *Get out and get to Catarina.* That's all that mattered. She was thankful the child had little hair to shave. Her lovely dark locks had long ago turned thin with malnutrition. Looking around at the women with shaved heads and bodies, Rachael realized they all looked the same. Would Catarina even recognize her after this?

After putting on a coarse dress and wooden clogs that were too big and instantly hurt her feet, she moved down the line. A guard with a bound notebook shouted a number at her. Rachael stared at her blankly, not able to decipher the German words in her daze. The guard struck Rachael across the face. She felt a tooth knock loose, but she was more appalled by the casual cruelty of the hit than the pain. The soldier again shouted a number to her.

"26947," she screamed, spittle flying out of her mouth and landing on Rachael's dress. "Your name?"

"26947?" Rachael repeated, still not comprehending.

The woman laughed loudly, scaring Rachael even further. "This dumb animal learns quickly," she said sneering. "You're right, your name is now 26947. But," she added, her scornful smile disappearing, "what is your filthy Jew name?"

Rachael obediently told her, all while thinking of Catarina's fear of speaking to anyone. She said a fervent prayer that the soldier Catarina was seeing did not continue to strike the poor child for not speaking. *Let her be merciful,* Rachael prayed silently.

The next soldier down the line roughly grabbed Rachael's forearm. Before Rachael could even think to protest, the numbers of her new identity were tattooed on her arm in thick, black lines. She could not bear to watch the process, but she felt every stab of the needle. When her arm was released back to her, she did not recognize it as part of her own body.

The Germans were efficient as they pushed the other new arrivals through the brick building and into the prison yard, but the process could not move fast enough for Rachael—she was impatient to find her daughter. As soon as she was released into the camp, she searched her newly assigned barracks. She looked into each bunk, finding only empty planks with a little bit of straw for padding or still figures that she could have sworn were dead. She knew even with these prison garments and shaved heads, she would recognize her daughter immediately. But Catarina was not to be found. Bunk after bunk, she looked, forcing her panic down as it tried to creep up from her stomach, through her throat, and out in an inhuman moan of despair. She refused to let herself panic, to let herself cry.

After looking through two barracks, an older woman took pity on her. She stopped Rachael as she rushed out of the second barrack, looking desperately for a third to search.

"Who are you looking for, dear?" the woman asked. Her voice was barely a whisper. Judging by her thin frame, Rachael thought a whisper was likely all she had energy for.

"My daughter," Rachael's voice cracked, letting through a hint of her fear. She swallowed and repeated her words with more strength. "My daughter."

"I can help you," the woman said softly. She kept a frail hand on Rachael's arm. Rachael stared at it, realizing that she hadn't been touched with kindness by anyone besides Catarina in years. "I've been here for some time. I know many people. I'm sure someone knows your daughter. What is her name?"

"Catarina," Rachael said, with even more strength. This woman seemed so sure they could find Catarina. The hope pushed down her panic.

"We can ask some of my friends." The woman's hand moved to Rachael's elbow and started to guide her away from the barracks. "How long has she been in the camp?"

"We just got here," Rachael answered. "The train, this morning." She paused. "I don't even know if it was morning. It already feels like I've been off that train for days."

The woman nodded kindly. "Time is frozen here, it seems." They walked in silence for a few moments. "We are going to see a friend of mine. She sees many of the new people as they come off the train. Perhaps she will remember seeing your little one."

Rachael nodded, pushing down the frantic doubt that one woman would never be able to remember all the despairing faces of the day.

"How were you separated from . . ." The woman trailed off.

"Catarina."

"Yes, Catarina," she repeated. "How were you separated from her?"

"In the line," Rachael said softly, replaying the scene in her mind. "She was scared," Rachael whispered, feeling the tears stream down her face. "She was scared, so I went first. They sent me one direction. When I turned around for Catarina, they had sent her another direction."

The woman stopped walking, and her arm fell from Rachael's elbow. "They sent you to the left." Rachael nodded. "And they sent Catarina?" She closed her eyes for a second, then opened them, also filled with tears. "They sent her to the right?"

"Yes," Rachael said so softly that she was not sure any sound came out at all.

The woman held Rachael's hands in her own thin and cold ones. "I know where she is."

Rachael heard the words. She wanted to believe they were words of hope and salvation. But the woman's face and her tight grip on Rachael's hands told her otherwise. Her knees started to buckle, and she sank to the ground. The woman continued to hold her hands and kneeled down beside her. She looked off to a distance, out past the prison yards, above the rows and barracks.

"Do you see that chimney?" she asked. Rachael just stared at the woman, not fully understanding what she was saying. She let go of one of Rachael's hands and gestured to a large smokestack with a gray cloud billowing out of it. "There. That chimney."

Rachael nodded.

"I'm afraid that's where they took your child."

Chapter 8

HANNA

After she said yes, the night was a blur. She and Samual found themselves still at Old Town Square after the astronomical clock hit eight o'clock and the sun had set behind the horizon. They were occupied, kissing and laughing and rejoicing—and building castles in the sky with their dreams of their married life.

Samual, to Hanna's unending delight, had already determined their number of children—three—and had selected their names—Adam, Ruth, and Benjamin, after his eldest brother.

"Don't I have any say in this?" she teased him as they watched the sun set behind the city skyline.

He shrugged. "I suppose the names are debatable."

She laughed. "That's fine," she said. "But I've already planned our house design."

"Do tell." He wrapped his arm around her as the little warmth of the night leaked away with the sun's descent.

"It will be in New Town."

"Closer to work for me. I approve," he said.

"The parlor will have thick, gold carpet."

Samual wrinkled his nose.

"I'll hand pick the Salvador Dalí reprints for the walls."

"Reprints?" Samual scoffed. "Nothing but originals for my wife."

Hanna beamed under the new title. "Save your art money for the honeymoon. It will be exotic. And expensive."

They both laughed.

They didn't taint their planning with any mention of the Nazis. This night was theirs and it was one of perfection, not to be touched by the outside, evil forces of the war.

She was so delirious in her happiness, she had forgotten all about eating, until Samual pulled her to a stop, then a long kiss, in front of the door to her apartment building. He chuckled in her ear and apologized for not taking her to dinner, as was the promise of the evening.

"You shall cook for the first month of our married life to make up for it," she teased him. With a soft kiss on her neck, where his lips made her tingle from ears to toes, he promised that he would.

Hanna didn't care about the missed dinner, or even the grumbling of her stomach as she lay on her bed in raptures of that blissful night. She was feasting on the future life she was going to have as Samual's wife. Her heart was full enough to ease the slight hunger pains she felt, and her eyes were full of the sparkling diamond she carried on her left hand.

The morning after her most perfect night, she lounged at one of the outside tables at Prague Kofe and marveled at the diamond. The many facets of the center stone refracted the April sunshine and left tiny rainbows on the tabletop—the tabletop she was supposed to be cleaning with the fresh dishrag in her hand. Instead, Hanna sat lazily in the warm sun, dreaming about the previous night and the thrilling thought of her fiancé.

She knew she should be making herself useful, but the café had been empty of customers for almost two hours. This was not unusual these days. A Jewish-owned café had no chance of getting Aryan customers as the Nazis slowly increased the pressure in Prague. This café was at even more of a disadvantage as it lay firmly in the middle of the Jewish Quarter. Two years ago, that would never have kept its loyal patrons away from the rich aroma of coffee, but Nazis now patrolled the streets, happy to find any sign of rebellion from the Jews or sympathy from the Aryans.

Hanna kept waiting for Mr. Weis to take her into the storeroom, which doubled as his wife's office with just a small desk under the west window, and reluctantly explain that he could no longer afford to keep her employed. But every day as she reported for her shift, Mr. Weis just smiled warmly, asked politely about her health, and expressed his hope that today was the day their business increased. Some days, Hanna toyed with the idea of just quitting, thus making the decision easier on poor Mr. Weis, who was obviously struggling to pay for the coffee beans delivered every week, but she, too, was desperate for any money she could make. Every day of work was one more day she could pay her rent.

As she turned her left hand back and forth, she smiled to see shades of blue in the rainbow that matched the corner sapphires of the ring. She and Samual had never discussed his finances—or their finances as a married couple—but if he purchased this ring for her, surely he could support both of them in a small, New Town apartment.

She knew she would always need a job or project to keep her busy. But taking the pressure off of keeping this job specifically would be a welcome relief. She knew Samual would not push her to make any major changes in her life. He didn't speak of his family much, especially his mother, but she knew her future mother-in-law was a loyal believer of the Reich's "*kinder, kuche, kirche.*" Just the thought of such a misogynistic motto forcing women to focus only on "children, kitchen, and church" made Hanna roll her eyes. She was relieved to know Samual felt the same way, but she knew he would support her if she wanted to relieve poor Mr. Weis of one more person to feed.

She could use this opportunity to follow her dreams—do something, a real something, with her art. If Prague wasn't ruled by the

Nazis, maybe she would look for a brilliant artist to assist, gleaning all the knowledge she could while mixing colors, setting up the correct lighting, and washing paintbrushes. Prague was the best place in the world to find a talented, artistic mind. Before the Nazis scared everyone into silent submission, the city overflowed with creative talent—minds that could conjure romantic landscapes in verse, hands that could bring ancient myths to life with a few brushstrokes, voices that could string together a song strong enough to knock a grown man down. The Nazis couldn't rule forever. She truly believed that they couldn't continue to push the Jews into poverty and despair. They would get bored of it eventually, or eventually be satisfied. Then they would ease up. Or maybe the rest of the world would tire of their tyranny and finally stand up to them. Things couldn't get much worse, and surely someday they would get better.

With those thoughts and more of her life with Samual, Hanna continued to play with the diamond and the sunlight, creating design upon design on top of the café table. She toyed with the idea of transferring the iridescent designs to an abstract painting of oils. Her artist mind thought through the color combinations while her heart imagined a typical Tuesday night—she and Samual married, him coming home from his drafting table and her cleaning the paint off of her hands, hoping to surprise him with a candlelit meal.

The crass clicking of boots on cobblestones broke her from her reverie. After two years with those soldiers marching through the city streets, Hanna was sure the sound could wake her from anything, even the final sleep of death.

They were half a block away, and there were four of them. They were briskly walking in full uniform, stiffly pressed brown jackets with clashing red armbands. They walked through the street, forcing traffic to halt and let them pass, all without making eye contact or pausing to ensure their presence was having the desired effect. Hanna's thoughts fluttered from fearing them to despising them—fearing their power and unexplained hatred, but despising their arrogance and brutality. Moving only her hands, showing no expression on her face, she slipped the engagement ring back onto her finger, turning the diamond inward toward her palm.

She kept her head down, sneaking only quick glances at the approaching soldiers—four sharp, dark figures cut against the pastels of Prague. The street had gone eerily silent. Even the wind seemed to stop in the soldiers' presence. Hanna found herself sinking lower in the chair, hunching her shoulders toward the table, trying to make herself as small as possible.

She hated her body for its reaction to the oncoming threat. She wanted to be brave. To be bold. To stand up in the face of injustice. But instead, she tried to fade into the backdrop of the city.

Her heart thudded in time with their steps. Closer and closer they came. She expected them to continue down the street and felt her heart stop when their footsteps ceased. They stood in front of the picture window looking into the café, where Mr. Weis seemed frozen behind the coffee counter. Hanna held her breath, silently praying for them to keep moving. Suddenly, the sun that played with her diamond just moments ago felt too hot. She felt it burn into her back, though fear froze her body. One of the soldiers glanced quickly at the café's sign, and another swung the door open with such force that it slammed against the hinges.

"Josef Weis?" he barked out. The sound of his rough voice pounded through the street, echoing off the buildings.

Hanna went cold at the sound of Mr. Weis's calm reply.

"Yes, sir. I am he."

Through the picture windows on either side of the café entrance, Hanna could see Mr. Weis stand tall and look the soldier in the eye, unflinching. His voice was its usual softness.

"You need to come with us," the soldier said.

Hanna slunk further into her seat.

"May I ask what this concerns?" Mr. Weis said. He sounded like he was taking a mid-morning coffee order. There was no quake in his voice, unlike Hanna's entire body, which seemed to be shivering.

The soldier unpacked his rifle and swung it around in one swift motion. Without pausing, he slammed the butt of it into the window overlooking Tynska Street. The glass shattered into millions of pieces, spraying like machine gun fire onto the sidewalk and café tabletops. Hanna screamed and covered her head with her hands. The sound of glass breaking and her scream reverberated down the block. The wind picked up again and seemed to carry the noise throughout the entire city.

Mrs. Weis came running from the back storeroom, yelling frantically for her husband. She stopped mid-scream as her eyes fell upon the soldier with his rifle still poised over the now empty window frame. She froze. Hanna saw that despite the violence and noise, Mr. Weis barely flinched. Her heart swelled with pride for his bravery.

"You may not ask what this concerns!" the soldier bellowed. He nodded quickly to the others still waiting at the door. Two rushed into the small café and surrounded the still unmoving Mr. Weis. They each seized an arm, pulling him in opposite directions like dogs fighting over a filet.

At this rough handling of her husband, Mrs. Weis snapped back to life. She fell upon the soldier with the rifle, grabbing at his arm desperately.

"Please," she cried. "My husband!"

He shook her off with hardly a look and almost no effort, like she was nothing more than a gnat to swat away. "*Los jetzt!*" he commanded.

The soldiers holding Mr. Weis started to move him to the door. To the astonishment of all, Mr. Weis dug his feet into the floor and fought against the soldiers' forward movement.

"Sir," he said firmly and louder than Hanna had ever heard the gentle voice. "I demand to know the charge you are bringing against me."

In the same fluid motion the officer used to shatter the front window, he wielded his rifle around his body again. This time, the butt smashed into Mr. Weis's abdomen, doubling him over and forcing a loud grunt from the man. Mrs. Weis rushed to her husband's side.

"I beg you," she cried to the officer. He didn't even deign her with a glance.

"Los jetzt," he said again. This time, he didn't use his commanding voice, but rather one that Hanna found much more chilling. It was quiet and firm. There was no arguing.

Mr. Weis was unable to stand straight, so the soldiers dragged him out of the café, his feet making trails in the shards of glass on the ground. Mrs. Weis followed, sobbing.

She clutched at the soldier's arm again. Without breaking his stride, he struck his hand against Mrs. Weis's cheek, sending her staggering backward. Hanna, who had been unable to move from the café table, stood up in shock, knocking her chair to the ground with a loud crash. The soldiers still barely noticed her.

Though Mrs. Weis's nose was bleeding and her eyes seemed unfocused, she reached for the soldier again. Hanna was amazed at her determination—and ashamed of her own passivity.

"He's my husband," she begged, once more. "My husband. Please." Her voice lost its wail. It was gentle and earnest. The soldier stopped and finally looked Mrs. Weis in the eyes.

"Your husband?" he said. His voice was quiet, as when he commanded the soldiers to move Mr. Weis. Hanna trusted this voice less than the bark he used when he first burst into the café.

"Yes, sir," Mrs. Weis said with hope. The blood continued to flow from her nose and puddle dripped onto the bosom of her brown dress. "Please, sir." This plea was only a whisper. Hanna didn't hear Mrs. Weis, but saw her lips move clearly with the words.

The soldier nodded, and Mrs. Weis heaved a visible sigh of relief.

The leader looked pointedly at the fourth soldier. He hadn't moved from his station by the door this entire time. Now he barely nodded acknowledgment of this unspoken order, took two long strides toward Mrs. Weis, and roughly grabbed her by the forearm. From across the tables, Hanna could see Mrs. Weis's skin instantly redden and start to bruise under the pressure. But the woman said nothing. She looked at the commander whose arm she still clung to.

"Sir?" Confusion flooded her face.

The soldier once again used his soft voice. "He's your husband? Fine. Then you can join him."

For the first time, Mr. Weis's stoic calm broke. "No!" his voice rang of desperation, pleading.

It was that voice that finally unfroze Hanna from her fear. She had been cowering, watching Mr. Weis with a mixture of horror and admiration as he bore the violence and unfairness of it all. She felt her heart crack as she watched him beaten and dragged away, but when he cried out in true fear for his wife, she felt it shatter into more pieces than the café window.

She found her feet. Somehow, she found her courage.

The fourth soldier was starting to pull Mrs. Weis past the outdoor tables. The woman was so stunned and confused that she simply followed without a struggle. Mr. Weis, though, was trying to shake off his guards, trying to fight his way to his wife.

"Stop!" she yelled to the soldiers. When the soldiers turned to her suddenly, she softened her face and her voice. "*Herr Offizier*," she addressed the man giving orders. She looked him in the eye, holding her head high, trying to put on a show of confidence, as Samual always instructed her. Surely, she thought, he could hear her heart beating out of her chest, but she steadied her voice as she walked toward Mrs. Weis. "This woman is distraught. Hysterical." She rolled her eyes slightly and cast a look of annoyance at Mrs. Weis. "I'll escort her home." She paused when the soldier narrowed his eyes at her. "So she can no longer disturb you."

"Run along, Fraulein," the soldier said, with a cold edge to his voice. But Hanna took heart that he called her "Fraulein" and not "Jewess" or "filthy Jew."

She nodded respectfully. But instead of leaving, she took the few remaining steps toward Mrs. Weis and the soldier painfully gripping her arm. She grabbed Mrs. Weis's hand and pulled the woman to her side. The soldier released his grip without comment or issue. Hanna tilted her chin up again, feigning confidence that she certainly did not feel. Before the soldier could change his mind, she decisively turned and walked Mrs. Weis away.

More than anything, Hanna wanted to turn her head to get one last look at Mr. Weis—she could not get the sound of his desperate voice out of her head—but she made herself keep walking with a posture of courage she knew was a fraud. Mrs. Weis kept pace with Hanna's quick steps, but her breathing was ragged, and she was emitting a strange, strangled sound from her throat. Hanna wanted to make eye contact with Mr. Weis—whether to assure him with a look that she would care for Mrs. Weis or to assure herself that he would come home soon. But she knew her bravery had its limits, and she had reached it. She was afraid to show the soldiers that she knew the café keeper. Though she had managed to retrieve Mrs. Weis from their grasps, she felt the fear down to the tips of her toes that they would realize she was just another enemy and take both of them into custody.

But more than her fear of the Nazis, she was afraid to see Mr. Weis's face and the fear and sadness that was sure to be written there. She felt the shame of her denial of him burning her chest, slowly licking her heart with flames of selfishness. So she continued to stare ahead, walking into the glaring sun.

She could no longer stop herself, though, when she heard the first crash. She and Mrs. Weis had made it to the street corner when the shattering reached their ears. Mrs. Weis turned toward the sound as well, but her eyes were blank and unseeing. Hanna saw the cause clearly—the fourth soldier who had grabbed Mrs. Weis had thrown one of the café chairs through the remaining picture window.

The two soldiers who had dragged Mr. Weis away were out of sight, but the leader and the fourth soldier were still at the café. The leader watched as the remaining soldier hopped in through one of the broken windows. Hanna heard him break the large glass jars holding coffee beans from all across the world, the pastel coffee mugs that were purchased to match the slate tiles of the Jewish Quarter roofs, and the plates meant to hold freshly baked strudels. Hanna and Mrs. Weis listened to the utter and complete destruction of the café from half a block away, while the Nazi officer stood with a half-smile on his stern face, watching the disaster engulf a place that Hanna had once considered home.

Chapter 9

RACHAEL

Rachael was haunted by memories of her daughter's last moments for the remainder of the day. The torture continued into the night with her dreams. She foresaw more of the same if she continued to converse with the little girl. Avoiding her, and the thoughts she brought about, seemed the best option for self-preservation.

Relative to her situation, Rachael almost considered herself lucky the next day as she sorted through the plunder and possessions of the most recent intake of prisoners and Jews. Until recently, she was able to go through the motions—clothes searched and left in one pile for sterilization; jewels and money handed to specific soldiers for safekeeping; other items like blankets, pots and pans, woodworking tools, books, hair combs, bits and pieces of what used to be a life sorted and stored in massive buildings. The plunder—Rachael heard people call it *kanada* because it was as big and unfathomable as that North American country—kept overflowing. She was starving with one cup of watery soup a day, while the food from people's pockets filled crate after crate. She was freezing most nights while lying on a hard wood bunk with bits of straw to cover her up, while she tossed warm blankets into a pile to be sent to German soldiers across Europe. Her feet often filled her ill-fitting clogs with blood from the blisters, while she sorted through worn work boots and women's leather pumps. There was so much abundance around her, yet she could not have any of it. She was reminded of some of the old poetry lines her father would recite to the family before bedtime on wintery nights. "Water, water everywhere, nor any drop to drink."

She could not afford to focus on the people whose lives were destroyed—like hers—to make this plunder possible. They were faceless, as long as she did not look too closely at the neatly printed names inside coat tags or book covers. Others had it much worse. She knew there were prisoners who were tasked with taking these items from the shrieking and terrified people as they walked off the train. She had heard there were prisoners who were forced to move dead bodies out of the chamber after the gas was pumped in and then to deposit the bodies into the giant furnaces. Once, she even heard whisperings that a prisoner was forced to cut open the stomachs of the recently murdered to search for swallowed valuables. Even in her hatred for everything at Auschwitz, she could admit this job was much better.

Yes, she was in constant pain—her back from bending over to sort, her feet from the blistering wooden shoes, her hands from the cold and dry air, her head from each errant strike from a cruel guard, and her stomach, always her stomach, from the lack of food and nutrition. And yes, she was in constant danger—not just from living in Auschwitz, which was a feat of survival every day, but because of her position in the plunder room. One whisper about what she had seen and she would be selected at the next roll call, never to return. One sideways glance at an item she found tempting and she would be beaten until she stopped breathing or the guards tired. That was why the ring that kept nudging against her leg as she moved around was such madness. Theft was punishable by a swift bullet through the skull. No trial, no questions, no mercy.

She was seeing things these last few days she had never noticed in Auschwitz—starting, of course, with the little girl. As she sorted and stacked, she could no long gloss over the possessions in her hands. They were no longer muted colors and blurred objects. They were people's prized belongings—items that someone had deemed special, important, sentimental enough to bring from their homes into the ghettos, then smuggled to this camp, where they had finally been wrenched from their owner's fingers.

She was sorting clothes. There were always endless piles of clothes to go through. She was to search the pockets, the hems, the linings for anything hidden. Today, she was working her way through a pile of threadbare dresses. They were of different sizes, colors, material, but in Auschwitz, all were ownerless and worn to the seams. Using only the sensitive touch of her fingertips, Rachael searched a long-sleeve dress. It was a deep burgundy with worn elbows and a mismatched patch on a side seam. Rachael could imagine this as a dancing dress at one point, a dress its owner had saved pennies to purchase for a special Saturday night. She ran her fingers under the collar, the sleeve hems, through the bust. That's where she found it. She almost always found something in a dress like this, a treasured item someone had tried to save. She rolled her eyes at the thought: nothing could be saved these days.

It was a picture folded into fourths, the crease worn. It had been tucked into a slim pocket, positioned, with purpose, above the dress-wearer's heart. It wasn't a particularly special photograph, not one worthy of accolades or a spot on a museum wall. It was just a worn picture of a woman, a man, and two little boys. It was a family—a family before war and hate and murder tore them apart. The man and woman sat on a park bench, with trees growing behind them and flowers growing in front at their feet. Sandwiched between the adults were two little boys, one smirking like he was about to cause no end of mischief for his parents and one squinting as if he was looking past the camera to the bright sunshine in the distance. The man was stern, with his lips pursed into a straight line, but there were laugh lines around his eyes. The woman had a tight smile, but dimples still showed on both of her cheeks. She had her head tilted down, so that her eyes were looking hard into the camera, into the face of onlookers, into Rachael's own eyes as she stared at this photograph.

She had seen hundreds of these same family photos—maybe thousands, possibly millions—not that she distinctly remembered a single one. This one, though, gave her pause. She was supposed to toss the picture into a pile of papers and trash to be burned. She was supposed to keep moving, not think about the family who were most certainly dead—if not at this moment, soon enough—and continue sorting through the never-ending piles. But she was unable to release the photo and unable to tear her eyes off the woman.

This woman, young and smiling and beautiful, had her left arm draped lovingly around the boy closest to her. And clearly shown, even through the worn creases, was a diamond ring on the woman's hand. Rachael's breath caught when she saw it. Could it really be the same ring that she held secretly in her pocket? She could look at nothing else, but her hand reached for the jewel. She felt the rough edges of the ring where dirt was still cemented around the scrollwork. Then her fingers traced the four corners of the ring, where, without looking, she could see in her mind the trine-shaped sapphires. Last, she ran the pad of her thumb over the smooth top of the sparkling diamond. Her touch measured the ring in her pocket with the one in the sepia picture. It was easy to see they were different rings. The one in the picture lacked the detailed work that made Rachael's ring so special. Even from across the camera, she could see it was a European cut diamond on a simple band.

Still, Rachael found herself bringing the ring slowly out of her pocket and holding it against the picture for closer inspection. She was never one to believe in fate, or truly, even miracles. Nevertheless, she could not help asking herself, what were the odds that she found this ring and only days later a picture of a ring? Were they connected?

"Dirty. Thieving. Jew." The words came along with a blow to the back of the head. The force knocked Rachael forward. Her hand holding the photograph opened to catch the ground, rather than slamming her face into the hard surface. Her other hand, clutching the ring, tightened instinctively around it. As she lay on the ground, her head spinning and a throb rapidly working its way down from her skull to her neck and into her back, she shoved the ring back into the safety of her pocket.

"Get up, you rat." The voice came from one of the more ruthless female guards. Rachael knew from witnessing firsthand, this Nazi loved to find thieves among the plunder. She searched them out—baited them, then pounced once someone fell into her trap. Unlike some of her fellow soldiers who shot anyone suspected of stealing before asking questions, this one seemed to enjoy the interrogation and torture. "Get up!" she repeated, this time at a yell that made Rachael's ears ring.

She struggled to her feet, black dots spotting her vision as she tried to look at the guard. "I wasn't stealing," she said, barely a whisper.

The guard kicked Rachael in the stomach. There was little protection from a good meal to pad the kick, so it took the breath out of her and threatened to send her into dry heaves. She forced herself back onto her hands and knees, doubtful that her legs would be able to support her. The guard grabbed Rachael's chin. She pushed her face into Rachael's until the two of them were nose to nose. "Don't lie to me, you nasty Jew."

Rachael tried to shake her head, tried to tell the guard she would never lie to her, but the woman's grip tightened on Rachael's face. "What did you take?"

"I didn't . . ." she started, but the grip made it so she could barely move her mouth to form words.

Without breaking the stare, the guard pulled a small gun from her belt. She lazily cocked it with a loud click. Rachael felt the dry heaves roil up in her stomach again. The guard pushed the cold metal barrel of the gun under Rachael's chin, digging it deep into her neck. Rachael knew she would never even feel the shot. It would pummel into her brain before she would be able to register the sound of the blast. And just like that, there would be nothing left of her.

The woman at the fence was wrong. They could kill all of them. Every single person in Rachael's family would be dead, gone, ashes scattered in the wind. There would be nothing left to bury, nothing left to mourn—certainly, nothing left to remember.

There was not a soul alive who knew her name. Her family had all been killed or lost. She certainly had not made any friends in the camp, though clearly her bunkmate had tried. If the gun fired into her skull, not only would her name be lost forever, but also those of her children and her husband. She could not shake her revelation from the night before: if no one knew they ever existed, had they?

Between the gun forcing its way into her neck and the hand gripping her chin, she could not speak, nor could she remember any German words to help her. Instead, she motioned her hand wildly toward the floor where the picture had fluttered to a rest. She pointed to it frantically, expecting with every second the shot to end her efforts. The cold of the gun barrel on the soft skin of her neck chilled her deep into her bones. The only warmth in her body was the hot tears streaming down her face.

It was days, years, decades before she finally felt the hand loosen around her mouth. Her body sagged with relief, instinctively moving away from the gun. She panted and tried to find her words.

The German guard walked over to the picture and slowly, methodically, picked it up for examination. "This?" she asked Rachael. "This is what you took?"

"I was just looking," she gasped. "I would never . . . I would never steal." The cold had passed through her body and now she felt fire everywhere. Adrenaline burned through her veins and pumped into her heart. She found her feet and stood to face the guard, despite her ribs screaming in protest. "I would never steal," she said with more strength and finality than she truly felt.

The guard crumpled the picture and tossed it at Rachael. It bounced off her chest and landed next to her foot. "No more looking," the guard said. "Or I'll pull the trigger next time."

Rachael had no doubt of it.

Though she was exhausted after fourteen hours of sorting through *kanada*, when she returned to the barracks that night, she set off immediately to track down the little girl. Rachael found her in the corner of one of the wooden barracks. The gray light from outside leaked through the gaps in the wall planks, forming a blurred, striped pattern on the floor. The child was crouching over them, bouncing her finger over the thin lines like she was playing hopscotch along the sidewalk. She was chatting quietly to herself, obviously engrossed in a game only she understood.

Rachael found herself smiling at the child's game. She sat on the floor, careful not to block the light and its pattern.

"What are you playing?" she asked.

Without looking up or pausing the bounce of fingers from stripe to stripe, the girl shrugged. "Just a game. One I made up at home." Rachael cringed at the mention of home. She never spoke of her own home.

"Tell me about the game," Rachael encouraged. She sat back against the wall, feeling a small relief in her sore feet. The wooden clogs, even if sized right, would never fit well enough to make any long-distance walking comfortable.

The girl stopped skipping the line with her first and second fingers and held them up for Rachael to see. "This is the momma," she said, holding up the two fingers on her right hand. "She's looking for her baby." She held up the first two fingers on her left hand, waggling them at Rachael. "She can't walk on these bright spots though. It's fire and will burn her dead."

"Oh my," Rachael said. "We wouldn't want the momma to burn herself dead."

"No," the girl agreed. "Then she would never find her baby."

"How did she lose her baby?"

She shrugged. "Mommas just lose their babies, don't they? All the mommas I know have lost their babies."

The tears were instant. They blurred Rachael's vision and burned her eyes. She did not trust herself to speak.

The child continued. "So the momma goes this way looking for her baby. But her baby is scared and looking for her momma. And she goes this way." The child demonstrated the right hand hopping from shade to shade, while the left hand jumped over the light going the opposite direction.

"So they never find each other?" Rachael asked in a whisper.

The girl shrugged again. "Not yet."

Rachael leaned forward toward the girl and moved her two hands together. "All the mommas I know never stop until they find their babies."

She was rewarded with a dazzling smile from the child. It brightened the room with the luster of a thousand diamonds.

She held out her hand to the girl. "I'm Rachael."

This time she was rewarded with a hug and a name. "Chaya."

Chapter 10

HANNA

The window was opened just a crack to let the morning air into the bedroom. The wind moved the soft yellow curtains, playing hide and seek with the stream of sunshine. Hanna felt the breeze on her face as she awoke. With her eyes still closed, she felt the flash of diamond sparkles dance across her eyelids. She wiggled her left ring finger and opened her eyes.

The glow of that perfect ring made her smile, but a memory of yesterday was starting to dawn on her. She first felt her swollen eyes and the headache behind them. Then she remembered Mr. Weis's stricken face and the full horror of what transpired.

She had gone straight to Samual's after depositing Mrs. Weis at the home of the poor woman's sister. Going to her lonely apartment never even crossed her mind; Samual was her home now. In bed next to him, she shut her eyes again, refusing to wake to reality. She absentmindedly wondered how she got here.

Leaving her hometown of Pribram was a matter of course for Hanna. For as long as she could remember, she knew she would leave as soon as she could. Her father used to take the family to the bustling city of Prague, only sixty kilometers away, every few years. Hanna was six years old when she remembered first seeing Maisel Synagogue, where her family would devoutly sit through hours of services. While she should have been seeking penance for her sins, like fighting with her sisters, her mind was filled with images of pastels and gold and sunlight streaming through stained-glass windows. Her young self never understood how she was supposed to focus on atonement in such a beautiful place.

From those visits, she knew where she belonged. It wasn't with her parents and five siblings in Pribram. Though her father amply provided for his family, she knew the best she could hope for in that town was to marry a man who made his livelihood in the silver mines. She wanted more. And she always thought her father wanted more for her too. He encouraged her curiosity and reading and art. He would tell her, "You can be anything you want to be." But when she turned seventeen and he started pointing out eligible Jewish bachelors, she realized that what he truly meant was that she could be whatever she wanted to be so long as she lived in Pribram, married in Pribram, had lots of babies in Pribram, and died in Pribram. At age eighteen, she left.

She didn't come to Prague to find a Jewish bachelor to marry. She came to find herself and to find her own way. She came because it was the center of Czech life and the center of art, music, and culture in Europe. And she did find all of those things. She knew she lived a small life—making meager tips from her café job, having few friends, and preferring to spend much of her free time alone, working on one watercolor painting after another. Her life may have been small, but it was hers. It was the life she had made for herself.

She had no intentions of changing that life, even when she saw Samual sitting at that outdoor café table. She would have been blind or a fool to not notice him. She recognized his type immediately: strikingly handsome, but with confident self-awareness of it; complete disinterest in the pretty girls around him, partly because he was engrossed in his own concerns and partly because he felt the pretty girls should be interested in him. Hanna knew that type well. She could only guess that he had renounced the faith of his family—he wore none of the traditional garb, yet here he was, frequenting the small, Jewish-owned café in the Jewish Quarter. It seemed he professed Christianity but preferred the comfort of Judaism.

Later, she would discover the extent to which she had guessed correctly. "It's like you are trying to straddle both worlds," she once said to him. He didn't understand what it truly meant to be Jewish. To her, Judaism was more than just a religion. It was community. It was lifestyle. Identity. It was a place to go to be welcomed without question when she stepped off the train in a new city full of strangers and unknown streets. It was a job that was waiting for her despite her lack of training or experience.

When she saw Samual the first time, she was inclined to ignore him. She could see his dual faiths were like two logs floating down a river with him trying to balance in between. He would eventually fall. She could quickly admire his looks and roll her eyes at his hypocritical arrogance when it came to life in the Jewish Quarter—where he took his daily afternoon coffee. Unlike most young men frequenting the café, he initially took no interest in her. Hanna found it amusing. With her thick, glossy hair, quick smile, and laughing eyes the color of melted chocolate, she was used to men staring at her. But she wanted to be admired for something more than her looks.

She remained indifferent to this stranger sitting at the café until he stuttered his way through a conversation with her after his third or fourth visit. She had no idea at the time, but she had made a lasting impression on him with her love for Prague. They were two drifting souls who had found themselves in the same place pursuing the same passion. She knew from a young age that Prague was where she could build a life for herself, as her own person but also as an artist. He made the same discovery on accident. And here they were.

She was surprised by two things when he finally approached her after she ended a shift one day. First, that he was even speaking to her at all. She had poured his coffee many times, but besides placing his order and giving a polite nod to acknowledge his refill of coffee, he hadn't spoken to her at all. Second, he was clumsy and nervous when asking her to join him for a walk that night. She had expected arrogant self-assurance. Later, when she knew him better, she saw that side of him many times, but only when he was trying to charm someone who meant nothing to him. When he craved real approval, he often stammered his way through the encounter. Hanna found that even more charming than his confidence with strangers.

On their first date, they chatted about the basics of their lives over warm bowls of *kulajda* to keep off the October chill. On their second date, Samual planned a somewhat disastrous night of dancing. Hanna had tried to explain to him that while she enjoyed all types of music, her feet were not made for dancing. He didn't believe her, insisted, and learned his lesson after she bruised his toes a few times. On their third date, he was resolute about his feet bearing no lasting damage, and they walked through Letna Park, bundled up against the coming dark and cold but sharing the view of Old Town from high atop the hill.

On their seventh date, he told her he loved her. He had brought her flowers when he picked her up from her apartment, the first time a man had done this for her. She never thought she wanted flowers, but the gesture made her heart beat just a little faster.

She was speechless when he handed them to her.

"I would have liked to bring you roses," he said, looking abashedly at the white bundle of flowers that he held out to her. "But," he shrugged. "Wartime. Rations. You know."

"I like these better," she said as she took the flowers. "You couldn't have known, but lilies of the valley are my favorite."

Samual rolled his eyes. "You don't need to say that."

Hanna looked him in the eyes. "Do you know me to say things just to be nice?"

He laughed. "To me? No."

He lingered by the door as she filled an old coffee tin with water and arranged the flowers on her small, two-person table. "So I chanced upon your favorite flower?" he asked.

She nodded.

"Why these?"

She smiled. She loved when he tried to persuade her to talk more about herself.

"For starters, they are a very hardy flower. They grow in rocky soil, in the shade, in the cold. You have to respect a flower that can thrive in such harsh conditions."

Samual nodded and took a step further into the apartment. Hanna looked up from the flowers and continued.

"They smell lovely—sweet and flowery. Not overpowering. When you walk into a room of roses, you know there are roses there. They take up all the space in the room. But lilies of the valley are subtle."

"You've put a lot of thought into this," Samual said.

"I put a lot of thought into everything," she returned. "They are white. And I love white flowers. And—"

Samual laughed at her long list of reasons.

Hanna shot him a teasingly dark look at his interruption and continued. "And . . . And in the language of flowers, they mean the return of happiness. These days, who wouldn't love a flower that means that?"

Samual walked across the small room and took her hand. "You've convinced me," he said softly. She gave him a quick kiss on the lips.

"I knew that I would." Hand in hand, they walked out of the apartment. As Hanna closed the door behind her, she added, "Oh, and when eaten, lilies of the valley can kill a grown man."

Samual's laugh echoed down the small hallway.

It was later that night when Samual held her face in his hands and whispered that he loved her.

That was only a few months ago. Now, here she was—in the arms of the man she loved (how her mother would be mortified!), with a sparkling diamond on her finger, imagining a future life of happiness though a worldwide war raged around her. The events from the day before made the risk of living through this war even more real. But while she still felt the trauma of Mr. Weis's arrest through every bone in her body, she also could not help feeling safe with Samual's arms tightly wrapped around her.

He must have been awake, because his arms pulled her closer—tighter and tighter until she knew he was being playful.

She let out a fake gasp. "Would you like to let me breathe this morning?" she asked him.

He gave her one final squeeze and nuzzled his head against her cheek. "How are you feeling this morning?"

"Awful."

"I thought as much. Stay in bed and I'll bring you coffee and a little breakfast," he offered.

"I'd rather you just stay in bed with me," she said. She pushed her body into his, wiggling back into his tight grasp.

"An acceptable compromise," he whispered in her ear.

They lay in bed a while longer, enjoying the warmth of each other and the sunlight as it continued to glow though the sheer curtains. Hanna kept positioning her ring finger into the sunbeams, playing with the light. Samual chuckled and held her hand up higher into the sunshine, moving it back and forth to reflect the rays.

"How are you feeling?" he asked again after a long, comfortable silence.

"Still awful," she said.

"Tell me."

Hanna sighed and rolled over to face him. His chin was covered with just the slightest stubble, and his eyes were fixed on her. He waited quietly for her to say something.

"I just stood there," she said finally. She kept her eyes on Samual's lips, not daring to look into his eyes. "I just let it all happen. They took him away, and I did nothing."

"You didn't do nothing. You probably saved Mrs. Weis's life. You were smart and brave, and I'm very proud of you." He tilted her chin up so she couldn't avoid his gaze.

"I wasn't brave," she said, trying to look back down, but Samual held her chin firmly.

"You were incredibly brave."

"It's not bravery when you're pretending," she said. She looked him steadily in the eyes finally. He released his hold on her. She kissed the tip of Samual's nose, though, to show she appreciated his words.

"Hanna, my dear," he said softly. "Pretending when in fact you are terrified, that is the exact definition of bravery."

"I don't feel brave. I feel like a coward." She tucked her head under Samual's chin—for the comfort of his closeness, but also to avoid letting him see her face, blushing in shame as tears formed in her eyes. "I didn't even admit that I knew Mr. Weis. I just sat there as they took him. I did nothing to help him." She snuggled even deeper into Samual's warmth. "I was no better than these people of Prague who let terrible things happen to us."

Samual moved away from Hanna's tight embrace. He craned his neck until he was looking at Hanna's face. "Stop," he said firmly. "Stop. You can't do that to yourself. What you did was one of the most selfless things I've seen since the Nazis took over the streets."

Hanna shook her head, but Samual stopped her.

"You could have walked away before the soldiers even reached the café. You could have escaped when you realized they were there to arrest Mr. Weis. You could have remained silent when they tried to arrest Mrs. Weis. But you didn't."

She tried to shake her head again, but Samual again stopped her with a small shake of her shoulders.

"You saved Mrs. Weis's life. And from what I know of Mr. Weis, that was the most important thing you could have done for him. It may seem like a small thing, but what you did is the exact reason why the Nazis can never destroy us."

"Us?" Hanna teased.

"Yes, us. People who care for others. People who are brave and selfless. Us."

"I didn't think I would see the day when you'd throw your lot in with us poor Jews," she said, still playfully.

Samual shrugged.

Her voice serious again, Hanna asked, "Are they going to just keep arresting us one after another? Are they going to imprison all of us?"

Samual shook his head decidedly. "They can't arrest all of us. Do you know how many Jews there are in Prague alone? Think about the rest of Europe. The world. They can't imprison all of us."

"And why would they want to?" Hanna asked. "I don't understand it."

Samual shrugged again. "Maybe they are just afraid of what they don't understand. Once things settle down, once they push us around enough to prove their point, the Nazis will start to ease up. You'll see. It's not like they can get rid of all the Jews."

Chapter 11

RACHAEL

Talking to Chaya, even just spending time with another person, felt unfamiliar to Rachael. She felt as if she was wearing a stranger's clothes, living a stranger's life. Most of the women in Auschwitz lived on memories—telling and retelling old stories. At night, they would walk their bunkmate through their old home, describing every squeaky stair, every scratch on the wooden floor, every picture hanging on the wall. When they were eating their allotted piece of bread, they would share family recipes, down to the pinch of salt added after stealing a taste from the wooden spoon. They would search each wave of new arrivals, looking for a familiar face with whom they could reminisce about better times.

Not Rachael. She had preferred to forget. Maybe that was why she had felt so close to death. Now, with Chaya, she had to use her voice, practice patience, and remember to care about another. It felt like a lifetime ago when she had last cared for anyone, including herself.

She could not lie; it was nice. It was nice to have someone smile at her, hold her hand, and look at her with intent, caring eyes. She had not realized how much she had missed it. But she felt the danger of this new friendship, too.

It reminded her of the last winter before the Germans came to Prague. Radek had rebuilt an old wooden sled that Alexey had from childhood. Her son had spent the fall sharpening and polishing the old runners until they cut through the first snowfall like new knives. They hiked to the tallest hill in Kralovska obora Stromovka, her favorite park in the city. He convinced Rachael to get on the sled, holding a very small Catarina between her legs. Radek gave her a push, and she found herself flying down the hill with Catarina squealing in pure delight. She felt them pick up speed as they hurtled down the slope. The cold whipped their faces, and their laughter was louder than the slice of the sled on the ground. As wonderful as it was, Rachael felt like they were on the edge of catastrophe the entire way down. One rock on their path, one snow-hidden hole, one unbalanced turn, and she and Catarina would lose control to land in disaster and pain.

Friendship with Chaya was like that—exhilarating and wonderful but balancing on the edge of complete disaster. Another heartbreak would kill her. Her heart would just stop beating and she would slump to the ground, another corpse to be dropped into a mass grave outside of the camp.

Despite the comfort of a relationship with another person and despite her resolution to forge a bond with this child, Rachael found it difficult to break out of her ways. She was short with the girl, often unwilling to play or talk. She wondered why Chaya continued to greet her every day as she came back from long hours of sorting through the remnants of people's destroyed lives. The unending patience Rachael had for Catarina, even in those darkest days in the Terezin ghetto, was hard to resurface for this new child.

Perhaps, Rachael thought, it was because the children were so completely different. This child was energetic, despite her near-starvation state. She lived in the worst place on earth yet always had a smile on her face. She was creative and happy—cheerful—constantly making up games with her fingers, or the shadows on the wall, or pieces of dried mud that she found on the barrack floor. Catarina, though, had been nothing but solemn and quiet since the beginning of the war. Chaya was always doing. Catarina had always been observing.

Chaya was a little older than Catarina, but still too young to really know anything other than war. Chaya was unsure of her age, her family, truly anything prior to hiding from the Germans in some family's basement pantry. From the bits of information Rachael coaxed out of the child's spotty memory, she determined Chaya was around nine or ten years old. The girl's complete lack of knowledge of her own mother and father cemented Rachael's fear of being utterly forgotten. If a daughter could not even recall a faded image of her own loving mother, what hope did Rachael have of living on in memory if she died at the hands of the Nazis in this godforsaken place?

So slowly, very slowly, Rachael tried to learn what she could from Chaya and share her own story with the little girl, who was eager to learn and remember. Bringing Radek, Catarina, and the baby back to life, in some small sense, had been Rachael's purpose, but she found herself unable to speak of them. It was too painful.

Instead, she spoke of her husband. She was sure a small girl had little interest in hearing an adult love story. Chaya was never told fairy tales before meeting Rachael, so the concept of "happily ever after" was as foreign to her as a land free of war. But she happily sat next to Rachael in the corner of the barracks, listening to the soft voice recount her courtship and early married life. She would lean her head against Rachael's side and play absentmindedly with the ring, which she often begged to hold. Just when Rachael was sure the child was no longer listening, Chaya would ask a question or pause in her admiration of the diamond, waiting for Rachael to continue.

"My mother, always playing the matchmaker, sent Alexey to the bookstore where I worked," Rachael told her.

"Bookstore?" Chaya asked.

"Bookstore," she repeated, before realizing the girl had little concept of books and none at all of a bookstore. It was not unusual for her stories to take detours such as these. "Bookstores are where books are sold."

"Just books?" Chaya asked. "A whole place with just books?" She shrugged, her little mind unable to fathom it.

The two of them were sitting hunched on Rachael's bunk. She could not sit up straight without grazing the top of the ceiling, but Chaya enjoyed sitting up so high with her feet swinging over the edge of the bunk.

"I remember bookstores," Rachael's lower bunkmate said, a heavy note of longing in her voice. Chaya doubled over so she could see the woman below them.

"Not me," she said, as if that ended the argument. "What's your name? I'm Chaya. She's Rachael."

Rachael almost laughed. All these months ignoring the woman who slept right below her, and now Chaya had destroyed Rachael's brick wall with a dip of her head and a few lively words.

The woman laughed as well, sounding as if she had just won a long-fought battle. "I'm Irene. Nice to meet you, Chaya. Rachael." She nodded at Rachael, who smiled back in surrender.

That night, Rachael, with input from Irene, tried explaining shelves full of books and confectionary treats and a Jewish wedding ceremony to Chaya. These trivial conversations, though, did not keep at bay the nightmares that came later. After the barracks quieted down, Rachael felt the sweat trickle down her neck, despite the dankness and draftiness of the barracks. She tossed and turned with restless sleep and dreamt over and over again about her destroyed family. The irony was not lost on her that her dreams were often of Alexey, the one person who was most likely to settle her when nightmares came.

She hadn't been prone to nightmares before the war. Even after Radek was taken, Alexey died, and she was living in the Jewish ghetto outside of

Prague, she usually slept soundly. She and Catarina huddled close in the small bed they shared—not so much because they needed the warmth or didn't have space for two beds, but because they needed each other's touch and comfort. She was usually exhausted from a long day of working with the clean-up crew to clear the ghetto streets and trying to find enough scraps of food to provide for Catarina. Sleep came easily and deeply. When she and Alexey shared a bed, she would often reach for him in her sleep. She'd wake up with her hand resting on his forearm or on his chest, like she needed to assure herself that he was still there. Now, he wasn't.

Rachael had first met Chaya in the autumn, and the days had turned darker and colder by the time the little girl asked Rachael the question she had been dreading.

She spoke the words as she did most conversations between them—half playing out a scenario with her active imagination and half listening to the stream of words coming from Rachael. "So what happened to your husband? Is he here?"

With exaggerated movements, Rachael looked around the barracks. Though the place was filthy and the smell made her eyes water every time she entered, it was a type of oasis, away from the ruthless guards. Rachael tried to keep Chaya away from the Nazis as much as possible. The fleas and stench kept the Germans far from this place. Chaya giggled and Rachael pretended to look for her missing husband under the nearest bunk.

"No," she said with forced playfulness. "It doesn't look like he's here."

Chaya was not to be distracted, though—the girl never bounced from one idea to the next when Rachael wanted her to. "Where is he?"

"He died."

Chaya stopped climbing her fingers over the barrack wall. She waited for Rachael to say more.

"It was a few years ago," Rachael started. She honestly did not know how long she had been living without Alexey. It felt like a lifetime. Or several, if life can be measured in sorrows and witnessed horrors. "He was hurt, and no one would help him."

"And he died?" Chaya asked.

Rachael nodded.

Chaya nodded too, knowingly. "They all die, don't they?"

How could Rachael explain the complete waste that was Alexey's death? In Chaya's short life, she had come to understand that death was to be expected at every turn. Maybe in the acceptance of this came her happiness. Rachael, though, wanted to shake the girl by the shoulders and make her see—Alexey's death was pointless and could have easily been prevented.

She hadn't heeded her husband's concerns that autumn when he worried over a new German leader taking over the city. She had never heard the rough German name, Heydrich, before, nor had she much bothered herself with politics or world news before the war. The change in the city was immediate though. Even she, a doting wife and mother with little interest in the affairs of military men, felt the cold wind sweep through the city that October. There came a new and far-reaching round of arrests, disappearances, and, if rumors could be believed, executions in the first week of Heydrich's reign. To be sure the Jewish people knew the extent of his brutality, rumors became fact as lists were posted around the Jewish Quarter of criminals shot in the distant Pankrac Prison. The list, though, did not contain the names of murderers or thieves, but teachers and artists and friends she had known all her life. Like Radek, she could not fathom what crime they could have committed besides being Jewish and living in this city.

"Keep your head down and stay out of the way of the Germans," Alexey advised. In her terror, she agreed with him. But the part of her heart that belonged to Radek felt that Alexey was being untrue to their son. Did he think, deep down, that Radek was to blame for his fate? If he had "kept his head down," would he still be with them? Rachael could not let herself consider those questions. The answers would only hurt her already broken heart.

That's what they were doing just a few months after Radek had been taken from them—keeping their heads down. It was coming up on curfew for the evening, and Rachael and Alexey had traveled the five blocks to offer comfort to old friends, two widowed sisters who had lived together for years. Their father had been taken from their home the day before by Nazi soldiers under the flimsy pretense of inciting a rebellion among his neighbors. The poor man was close to seventy, nearly blind, and just as hard of hearing. The truth of the matter was he had spoken loudly—as all his words were spoken—about the unjustness of the treatment of Jews. "He wasn't wrong," Alexey whispered to Rachael as they made their way back home, "but he was foolish. No good can be done with such words. Poor Mr. Kohn did nothing except sign his own fate. And without him, what will happen to the sisters?"

Before Rachael could answer, though she really did not have an answer, Alexey squeezed her hand, a quick warning of what lay ahead of them.

Two German soldiers were standing stiff as statues at the corner they were approaching. They stood in the middle of a glistening sea of broken glass from the shop windows just beyond them. The sounds of more destruction—shattering china, sturdy furniture toppling over, cries of mercy—wafted onto the street from the Jewish-owned shop that was being wrecked.

"Let's cross over," she whispered urgently to Alexey. She tried to veer toward the curb and across the street to relative safety, but Alexey's hand held her firm.

"They've seen us," he said, barely moving his lips.

Rachael looked up to find he was right. While still at perfect attention, both soldiers had narrowed their stares to Rachael and her husband. It happened in an instant, but she was sure she saw one of them crack a malicious smile before resuming his bored, blank expression. Like a rabbit crossing paths with a lion, Rachael hoped to keep her head down and walk by, unnoticed, or at least noticed as not a concern.

Alexey did not allow them to slow their pace. They continued walking, her hand on Alexey's arm, his other hand covering hers. They were connected in every way possible as they approached this danger. He kept tightening and loosening his grip on her hand, trying, she thought, to give her reassurance.

Time slowed for her as they walked those last dozen steps to pass the soldiers. Glass that would break in only seconds took four times as long. She saw pieces of plates and teacups scatter into the street, noting every individual shard as it flew through the air. People across the street scurried quickly away from the soldiers and the carnage of the shop, but to Rachael, she and Alexey seemed to move toward them in slow motion. She heard vehicles driving down the street, some full of soldiers, some splashing through puddles from a cold downpour earlier in the afternoon. She felt Alexey's hand loosen once more, like a Morse code message sending her wordless support as they neared imminent peril.

In real time, Rachael was sure the action took a fraction of a second, but when she relived the moment over and over in her mind, it slowed down more every time, until she could see every millisecond in perfect clarity. As Alexey and Rachael walked past, neither of the soldiers seemed to look in their direction. She was about to exhale the breath she had been holding. Then the hand of the nearest soldier shot out in front of her. She had to stop abruptly to keep from running into it. In the slowed down versions of events in her mind, she could see the perfectly ironed crease running along the length of its sleeve, brown like the shirts worn by all the vicious SA soldiers, only impeded by the red Swastika armband. She stutter-stepped to miss hitting the soldier's arm, but the hand connected with Alexey's shoulder. He stumbled to the side, tried to correct his footing, then lost all balance as he fell off the curb. His arm pulled from Rachael's grasp and he stumbled into the street.

Not just into the street, but into a speeding truck full of German soldiers.

She saw every detail of the collision. The bumper hit Alexey's legs first, with a sickening crunch. The force of the moving vehicle spun him so that the next collision was his head and chest hitting the windshield. As the truck continued without slowing, Alexey was pushed several meters down the street before rolling off the front of the truck into the gutter.

From there he made no sound, nor moved at all. Neither did Rachael. She stared in horror at her husband's broken body, his blood already mixing with the puddle on the side of the street, turning the rainwater a sickening red. The truck continued down the road, with only the laughter of the soldiers in the back showing that anyone even noticed what had happened.

Rachael was frozen, looking at Alexey as he lay in the gutter. She heard a moan, a sound that she didn't realize humans were even able to make. It was beastly, like an animal caught in a metal claw trap. It was another moment before Rachael realized the sound was coming from her.

She rushed to Alexey's side, but stopped herself from touching him. She knew very little about nursing someone through a trauma. She could clean a bloodied knee or offer some small remedies for a cough or head cold. But Alexey was a ruin. His limbs were bent in angles unnatural to the human body. Blood was everywhere. Rachael could not determine the source—head, abdomen, leg. It seemed like he was a faucet spurting blood rather than clean water.

Rachael's hands were frozen above Alexey as he lay face down. It was hard to tell if he was breathing. She wanted to turn him over and see in his eyes that he was still with her, but she was terrified to hurt him even further. More than that, she was terrified at what she might see.

"Get him out of here." The words were hissed into her ear, making her jump to her feet in surprise. By instinct, she stood over Alexey, guarding him from further danger. It was the Nazi soldier who had pushed her husband into a moving vehicle. She wanted to fly at him, turning her hands that were useless to help Alexey into weapons to ravage this soldier's face. His expression of pure hatred and barely suppressed violence, though, kept her from making such a fatal move.

"I need to get him to the hospital," she said. The words were barely audible over the normal bustle of the street. To her horror, life seemed to move on around her, unheeding of the dying man at her feet.

The soldier laughed. "You need to get him to a morgue."

Rachael shook her head desperately. "He's alive," she said. "He's alive and he's a fighter, and—"

Rachael broke off her words abruptly when the soldier swiftly turned the gun hanging off his soldier onto her husband. "He's a dying dog making a mess of my street. Get him out of here." The soldier moved the barrel of the gun so it pushed into her stomach. She tried to take a step back but would have tripped over Alexey. "Get him out of here or join him."

She nodded dumbly. She turned back to face her husband. Tears blinded her sight. She wanted to scream with frustration but decided to use that rage to save Alexey. She, like any mother, knew that when her family was threatened, women were capable of unbelievable strength. As a woman who had to keep life moving along after her son disappeared at the hands of the Germans, she always thought it was a metaphysical rather than a literal strength. Her opinion was changed as she grabbed Alexey underneath his arms and started to pull.

Besides a grunt that escaped from already parted lips, Alexey made no sound or movement as Rachael struggled, step by step, to pull her husband out of the street and around the corner. She did not look behind her, at the endless blocks and streets of Prague. She had no idea how long her strength would hold out, but she silently prayed she could at least get out of sight of the German soldiers. She could feel the eyes of the one who shoved Alexey. He was watching her every movement, but she would not give him the satisfaction of looking his way.

Panting and sobbing, she made it around the corner. The muscles in her arms and legs screamed for her to stop, but she feared if she did, she would never find the power to start again. With every step she took, her cries grew louder. She jumped when she felt a soft hand on her back.

She looked up and realized she had rounded the corner onto a quiet side street of the Jewish Quarter. Two men stood behind her. Both were undistinguishable in their expressions of pity and shame.

"Let us," one of the men said. Like her and Alexey, they were both wearing new yellow Stars of David on their outer coats.

She wanted to scream at them: *Where were you when they pushed my husband into a truck? Where were you when I had to pull his broken body down the street? Where was your pity and help then?* But she had no voice, and she knew it was no use. Even though every rabbi in the quarter would preach that the Jewish people needed to stand together to fight this enemy, Rachael knew her people were as human as the rest. They would stand only for themselves. In this quiet street, without the watchful eyes of the Germans, they would help in secrecy. Screaming and unleashing her rage on these men was both unfair and unhelpful to Alexey. So, she straightened her already aching back and reached for Alexey's hand that was dangling from his body, like the top button on Catarina's blouse, hanging on by only a thread so it swayed with every movement of her body. His hand was wet, both with rain from the puddle and blood still flowing.

"We need to get him to the hospital," she said.

The man nearest her shook his head slowly. "They will not help you," he said.

"What are you talking about? My husband—"

"I understand, but they will not help Jews."

"That's ridiculous," Rachael said. "If you will not take him, then I will."

The second man answered. "Of course, we will take him for you. But prepare yourself."

Neither of them spoke any further. The only noises coming from the slowly proceeding foursome were the grunts of effort from the men and Rachael's sharp intake of breath whenever she worried Alexey was jostled more than his body could handle. Her husband never woke up nor made another sound, which Rachael counted as a blessing. She would not even let herself imagine the pain he would have been in were he conscious.

As they made the slow and torturous pilgrimage to Na Frantisku Hospital, the nearest one to the Jewish Quarter, Rachael took inventory of Alexey's injuries. Most of the blood, which dripped a trail from the scene of the accident to their current course on the street along the Vltava River, seemed to be coming from a cut near his temple. From broken windshield glass, Rachael assumed. She knew that head wounds gushed exorbitantly. She had seen enough from Radek's rough and tumble days. Aside from this and some other gashes, everything lay at odd angles—she was sure, if not broken, both his right arm and leg were severely strained. With his clothes on, she could not assess the damage to his torso, where she thought the impact of the truck hit hardest. His breaths were shallow and rasping. Were his ribs constricting his lungs? Until a doctor at the hospital examined Alexey, she could not be sure.

As the familiar red roof of Na Frantisku came into sight from around the bend, Rachael knew they had made a mistake. She knew this place well. She had delivered Catarina in this hospital and visited many unwell friends here. Rachael always found the hospital inviting and friendly, with its red roof and sunny yellow walls. But she'd had no reason to visit it in months, maybe even years, and now it was anything but welcoming. The door was guarded by two armed Nazis, checking everyone's papers before allowing them inside.

"They'll never let you in," said the man nearest her. She did not even bother to note anything of either man's appearance. "I have heard they only care for Nazis, especially wounded pilots."

"Then why did you bring me here?" Rachael wailed the words more than spoke them. They had carried Alexey in this state for blocks upon blocks, and now the man was telling her it was for nothing? She felt a bubble working its way up from her gut, about to explode.

"Ma'am," the man said, "it would not have mattered. Hospitals will not admit Jews. None of them. Herr Heydrich's orders." He hung his head in shame that was not his.

"They have to." Rachael swallowed the bubble back down. She held her head up. "It is a hospital, is it not? They help the injured and"—she steeled herself—"dying. Clearly my husband is both." She took the lead of their small procession and marched up to the soldiers. She kept her eyes fixed on the door between them, not intending to stop unless they physically forced her to do so. She felt the men following behind her with the shattered body of her husband in their arms.

With her eyes fixed ahead, she did not see the soldier's swift movement, but she felt an iron grip close around her upper arm.

"Where do you think you're going?" he snarled. He looked at her like she was dirt, yet he was nothing more than a rabid animal.

She tried to shake her arm free from his clutches but only succeeded in making the hand tighten even further. It registered that such a hold should hurt, yet she felt nothing. She finally made eye contact. She knew that one look conveyed everything she was feeling—rage, helplessness, despair, hatred, and courage like she had never known. The Nazi must have read her flood of thoughts because he dropped her arm but continued to stand in her path to the door.

"Papers," he said, holding his hand out. He had already eyed her yellow star.

She pushed his hand away and tried to sidestep around him. "There's no time," she said, the panic forcing her voice to betray the unsurety that she was suppressing. The soldier matched her step for step, like a terrible dance of life or death.

"Papers," he said again. "Now."

"Look at him!" she yelled. "Look at what you've done to him! I have no time—"

"I *am* looking at him," the soldier said. His face was mere centimeters from her own. His voice had gone deadly quiet. "I see him, the filthy, dirty Jew." His hard stare moved from Rachael's eyes to Alexey's body. He pulled a handgun from inside his brown coat and pointed it straight at her husband's chest, which trembled every time he took a breath. The soldier aimed it directly at the Star of David. Rachael moved instinctively between Alexey and the soldier. He moved his eyes back up to Rachael's, bringing the aim of the gun with him. Rachael stood facing him, staring down the barrel of the weapon.

"I had a teacher once who was a Jewess." The soldier spit onto the cobblestones in front of the hospital entrance. "I'm sure she's dead now." He smiled slightly. "But she was kind to me and my brother. So, in honor of that bitch"—Rachael cringed at the word—"I'm going to help you."

She felt no relief at his words. She heard the men carrying Alexey stir behind her.

"Here are your choices," the soldier said. The other soldier guarding the door, who had watched this scene unfold with disinterest, chuckled. "You can take the rat home to die slowly as the blood runs out of his disgusting body . . ." Rachael fought the tears. She would have begged this man on her hands and knees to let her into the hospital, but she would not let him see her cry. "Or you can drop him at my feet, and I'll finish him off nice and quick. The second option would be a mercy, but I don't care either way." He tilted his head, looking back to Alexey behind her. "By the end of the day, there will be one less Jew for us to worry about."

They made it home—Rachael, Alexey, and the two men acting as his stretcher. Turning her back on the soldier at the hospital was, she thought later, the single hardest thing she had ever done. She knew turning away from the doctors inside was condemning her husband to death, one that surely could have been prevented if she had been allowed just a few paces further. She was also sure, as she stepped away from the soldier, that she would be shot in the back of the head at any moment. Though she backed down and away from the hospital entrance, the Nazi never lowered his gun. When she glanced back toward him as she walked around the riverside bend, he was still tracking her with his aim.

When Rachael later dreamed about that trek through the streets of Prague, silent and empty as curfew had taken over, it was a nightmare that never ended. She walked and walked and walked, holding Alexey's hand as it became colder and colder. His face became white like the sheets she once hung in their small backyard. She urged the men to move faster, to do anything to help him, but the sidewalk continued to extend in front of them without end. The faster she tried to move her legs, the slower they actually carried her, until she would finally wake up in a cold sweat on the bunk in Auschwitz.

In real life, Rachael finally brought her husband home. The men laid him as gently as their exhausted arms would allow on the bed that she and Alexey had shared since moving into this snug house. No amount of tears, pleading, or bribery could convince either man to take any further risk by running through the dark and patrolled streets in search of a doctor. They had already endangered themselves far more than they had wanted when they first offered assistance. Rachael had no emotions left to spare for them, either to feel grateful for their efforts, however ineffective, or guilty for the trouble they would certainly meet if discovered on their way home at this late hour.

Rachael had just enough mind left to consider her daughter. The effects of Radek's arrest and deportation were deep and long lasting in Catarina. As Alexey lay in their bed, where they had shared so much love and tenderness, writhing in pain, Rachael picked up her child and ran her to the neighbor's house. Though she was not sure she spared Catarina much trauma, as she knew the moans from the house could be heard many doors down. It was the mournful harmony of

Alexey's cries of pain and Rachael's wails of despair as she helplessly watched her husband die.

The doctor came with the first rays of sunshine breaking through the darkness of her bedroom. He was Jewish, out of work, and mostly useless. Yes, he told Rachael, Alexey was gravely injured. Yes, to her unasked question, the hospital would have been able to help him more than he ever could. But, he assured her, he would do his very best to save her husband.

He placed his ear close to Alexey's chest. Throughout the night, his short, wheezing breaths, broken intermittently by painful gasps, became more of a rattle. Rachael could not stop herself from thinking this was the "death rattle" she often heard people speak of. The doctor placed his stethoscope under Alexey's shirt and listened for just a moment before shaking his head sadly. A collapsed lung, he told her. But whether from the impact of the vehicle or a broken rib that had ruptured the organ, he could not say.

Next, the doctor examined Alexey's head. Rachael had tightly wrapped a bandage around his head when first arriving home. By that time, though, the bleeding had mostly stopped. She had found several cuts on the right side of his temple, but none alarmingly deep. She hunted for remains of glass, cleaned the wounds, and washed the remaining traces of the accident from her husband's hair and face. The rest of his body, she dared not touch.

Last, the doctor pulled down the blanket that Rachael had lovingly tucked around her husband when the chill of the room nipped at her own hands and feet. He unbuttoned Alexey's collared shirt, once white but now stained a stiff brown from the dried mud and blood. Using a small pair of shears from his black bag, the doctor cut away his undershirt, slowly unwrapping it from Alexey's body.

Rachael looked away at the last second. She did not want to see his strong torso demolished by the Nazis. When she heard the doctor's gasp, though, her head instinctively turned to see the cause, despite her heart's pleading.

She had never seen anything like it. Her quick mind, the one with a wit so sharp Alexey told her he loved it more than all her other traits, saw and thought so many things at once that she could not keep up. It's a bruise, not so bad. It's the most beautiful array of reds and purples that she had ever seen. That's not her husband's body. It's the color of the plums she used for pastries in the spring. Bruises heal. If she could paint, this would be a color that would make people stop in their tracks and admire it. Her husband's body could not take such damage and still live. Not exactly like a plum; a bruised plum. He can heal. Thus, that is not Alexey's body because Alexey must live. But a bruised plum would turn wrinkled and brown. She had seen terrible bruises on Radek's knees, and he continued to run through the street playing as if nothing was amiss. Whose body is she looking at if that is not Alexey?

Rachael's mind took these thoughts and tangled them together, braided them so they were interwoven with each other.

It was just a bruise.

The colors were beautiful, worthy of a canvas.

It was not her husband.

It was a dropped fruit.

That was the thought her mind decided on in the end. Damaged and bruised fruit.

She heard the doctor say something about internal bleeding.

Once she had let Radek help her at the market. He carried home a dozen apples, bought at a good price from a local farmer. As they entered the kitchen, he dropped three of them. He laughed at the plop, plop, plop they had made on the floor. But Rachael was angry with him.

He could have a ruptured spleen, the doctor said from far away.

Radek picked the apples up from the ground and showed her that they were still red and delicious. They placed them in the bowl on their small wooden table.

Maybe a ruptured liver, he continued.

A few days later though, Rachael turned the apples over in the bowl. The entire sides of those three apples were brown. Rotted. Damaged beyond saving. Radek cried.

Possibly both the liver and the spleen. It was impossible to tell.

Rachael had Radek help her make applesauce that afternoon. They cut the spoiled parts from the apples, diced the good fruit into fine bits, and boiled it on the stove. That evening they desserted on sweet, tangy applesauce with touches of cinnamon.

"The hospital may have been able to stop the bleeding, but there is nothing I can do in this bedroom."

Rachael remembered what the insides of those apples looked like, how she had cut the ruined parts from the healthy parts. She could not cut the ruin from Alexey's body. It was half of his body and growing. There were red fingers of blood clawing their way up from his abdomen into his chest.

"Even if I could operate," the doctor continued, "I couldn't stop the bleeding at this point."

She would never eat applesauce again.

The doctor left soon after. His parting words were something about how he didn't even have morphine to stop the pain. As she closed the door behind him, she thought, he truly was useless.

She held Alexey's hand as he died. She was afraid to touch any other part of his body. She listened to his breathing, short, painful, soon to stop. She watched the clock.

Thirty-one hours. Alexey left her and this world after thirty-one hours. Rachael did not mark that time on the clock as time of death, like a medical professional would have. Instead, she thought of it as a milestone for the Nazis to celebrate. It took them thirty-one hours to kill this Jew. Was that a record for them to cheer? The longest they had ever made one suffer?

At the thirty-one hour mark, Rachael watched Alexey start to cough. It was weak and faint at first. She sat up straighter and held his right hand with both of hers. The coughing intensified. Though he had no strength left, his coughing grew stronger. His body would not give up that easily. Then blood started to spew out of his mouth. It sprayed onto his chest, leaked from the corners of his mouth down his cheeks; it flew through the air, peppering her own body. She rushed to turn him over, to let the blood flow out of his mouth, away from his lungs, but as she placed her hand on his destroyed right side, she stopped. The bruising covered his entire torso, with those red, bloody tendrils now working their way up his neck.

She could have rolled him over. She could have saved him in that moment. She could have given him more time, more minutes, maybe one more hour. But she did not. She watched her husband choke on the blood that had filled his body. She did not let herself look away, because she deserved the torture of this sight. She wanted it to haunt her for the rest of her living days.

As she stared at Chaya, who waited with uncharacteristic patience for her to continue, she considered what she should have done differently. But there had been no helping him from the moment they saw those Nazis standing on the street corner. She should have let them shoot Alexey as he lay in the gutter. Or she should have let the soldier at the hospital put a bullet through his chest. Or she should have been the brave and merciful one and placed a pillow over his face when the doctor told her it was too late.

But how could she say that to Chaya? How could she explain to this child the pointlessness of her husband's death and her own uselessness since that instant?

"They all die, don't they?" Chaya asked again, breaking Rachael from her terrible memories.

A good mother would have put her arm around the child, said some comforting words, corrected this all-too-cynical view of the world. Rachael, though, did not see herself as a good mother, or even a mother at all, anymore. Instead of bringing the child close, she shrugged. "It seems that way at times."

Chaya looked down. "Did you ever hear the story of the wicked witch and a house that dropped on her? Irene told me about it."

Chapter 12

HANNA

That spring and summer, Hanna fell into a contented routine as a newly engaged woman. Life was by no means easy; she struggled to replace her work at Prague Kofe, so money was a day-to-day fight. But, as terrible as she knew it sounded, she was getting used to it. She never thought she could grow accustomed to war or living under the constant threat and terror of the Nazis, but by autumn, she started to feel something akin to normalcy.

She knew, despite the horror of the war, she was making memories that she would cherish all her life. Mainly she knew she would treasure the smoky and lazy Saturday nights, like this one, with Samual and his friends.

"I have to say," Werner said as he and Greta, his long-time girlfriend, came through the door, "I really thought the two of you would have killed one another by now. This two-bedroom is awful small for both of you boys."

Samual laughed at the teasing. "Maybe we are just easier to get along with than you," he quipped back. David, the other roommate, remained quiet. Hanna noted his patchy beard; Werner, on the other hand, was clean-shaven as always with his blond hair thoughtlessly pushed to the side.

David scowled hard at his cigarette. Hanna felt rather than saw his desperation. She knew he would never admit it, but he hadn't worked for over two years. It wasn't just the dependency on Samual and his other friends that broke David's spirit, but the lack of doing anything productive. These nights with friends were different though. Despite Werner's jokes, David started to relax into one of the small wooden chairs in Samual's living room. Werner, still employed at a small machine shop in New Town, carried two bottles of cheap wine and a pack of cigarettes, which he set down on the coffee table. He and Greta quickly joined the rest of the group, sitting around the small living room, taking long, luxurious drags at their cigarettes, listening to old records—no one had the money to buy anything new—and reminiscing about easier times.

It was not an easy life for any of them, though some certainly got on better than others. David never complained about his lack of work, but the patches that slowly took over his shirts and pants told the complete story. Hanna, also in the beginning, tried to avoid talk about her unemployment at those Saturday night gatherings, but her experience at Prague Kofe when Mr. Weis was arrested was common knowledge in their group.

"Speaking of roommates," Werner continued, "how is your new place?" he asked Hanna.

She groaned on reflex, then laughed at herself to lighten the mood. "Pretty awful," she said, hoping her forced smile would make her complaints seem more like a joke. "Freezing floors, shared washroom, bland food. And worst of all," she lowered her voice and leaned in conspiratorially toward Werner, "enforced curfew without male visitors."

"Oh the horror!" he said, laughing.

Hanna took a small sip of her wine. "At least it's a place to stay." She nodded at Werner. "And thanks to your suggestion to tutor your boss's daughters in art, I can actually pay my rent." She raised her glass to him in a small toast. "So I know I'm luckier than most."

As much as she adored Samual's friends and more and more considered them her own, she did not want to tell them the whole truth: that her entire body felt like ice when she was in her boarding house; that fifteen women were expected to share one small washroom; that the little money she earned scarcely covered the watery oatmeal in the morning and, if she was first in line, a bit of bread and cheese for lunch.

Nights like these were a salve to her wartime wounds. Here they were all equals—pitching in what little they had or could scrounge up, enjoying the music and company. Most of all, they would laugh. Hanna knew that they laughed too freely and too easily. But, as they saw it, Prague lost a little bit of color with every new Nazi who stepped into the city, so was it possible to laugh too much?

Hanna had to admit, the summer Saturday nights had seemed easier, but the warm weather and glow of friendship could not last forever. By now, the leaves from the beech trees had turned from brilliant greens to bloody reds, then faded yellows. The wind started to bring in the chill, first from the North Sea, then from Germany. Tonight, Hanna had set out extra blankets before Werner and Greta arrived, to make up for the coal or firewood that should have been in the small stove. She felt, though, that the chill in the room was from something more threatening than the falling temperatures.

"Werner," David said, his tone serious. He had been sitting quietly near the window all evening. Hanna and Greta had been chatting about how to make their summer wardrobes fashionable and warmer with their meager to nonexistent budgets. She paused midsentence when she heard the change in David's voice.

"Werner," David repeated to a now silent room. "We are going to need identification papers to get out of Prague."

Werner laughed. "If you say so, my friend. I shall oblige immediately." He rolled his eyes at the rest of the friends. Samual laughed, but Hanna felt a tightening in her stomach.

"Werner," David said a third time. "We need to leave Prague. Actually, we need to leave anyplace where the Nazis are in power."

"Why the sudden sense of urgency, David?" Samual asked. "I know things are not good here, especially for Jews." His voice was gentle. "But things are much better here than many other places."

"It's true," Werner said. "Hitler has a soft spot for Prague. He will protect it."

"You don't understand!" David yelled, standing up so quickly that the chair crashed against the windowsill.

"Explain it to us, then, David," Hanna said.

"Heydrich," he said. He looked from face to face, waiting for their reactions. When he found nothing, he repeated with force, "Heydrich! Reinhard Heydrich!"

Werner said, "David, we are not as well versed as you in conspiracy theories and the quirks of certain German officials." Hanna thought he looked weary all of a sudden, as all the stress of war and occupation settled on his shoulders with David's last sentence. Despite his clean appearance, she saw worry lines around his eyes.

David spun a hard gaze onto Werner. "You, of all people, should know who Herr Heydrich is."

Werner's tone matched David's frosty glare. "Of course, I know who Heydrich is. What I don't know is why he has put you in such a foul mood this evening."

"I'm sorry, but I do not know who this Heydrich is," interjected Greta softly.

David started to pace around the small sitting room. With his long legs, he covered its length in three steps and was then forced to turn the opposite direction. "Heydrich is head of the SS." Hanna drew in a sharp breath. "He is one of Hitler's more effective mad dogs. He is vicious and cruel and a danger to all of us." He looked around the room quickly. "He's a danger to all of us Jews."

"What does he have to do with . . ." Greta paused. "With us . . . you . . . the Jews here?"

"Hitler has let this mad dog off his leash, and he is coming to Prague. He is the new protectorate." David spit out the last word with disgust. "But, I assure you, he will not be protecting anyone." David sat back down in his chair and leaned forward, toward his friends, speaking softly. "It is rumored that when he was in Poland, he led a string of arrests against Jews, taking them from their homes in the middle of the night. People woke up the next morning, and friends, neighbors, family members had just disappeared." He snapped his fingers, making Greta and Hanna jump. "Like that. Gone."

David stood up again and continued his pacing. "Hitler sent him here to take care of the Jewish problem."

"Take care of . . ." Greta started.

"Kill! Kill, Greta, kill! He wants Heydrich to systematically and completely kill all of the Jews in Czechoslovakia, beginning in Prague!"

Greta gripped Werner's hand tightly. He gave her a small smile of reassurance. Hanna just stared at David. She knew he was quite the pessimist, more distrustful than all the rest of them when it came to the Nazis. She blamed it on his experience during the initial occupation and his resentment over being without work for two years. But she also knew that he spoke with more people across the city and had his ear to the ground, while she tried to keep her head high and out of the politics of the war. Was he right that something—or someone—truly terrible was headed their way?

"You're frightening the delicate ladies," Samual said softly, then added a smile to show Hanna and Greta he was teasing.

"Good," said David. "They should be frightened. Hell, we should all be frightened." Again, he sat down. "That is why, Werner"—he enunciated his friend's name with perfect emphasis—"we need papers to leave Prague. We should all go, but myself, Hanna, and Samual need them immediately."

Werner just shook his head. "You're crazy," he muttered.

Before David could jump up again in outburst, Samual broke in calmly: "Let's just slow down, David. I hear what you're saying, but we don't even know if this Heydrich is actually coming to Prague. I've heard nothing of it." He raised his hand as David's mouth opened to interject. "And if he does, what is he going to do here? What can he do? It's not like he's going to come here and kill all the Jews. He can't kill all of us."

David turned to look out the window, and Hanna followed his gaze. Prague was black—darkened streetlamps, dark Swastika flags moving in the fall breeze, people hiding in the safety of their homes. Without facing them, he said, "He can. And he will."

♦

It took mere days after Herr Heydrich stepped his boots onto the streets of Prague for Hanna to realize they should have listened to David's warning. But even Werner, with his German origins and Lutheran upbringing, could not have secured papers for them to leave the city. And even if they escaped Prague, where else could they go? Hitler ruled all of Europe, it seemed.

She and Samual discussed it in the security of her small bed, with the covers pulled over their heads like the blanket forts Hanna used to make with her sisters when they were children. "He's executed almost a hundred people," Samual whispered as they faced each other, heads bent close together. Hanna could feel his breath on her cheek as he spoke.

"He's only been here three days! Who could he possibly have found in such a short time to kill?"

"Anyone. He doesn't need a reason. It's mainly been leaders of the city before he even arrived. Many have been in prison since the Nazis took over. But some college students. People who were caught with radios. Communists."

"Jews?" Hanna snuggled closer so their lips were almost touching as they spoke.

"Of course," Samual answered. "But not because they were Jewish, I don't believe. They were charged with some sort of crime first. Sabotage. Espionage. Some sort of resistance work."

"Resistance work?" scoffed Hanna. "What resistance work? I'd love to see Prague stand up against the Nazis. If everyone worked together . . ."

"No," Samual said sharply. Hanna pulled away at his quick change of tone. "Fighting back isn't the answer right now."

"How can you say that? You're as frustrated with the people as I am. They've done nothing to stop the Germans from ruining this city."

"When you see a hornet's nest, you don't kick it. You walk away. Why anger the Nazis?" Samual closed the gap Hanna had put between them in her surprise. "Heydrich is showing off right now. He's making sure we know what he is capable of. Things will settle down, you'll see."

"I don't know . . ." It was best not to argue. She wanted to believe Samual. She wanted his words to comfort her. She moved into his arms, resting her head on his chest.

Speaking into her hair, Samual said, "Don't bring attention to yourself. If they don't know you're Jewish, the soldiers should leave you alone."

She nodded into his chest.

After a few minutes of comfortable silence, Samual spoke in a soft voice. "I haven't seen David in days. Not since that night with Werner and Greta."

"He often wanders the city, staying away for days at a time."

Hanna felt Samual nod once in agreement. "This feels different though."

♦

Hanna did not get much opportunity to put Samual's theory into practice. He wanted her to avoid the Nazis, hide her Jewish-ness, stay out of trouble. She was willing to give it a chance, but two weeks after that night when she smuggled Samual into her room, the order was given for all Jews to designate themselves as such by wearing a yellow Star of David.

"It's humiliating," Samual fumed as he paced the few steps back and forth in his sitting room, retracing David's same restless movements from a few weeks prior. Hanna sat nervously in one of the wooden chairs, twisting the engagement ring around her finger. She noted that it spun much easier recently. The weeks without a filling breakfast or any lunch at all were starting to show in her figure. "He wants to point a finger at the Jews of the city . . . point a finger and laugh."

"It's not just in Prague. It's throughout all of Europe. Any place run by the Germans now," Hanna pointed out quietly.

"It's cruel, is what it is," Samual snapped. "What does he think he's playing at?" He continued to take three long steps, reach the wall, and turn around. Hanna watched him complete a few more laps. His hair was ruffled where he kept running his hand through it. He looked like a caged animal. "I hate that he's making you wear a bloody Star of David." He kneeled in front of Hanna, taking both of her hands in his own. "We will figure something out."

"And it's not just me. Not just Jews who have to wear it." She waited for Samual to respond. He said nothing, just resumed his pacing. "It's anyone born to a Jewish father."

She waited longer this time for a reaction. She counted Samual's frustrated steps. One, two, three. Turn. One, two, three. After two more turns around the room, he sat heavily on the chair next to her.

"Anyone born to a Jewish father?" Samual's voice was so soft that Hanna barely heard it. "Anyone born to a Jewish father?"

She nodded. Her eyes filled with tears. She had been coming to the resolution of what life was like for a Jew in Nazi-ruled Prague. She knew Samual had seen what it was like; she knew he was compassionate for her and the Jews; but she also knew that he did not consider himself part of it. He breezed through checkpoints and pretended the "No Jews Allowed" signage did not apply to him. Thus far, it had served him well.

Samual's head suddenly dropped low. She knew, then, that the realization had hit him completely. He put his face in his hands, his voice muffled. "I have to wear this star. I have to label myself as a Jew in front of the entire city."

Hanna nodded. She preferred Samual's frustrated pacing over this resigned sorrow. He looked up at her.

"I'm more than my father's religion." He looked intently into her eyes. "Hell, I'm more than my own religion. I can't be labeled by this one thing. It's not me." He looked as though he was pleading with her. "This isn't me."

"I know." She laid her hand on his arm. "I know. We're more than this one thing."

"But not to the Nazis."

"No, not to the Nazis."

Samual stood and commenced his three-step journey from wall to wall again. Hanna breathed a small sigh of relief.

"I'm not going to do it," he said. "I'm not going to wear it." He stopped in front of Hanna. "How will they know? What can they do to me?"

"They say if a Jew is found without the Star on their outer clothing, they'll be deported to the East."

"They can't deport all of us."

"Maybe not . . . but they can deport you."

Samual shrugged.

Hanna stood up, blocking his path. "They can deport you," she repeated with more force that she intended, but her tone snapped Samual's eyes into place within her own, so she continued in the same vein. "And then, where will I be?"

Samual argued incessantly with anyone who would listen about why he should not be forced to wear the Star of David, but when the day came for the Jews of Prague to line up outside the offices of the Jewish Community in Josefov, he stood next to Hanna, gripping her hand so tightly that she thought the band of her engagement ring might break right through the soft skin of her finger. She said nothing though, because she knew they were both holding on to each other as their only lifeline in this storm of hate and discrimination.

They moved slowly, one step at a time through the mass. Around them were all the people of the community that Hanna had gotten to know and love over her years in the city, and so many others. She saw Mrs. Weis's sister many people behind her, but there was no sign of Mrs. Weis. She had heard rumors that Mr. Weis had been sent to Russia. Others said he had been shot. She refused to believe in such a terrible fate, but Mrs. Weis must have believed it, as Hanna also heard she had taken to bed and was not expected to rise again.

In front of and behind Hanna and Samual were families, young couples, children, elderly, Orthodox, Germans, Czechs, the poverty stricken, the well-to-do bankers and lawyers. It was a beautiful display of the diversity that Prague had become known for, but the war had started to wear away the features that made the people unique. Suffering and hardship were like a relentless wind, slowly chiseling at a cliff face—smoothing its edges and eroding the ground beneath it. The people waited in line, silently for the most part except for the outcries of children, too young to understand what was happening around them yet still feeling the cloud of misery that hung low over the Jewish Quarter.

Hanna squeezed Samual's hand harder. She didn't feel much differently than the six-year-old in front of her clutching his mother's skirt. She needed Samual's reassurance and comfort. She also needed him to explain this to her. Why? Why them? How could people hold so much hate in their hearts? How could human beings treat other human beings in this way? But she didn't ask. There were no answers to such questions.

"There's been a mistake," Samual told Hanna after they received their matching stars, made of rough sackcloth. "We shouldn't be on this list."

"Shhh . . ." she whispered to him harshly. She crumpled the Star into a scratchy ball and was trying to fit the entire thing in her fist. "We are Jews. We should be on this list."

"No," he said, firmly. He pulled her away from the crowd in front of the community office. He didn't stop pulling until they stood directly in front of a German soldier standing at attention near the entrance of the Josefov square. "Excuse me, sir," Samual said in his perfect German.

The soldier turned his head from his alert posture slowly and deliberately to Samual. Hanna felt her breath catch. "No!" she whispered to Samual.

She wanted to pull him away. She wanted to remind him to not draw attention—to avert his gaze, put the Star on, and walk away. Was not staying out of sight of the Germans his own plan? But it was too late. Samual had the soldier's intense stare now.

"Excuse me, sir," he said again. "I'm sorry to trouble you, but there's been some sort of mistake with these Stars of David."

"A mistake?" the soldier asked.

"Yes, my fiancée and I"—he tugged on Hanna's hand again, forcing her to take a small step toward the soldier—"we should not be on that list."

"No?" the soldier asked. An amused smile was starting to play at the edges of his mouth.

"No," Samual continued, forging forward as if unaware of any indiscretion or danger. "I am German. And a Christian." He paused, looking at the soldier intently. "And this is my fiancée. We're to be married in just a few weeks."

The soldier appraised Samual, taking in his Aryan looks, his perfect German accent, and his confidence. "Then how did you get on the list?"

For the first time, Samual stuttered, giving himself away for just an instant. Hanna was sure the soldier caught it. "Well, my family is Jewish. But I converted. Years ago. And Hanna and I will be married . . . in the church . . . in just a few weeks."

"Your name?" the soldier asked. Then he smiled, but Hanna found no comfort in it.

"Samual Hamel."

The soldier nodded. "I see. And you're German." Samual nodded. "I grew up on a farm outside of Munich. In Otterfing. You've been?"

Hanna felt Samual allow a small breath to escape his lungs. Perhaps he had been holding it. "I've never had the pleasure."

"Lovely place," the soldier said serenely. "Very lovely."

"I'm sure."

"We had animals on our farm. When I was younger, I had to care for many of them. Have you ever cared for pigs?" he asked, cocking his head and looking pleasantly at both of them.

"I have not," Samual answered.

"Lucky you. Nasty creatures, pigs are. Filthy. Smelly. Loud."

Hanna took an involuntary step back. Samual squeezed her hand to reassure her.

The soldier continued. "My littlest sister took a liking to the pigs after one of the sows had a bunch of piglets." He chuckled. "She wanted to keep the babies as pets. She would get up early every morning, feed the little ones, play with them in the mud. She was such a sweet thing."

Samual smiled.

"But the piglets got bigger. And smellier. And louder. In a last attempt to keep them as her pets, my littlest sister spent an entire afternoon cleaning them—washing them down with buckets of water, scrubbing them." He chuckled again. His eyes were far away, back in Otterfing. "But do you know what happened the next morning when I went out to the pen to feed those little pigs?"

Hanna felt the fear then. It was a physical thing. It started in her toes, making them curl inside her black pumps.

"They were dirty again." He laughed this time. "Like my sister hadn't spent the entire afternoon cleaning them." His eyes narrowed at Samual and any trace of fond remembrance had vanished from his face. "They were pigs after all."

The fear worked its way to her knees, making them buckle for a fraction of a second.

"Filthy. Stinking. Squealing. Pigs."

Hanna felt it in her stomach. Samual squeezed her hand again but didn't even blink in the face of the soldier's sudden hatred.

"Because you can't clean a pig and make it something else." He paused, letting his words sit in the air, and Hanna felt the fear start to grip her lungs. Then he leaned close to Samual and whispered, "And do you know what we did to the pigs when their time came?"

Samual stiffened. "No, sir, I don't."

There was no tremor to his voice. She had never been so proud or so in love with this man as she was at this moment—his courage and poise when facing down this enemy.

"We slit their throats and feasted on their carcasses."

Hanna thought the fear might stop her heart. But she would not let Samual down. She forced her face to stay neutral, impassive at this threat. Samual said nothing but continued to look straight into the soldier's eyes.

"So, Samual Hamel and his fiancée Hanna." His tone changed suddenly, making Hanna jump, though she instantly hated her body for giving her away. "Put your stars on and go back to your pigsty."

Samual nodded curtly and led Hanna quickly away.

The soldier called after them: "I'll be sure to find you when your time comes."

Chapter 13

RACHAEL

She woke with her cheek stinging. The merciless shouts of the guards had not yet rung through the barracks for morning wake up. It was the pain in her face that brought her back to consciousness. She lay on her side, keeping her eyes closed, trying to discern the source of the sting. It could have been tears that had found their way down a well-known path. Crying in her sleep happened often. It could have been the freeze in the air. Though it was late spring, the nights were still cold. But, as Rachael mentally examined the rest of her body, it was her cheek specifically that awoke her.

She rolled onto her back carefully, hoping to not shake the bunk and disturb Irene and the other women sleeping below her. That move brought instant relief—she had been sleeping on her hand, the ring placed on her finger sometime during the night. She must have done it in her sleep. When she was awake, she never wore the ring—not even if it was just her and Chaya talking in the barrack corner.

Chaya never wore it either. It seemed to be an unspoken rule between the two of them. The girl saw the ring as a toy—a glorious, beautiful toy. She would spin it on the ground like a top. She ran her fingers over every facet of the stones, every engraving, every angle she could feel. Rachael was sure Chaya would be able to pick this ring out of the pile of plundered rings by the feel of her index fingers alone. Mostly, though, Chaya used it to reflect bits of sunlight, making tiny dancing rainbows on the dirt floor.

Before meeting Chaya, Rachael was sure the sun had never shown in Auschwitz. Logically, she knew this could not be true. There was light in the morning that hurt her eyes during roll call, there were shadows in the afternoons reflecting the angles of the various camp buildings, and there were sunsets where she briefly noticed the darkness before finally closing her eyes to another dreamless night. So yes, she knew there was sunlight, but somehow, without the diamond ring to turn that light into colorful rainbows, she had never considered it as such; it was just a glare that had broken through the dark clouds, more of a spotlight on the darkness, making it more foreboding. But Chaya saw brightness. She did not discriminate between the sunlight before the war and this gleam she played in day after day.

This was not one of those days where the sun was going to make any sort of appearance. Rachael barely had time to rub the impression of the ring from her cheek and pocket the diamond safely in her dress before the first gong rang loudly throughout the camp. It was followed quickly by the harsh voices of the impatient guards. She quickly tidied up her small bunk by sweeping up the straw with her hand, pushing it back to the center. She never thought she would be so concerned about every piece of straw, but it was all she had, as both padding and blanket. She shook Chaya by the shoulders, as the child was slow to wake in the mornings.

Rachael waited in the long line for her turn at one of two buckets of fresh water set outside the barrack. The temperatures reminded her of winter afternoons where she would take Radek and Catarina to the park for the excitement of sledding down one of the many hills overlooking the city. Despite the cold, she splashed some of the water on her face, trying to rub off bits of grime from her cheeks. She ran her wet hands through her hair, drying them in the short locks that had started to grow back. This bit of hygiene would never be enough to rid herself of the dirt and stink and lice that resided permanently in her scalp.

The second gong rang before Rachael had a chance to get her morning ration of coffee. Her stomach had long ago stopped growling at the lack of food. Those sounds of hunger, Rachael had realized, were for those who had never really known true starvation. She could not really lament the lack of breakfast on this morning, since she was sure there was no nutritional value to the swill that was called coffee. It was water—she supposed that was something—flavored with some sort of root or grain, bitter and unsweetened. Rachael forced herself to swallow it since it was at least lukewarm, but it was not unusual that prisoners should go without. She often had to choose between getting her cup of dirty water or washing her face with dirty water.

The ringing of the second gong summoned most of the women to roll call, though some stayed behind to work in the kitchens or hospital. Rachael stood with as much attention as she could muster. Chaya stood beside her. The child had taken to following Rachael around everywhere—in the mornings, after she returned to the camp from long days spent sorting through *kanada*, even sleeping in the bunk with her at night. On this morning, the gray clouds were so heavy it seemed like the sky had come down to meet the earth. It gave Rachael a feeling of being inside a box that was slowly but steadily growing smaller each moment.

As Rachael and Chaya stood side by side for roll call, Rachael thought about how she spent the majority of her life waiting in lines—waiting for her meager rations, waiting with the other dirt-ridden women to relieve themselves or wash themselves with a single bucket of freezing cold water, or, the worst, waiting for roll call. She had learned to read the morning moods of the guards in the same way she knew Alexey's or Radek's disposition when they first came into the kitchen for breakfast. Radek's blinks would become longer and longer as he waited for Rachael to place a warm piece of sourdough bread in front of him, topped most often with his favorite, a thin layer of butter and a generous pour of honey. His grumpy mornings involved grunts more than words, and Rachael learned, as he got closer and closer to manhood, to give him a brief scratch on the back and then let him stew in silence. Alexey's dark moods were more difficult to manage. She identified it easily with his morning kiss. On his grumpy days, it was a quick, lackluster peck on the cheek. When he woke up with a smile though, it would be a long and sloppy kiss on the lips, with his arms enveloping her into his warm body.

She hated that she could read the guards' moods like she once did her family's. But it was necessary for survival. This was a bad morning. Before the women could get in their many lines, waiting to be counted, guards were already screaming into faces and throwing punches. Rachael had tried to strategize the safest place to stand during these torturous queues, and had determined there was no such spot. The women in the front lines and on the outside edges were, of course, the first to fall under scrutiny. The guards, though, were no fools. They knew women tried to lose themselves in the middle of the crowd, so the female soldiers were even more brutal with those women. Staring at the ground did not make the prisoners invisible, but Rachael had never seen it end well for a woman to look the guards in the eye either. The only hope was to pray, if one still believed in such things. She did not.

In the months since Rachael had been with Chaya, the girl was finally learning the seriousness of roll calls. She stood mostly still, like her fellow inmates, but that was not until Rachael changed her tactic for impressing the danger of the situation on the child by telling her it was a game of who could stand the stillest. Chaya spoke the language of games, and she loved winning. She had also seen enough women lose the game to know it was more than idle play. As one of the guards walked in front of Chaya and Rachael, screaming out numbers of the missing prisoners, Rachael felt Chaya stiffen. They both held their breath. Like a dog sniffing out fear, the guard stopped suddenly.

She turned viciously on Chaya's neighbor. With no warning, she slapped the woman across the face. Rachael could never get used to the casual violence of this place. To hurt someone as if it was nothing—or rather, as if that person was nothing . . . that was how the guard attacked the woman next to Chaya. The prisoner cried out from the pain and shock of the slap. She staggered.

"Get back in line!" the guard shouted at her.

This was the cruelest torture of roll call, Rachael thought. There was nothing a person could do correctly when the guard decided to attack. The prisoner stood back at attention, staring straight ahead of her, past the guard's ear.

"Look at me when I'm talking to you!" the guard yelled. She slapped the woman again. Her cheek was already aflame between the heat of violence and the cold of the air. "Where is the prisoner 1265?"

The woman, clearly unsure as to the right action to take, glanced quickly at the guard's face, then to her feet, back and forth. She looked like a wooden toy that Catarina used to play with, a hand-carved bird that was weighted so it would bob back and forth like it was pecking at the ground. Chaya would have fallen into a heap of joy and giggles if she ever had the chance to see such a toy, Rachael thought fleetingly.

"I do not know this prisoner . . ." the woman stammered.

Her words were rewarded with a punch to the stomach with the guard's fist. She doubled over, trying to breathe. "I do not know this prisoner either," the guard said in a mocking tone, mimicking the woman's stuttered speech. Yelling again so that the prisoner jumped at the sound, she shouted, "You all look the same to me! How can I tell one pig from another?"

The prisoner nodded her agreement, still struggling to catch her breath. It was terribly unfair, but in that moment, Rachael hated her.

She hated the woman's timid, stammering voice; she hated her body's reflexes; she hated how the woman reminded her of a small puppy, begging for scraps outside a deli or running back with its tail wagging when its owner kicked it away in frustration.

"Yes?" the guard shouted only a hair's width away from the prisoner's face. "Yes, I should be able to tell you pigs apart?"

The woman shook her head frantically.

"No?" the guard bellowed even louder. Rachael's ears hurt, and she noticed Chaya was leaning away from the scene unfolding right next to her. "No, you're not pigs?" She punched the woman again, and she crumpled to the ground at this blow. "Get up." The woman made a slight movement. The guard gave her a ferocious kick, landing somewhere between the ribs. The woman screamed but put more effort into standing back in her place. "Where. Is. The. Missing. Prisoner?" Each word was staccato, emphasized.

The prisoner could only shake in terror.

Rachael was all of a sudden very aware of the tiny weight in her dress pocket. Not for the first time since finding it, she was panicked that the guards could see the object through the rough fabric of her dress. She wanted to glance at her pocket, to assure herself that her treasure remained invisible, but she knew even the slightest movement of her eyes could invite the guard's attack. Even more, though, she wanted to reach her hand into her pocket to feel the cold metal and the square edges of the diamond. When she first found the ring, she thought it was the height of vanity and pridefulness that would make a person risk bringing such a useless thing all the way from their home to the ghetto and, lastly, to this place. Now, though, she thought it more like an act of bravery. And holding the ring in her hand made her feel brave.

The guard grabbed the prisoner's hair, getting a handful of loose-skinned scalp more than hair, and pulled the woman to her feet. Rachael had seen the movement many times over, but not in Auschwitz, rather in a cozy cellar where children picked out new kittens and the seller picked them up by the scruff of the neck. Pushing her face into the prisoner's, the guard yelled, "You're useless to me." She looked down at Chaya then, and Rachael's heart stopped. "What do we do with useless Jews?" Chaya continued to stare straight ahead.

In one swift motion, the soldier pulled out a small gun from inside her long winter coat. With the fluidity of a dance, she shoved the barrel under the woman's chin and pulled the trigger. The soldier let the body fall to the ground. She placed the gun back into its hiding place and used her woolen sleeve to wipe the drops of blood from her face.

"We're short one more Jew for roll call," she yelled to her peers, laughing and walking away.

Rachael dared a movement. She reached out her hand, just for an instant, and touched the outside of Chaya's arm. She was not brave enough to venture any more comfort for the child. Not for the first time, Rachael had to wonder about the German people. Before the war, she had met few Germans. She stayed fairly secluded in her Jewish Quarter, though she knew her hometown of Prague was a melting pot of difference races, cultures, and people. The soldiers who marched into her city were the first true interaction she had with the nation to the west. They said her people were vermin, animals, beasts. She had never in her entire life seen a single Jew treat anyone the way all Germans treated her. Were the German people naturally beastly? Or did the Nazi regime train them to be this way? Or maybe they only recruited truly degenerate people to serve as soldiers?

The woman's life continued to leak onto the ground while the roll call continued. The red seeped into the earth and created a stream trickling its way toward Rachael's and Chaya's feet. The girl tried to shuffle her feet away from the flood, but before the missing inmate was found, her shoes were soaking up the blood. The missing prisoner had been dead on her top bunk the whole time—not an unusual occurrence. But the guards loved making the women stand at attention for hours before letting a prisoner check the barracks, then laughing as she struggled to bring out the stiff and frozen body of her friend.

While Rachael sorted through the newest arrived plunder in *kanada*, she forced her mind from wandering to the woman fallen facedown with blood blooming from the place her head should have been. She focused instead on Chaya's shoes. The girl's toes were cramped inside her wooden clogs. Despite the lack of food, she continued to grow, as if she drew nourishment from sunshine and water like a flower of the fields. Her body stretched taller, but she had no hearty meals to give her weight. Rachael thought she might stretch as tall and thin as a black spruce tree—skinny trunk and drooping branches. A strong wind blowing west from Germany could knock her down and trample her to the ground.

What she needed, Rachael thought, was more food. She almost smiled to herself. More food—as if it were that easy. Everyone in Auschwitz just needed more food. And more shelter from the elements. More clothes. More kindness and compassion and humanity. Rachael could not procure any of those things. Could she? She was currently sorting through plunder from the newest inmates—most of them probably dead already and nothing more than ash. But before they became part of the choking and sickening air around the camp, they were people with hopes for the future, despite all the signs saying there was no reason for such hopes. They were people who hid their most prized possessions, carried their most sentimental treasures, and packed meals to be enjoyed in a better place than the ghettos.

She could steal food. She was currently working in a place named after an excessively large country full of goodness and riches. She had her hand inside a long blue woolen overcoat. She could find scraps within the plunder, hide bits in her dress. They could stow away next to the diamond ring until she found Chaya later that night, and then they could feast. Rachael knew some prisoners stole from *kanada*. She knew they stole a few items each day to either enjoy themselves or to trade with others on the black market. She also knew many were caught, humiliated, beaten, whipped, sent to the gas chambers.

But some were not. Some took food and tools and books and clothing with no repercussions. They were not caught. Did not she hold in the pocket of her dress a valuable ring? She had had this ring for months with no one knowing. She could only imagine what the SS guards would do if they found such a treasure on her. She had seen people killed for the gold fillings in their back molars. Just this morning, she watched a woman shot in the face for no reason other than the guard was in a foul mood. What would they do if she was found with a diamond and sapphire ring? Death, of course, was the German answer to any question concerning the Jews. And yet, she had the ring. It did not adorn the finger of a soldier's girlfriend or wartime mistress. It was in her pocket, on her own finger sometimes in the dead of night, enjoyed and admired by Chaya on sunny afternoons.

Rachael went about her work with more purpose. Instead of letting her eyes blur over as she worked, moving mindlessly from one sorting pile to the next, she was keenly aware of her surroundings. She was sure her racing heart could be heard by her fellow workers and the guards meant to watch for such thievery. But her hands were steady. She searched the giant pile of leftover belongings, cognizant of every move the guards made—when one was watching her, walking near her. She was mindful of the prisoners sorting alongside her, too, as one never knew which inmate would look the other way, understanding her plight, and which would turn her in for the hopes of a favor from the guards.

As her pocket was not large, she chose two items carefully. She found a piece of dried meat. Her mouth watered at the thought of the jerky, tough and dirty as it was. She held on to a piece of stale bread most of the afternoon but discarded it in favor of a chunk of hard cheese, wrapped lovingly in a handstitched handkerchief. Rachael could not remember the last time she had cheese, and she wondered with some excitement if Chaya had ever tasted such a treat. Rachael was still surprised by the things Chaya did not know. She felt a semblance of the excitement she used to feel on the first night of Hanukkah when she laid out the small gifts she had thoughtfully found for Radek and Catarina.

As the workday ended and she joined the line of other women to make the trek from *kanada*'s storerooms to the prison yard, she forced herself to act normal. She kept her eyes trained to the ground, watching it slowly pass under her feet as each step brought her closer to Chaya and their relative feast.

It was impossible to look down when she heard the cries. It was a man pushed up against the wall of one of the many buildings in the men's camp. Rachael passed near the men's camp twice every day, but she never took much notice of the prisoners on that side of the fence. Today, though, her eyes went ahead of her to a man shoved face first into the wall. Two SS soldiers stood behind him, both shouting simultaneously in German. Rachael, though she knew a fair amount of the language, especially the curse words yelled at the Jews, was unable to discern one voice from the other. Clearly, the man had broken a rule. *Stolen, perhaps,* Rachael could not help but think. She had to will her hand to stay firmly at her side and to not stray to her pocket.

As she neared the man, now whimpering like a child, she saw the action clearly. One of the soldiers roughly shoved the man in the middle of his back every time he tried to move away from the wall or turn to face his persecutors. The man's nose was bleeding from the repeated blows into the unforgiving brick wall.

The cries of the man, and all sounds of the camp around them, came to a halting silence when the second SS soldier pulled out his sidearm and shoved the cold barrel into the back of the man's head. Rachael stopped walking, forcing the woman behind her to stutter in her tracks. The man stopped struggling. His face was pushed so hard against the bricks that his broken nose pushed to the side under the pressure of the gun.

The silence was broken by the soldier's execution proclamation: "On three, you filthy Jewish swine. I pull the trigger on three."

The prisoner started muttering his prayers in Hebrew. He seemed to have realized that his pleas would never be answered by the Germans, so he changed the recipient to a god who had abandoned him long ago.

"One."

Rachael knew no one would intervene, but still, she looked around anxiously for a savior to stop this cold-blooded murder.

"Two."

There was no one around besides the other soldier. He had left off shoving the man against the wall as the prisoner stopped struggling, resigned to his fate, and had walked a few paces away to a pile of tools and scraps from a repair project.

"Three."

Rachael closed her eyes for a second but did not hear the gun shot. As she opened them, she saw the second soldier had taken a large wooden board and had hit the prisoner in the back of the head, swinging the board like a bat. The man's face made a horrifying crack as it banged into the solid bricks. His body slumped down to the ground as the soldiers laughed.

Rachael began walking slowly again, keeping the SS guards' antics in sight. She knew this trick. She had heard it play out before. The guard with the gun was already grabbing a nearby bucket—probably full of human waste. The shock of the waste, thrown into the man's bloodied face, woke him from unconsciousness. His confused expression at seeing the Germans, when he was certain he had just been killed with a gunshot to the back of the head, was the last thing Rachael saw as she continued her march back to the barracks.

She heard the end of the joke from a distance. The Germans laughed uncontrollably after telling the man, "You thought you could escape us in death? Germans are in the afterlife, too!"

With that terrifying thought, a gunshot echoed through the camp.

When she got back to the barracks, she forced up the feeling of excitement again as she prepared to show Chaya the food she'd smuggled. Excitement. She didn't know such feelings were possible anymore. Chaya had gotten into the habit of waiting for Rachael after a long day of work. But she was not there to greet her this evening. Rachael went to the back wall of their barracks where the girl often played by herself, wondering, with the start of a smile, what mischief or game Chaya had discovered.

It was eerily quiet as she looked around the yard. She saw no guards patrolling, holding back their blood-hungry dogs, or, worse, not holding them back as they snapped at someone's legs. The patrols were silent; there were few people milling about, not even tired prisoners moving toward the line for watery soup with small chunks of turnips.

Rachael carefully wound her way through the nearest barracks, looking to see if Chaya had hidden herself in a corner. She saw only a few women, who all avoided her eyes. She worried about missing the queue for supper. She had the pocketed meal, but she and Chaya needed all the food they could get, even the meatless, tasteless cup of soup every night. As she trudged toward the queue that was oddly subdued, she passed Irene. Irene stared out past the first fence to a cloud billowing from the ground and moving high into the sky.

The chimneys were running again. The furnaces were burning.

"Where is everyone?" Rachael whispered. She half hoped Irene would not hear her, but she responded quickly.

"They came this morning."

"Who came?" Rachael asked.

Irene tore her eyes from the rising ashes to give Rachael a look of despair. Of course, Rachael knew. The soldiers. The Germans. The Nazis.

"Selection?" Rachael asked, barely saying the word.

Irene looked back at the only remains of the burning bodies. "Selection," she confirmed.

Chapter 14

HANNA

She refused to be ashamed any longer of her poverty at the hands of the Nazis. Of her constant fear. Of standing in line day after day, dependent on the small handout of food. She decided, as she stared at the Star of David sitting on her nightstand, that she would not be ashamed of being Jewish. She knew Samual advised discretion and passivity, but she could no longer stand aside. She needed to stand up.

For the first time since Prague Kofe was violently shut down before her eyes, Hanna felt the urge to do something. She flipped quickly through her wardrobe. She had been forced to quietly pawn many of her favorite dresses throughout the summer—to buy a much-needed lunch, coal for the small stove in her room as the nights turned colder, more sensible shoes in anticipation of the snow. But she had managed to hold on to her favorite dress—a white, knee-length satin number with puffed sleeves ending above her elbows. It had small, light purple flower buds sprinkled over the fabric and matching pastel gloves. It was a spring dress, not usually acceptable for October, but Hanna reminded herself that wartime made many things admissible.

Though it hurt her to do it, she picked up the Star of David and, with careful and tiny stitches, attached it to the satin dress, directly over her right collarbone. The rough yellow patch shone brightly against the white fabric—like the noon sun on a clear day. Despite the care she took, she knew the needle and the patch would ruin her dress. When she returned home later that day and meticulously removed the stitches, small pulls and tears in the fabric would remain. They would form an outline of the star, like a painting that hung for years on a wall leaving its shadow behind when removed.

With the Star attached, she dressed slowly, precisely. The white satin did not showcase her curves as well as it did many months ago when she wore it for a quiet dinner with Samual. The skirt, straight cut but with pleats peeking out from slits over her legs, still flared flatteringly as she walked around the small room. She cinched the belt a little tighter, hoping to show off a more attractive waistline rather than what she feared bordered on an emaciated frame. She hadn't been able to afford new make-up in ages, nor did she see much reason to wear it lately, but Hanna still had some rouge for her cheeks and red for her lips. She had pinned her hair into curls the night before. This morning, she swept the once-glossy curls far to the side and topped them with her favorite wide-brimmed hat in beige.

Her small room didn't possess a mirror, but turning her head back and forth, she was able to glimpse enough of her reflection in the window. Two years ago, she would have laughed at her attire—a woefully out of season dress that was nearly a size too big, a mismatched hat, and half-completed make-up. But today, she felt proud of the outcome. Her face was set, determined. Her eyes were bright—partly in anticipation and partly in fear, but she decided the look agreed with her.

She had one finishing touch. She used the edge of her pillowcase to polish the silver on her engagement ring. Using her fingernail, she rubbed the fabric around the cuts of the diamond, between the edges of the design work, over the corner sapphires. Not for the first time, she wished for a silver polishing cloth, but such things were not to be had these days. She was immensely blessed to even have a ring to polish. As she glanced at her scarce wardrobe, she knew she would rather dig through garbage cans for scraps than have this ring join her dresses in the pawnshop.

With the diamond sparkling, she was ready.

She had come up with this plan after she and Samual had escaped from the Nazi the day before. She knew she had nothing to offer the fabled Resistance in Prague, and she had no grand gestures of defiance against the Nazis. But she was inspired by one of her favorite buildings in the city.

She and Samual had walked back toward her boarding room, hiding their new Stars of David in their pockets. They hadn't spoken since the soldier had shouted his final threat to their retreating figures. Hanna watched the sidewalk under her feet as they hurried, not wanting to see Samual's face. She didn't know if he was angry, humiliated, or terrified, but it was probably all three.

She knew the sidewalk in front of Maisel Synagogue without having to look up, though. The normal cobblestones transitioned into a gray and blue design that mirrored the blue iron fence surrounding the synagogue's front entrance. She walked past this building every day, and it had yet to cease to impress her. She loved the subtlety of High Synagogue and the outlandish color of the new Jerusalem Synagogue, but it was Maisel, with its classic Gothic look, that always captured her attention. She envisioned castles in the rolling moors of England, and she pictured knights of the Round Table and the legendary Camelot. It brought to mind favorite romance novels and bedtime stories. It sent her mind spinning back to easier times. Very little of the building said Jewish or Czech even—except for the gold Star of David standing proudly above the entrance. It was a small adornment, but strategically placed in the center of the synagogue where it would reflect brightly from the glowing sun and announce proudly that this was a Jewish place of worship.

Hanna paused as they reached the small wooden front doors. Though the sun was starting to set—they had spent most of the afternoon in line at the Jewish Community offices—the light still gleamed off of the gold Star of David, giving it one final glow before the sun snuck below the horizon. Unlike many of the buildings in Prague, Maisel Synagogue's lack of gold made it stand out. And since the Star of David was the only gold in the building, it spoke loud and clear to Hanna.

Hanna stopped in front of the synagogue. She stood looking at the Star at the top of the building. Samual had not noticed her pause at first and was ten steps ahead of her before he stopped. He slowly walked back to her side, his gaze joining hers as she looked up.

"Maisel wears the star with pride," she said quietly. Hanna felt, rather than saw, Samual's head nod in slight agreement. "If she can wear it with pride . . . so can I."

After making an initial, and probably ill-advised, plan, Hanna spent most of the night in bed, mentally preparing herself for this moment. She walked though the different scenes that could play out, trying to focus on the worst-case scenario. After witnessing the senseless arrest of Mr. Weis—people in the Jewish Quarter heard a rumor that he had been turned in by a neighbor for possessing a short-wave radio—Hanna knew the Nazis could strike for no reason at all. But to arrest a young woman for walking the streets of Prague, unjustified, she was sure that would not stand. All of the other worst-case scenarios, she decided as the sun started to peak over the horizon, she could survive. What she could not survive was living in silence anymore. She had once told Samual that they were like frogs in a pot with the water slowly heating up to boil. She felt the heat now, and she was going to jump out.

So, with only her white dress and a little make-up as her armor for the day, she took a deep breath to steady her nerves and stepped out of her small room in the run-down boarding house. She remained grateful for living in the Jewish Quarter, even now when such association held danger. She loved the community of her people. She was ever more appreciative as she walked those first few blocks.

She saw a friendly face almost immediately, a woman who regularly bought her morning pastry at Prague Kofe. She nodded at Hanna and gave her a genuine smile.

"Lovely dress," she said as the two women paused on the sidewalk. "It makes a dreary day much brighter."

"That was my hope," Hanna replied, then continued on her walk with more confidence. She was especially grateful for the praise, as she knew this woman had seen her in this dress before—when both dress and wearer were in much better condition. She even received a whistle of admiration when she passed three teenage boys lounging around the corner of Praizska Street, right before she crossed the unmarked border between the Jewish Quarter and Old Town.

Hanna felt the air change when she stepped into Old Town Square. The Jewish Quarter certainly did not house the hustle and bustle that was common three years ago. She wondered if she was the only one to feel the tension that blew through Old Town like a chilling northern wind. It was physical—there was an icy breeze on the back of her neck; she felt goosebumps on her arms as the cold cut through the satin of her dress. But the Star positioned over her collarbone, that burned. It was fire, searing the sensitive skin of her chest. Heat rose from it, like the wavy air above a flame, burning her cheeks, making them flush with warmth and humiliation. Her instinct—one she had never known before the occupation—to blend into the background, to make herself as small and hidden as possible, started to take over. Self-preservation was fighting pride.

Nevertheless, she persevered. She had planned for this feeling as she lay awake in bed the night before. She knew enough about her body's response when she was around the soldiers and unfeeling people of the city to know she would have to fight this. How could she fight the Nazis if she couldn't even win the battle against her own fear? So, she kept walking. One foot in front of the other. She repeated the mantra in her mind: head up, one foot forward, eyes up, one foot forward. On and on. She walked through Old Town Square. People avoided eye contact, as she knew they would. This was her best-case scenario—that she make it through this day and this walk through Prague with only diverted gazes.

She held her head up high as she walked over the giant black V the Nazis had painted onto the cobblestones months earlier. David had shared during one of their idyllic summer nights that the Allies posted "V for Victory" signs in their shop windows at the urging of the British prime minister. The Germans, though, never to be outdone, claimed the V as their own symbol and superimposed it over Prague's cobblestones. Hanna remembered David saying he spit on the V every time he walked over it, and though her mouth was starting to fill with saliva, she decided this stroll through the city was enough rash action for the day.

She continued on, down Linhartska Street, turned onto Karlova, and over the Charles Bridge. She didn't loiter to admire her favorite statues lining the bridge or watch the swans on the banks of the Vltava River. The swans had not abandoned the city, but they seemed to be indifferent—like the people. She turned south onto Certovka Street, intending to walk through Kampa Park. The flower-lined walking trails were a favorite stroll for her and Samual, but Jews had been banned from the public parks months ago. Her courage wavered as she approached the entrance. The smell of falling leaves greeted her. She used to think she could smell the leaves turning, first from green to yellow then brown. Today, the scent of autumn gave her a little more strength to keep moving past the park, past the "No Jews Allowed" sign.

With her head up and eyes scanning all around her, she saw a group of young women from a block away. From their dresses and the books in their arms, Hanna supposed they were university students. They were deep in conversation as they strolled down the street. They were only steps away when one of them—a pretty girl with thick blond waves framing her face—made quick eye contact with Hanna.

It took all of Hanna's willpower to keep her hands by her side and not cross them protectively over her chest, trying to hide the Star. Instead, her hands clutched at the skirt of her dress. She forced her fists to relax—she didn't expect trouble from such an innocent gathering of girls near her own age. She expected womanly support, solidarity, compassion. Instead, the blonde wrinkled her nose in disgust, grabbed the hand of her nearest friend, and dragged the two of them off the sidewalk and across the street. She gave no heed to the street traffic, only glared at Hanna as she whispered something into her friend's ear. The rest followed her, none offering a shred of compassion.

Hanna felt hot tears prick her eyes. She took a few deep breaths to steady herself and continued on. She crossed the river again by another bridge and found herself walking through the streets of New Town.

She hadn't found many reasons to walk New Town since the occupation. There were no longer any shops that didn't hang the "Aryans Only" sign, and even if she could find a sympathetic shopkeeper, she had no money to purchase anything. But shopping was not the purpose of today. The purpose was proving that she could do this—live in a city where people had forced her out of her home, forced her out of her job, and now forced her into a state of humiliation.

As she walked down Nardoni Street, she saw a young mother holding the hand of a little boy in a threadbare sweater. From a few shops away, he made eye contact with her, looking at her questioningly. Hanna smiled reassuringly at him, grateful to finally have someone outside of the Jewish Quarter acknowledge her existence. His mother, Hanna noted, glanced up and saw her walk past, but quickly looked away toward the shop windows on the other side of the street. When Hanna was barely three paces past the little boy, he asked his mother, "What is she wearing on her dress?"

"Shhh," the mother scolded. "It's so we know not to talk to her."

Hanna knew that was what people would say about the Star. That was the whole purpose of it. To hear it whispered to such an innocent boy though, already poisoning him with discrimination—that was heartbreaking. The burning from the Star that she felt once she left the safety of the Jewish Quarter pulsated again, making her cheeks flush. Still, she continued on. This was the pain she was welcoming with this walk. It was like holding a rag of alcohol on a cut. It burned but was necessary.

She could feel the boy's questioning eyes on her back as the gap between them grew. She snuck a glance behind her, seeing that he was doing the same. His mother held his hand tightly, pulling him along. His feet moved him forward, but his eyes looked behind. Hanna gave him a slight nod and a small smile. When she turned back around, ready to return to her boarding room, she saw three men standing only steps in front of her, blocking her path.

"What do you think you're doing here?" the man in the middle snarled. He looked like a rabid dog, baring his teeth and readying for an attack. Hanna felt the immediate spike of fear pulse through her body, making her heart race and her breath stop.

"Excuse me," she muttered, trying to sidestep around the trio to continue on her way home.

The man closest to the street matched her step for step, staying directly in front of her. "Don't you dare talk to me," he said. His voice was so thick with hatred that Hanna had to look deeper into his face. That he could hate her so much for no reason was confounding. Did he confuse her with someone else? Did she look like a lover who had jaded him, a mother who had abandoned him, a sister who had mercilessly teased him?

He shoved her, both of his hands contacting with her collarbones. Hanna felt the rough fabric of the Star of David scratch against her skin. The force and surprise of his attack made her reel back, losing her balance. She took two staggering steps, unable to catch herself, and fell. The cobblestones were cold and still wet from the previous night's light rain. She felt it seep through her dress and into her bones—the chill of the stones and all the city around her.

The rabid dog stood over her, ready to attack. "Dirty, filthy Jew." In horror, Hanna heard him cough deep from the bowels of his body. He spit all the vile and poison he could muster onto her bowed head. She felt the saliva—hot and sticky—land on the back of her head and dribble down her neck.

She could not understand it. Her eyes reacted, tearing up. They were controlled by her heart, which was breaking. Her mind was reeling. To her, the man was a dog, unleashed by the Nazis, his hard eyes constantly searching for prey—someone weaker, someone vulnerable. With her obvious yellow star, he no longer had to hunt. It was open season for hate.

The man's friends laughed. She didn't hold her head up to see them walk away but listened as their laughter and steps faded into the other sounds of the city. Her tears flowed slowly. She knelt on the cold ground. The dirt and dampness had soaked through the back of her dress and now she willingly let it ruin the front as well. She could never wear this outfit again anyways. She'd never be able to recall the lovely stroll, hand in hand with Samual, wearing this dress. She would always look at it and think of spit and hatred and humiliation. She might as well let Prague ruin it completely so she could ball it up and burn it in the small stove in her room. She looked forward to letting the flames eat up the white satin, fill the room with its stench.

She took two more deep breaths before standing up. She glanced around quickly, instinct making her search for the rabid dog and his friends. They were out of sight. So was the curious boy. Hanna was both relieved that he did not see her scene of degradation and also disappointed that the small friendly face was not there to give her another smile of encouragement. Again, she took two deep breaths before forcing her head back up to its proud position and walking onward.

She only had a few more blocks until the relative safety of the Jewish Quarter. Her high heels clicked on the sidewalk, and she increased her pace. *Not as bad as it could have been*, she kept thinking to herself. She timed each word with the sound of her footsteps: *Not. As. Bad. As. It. Could. Have. Been.*

She knew what she could survive. She had anticipated the diverted glances, the whispers, and the movement to the other side of the street. Even the shove from the man hadn't surprised her much. She had expected some minor violence. Though she thought arrest unlikely, it still held a place in the back of her mind. But this. The spit. She did not see that one coming. But she would not let herself think about it, about its humiliation, about its inhuman hatred. She reminded herself: *Not. As. Bad. As. It. Could. Have. Been.*

That mantra, those steps carried her home, to Samual's apartment where he would be waiting with a warm blanket and a clean shirt that smelled of him.

Hanna felt the footsteps dogging her own before she ever heard the sound of feet meeting the cobblestones. She felt the presence of eyes and a shape following behind her. She was only a few buildings away from Samual's apartment, so she tried to subtly increase her walking pace and make it to the security of her fiancé before any more harm could befall her. She hurried past the last few shops and abandoned storefronts, into the quiet and empty lobby of Samual's building. She forced herself to take the steps one at a time, especially when she heard the stairwell door close again after she turned to start the second flight. *One more*, she told herself. One more, and then she would be in Samual's arms. She could no longer contain her panic when she reached the hallway leading to his door. She broke into a run and banged on his door frantically.

"Sam!" she called with desperation. "Sam, please!"

He opened the door wide, a look of worry coming over his face when he saw her ruined dress and flushed face. She rushed past him and tried to slam the door shut, but an arm stopped it mid-swing.

"Wait!" the voice said, hoarse like those were the first words it had uttered in days. "Let me in!"

Hanna thought she would faint from the stress and worry of her morning. She never dreamed that a Nazi, or one of those terrible rabid dogs, would follow her home. This was supposed to be her sanctuary. She pushed at the door again, hoping to slam it shut against all danger.

This time, it was Samual who stopped the door from closing out the world. He caught it before it hit the man standing in the doorway—before it hit David.

"David!" Samual said, in obvious surprise. He hadn't seen his friend since the night he announced the arrival of Reinhard Heydrich. It was almost a wonder Samual recognized him at all. The man had the face of a soldier, hardened from battle and gruesome sights.

Hanna had never known David to be especially well groomed. His dark, curly hair was often too long, weeks or even months past needing a trim. His beard was, more often than not, unruly and uncombed. But this David standing in the doorway was more than unkempt. He was almost savage. Upon looking into his eyes, Hanna thought that this man had seen things—things no man could see and come back from unchanged. But how, in such a short time? But a glance down at her ruined white satin dress answered the question for her. Hadn't she just, in a short walk around the city, seen things that would haunt her for years to come?

"Quick," David said. He dove through the door and slammed it behind him. Before Hanna could reprimand him for the scare he caused, he had bounded through the small sitting room, pulling shut the blackout curtains. He ran through the apartment, blocking out all life and scenes from the outside city. Only then did he return to them and take up his nervous pacing of the small room like it had only been minutes, not weeks, since their last conversation.

Hanna collapsed on the small couch, but Samual remained standing at the door, shocked and looking quickly from his friend to Hanna, obviously unsure who to address first.

"I've got to get out of Czechoslovakia," David said, breaking the silence.

"Don't we all?" muttered Hanna. She had lain down, burying her face in the crook of her elbow.

"I've got to get out now," he said earnestly. "The Nazis are looking for me."

That statement broke both Hanna and Samual out of their stupors. Samual finally moved from the door to join his friend, taking him by the arm to stop his panicked pacing. Hanna sat straight up.

"Why are the Nazis looking for you?" she asked, enunciating every word.

Samual ignored Hanna and said, "You can't get out of the country. You can't even get out of the city. All the trains are searched. The borders are secured."

"I just need German papers," David said.

"Why are the Nazis looking for you?" Hanna repeated.

"You just need German papers?" Samual scoffed. "You're not German. According to the Germans, you're not even human."

"We need Werner to help us," David said, resuming his pacing. Hanna watched him move through the small apartment, just like he did on their last pleasant Saturday night together. Three long strides, then he would hit a wall. Three more long strides, and he would be stopped by another wall. Hanna thought she might get dizzy just watching him.

His clothes were filthy. The back of his shirt—she assumed it had been white or beige at one point—was completely ruined. It was crossed with browns and blacks and greens, reminding her of the back of a ruthlessly flogged man. It looked as though he had been lying in the dirt and grass, which she assumed wasn't out of the question. His pants had holes in the knees and were streaked with thick black stains. *Tar, maybe,* Hanna thought, *possibly oil.*

"I don't think Werner can help you," Samual said. He shook his head.

"I have it planned," David said. He stopped walking and stood, center stage, in the room. "I'll take Werner's papers. I'll pretend to be him, just to get out of the country. I'll go to Switzerland."

"You'd never pass as Werner," Samual tried to reason. "There's at least fifteen centimeters between your heights."

"I'd never pass for Werner under tight scrutiny," David clarified. "I certainly look close enough like him at a glance."

"The Nazis aren't known for glancing these days."

"Why are the Nazis following you?" Hanna asked once more, but they continued to ignore her. She laid back down on the sofa, covering her face again. She was too tired to truly care about their lack of attention.

"The Nazis are known for being easily distracted," David said, with a bit of a wicked grin. Hanna poked her eyes out from under her arm to watch him. "Put a pretty girl in front of them and they will let a lot of things slide."

"No," said Samual forcefully. "No, no, no." He gave Hanna a look of pure terror.

"No," agreed David. "Not her. Greta."

Samual released his breath in relief. "I can't imagine Werner will feel any differently about putting Greta in danger."

"She won't be in danger. She's a pretty, Czech girl. A pretty, Christian Czech girl." David emphasized "Christian," as if that word made all the difference in the world. Perhaps it did, but Samual did not look convinced. David looked Samual hard in the eyes. "I'll take Werner's papers. Greta and I will take the train out of the city, all the way to safety. Greta will be able to distract anyone from looking too closely at my papers. She'll be perfectly safe. She's allowed to travel."

"Then Werner has no papers," Samual pointed out. "It's not like he can walk around Prague with yours."

"I'll send them back to Werner with Greta."

"It will never work," Samual said. "It's too . . . simple."

"Maybe simple is best."

"Why are the Nazis following you?"

Chapter 15

RACHAEL

Selection. It was as dreaded a word as "furnace" or "gas shower" or "Mengele." She had heard stories of the Germans coming in the middle of the night, literally pulling people off their bunks and throwing them onto trucks headed for the "showers." In her experience, though, selection came during either the morning or evening roll call. The soldiers did not want to do the work of burning bodies late into the night, so they typically chose to get the necessary business done during the daylight hours. Selection took place frequently in the hospital, which was why no cough or fever could ever be enough for Rachael to voluntarily set foot into that building. Once, she had seen an entire barrack get selected by the guards, who marched every last woman, child, flea, and tick straight to an uncovered truck, then to the gas chamber.

But Rachael had never heard of selection taking place during the day after morning roll call, while people were off at their assigned tasks. If she was her old, curious self, maybe she would have ruminated on what was happening on the German front lines to cause such an act of desperation. No, she thought, she would not have given it even that much thought. Before Chaya, she would have barely noticed that the soup line was shorter than usual.

Today, though, she felt the lingering effects of the day's selection acutely. It was making it hard for her to breathe. She sweated as she forced her legs to move at a normal pace from barrack to barrack, calling Chaya's name urgently, but softly. She knew running, even away from the fence, from building to building, was an easy reason for the soldiers in the high watchtowers to practice their sharpshooting skills. A thought tickled the back of her mind: if she did not find Chaya, maybe running across the yard would be her next step.

Not yet, though. Chaya had long since proven herself to be a master hider—finding any nook or cranny in this prison to burrow into, like a hibernating fox. Chaya did not speak much of it, but from her comfort in tight, dark areas, Rachael suspected the child spent most of her formative years in such places. The cellar that Chaya called "her room" must have been no bigger than a pantry or a washroom. So, she just needed to look in Chaya's favorite hiding places. She had already searched one or two since arriving back from work detail, and then a few more with an air of rising panic since Irene told her about the day's selection, but no sign of the girl yet.

Like everyone else who had been in Auschwitz for more than a few days, Rachael knew what happened in the showers—the small rooms with signs in all languages proclaiming "shower" and the value of cleanliness. She had heard rumors that the Germans, ever considerate of efficiencies, would only run the showers full of deadly gases if they had more than two hundred Jews. Otherwise, they simply shot the selected individuals in the back of the head and ordered other prisoners to clean up the blood and brain tissue. On top of that, the Germans would not run the furnaces for less than one thousand bodies. Rachael shuddered at the numbers running through her head—hundreds, thousands of Jews in a single day, in a single sweep of the camp.

Her sweet Catarina had died in such a selection before even stepping into the camp. For that reason, Rachael had closed her mind to the thought of what those people suffered when gas came seeping out of the shower heads rather than clear water.

A metallic, steady roar rumbled through the camp—the furnaces had started to burn. Though she was never sure if it was the crematoriums making such noise or the Germans trying to drown out the sound of the blazing fires and burning flesh.

Did Chaya get caught up in the stream of people being pushed and shoved toward an open-air truck bed? Was she trying to hide in the crowd, away from the snapping and snarling dogs? Or did a guard single her out—find her playing in a quiet corner with bits of rubbish and scraps of materials? Did the guard grab her roughly by the arm and throw her—literally—to her doom? Did Chaya call out in fear, or did she go willingly, as she seemed to with so many things around the camp, having no life experiences to tell her to do otherwise? Did she look for Rachael? Did she cry out for her, wondering why she wasn't there to hold her hand through this ordeal?

Her vision of a scared Chaya riding the truck to the gas showers blurred and changed. It was Chaya; then it was Catarina; back to Chaya. Her legs gave out as she searched behind another barrack. She sank to her knees on the cold ground. She was physically sick, feeling dry heaves start deep in her stomach. The fear and confusion and abandonment that she knew Catarina felt in her last moments . . . she could not bear to think Chaya felt the same.

Dry sobs wracked her body. She gasped for breath and squeezed her eyes shut. She did not know, until Auschwitz, that there was despair and sadness too deep to even bring tears. When Radek was taken and when Alexey died, choking in his own blood, Rachael thought her body was made of tears. She smelled tears when she lay in bed at night, placing her hand where Alexey should lie. The tears smelled of warm summer showers, but instead of growing flowers full of color and vibrancy, her tears gave life to a monster of sadness. Here, in this death camp, the monster should be bigger than the soldiers, bigger than the chimneys, bigger than the guard towers. She had no tears in this place. Yet, it grew without them. The monster of sadness took over her entire body as she knelt behind the barracks, trying to think of anything besides Chaya's terror as she was led into the hygiene room, given a small piece of soap, though the pretense was wasted on inmates of the prison, and closed into a fake shower room with hundreds of strangers. Rachael saw Chaya's small body shudder as the oxygen in the room was replaced with poison. Chaya's face twisted. It became Catarina's again. She clawed at her throat, she tried to push toward the door to feebly bang on it, begging for release. Catarina fell to the freezing cement floor, on her hands and knees—unable to get back up but unwilling to give up completely. She looked up, searching for Rachael's comfort. The face morphed back into Chaya's.

Rachael wanted to scream. She wanted to beat her head against this barrack wall until she dropped into blissful unconsciousness. She shoved her fist into her mouth and vented her rage. She screamed and screamed, silently, into her hands. Her body would not let her make a sound, instinctively knowing the danger in such an action. But her heart needed the release. So she screamed inside her head until the images were pushed away. By the time she finished, her hands were cramped from covering her mouth so tightly. She got back to her feet, took several steadying breaths, and continued her search for Chaya, knowing she had only a few more minutes before the curfew bell sounded and she was expected to spend a sleepless night not knowing where her small friend was laying her head.

There were certainly worse ways to die. She had heard some—not all, though—say the gas in the showers was quick. Not painless, but fairly fast. Of course, no one but those in the ashes truly knew. Maybe if Chaya had been killed that way, maybe she did not suffer. Rachael had witnessed, and lived, the slow and torturous death by starvation ever since she moved to the Terezin ghetto outside of Prague. She had thought she was hungry in the last months in the city. Then, she was sure she was starving when she, the baby, and Catarina lived inside the walls of Terezin. But she knew nothing back then.

It was not quick; and it certainly was not painless. True starvation was like a parasite that attacked the body. It started with the stomach, which fought back with growls and aches. By the time the parasite struck the rest of the body, the stomach had been silenced and defeated. The hunger attacked what bits of flesh the body had left—the arms, the legs, the cheeks. It ate away at those parts until limbs became bone thin and cheeks turned to sunken holes in a face that once smiled. Pink, rosy, and tanned complexion turned yellow and dry. And the pain—it traveled out from the stomach until every part of the body hurt. Starvation—the parasite—was slowly eating the entire person.

Rachael saw those signs on Chaya. She was supposed to be growing, supposed to be filling her stomach, supposed to be active and energetic. Instead, the parasite had taken hold—first the flakes of skin peeled off from her hands and knees and face; then her stomach bloated, giving it a deceptive look of fullness; and lately, the listlessness was starting to win the battle against Chaya's natural playfulness and energy. Withering away from lack of meal after meal—maybe that was worse than a poisonous shower.

Having searched the meal queue and Chaya's favorite hiding places, and having exhausted her own show of anxiety, Rachael walked into the barrack that she now shared with the girl. No matter how many times she walked into this building, the smell of vomit and feces and blood made her stagger back a step. She glanced at the bunk closest to the entrance. To Rachael, the body lying in the straw was another nameless prisoner, but she also saw blurred memories of Alexey in his final moments, and a horrible premonition that it could soon be her, or worse, Chaya.

The woman was shaking violently from fever. Even in the dim light, Rachael could see sweat covering the woman, soaking into the straw around her. Her face was buried into the sharp crook of her elbow. She moaned softly.

"Too bright," she cried, though the light of the barracks was weak and gray.

Another woman gently rubbed the sick prisoner's feet. "Let me take you to the hospital," she pleaded.

The sick woman shook her entire body back and forth, a desperate no. "Not there," she whispered. "I'll die there."

Rachael knew the truth in that. Very few women returned from the hospital. Those that did had stories worse than death by illness—medical experiments, operations with no pain relief, a doctor whom some called the Angel of Death. Rachael thought she would lose her mind if she had to watch Chaya die slowly from an illness that was treatable, if she had to carry the child out for morning roll call when she was too weak to even stand, if she had to watch coughs torture her small body as they were doing to this woman in front of her.

She could not take this sight any longer, or take the thought of Chaya dying in this way. She rushed back out of the barrack. Darkness had fallen like a curtain. There was no gradual sunset of reds and oranges and violets. It was light when Rachael entered the barrack, now it was dark as she walked quickly back out. She stood outside the entrance. She felt the night closing in on her. She wanted to be brave enough to run to the fence, to end it all, but she lacked even the ambition for that. As she stood, paralyzed by worry and indecision, a guard turned the corner, almost running into her. Rachael instinctively placed her hand over the dress pocket, hoping to hide any hint of her contraband—the ring, mainly, but also, she just remembered, the feast she had prepared for Chaya. To her relief, it was a guard known to have something resembling mercy and kindness, though Rachael found it hard to believe the rumors that this guard would even give an extra piece of bread to the especially sick. The woman did, after all, carry a bullwhip with her everywhere she went.

"What are you doing?" the guard asked sharply. Rachael's eyes immediately fell to her feet. "Curfew is in just a few moments. Get to your bunk."

Rachael nodded furiously, but there was something in the guard's words that dared her to hope—perhaps not so much the words but the fact that the guard did not even threaten to use that terrifying bullwhip on her if she did not hurry.

"Please," Rachael muttered, just loud enough for the guard to hear her and pause. "There was a little girl, Cha—" She stopped herself. The inmates here did not have names to the Germans. "A little girl," she repeated. "I can't . . . I can't find her. Do you know . . ." She stopped, sure she had gone too far.

The woman was quiet long enough for Rachael to dare a glance up. She looked at Rachael with a mixture of puzzlement and anger, but Rachael was sure she could detect a sliver of something else . . . sympathy.

Finally, the guard spoke softly. "I know the girl you mean. I did not see her."

Rachael's heart leapt. It was vague, but it was enough to give her hope. Did that mean she did not see Chaya on the selection trucks?

"But . . ." the guard continued, this time grabbing Rachael's arm and forcing her to look into the woman's eyes. They were intense. "There are many ways to die in this place. A broken heart is the most painful." Then, she pushed Rachael roughly toward the barrack door and walked away.

Rachael felt the despair in her chest turn to rage. What did this woman know of heartbreak?

She thought about lying in that bunk all night, alone, without the soft breathing and warmth of Chaya next to her. But as Rachael finally made her way to the bed and raised her eyes to the hard planks with a neat pile of straw in the middle, she saw Chaya curled tightly into a ball, shoulders shaking with sobs.

Rachael softly placed her hand on Chaya's body, like she used to with Alexey late in the night. When Chaya looked up, Rachael saw clean, pink lines on her cheeks where the stream of tears had washed away weeks of dirt. Chaya threw her arms around Rachael, almost launching herself out of the bunk.

When the cries subsided enough for her to speak, Chaya said, "I thought you had left me."

"Never," Rachael said softly into her hair.

Chapter 16

HANNA

David's story came out in bits and pieces over the next two days—many of the pieces Hanna had to fit together like a puzzle. She was somewhat surprised to hear that there was a resistance ring inside the city. Apparently, not all of Prague had decided to stand by and stay silent as the Nazis claimed power. Not everyone would remain passive as beasts disguised as men tortured, imprisoned, and humiliated innocent people.

"There's really a resistance?" Hanna asked. "I thought it was a rumor. Wishful thinking."

"There's been an active resistance since the Nazis first walked into this city," David said. Hanna reassessed the damage done to his clothes under this new lens—dirt and grass stains, oil and grease. She smiled knowing that despite most of the city's indifference to the plight of the Jews, at least some people were doing something about it.

"Maybe there's hope for humankind after all," she said.

David nodded once in agreement. "I got involved in the beginning." He shrugged with a half-smile. "What else did I have to do?

Unemployed as I am. But when Heydrich arrived"—he sneered at the name—"I increased my activity. Substantially." He smiled wide. Samual, who'd been listening quietly, matched the grin.

"Activity?" Samual leaned in, looking like a boy planning a schoolyard prank. "Such as?"

David shook his head, his long hair whipping his face with the motion. "The less I say, the less danger you are in." Hanna shivered at the word "danger." "If the Nazis come looking for me, you honestly don't know anything."

"True." Samual glanced at Hanna, agreeing too quickly to David's secretiveness. She suspected that he wanted David to remain tight-lipped, not only for their protection but also to keep her from getting any ideas. He had been less than pleased after her walk around the city. He hadn't scolded her too much because David was taking up most of his attention, but Hanna knew he disapproved. He was still preaching for her to keep her head down and stay out of the Nazis' way. David was telling a much different story.

"I'm not afraid to die for what's right," he said, after they had gone over his plan for what seemed the hundredth time in two days.

"If that's true," Samual said, "why don't you turn yourself in? I'm sure the Nazis will be happy to oblige your wishes."

"Just because I'm not afraid of dying doesn't mean that I'm willing to give up," David said sulkily. Samual had agreed to help him implicitly, but it was clear David knew his friend still disagreed with his actions and his plan. "We have to stand up to them," he urged, not for the first time. "Even if it's dangerous."

"Dying is easy, David. Fighting back is much harder." Samual's tone darkened. Gone was the earlier lightheartedness, the sneaky smiles when talking about how they would make the Nazis pay.

Not for the first time in the days since David showed up at their door, Hanna noted the difference between Samual's reactions. To her, he was protective—dismissive of the Nazis even. His advice boiled down to: don't look at them and they won't see you. To David, he was impressed, maybe even jealous of David's bravery. He had laughed at David's daring and always wanted to hear more. Now, though, as the plan got closer to implementation, Samual seemed to get nervous, to rethink his support of his friend's defiance.

"What does that mean?" David asked.

"It means," Samual said with exaggerated patience, "that any fool can stomp his foot and throw a tantrum in the face of the Nazis and be rewarded with a gunshot to the head. But it takes a lot more courage and brains to survive this war. Which will really show the Nazis?"

Hanna had been preparing a small meal for the three of them as Samual and David talked. She had boiled four potatoes and felt lucky to be able to add a little crushed garlic for flavor. Getting food was becoming more and more difficult, and since David was in hiding, it was not as if he could collect on his small rations.

Hanna was impressed by David's determination to do what little he could to fight the Goliath of the German Empire. But she was not impressed by how small their efforts seemed. Cutting brake lines, passing on news about the Allied troops, severing telephone cables—it seemed like little more than a housefly buzzing around the head of the giant. Annoying, yes. Distracting, maybe. Winning the war, definitely not.

David was doing something, though, and much more than strolling through the city with his head held high. Hanna felt the pull to follow suit, like a siren call luring her away from Samual and into the arms of the dangerous and unknown. She wanted to ask David to help her get involved, but he was in no position to do that right now. Plus, she was terrified. She thought she could deliver messages, but also worried that she would wear her terror on her face like a beacon. Then, she would be no help to anyone.

The plan was set to move forward the next day. Hanna had no idea how Werner felt about it, since Samual had refused to let her accompany him when he snuck to Werner's apartment after curfew. Hanna thought she could help convince Werner, but she was not very convincing even to Samual, as she still wore the shell-shocked look from her experience with the rabid dogs on Nardoni Street.

As this was his last night before his escape from the city, David fell into a restless sleep on Samual's bed, his stomach still grumbling after the meager dinner of Hanna's potatoes. After he was soundly asleep, Samual and Hanna sat down in the sitting room, and Samual conveyed to her in whispers part of his conversation with Werner from the night before.

"He wasn't happy," Samual confided. Hanna was not in the least bit surprised.

"Of course he wasn't," she agreed. "Though David says Greta won't be in any danger, I'm sure that's not completely true."

Samual nodded. They had snuggled themselves onto the sofa. It was too small for even one of them to lounge comfortably, but after the last few days, Hanna did not mind being as close to Samual as possible. His arms held her tightly to the entire length of his body, and she kept burying her nose in his chest to take in the smell of him. He always smelled like spearmint and slate, from the pencils he used at his drafting table. He had a habit of rubbing the excess slate on his shirt front when he was thinking through a particular design.

"Keeping Greta safe is a big part of it," he said. "But overall, Werner does not agree with anything David's doing."

"You mean the resistance work?"

"Exactly," Samual whispered. "I didn't share any details with Werner, but it doesn't take much detective work to realize David needs to get out of the country because he's causing trouble for the Nazis."

"How can Werner object to causing problems for the Nazis? He's no sympathizer," Hanna said.

"I wouldn't be so sure." Samual paused. She could feel his chest moving up and down in time with hers. She was staring up at the dark ceiling. With the blackout curtains pulled tight and all light extinguished from the room, it was no different than if she had her eyes closed. Though she could not see Samual, she could feel him struggling to find the right words.

"You think he's coming around to the German way of thinking?" she suggested.

"Perhaps something like that," he said finally. "For everyone around us, life has only gotten worse. Worse since the Nazis arrived, but even worse still since Heydrich showed up. David had it right when he warned us a few weeks ago." He was quiet again. "But for Werner . . . Things for Werner have gotten suddenly better." She felt him shake his head, maybe trying to knock out the bad assumptions. Hanna remained silent, letting him gather his thoughts and continue.

"His factory started serving midday meals to all the workers. Good meals, too. With meat and seasonings. He got a pay increase. He's making more now than he ever did before the war broke out." Hanna knew that Samual said this with a heavy heart. He wanted to be happy for his friend—at least life was moving along in the right direction for someone. But what did it mean that Werner was thriving when David was running for his life? And how could they be happy for Werner's good fortune when they were barely surviving?

"I didn't tell David these things," Samual continued. "He's suspicious enough."

"For good reason, it seems," Hanna finally broke in.

She felt Samual nod once. "Yes, for good reason," he agreed. "Werner is afraid that the Jews are causing these problems. That if we would fade quietly into the background, things would start to return to normal. He thinks that Heydrich is doing the best he can to help the people of Prague."

"So he *is* a Nazi sympathizer?" she barely whispered.

"Maybe worse," Samual said, his voice equally low. "Maybe a Heydrich sympathizer."

Hanna shuddered, though she was anything but cold inside the warmth of Samual's arms. "Yet he agreed to help David?"

"Not without much persuasion." Samual laughed ruefully.

"Tell me again that this is going to work," Hanna said. "I think I need to hear it from you, not just David."

Samual was quiet for a long time. He was quiet for so long that Hanna thought he may have fallen asleep from the stress of the past few days. Finally, he sighed. "I can only tell you what I know." He started reciting the plan, even through Hanna had heard it numerous times. "Tomorrow morning, David is going to meet Greta at the train station."

"She's going to have Werner's papers?"

"I can only pray so," he continued. "They won't have any luggage, since they are traveling under the guise of a day trip. They are going to head first to Salzburg." Hanna closed her eyes, imagining the train ride south: Greta's hand in David's, holding their breath every time a Nazi boarded the train car or when another passenger gave them more than a passing glance.

"Once they are sure no one from Prague has followed them," Samual said, "they will head west. Once David gets to Zurich, he'll be free. Greta will stay long enough to get a change of clothes, a hot meal, and a little rest."

"So she won't look suspicious?"

"Exactly. We need Greta to blend into the crowd. She will still have to get home safely, smuggling Werner's papers back to him." Samual was quiet again for a moment. "I don't think carrying another person's papers is illegal, exactly, but it certainly would raise a lot of questions if she was caught with them."

"I have to admit," Hanna said, turning her head into Samual, "I'm very impressed by Greta. This is incredibly brave of her." She felt Samual nod in agreement. "If I'm being honest, I never thought she had it in her. But I guess I never had occasion to see it. It always just seemed that everything was so easy for her. She's lovely, has the right golden looks. She's Christian and Czech. How nice to have all that going for you . . ."

Hanna could not deny that the girl had suffered during the Nazi occupation, but she certainly had never undergone any of the humiliation or persecution that Hanna, Samual, and David felt every day. It wasn't Greta's fault, but Hanna couldn't stop herself from thinking that Greta was like the teacher's pet in primary school. Her place in Prague was like the front seat of the classroom, where the teacher offered only smiles and praise for correct answers.

But now, Greta was risking arrest, punishment, maybe even her life to help David—a man she had only known for a few years.

Was everyone braver than herself? Did everyone else know their place in this world, where they could stand up and be heard? Was it just her who was searching for a lighthouse in this dark, stormy sea?

♦

When Hanna awoke on Saturday morning, her stomach was already in knots. She dressed quickly, pinning her hair under a plain brown hat. She did not even attempt a small breakfast, as her nerves would not allow her to keep anything down. She did drink half a cup of weak tea to stop her stomach from grumbling as she walked with David and Samual to the train station.

Though movement out of the city was becoming more and more difficult, the train station was still bustling with travelers. If Hanna were to stand in the middle of the train platform, perfectly still, with her eyes closed, she thought she might be able to hear the sounds of the station before the occupation—families parting ways with tearful goodbyes; lovers united in passionate embraces; heels tapping quickly as one or another person rushed to catch their train. The scene in front of her eyes, though, told the real truth. The Nazi flag hung everywhere, making sure no outsider could claim ignorance as to who ruled the city. Soldiers patrolled up and down the platform, giving penetrating stares to all who stepped off a train into Prague and glaring at the betrayal of any who dared leave it.

It was the faces of the people that were the most disturbing. They reminded Hanna of unfinished portraits. Whenever Hanna painted a scene with human faces, she painted all else first—the landscape around them, the details on their clothing, down to the last black button. When all else was done, she would finally fill in the facial features—the details that turned faceless figures into real people. She would add the brown eyes with specks of gold, the faint lines of wrinkles around the eyes as one would smile, the tinge of red on a girl's lips, the slight pink to rosy an energetic boy's cheeks. Those were the details that turned something into a someone. Those were the details that the people around Hanna were lacking.

As she looked around her, Hanna knew even closing her eyes would not bring back the days of old when the station rang of partings and reunions. The luggage could still be heard thumping the ground as a person tired of holding it. The harried steps of someone running late still echoed through the platforms. And the voices still combined to make a general hum of human sound. But it wasn't right. The details of the painting were missing. The sounds were like a recording.

Hanna and Samual walked with David through the station, though David insisted they not follow him to the last platform. He did not want them near if he was unable to board the train with Greta. Samual had agreed wholeheartedly when he realized Hanna could not be persuaded to stay home. As they approached the third platform, David stopped and turned to them.

He shook Samual's hand earnestly. "You've been a wonderful friend these years, Samual," he said. Hanna found that this, more than any other conversation of theirs she'd overheard over the last few days, unnerved her. David was many things—anxious, passionate, opinionated, but never sentimental. This was truly goodbye, she realized. Though David had always been Samual's friend and not quite hers, she still felt her throat start to close up at the thought of forever parting with him. This was the end of their Saturday night group. This was the start of something completely unknown and unwelcomed.

"Get yourself and Hanna"—David gave her a small, but warm smile—"out of Prague as soon as you can. Find me in Zurich. The Swiss will never fall to Hitler. You'll be safe there."

Samual nodded, but Hanna could tell there was no conviction in it. Whether that was because Samual still did not believe escape was necessary or because he did not believe it was possible, Hanna couldn't say. David must have felt the lack of conviction as well. He smiled slowly.

"Whatever you do, Samual," he said softly. "Whatever you do, do not let them send you east. Do not go east."

Hanna reached for David's hand and held it for a few seconds. She gave him her best reassuring smile, though she was sure he could see how forced it was. "Take care of yourself, David."

"Always." He responded with an equally artificial smile, meant to reassure. Then he added urgently, "Don't go east."

"What's east?" she asked. She knew the answer but, somehow, needed to hear him say it.

"Death."

David turned without another word and, without looking back, camouflaged into the crowd of lifeless people. As she held Samual's hand, watching David go, she felt that—for the first time in years—she was a part of something bigger. She was just one of the many in the train station, shell-shocked by the way her life had turned out since the occupation, saying goodbye to someone she cared for, hoping for the best or at least better than what she had been dealt.

David, too, became part of something, for after just a few steps, she lost him in the crowd. He had been without proper clothing for some time, but for the occasion, he borrowed one of Werner's hats. His sloped fedora became one of many on the platform; the black wool faded into one large mass, and Hanna could no longer distinguish his form from the other men. She smiled, knowing his escape plan hinged on just that, and also knowing that David wanted to be just one of the free men of Prague. Now he was.

Samual and Hanna continued to stand on the platform, searching for another glimpse of David. Samual squeezed her hand before releasing it quickly. He pointed across two platforms to a corner by the ticket counter.

"There," he said. Hanna's eyes followed his finger to Greta. She stood with her back against the wall, nervously wringing a pair of ivory gloves in her hands. Hanna could feel her anxiety from across the train station. In response, Hanna found her hand nervously twisting her engagement ring around her finger. Greta's eyes moved just as quickly as her hands, scanning the crowd for David's familiar face. She must have seen him because her eyes suddenly widened, and Hanna could swear she saw the girl tremble from head to toe.

"She'll never convince the Nazis like that," Samual said quietly. "She looks guilty from all the way over here."

Hanna nodded, still spinning her ring, her stomach knotting even further.

Hanna assumed that David had nodded or waved to Greta, because she started to raise a hand, but brought it back down to her gloves before it even reached shoulder height. She may have nodded in response, but Hanna could not tell if it was an involuntary quiver of fear. The girl took a step forward, then violently slammed herself back against the wall.

"Something's wrong," Hanna whispered. "Something . . ."

She and Samual saw them at the same time. Samual hissed in a deep breath. She barely had time to register what she was seeing when she felt Samual's crushing grip on her hand. He jerked her so ferociously that she stumbled backward. He did not give her time to catch her balance as he was pulling her roughly through the crowd. Her shoulders smashed into strangers, her feet tread on others' toes. She was lurching forward rather than walking, but still, Samual pulled. Blank face after blank face passed her. Hanna could barely keep up, and she could not process what was before her eyes, let alone what had been behind her.

Nazis.

Four of them. There had been four Nazis emerging from the shadows of the train station. Emerging right next to Greta.

Hanna continued to bang into people as they rushed through the train station. She could not catch her breath, she could not pause to apologize, she could not stop. She knew if Samual let go of her hand, if they stopped moving, if she turned to look behind her, all would be lost. Maybe the Nazis were coming after them as well. Maybe they knew about Samual's involvement with this escape plan. Maybe not. But she knew for certain that she would not be able to control her terror and her tears if they stopped moving.

So they did not stop. Not until Samual slammed his apartment door behind them and pushed the sofa in front of it.

Chapter 17

RACHAEL

Chaya just kept crying: "You didn't come for me. I waited, and you didn't come!"

"Shhh," Rachael said as she stroked the girl's hair, careful not to tangle the ring in it. For months, Rachael had tried to impress upon the child the seriousness of their lives in Auschwitz, but everything was a game to her. Now, in one evening, Chaya seemed irrevocably changed.

Rachael still didn't know how Chaya escaped the day's selection.

"I didn't think you were coming back," she sobbed into Rachael's dirty dress. "I thought I would be here alone forever."

"I know, dear," Rachael whispered, hugging the girl even tighter. "I was terrified of the same thing." Before this, Rachael thought nothing scared the girl. Or maybe, everything scared her. Maybe the girl's terror was like a field hand's calluses—open and bleeding at first, but now toughened and dead to the touch after years of nonstop fear.

It was Rachael's job to save Chaya. It had never made sense to her why she was still alive. She had watched every member of her family be taken or killed. She was the mother. A mother should die before her children. Clearly, she was a terrible one, and an even worse wife.

She had not been able to save anyone. Yet, here she was again, in the same situation: a helpless child in her arms with an entire world working against her, trying to destroy that child.

This time, though, she would not let the Germans win. Yes, she was in a place where success was even less likely. Everything in Auschwitz was meant to kill her and Chaya—the cold, the heat, the lice, the illnesses, the work, the lack of food, the guards, the electric fence, the gas chambers. She had been unable to save Radek and Alexey when they were tucked safely in their own home. She had been unable to save Catarina and the baby when they were firmly in her arms. But, despite those failures, she knew she would not let Chaya down. She felt her confidence grow with every stroke of the girl's hair. This was why she had not succumbed to despair and death yet; she was meant to save this child.

The last time she had a child sleeping in her arms was her last night in Terezin. By the time she had received the pink slip of paper telling her to pack up her few belongings and be ready to depart for the train station the next day, she was a realist. Life in Terezin had been horrible. They struggled for food every day, and she feared constantly that disease or starvation or the Germans would take one or both of the children. But they did live. Catarina was tucked in with her in the small room they shared with another mother and her three children. The baby was in her arms all day long, alarmingly quiet and still. Rachael matched her breaths to the baby's short ones—two of the child's to one of hers.

She had found out she was pregnant only a few weeks after Alexey died. She thought the nausea was from watching her husband choke on his own blood. The part of her that would have seen this baby as a final gift from her husband, a blessing among so much death and destruction, had been buried with Alexey's body. She loved this new life in her belly, but she knew this child would never have a life worth living.

There were nights when she contemplated ending it before it began, but every morning, she realized the unborn child was a part of Alexey, and she could no more kill it than she could have killed her husband.

Maybe this baby was a fighter—stronger and more stubborn than Rachael could ever be. Maybe, despite everything the Nazis would try to do to destroy it, this baby would find a way to live. That was the thought she held on to when she moved from Prague to the ghetto outside the city, visibly pregnant as she held Catarina's hand on the train platform, quietly allowing the Nazis to transport them from their home to a cage. She gave birth inside of an open room with rows of beds and sick patients all around her, in what constituted as a hospital in Terezin. She considered herself lucky, as she had a nurse delivering the baby and her daughter standing next to her. Rachael was terrified to leave Catarina in the small home they had made with other families, worried that a round-up of Jews in the middle of the night would happen while she was away. Better to have the girl with her at all times than to risk her disappearing forever.

Catarina said nothing as she watched her mother endure eight hours of labor—sweating, screaming, and cursing God. She said nothing as a tiny boy emerged into this world, mostly silent but squirming, covered in blood and a white, creamy substance. She continued to say nothing when Rachael introduced her to her little brother.

"What shall we name him?" Rachael whispered as she and Catarina looked at the baby for the first time. Catarina stared at him, her brown eyes large and wondering. She shrugged. "I don't know either," Rachael said gently, resting her tired head against the girl's side. "You decide."

Catarina shook her head.

"No, I want you to name him." Rachael nudged her daughter with her head. "You can take your time and think about it."

Almost a year later, Catarina was still mostly silent, and the baby was still nameless. Rachael knew Catarina loved her baby brother. She cooed to him and tenderly held him at night as Rachael tried to prepare small meals. Rachael wondered if Catarina's reluctance to name the baby was because the girl saw no future for him. Lying in bed that last night, waiting for the sun to rise and a train to take them east, Rachael had thought her daughter might be right. They were preparing to go out into the great unknown again. Rachael held little hope that this journey would end well for any of them.

The next morning was even worse than Rachael imagined. She had thought the journey from Prague to Terezin was traumatic—the long line, the waiting, the inhumanity of the soldiers, the degradation they threw at almost every woman who passed by. This journey to Auschwitz, though, was madness, chaos, torture, depravity—worse than any of the awful words she could think of.

Rachael had always thought her people, the Jews, a stoic people. They were used to oppression; they had become desensitized to discrimination. She had even heard that the mass round up of children, led—voluntarily—by their teachers and guardians, was a solemn, quiet event, with the children marching onto the train without tears, without cries, without protests. This train station was not that. It was pandemonium. All the self-control these people once had was used up under Heydrich's rule in Prague and then under the invisible, but still persecuting, rule of the Nazis in the ghetto. Rachael had never heard such cries, never seen such violence in one place. She was frozen with horror and fear at what she witnessed around her.

The baby, of course, cried. He had spent his first eight months in one tiny room, surrounded by only half a dozen people. Rarely did he see anything but those four walls. His eyes were overwhelmed with the sights around him and his ears could not process the sounds. He flailed and screamed in terror. It took both of Rachael's hands to keep him in her arms. More than the scene around her, she was terrified of being separated from Catarina. She placed the girl's hand in the crook of her elbow and ordered Catarina to grip so tightly that the loose skin on Rachael's arm puckered red and started to bruise. Still, Rachael worried it was not tight enough.

So concerned was she at being separated from her daughter, Rachael was taken by surprise when she was parted from her baby son. That the Nazis could be so beastly that they would take a baby from his mother had never even crossed her mind. As she lay in bed in Auschwitz, she admonished her naïve self. Had she been wiser, had she been more on guard, had she been who she was now in this death camp, maybe she would still have her nameless baby with her.

Catarina was gripping Rachael's arm tightly, and Rachael kept stealing glances at the girl. "Hold on," she whispered. "No matter what, don't let go of me."

She looked from Catarina to the ghastly scene unfolding around her on that train station. She saw frail old men lifted from the platform when they had refused to step any closer to the train. The Germans lifted them up with no more strength than was necessary for a sack of flour and threw them into the open train car. She saw women—mothers and daughters, sisters, best friends—hold on to one another's hands, screaming and gripping wildly as Nazis tore them apart. She saw whips fly through the air and heard their cracks and screams. She saw two dogs rip into the arm of a woman who had fallen and was too slow to get back to her feet. All through this, she struggled with the baby, writhing from side to side in terror.

She was losing her grip on him. She paused in the chaotic queue to readjust her arms around him. Catarina took a step further.

"Catarina!" she said sharply, "Stay by my side!"

She felt the baby slide from her hands. In a panic, she turned back and flailed fiercely for him. He had not fallen though; he was now in the hands of a Nazi soldier with sweat dripping and an odd smile on his face. Rachael lunged for her baby, but the soldier pushed her away with an easy swat of his hand. She fell to the ground.

From the wooden planks of the train platform, she watched the Nazi look at her with a mixture of amusement and pity. He raised his eyebrows and the corners of his mouth. With the same hand he used to push Rachael away, he grabbed the baby by the thigh. He swung his arm back violently then up into the air with as much force as he could manage. With a grunt from the soldier and a scream from the baby, he threw Rachael's son high, high into the air, over the heads of all on the train platform.

The sound she made when she saw her baby launched into the air was deep and savage. She could not believe such a sound could be made by a human. But she was no longer human. She was no longer herself.

She did not see where her son landed. In his final moments, she was a coward. She had not the strength left in her to see what remained of his small body. She knew others saw it though. She screamed and screamed until her voice gave out, and when she finally stopped, there was a strange hush throughout the crowd. It started from those closest to the tragedy and expanded outward like ripples in a pond when a rock slams through the still surface. The crowd was silent and respectful to her grief, but only for a moment. Then life—life as it was on this platform, which was really no life at all—resumed. The people had given her nameless son the only tribute they could—a quick moment of stillness. Then he was forgotten, like the many lost before him. The Nazis had killed all of him.

Chapter 18

HANNA

She and Samual cowered in his apartment for the next two days. Hanna thought that "cower" was an ungracious word, but it was the right word. She strained her ears for any outside sound, constantly questioning if that was the click of Nazi heels on their stairs, or the whispers of neighbors turning them in to the German authorities. The dark of night was no relief, as soldiers were known to barge into homes under the cover of midnight and take away entire families—and none would be heard of again.

Finally, early Monday morning, they agreed something had to be done. They reasoned that the Nazis had had two days to search them out and arrest them along with David. There wasn't much searching to be done, because they only had Samual's apartment or Hanna's boarding room in which to hide. It was obvious to Hanna that they could not go to Werner for any kind of assistance, though Samual would not speak of his friend.

She had tried to broach the subject as soon as they barred the door after their frantic escape from the train station.

"Werner—" she tried to say.

"I can't," Samual said, stopping her.

"But, if Werner—"

"No, Hanna!" he said sharply. "I can't think about it right now."

Hanna found it was the only thing she could think about. Greta's face of misery and guilt screamed what Werner had done, but she understood Samual's reluctance to discuss it. He may have just lost one friend; he could not yet face that he had lost the other. But in the darkness and silence of Samual's apartment, her mind kept thinking: *If Werner turned David in to the Nazis, would he do the same to Samual?*

As the hours ticked by and it was only in their paranoid minds that they heard the Nazis coming, it appeared that Werner would not.

On Monday morning, they decided to try to live life as normally as possible. To not do so might bring more suspicion upon them. With that decision made, Hanna felt better. She could see in Samual's face that he did too. Having a plan, a purpose, made a world of difference. His eyes had been strained since they hurried from the train platform. His mouth had been drawn tight, his jaw clenched. Now, as he put on his brown suit for another day of work, he seemed to relax. Maybe he was heading straight into a German trap, but at least he was doing something.

Hanna was tasked with discovering what had happened to David—a job that neither of them wanted. The list of terrible things that could have befallen him was something they couldn't dwell on for long. "But not knowing is worse," she had said. She planned to appeal to the Jewish Council. They were often informed of arrests or at least able to gather what bits of information the Germans would allow.

It took most of the day at the Jewish Council for her to get any information at all. She waited as patiently as she could while the officials begged the German authorities for answers, bartered for information, and offered favors to discover David's fate. Hanna sat in a hard wooden chair in the small waiting area with many others. As she was beginning to feel her toes tingling from sitting still for too long, a woman came in with three young children in tow. The woman did not even see Hanna; her desperate eyes went straight to the young rabbi at the front desk.

"Please," she said, her voice already breaking. "My husband. He has not been home in three days. Please. Can you help me find him?" The children stood by the door, silent, but their eyes pleaded as fervently as their mother's.

"Of course," the rabbi said gently. "I need your husband's information—name, description, where he works, where you last saw him." The woman nodded furiously. "You can wait in that seat over there." He motioned to a chair similar to Hanna's, but next to a man who came in asking for a paying job—any paying job.

Hanna could witness no more misery, so she exited the building, allowing the gray skies and the sharp wind that rustled up leaves and trash on the streets of the Jewish Quarter to distract her. A walk around her community did nothing to lift her spirits, though, so she quickly returned to the wooden chair. At least while she sat in the Jewish Council office, she felt like she was doing something to help David.

When she returned from her walk, the young rabbi was comforting the wife. Hanna waited patiently until the woman, stumbling from grief and eyes swollen shut with salty tears, left the small room. When the rabbi approached her, Hanna steeled herself for his news.

"I'm afraid I don't know much about your friend," he said. Hanna let out a small sigh of relief. Perhaps the unknown was just putting off the inevitable bad news, but after seeing the wife so distraught, Hanna was happy to buy a little time. "He was taken immediately to Pankrac Prison, on the south side of the city." The rabbi paused. "You have heard of Pankrac?"

Before the war, Hanna had no impressions of the name. But since the Germans entered the city, she had heard the place mentioned too many times to ignore it. Now she knew enough about the prison to make her shudder, thinking David was sent there.

"The Gestapo take prisoners there." The Rabbi lowered his voice. "Usually resistance fighters, black marketeers, Jewish sympathizers..."

Hanna nodded. "Is it true"—she was whispering, though the room was empty now—"that they built gallows and a shooting range? Because they couldn't keep up with the number of executions?"

"Let's not think the worst," the rabbi said. "Those could be rumors. I've also heard that many of the prisoners are sent east."

East. Exactly where David told them to not go. Hanna did not know what happened when a person was sent east, but if David's last words could be trusted, it may have been worse than death. What Hanna did know was that once a person was sent east, he never returned.

"What is going to happen to my friend in that prison?" she asked. The rabbi only shook his head sadly and patted her arm.

That was as much comfort as she could offer Samual. She was surprised to find him already in the small apartment when she walked through the door with the news of David bearing down on her like a heavy burden.

Samual had his back to her when she entered the apartment. He was looking out the window, at what, Hanna could not imagine. The view was no longer of the city they had both fallen in love with. The colors and structures were still the same, but the essence of the city, the spirit that gave it a glow, had gradually been extinguished by the Nazis. Still, Samual stood like a statue on the Charles Bridge in front of his small view of Prague. He seemed not to hear her enter.

"Samual?" she asked tentatively.

She was sure he heard her, but he did not turn around or greet her. His stillness was unnerving. Samual was not a still man. He was always busy—fidgeting, pacing, doodling, smiling. This statue of her fiancé terrified her.

"Samual?" she tried again. There was still no movement. She walked quietly behind him and placed her hands lovingly on his back, feeling the taut muscles underneath his shirt. He did not respond to her touch. "Samual!" she said more firmly, fear leaking out around the word.

Finally, he gave some sign of life, though Hanna might have preferred his stillness. He hung his head and his shoulders felt like they were shaking. She did not understand what she was looking at. If this was anyone else in front of her, she would think that the person was sobbing. But this was Samual. Surely, he was not standing in front of her, weeping.

But the tremor of his body and the soft sounds—like wind blowing in bursts through a back alley—gave every impression that, yes, he was crying. Hanna struggled to understand what could cause Samual so much grief. Did he know about David already? Though the news was grim, Hanna thought, it was not desperate yet. Was it news from his family? True, he was not close to his siblings or parents anymore, but if something terrible had happened to them, he may feel the pain more acutely because of their estrangement. Was he hurt? Hanna moved her hands from Samual's back to his shoulders, down his arms, around his waist. He felt whole. He felt unharmed.

Suddenly, he turned into her and embraced her, like a drowning man grabbing on to a floating log in a churning river. He held her as though her body alone could prevent him from going under. Her legs almost buckled under the weight and suddenness of his grip, but she held her ground. If ever Samual needed her to stand tall, it was now.

She was not sure how long they stood like that—a drowning man, holding tightly to his lifeline, in front of the dismal scene of Prague in 1941. Hanna just held him. She did not ask what was so terribly wrong, for she knew he would share when he was again able to form words. She did not give him false words of reassurance. As strong as she had to be to hold him up, she did not have the strength to lie to him. But she did grip him back with the same intensity, and she did offer him soft sounds of love and encouragement—no words, just murmurs and hums that she hoped would calm him.

Eventually, the flood subsided. He loosened his grip and turned away with embarrassment. But Hanna would not let it be so. She forced him to look at her, forced him to see the love and understanding that she felt. She waited patiently until he could meet her eyes again and tell her what had broken him.

"My job," he said gruffly. "I lost my job today."

Hanna felt her heart sink and her eyes fill with tears. The thoughts she had of bad events had not included this, but she knew how this would affect Samual. It was not the loss of independence, the humiliation of poverty, the unfairness of discrimination, though, of course, those things weighed him down. It was the loss of his essence. Just as Prague had lost its glow and appeal when its freedom was signed away, Samual had lost the light in his eyes when his work was taken from him. Hanna missed her job terribly. She missed the purpose to her day. She missed the normality of going to work, flirting with the customers, and coming home with weary feet. But working at the cafe did not define her.

Samual's love for his work was his foundation. It was his love and passion and art. She understood that and loved him for it.

And, like everything else, the Germans had just taken it away from him.

♦

Idleness did not become either of them. Hanna gave up the pretense of staying in her own boarding room and moved in with Samual to save any small amount of money they could. She hadn't realized how much time she had spent frivolously throughout the day while Samual was at work.

For the first day of his unemployment, they stayed in bed late—though not lounging or making love. Samual was restless, tossing and turning, but found no reason to remove himself from under the covers. Hanna had nothing to do. There was no food to prepare for meals and no money to shop for food. They had little clothing and less to repair it if it needed mending. So she fretted around, hoping Samual would find the motivation to leave the apartment, or at the very least, leave his bed.

On the fifth day of his unemployment, she pulled the quilt off Samual's bare back and tried to entice him out of the apartment.

"Walk with me to pick up our rations for the day," she asked sweetly. "We can take the long way through the Jewish Quarter and walk the city like we used to."

He did not even answer her but tried to pull the blanket out of her hands.

"Samual," she said sternly, quickly keeping the blanket away from him. "Get out of bed."

"Why?" he asked, as he settled his head back onto the pillow, resigned to resting without covers.

"Why?" she asked incredulously. "Why? Because you can't spend the rest of your life in bed." She sat next to him, softly scratching his back. "Come walk with me. I miss you."

He shrugged her fingers off.

She took a deep breath, trying not to lose her temper. "Fine. Then get up and find a new job. You obviously need something to do. And we obviously need the money."

He rolled over suddenly and glared at her. She had never seen his eyes so hard or dark before. "What's the point?" he practically spat at her. Involuntarily, she moved away from his anger. He sat up, bouncing the mattress violently. "What's the point, Hanna? Find a job so I can just lose it again? And that's being optimistic. You know the Nazis won't let me work anywhere, unless it's picking up the trash and shit from the streets."

Hanna took a deep breath. She fought down her temper and tried to conjure up her compassion. "I know how you love your job," she said with much effort. "But I, too, lost my job. Both of my jobs, in fact," she reminded him. "I haven't been able to work as an art tutor since Heydrich entered the city." Samual did not seem to hear her.

"But," she continued with slightly gritted teeth, "I considered every lesson I was able to teach a small miracle. I'm happy that it lasted as long as it did."

Samual threw himself back down on the bed. "I never thought I would lose my job," he said. The anger and the color in his cheeks both drained out of him. "I just . . . I didn't see it coming."

"Because you aren't a Jew?" Hanna snapped. She took another deep breath and calmed herself. Samual rolled over so his back was to her. "We Jews"—she gently rubbed his back again—"we are all suffering in this way. But *we* can persevere."

Samual said nothing.

As a final plea, Hanna said, "If you won't get out of bed for yourself or for me, do it for David."

Samual hung his head, and Hanna felt guilty for needling him in such a tender spot. "What's the point of that either, Hanna?" This time, his words rang of despair and hopelessness. She preferred the venomous tone he had when talking about the Nazis. "We can't help him. We were never able to help him. But foolish as I was, I thought I could."

"We did everything we could for him," she said gently. "And now, it's time to do whatever we can again. Maybe the Jewish Council has more news about him."

She was able to entice Samual out of bed and into the same brown suit he wore on his last day of work. Though it felt automatic and insincere, he offered her his arm as they walked out of his apartment building, toward the center of the Jewish Quarter.

Hanna had hoped that the streets of Samual's beloved city would restore his spirit. Walking through Prague used to be like a seduction—its beauty and colors and life bringing her in closer and closer until she felt like she could not live without it. Now it was a disappointment—like a lover seeing his long-lost lady after years and hardships had chipped away her beauty.

Her hopes of breaking Samual out of his sadness diminished as they made their way further into the Jewish Quarter. Hanna was sure this area had not undergone such a drastic transformation in the few days since she last walked this path—surely, she was just being hyper-aware of her surroundings as she held on to Samual's arm. She was noticing different things today, like the trash that had blown into the doorway of the used bookstore on Siroka Street. There was no longer a proud shopkeeper to clean out the debris and tend to his storefront.

As they neared the Jewish Council, a small white terrier staggered up to them. Hanna could not be sure, but she thought she recognized the dog as the beloved pet of a couple down the street—a banker and his sweet wife. This dog, though, by the look of its coat, had not been loved by a family in some time. It was not unusual these days to see once-doted-upon pets roaming the streets of Prague, turned out when their families were forced to move or flee or beg for their lives. Hanna had seen former housecats scratch at a child to steal a few crumbs. Dogs who used to trot alongside their owners, heads held high, now formed feral packs, claiming communities as their own.

This dog, once called *Snehova Koule*, however, had not gone the way of the wild ones. Instead, it continued to rely on the kindness and generosity of Prague citizens. By the looks of it, though, that kindness and generosity did not amount to much. The dog, once a glowing white specimen well deserving of its name, Snowball, now wore a shaggy coat caked with hardened mud. The fur around its neck was matted around the collar, yet a small identification tag still dangled out of the mass of muddied fur. The tag was cut in the shape of a diamond and caught prisms of the sun as the dog moved its head from side to side, whimpering for assistance. It reminded Hanna of her engagement ring. She thought distantly of the picture she meant to paint, showing the iridescent rainbows created by the ring's cut.

Samual barely noted the dog as it followed behind them, whimpering and, once, nudging the back of Hanna's legs. She tried to reach down to pet it, but Samual stopped her hand.

"You can't help it," he said. His voice was flat, lacking sympathy or anger.

"It probably doesn't have a home anymore," she said. "It has no one."

"We can barely feed ourselves. We can't feed a dog, too." Hanna knew Samual spoke reason, but this dog was just one more wrong in the world that no one was trying to set right. She remained unconvinced and attempted to pat the top of the dog's head. Once again, Samual stopped her hand from reaching the white fur. "My apartment does not allow dogs, either. Where would you keep it? Better to leave it here. Maybe someone else will help." He pulled her away from the dog.

The white terrier knew when to give up. As they approached the corner, Hanna turned to look back once more. The ghost-animal stood cocking its head and watching them, its eyes almost completely hidden under untidy hair.

She wanted to make one more effort to convince Samual, but the dog began crossing the quiet street, already looking to another potentially sympathetic human.

She stopped walking when she saw whom the dog was approaching—a pair of soldiers looking, in her opinion, particularly ruthless. They were lounging against the boarded-up windows of a grocery store. One was smoking a cigarette while the other lazily surveyed the street. Both looked at ease around the destruction of a shop Hanna once knew so well. Both looked bored. In Hanna's experience, bored Nazis spelled trouble.

The little white dog trotted up to the soldiers, seeming to perk up with the prospect of new people. It sat down in front of the soldier with the cigarette and gave a small yelp for attention. The soldier took a long drag on his cigarette before looking down to the white terrier. The dog cocked its head to the side. The soldier mimicked it by also tilting his head, as he blew out smoke. The two looked at each other. The dog broke the spell by giving that same little yelp again. The soldier brought back his foot slowly, then released it like a spring. The sharp toe of his boot swung into the dog's belly, connecting right in the middle. The force of the kick lifted the dog off all four of its legs and it landed flat on his stomach with its legs splayed out.

Just as quick as the kick came, all was still again. Hanna and Samual were both watching from across the street. The soldier with the cigarette continued to lean against the grocery store, his foot resting against the shop wall. His shoulders seemed to shake, but Hanna could not hear his laughter from where she stood.

The dog didn't make a sound, besides a surprised, involuntary yelp when the kick connected. It got up and sidestepped away from the smoking soldier. It looked around the street, mostly empty, then walked gingerly up to the second soldier.

This one had been watching the whole time; his face was impassive when the dog begged and when the soldier kicked it. He watched the dog approach. As the soldier did not make any sudden moves or any harsh sounds, the dog seemed to think this person would help. The dog walked closer and closer to the soldier's legs, until it gently nudged the shin with the top of its scruffy, muddy head. The soldier still did not respond. The dog took this for encouragement and rubbed against the soldier's boot, begging for some form of affection.

This time the terrier was completely silent when the kick came. Again, the blow lifted the dog off its feet, but when it landed on the ground with a thud that Hanna could hear from across the street, it didn't get up. When it tried to lift its head, she started to go to its defense, but Samual's firm grip on her arm stopped her.

"No," he whispered. "We can't do anything."

"That seems to be the motto of everyone around us," she said angrily, but let him pull her away from the scene.

She stumbled after Samual, her eyes filling with tears, as she thought about the dog as she had last seen it—lovingly groomed, prancing around the street with its owners, trying to investigate the delicious smells emulating from the baker's shop. She didn't even realize where they were walking until they reached the Jewish Council. In front of the building, Samual held her tightly until she emptied her eyes of all the tears—not just the ones for the white terrier but for herself, Samual, and all the people who were suffering the same fate as Snehova Koule. When she stopped, she looked into Samual's eyes and nodded. They did not need words to understand one another. He kissed her softly on her forehead and grasped her hand as they walked up the steps.

They stopped again, mid-step. On the door of the Jewish Council was a large poster with a list of names. Hanna saw only the white paper—a blank canvas—at first. And then two words stood out. David's name.

It was the list of prisoners recently executed under Herr Heydrich's orders.

Chapter 19

RACHAEL

It was as if she had been living in a dense morning fog and the bright sun had finally burned it off. She knew what she had to do, and nothing—not the Nazi guards or the fear of torture or even death—could stop her. They mattered not in her new clarity.

Rachael never had much in her life. Her family was respectable but never wealthy. Her life with Alexey had been the same; though they had few luxuries, there was always enough food to fill their bellies and clothes to keep them warm. Before the war, she had never done without. Life in Prague under the Nazi occupation was hard. She wore shoes with holes that let the cold and wet from the pavement seep into her socks. She was unable to put green vegetables and sweet fruits on the table to feed her growing children. The family huddled in one room around the corner heater on the most frigid of winter nights to save on the cost of heating the separate bedrooms. Life in Terezin was even worse. She and Catarina experienced true hunger, cold, and poverty.

Now, though, she had nothing. In the ghetto, she and Catarina had two small suitcases holding some clothes, a blanket each, and some small mementos of a happier life—nothing valuable, as that was taken from her when she entered the ghetto. She often wondered how the previous owner of the diamond ring ever held on to such a treasure, entering the death camp with it still in her possession. That woman, whoever she was, possessed more courage and cunning than she herself did. Until she pocketed the ring, the only possessions Rachael had to call her own in this place were the coarse dress on her body and the wooden clogs that plagued her feet.

Standing in the middle of the plunder of *kanada* though, she felt a hot rage in the depths of her stomach. It was obscene that the Nazis had so much—had stolen so much—when she had nothing. Compared to the little she had, the injustice of this opulence, the unfairness, the plain cruelty of it made her legs and hands tingle with anger. That fury, along with the absolute terror of losing yet another child, losing Chaya, gave Rachael the courage she needed to smuggle food—or something that could be bartered for food in the barracks—every day. The thought of Chaya's possible death, by starvation especially, made this small act of defiance easy. She had followed the rules, obeyed those around her, and now had nothing to show for it except three dead children and a dead husband.

She no longer sorted through the stolen goods with sweaty palms and nervous glances over her shoulder. She was shocked at how easy it was. Unlike the first day when she stole the bit of dried meat and cheese, she did not waste time, or risk getting caught, by carefully weighing every option. She had more than enough choices in front of her on a daily basis—when you had nothing, anything at all was a treasure. So, she would bide her time—carefully sorting and piling the stolen goods until the guard watching her would turn to joke with another Nazi or yell and beat a fellow prisoner or close her eyes for an afternoon nap. Without breaking stride, she would slip the first few items within reach into her pocket, joining the ring as they gently bumped against her body with her movements. She did not worry whether it was edible or not. Even the most disgusting bits of food—stale, moldy bread that had been carried in a stranger's sweaty palms or crushed in a dirty pocket—seemed like a feast in her and Chaya's starved eyes. When Rachael palmed anything other than food, she had no trouble turning it into something to further their survival for at least another day. Bits of thread, scraps of fabric, pencil ends, things Rachael considered garbage in a past life could be used to make Chaya's life better. Usually, she traded the items for an extra ladle during the evening meal—and she insisted the spoonful come from the bottom of the pot, where the true substance lay.

Every evening, she walked past guard after guard without having to calm her heartbeat or force slow, even breaths, despite the half-eaten chocolate bar or crusts of bread or small sewing kit or, once, soft but dirty children's slippers that Rachael knew would warm Chaya's feet and make the adult clogs fit a little more comfortably. She had to wonder if the guards were not as terrifying as she had previously thought or if she was just truly that much braver. Perhaps they were getting lazy, but she was never questioned, searched for contraband, or even given a second glance. But still, walking from *kanada* back to the barracks was a test of nerves. The secret of bravery was complete disregard for the consequences. She knew the punishments for stealing; they were plenty and varied and always unreasonably cruel.

Along with feeding the small girl's stomach, Rachael fed the child's mind and spirit as best she could every night as they lay together on the hard bunk. She told Chaya stories, all the happy-ending fairy tales she could remember, silly remembrances of her children before the war, and, sometimes, even make-believe tales of what they would do when they were finally free from this prison. Mainly, though, she tried to teach the girl something, anything. She was shocked at Chaya's complete lack of learning. From the bits and pieces Rachael gleaned from Chaya's history, she knew the girl had very little memory of her parents. "They love me," she had said, "and will come find me one day." She spoke of them always in present tense, though when pushed for details, she could not even remember the color of her mother's hair or the games she played with her father.

"When we leave here," she told Rachael one night, "you, me, Mama, and Papa will find a pretty house by the sea." The sea was something Rachael had told her about a few nights prior. Chaya was fascinated with the idea of water all around, enough for swimming and fishing and boating. Rachael had explained to her that the sea was as large as the night sky that Chaya knew with great familiarity, and that the stars were like the waves in the water—uncountable, dazzling, and constantly in motion.

"When we leave here, we will all be able to play outside in the sun every day," Chaya dreamed. "At night, we will all snuggle into a bed like this. But maybe with blankets?"

When Chaya spoke like this, Rachael thought she could not love this abandoned child any more if she had birthed her from her own body—her spirit and resilience, how her dreams consisted of nothing more than the chance to be out during the sunlight hours and to have a warm blanket for the cold nights. That this should be a small child's only hope in the world filled Rachael with sadness. It was like a pail full of water, with the edges overflowing every time the child spoke. Rachael understood small dreams though. She dreamed of feeding Chaya enough food that the beautiful diamond ring they both admired so much would fit on one of the child's fingers. Rachael's own finger had long ago become too thin for her to wear the ring without terror of it slipping off and being lost forever. She would, she determined, fatten this girl up like a little sausage so she could wear the ring one day in freedom.

"Do you think Mama and Papa will be at the house when we get there?" Chaya continued. "Maybe they are there right now, waiting for us?"

"I'm sure you're right," Rachael agreed, stroking the girl's hair. She did not dare tell Chaya the practical truth that her missing parents were likely dead or had abandoned their child at the first sign of danger.

She felt her own failures as a mother all the more, especially to her sweet baby boy, every day. She was unable to save her children from the terrors of this war. Yet, Catarina and the baby had looked at her with nothing but trust and love, even up to their last moments together. Chaya was the same. She had clearly been left to strangers years ago—maybe for her protection, maybe not—but the child had nothing but overwhelming love in her heart for her parents, and for Rachael, too. Feeling the love of this child was both a burden that wore her down and a lift that brought her up.

She had learned such hard lessons about the futility of hope but did not want Chaya to think in such a cynical way. So Rachael encouraged the girl's dreams, while trying to suppress her own rising wishes to see life after Auschwitz and after the war.

It was as if the sky itself knew that good fortune was on its way—the weather warmed up, distant greens beyond the prison fence were peeking through. Everything urged Rachael to keep living and keep hoping. Rumors were starting to fly through the camp with buoyant wings.

"I heard the United States has joined the fight against the Nazis," Irene whispered to Rachael one night. Chaya had fallen asleep in Rachael's arms, and the bunkmates were talking quietly before sleep overtook them as well. "I heard others talking today. The Americans have invaded Europe and are fighting their way across the continent."

Rachael shrugged. "It's a nice thought, but I don't put much faith in these rumors. It's dangerous to live like we may actually escape this place."

"It's dangerous to live like we won't," Irene replied.

Rachael wanted to continue her role as a cynic, but she started to listen to these whispered hopes. She started to believe in them.

"I see evidence that the war is nearing an end every day," Irene said. "The guards are more lenient, maybe even kinder."

"If by kinder you mean they only shoot a man in the head rather than beat him until he begs for death, then yes," Rachael said. Irene clucked her tongue, probably in frustration at Rachael's perpetual pessimism. They both knew it was more for show than genuine these days. "I'll admit, they seem nervous." In the dim barrack light, Irene smiled a little. "And there's definitely more movement in the sky." Rachael was warming up to the signs of a ceasefire. "I've seen airplanes much more."

"Yes," Irene agreed. "All heading west."

Rachael left it unsaid, but just as the guards seemed to be acting better, the ruthless machine that was the crematorium ran even more frequently. "What happens if the Americans and the rest of the Allies do come? You think the Germans will just lay down their guns and flee for their lives?"

"Maybe," Irene said. "Maybe we will finally be released and be able to go home."

Rachael nibbled on this hope, hesitantly, as one would take small bites of an unknown food. She wanted it to sustain her, but the practical part of her mind, the part that had been living in Auschwitz for two years, expected it to turn bitter and poisonous in her mouth. She could not stop herself from saying, "Or the Nazis make sure Auschwitz and its uncountable prisoners are never found. They could run the gas chambers and those furnaces of hell until there's no one left to stoke the flames."

Both of them were silent for a moment. Rachael didn't know what to believe. She just knew if anyone was going to be free of this place, it would be Chaya—the girl whose name meant life itself.

For the first time since arriving in Auschwitz, maybe even since arriving in Terezin, Rachael found she was doing more than going through the motions. She smuggled food out of *kanada* every day and had a quiet picnic with Chaya on their shared bunk in the setting sunlight. As they nibbled on small bits of sausage or dry cheese, Rachael would tell Chaya recipes that she used to make for her family, walking her through each step, having the child close her eyes and imagine the movements in the warm, bread-scented kitchen.

Rachael took pride in her efforts—both to shower the girl with love and to fill her stomach. With every bit of stolen food, Rachael tried to keep the parasite called starvation at bay. Chaya was still not as filled out as a young girl should be, but Rachael thought, maybe only wistfully, that the girl's wasting away had stopped. Rachael, on the other hand, felt an eternal weakness from the moment she opened her eyes to the moment she closed them in a restless sleep.

At first, she had tried to give all the stolen food to Chaya alone. But the child, partly because of her love for her surrogate mother and partly from natural generosity, refused to eat the treasures by herself. So Rachael took a few tiny bites every night, thinking that the extra food should give her enough strength to last one more day. She was resolved to not make the same mistakes as she did in Terezin, especially now, when there was so much less to share.

When she thought of the food she ate while in Terezin, it seemed gluttonous now, compared to the meager bits she and Chaya received from the kitchen queue in Auschwitz. What was worse was she ate it all. Rachael and Catarina each received their own shares from the handouts. Both ate their meals eagerly, no longer caring for taste, only trying to find enough to stop the constant ache in their stomachs. Rachael could argue with herself that she was growing a child inside of her and, later, feeding that child from her own breast. But did it really excuse her? The food she ate could have gone to Catarina's plate. Knowing how life ended for her nameless baby, should she have just starved him and herself in the ghetto? Now she knew on just how little she could survive.

As the weather turned warmer though, Rachael found that sharing her food with Chaya was not such a sacrifice. She had no desire to eat, not even the treasured morsels she brought home every night. For the first week with no appetite, she worried that she was in the last stages of starvation, the point of no return where food, no matter how enticing, could not bring her back from the brink of death. She was exhausted all the time, though she knew working fourteen hours a day and subsisting on a few bites of stale bread and a bowl of watery soup was sure to drain all of her energy. She felt, though, deep down, it was more than that.

She lay in bed worrying and trembling. At first, she thought the shaking was from her concern over finally dying, but as the air blowing through the glassless windows and chinks in the wooden boards grew warmer, she feared it was one of the silent killers that claimed many of the women around her. The irony was not lost on her, of course. She had wanted nothing more than the sweet release from this life since she entered Auschwitz. Her only hope had been for it to be as painless as possible at the hands of the Germans. Since she met Chaya, though, she found a renewed vigor, a will to live. Yet it seemed her body was finally giving in to her original wish.

Her fears were confirmed in the heat of the summer when her chest started to ache and coughs started to wrack her body. She spent large parts of her time with Chaya simply trying to hold back the coughs, partly because she was sure they would scare the child and partly because it was so painful. Her chest muscles ached with the strain of the cough; her throat was dry and raw from the action; and more and more frequently, she was forced to spit blood onto the dirt floor.

She had seen this killer. She was just as, if not more, familiar with it than she was the Nazi guns and clubs and gas chambers. She had seen women work through the same cough. She had heard them shaking from chills in their bunks even when the nights were sweltering hot. She had seen their hands dark with dried blood that was forced up with every cough. She had seen them move stiffly, hunched over from the pain the disease caused in their back and hips and knees. She watched many of them get weaker and weaker until bunkmates had to carry them to roll call. Some were fooled into thinking there was a better place in the medical barracks and were never seen again. No one ever mistook their disappearance for a cure or a better life. Those women just died quicker, either from a shot to the head in a hospital back room with a drain in the floor or rounded up during a selection and sent to the gas chamber.

Rachael knew what to expect; she just did not know how much more time she had. Even in the best of times, before the war, consumption killed people—people who were afforded real medical care, people with healthy diets and warm beds at night. Sometimes they lived for years longer, sometimes not. These were certainly not the best of times. Could she survive until liberation came or the Germans conducted a mass murder of all remaining in the camp? Could she fight long enough to make sure Chaya walked out of this camp free and alive?

Chapter 20

HANNA

They probably would have stood staring at David's name on the list of condemned, and now dead, prisoners for hours, maybe even days. It felt like time stood still as she held Samual's hand, looking at the white paper hanging on the Jewish Council door, hanging everywhere around Prague. Minutes turned to hours and the color of everything around her slowly drained out, like the paint on a brush as she ran it under a steady stream of water.

It was not days that they stood there, looking at David's name, but only a few minutes. The door opened on them. The shellshocked survivors that Hanna once knew as herself and Samual were tenderly ushered inside. She remembered hushed condolences, a glass of water placed into her hands, and loving pats on the back. Finally, as the sun began to set in the west windows, Hanna came back to herself. She felt the hard wooden seat beneath her and noticed the colors in the small room. She felt the steady breathing of Samual next to her. It was too steady. She watched him methodically take a deep breath in, hold it, and then exhale, all in perfect rhythm—inhale, one; hold, two, three, four; exhale, five. Again and again.

When the two of them were led into an office, Hanna kept the breathing pattern going. Samual was distracted by the man behind the desk—a short man with wire glasses. Hanna continued the five-count breath while Samual spoke back and forth with the man, stood up, and shook his hand. Then he placed his hand gently on her back and moved her out of the room, down the hallway, and out onto the darkening street.

It was in the setting glow of the sun that Hanna was fully herself again, and only when she looked up into Samual's face and saw that he was smiling. True, it was a smile tinged with sadness and worry, but seeping in around the edges was something else, something Hanna had not seen on Samual's face in days: hope.

"The Jewish Council asked me to go to Terezin, to help design a town for just Jews," he told her when they arrived back to his apartment.

"The Germans want to design a town just for the Jews?" she asked, skepticism dripping from her voice. She knew very little about Terezin, just that it was a small fort town outside of Prague. She had never been, never had a reason to visit.

"Complete with schools, homes, parks, everything," Samual said. Hanna smiled at the eagerness in his face. "They called it 'the Fuhrer's Gift to the Jews.' They need engineers and architects to work as the building commando. They want Jewish ones specifically."

"They want Jewish architects and engineers?"

"I know it sounds crazy," Samual admitted, "but with the responsibility would come future rewards—positions of power within the new city. Extra privileges. Safety."

While Hanna sat in a stupor, unable to process her surroundings or what had just happened to David, Samual was working to build their future back up. She did not trust any promises made by the Nazis, especially the Fuhrer.

"I agree," he said. "We can't trust the Nazis. But the city will be run by Jews, a new administration called Judenrat. We can trust our own people."

When Hanna sat silently, chewing on his words, he continued.

"They realized they cannot continue to torment us and torture us." Samual was already packing a small bag of belongings as he worked to convince her. "I said it when they first came. They want to show us who is in charge, but now they are letting off the pressure. They will send us to Terezin, where we can live in peace by ourselves."

"How can you leave Prague, though?" she asked him. "You love it here. I often think you love Prague more than you love me," she teased.

He laughed and kissed her on the forehead. "True," he said with a smile. "But we are not welcome in Prague right now. I'll send for you when I'm settled in. We'll wait out the war safely in Terezin and, when it's over . . ."

"Exactly," she said. "When it's over? Then what? You think all the people who have stood by and let these terrible things happen will welcome us back with open arms and smiles?"

Samual gave her a dismissive wave of the hand. "What else can they do, love?"

♦

A few days later, he left for Terezin, with a small bag carrying two changes of clothes, his drafting supplies, and a picture of Hanna. He left her with the apartment, a kiss, and a promise to send for her as soon as possible.

Life was not easy without him. Hanna busied herself by collecting her food rations every day. Besides that short walk through the Jewish Quarter though, she no longer felt safe traveling throughout the city. She had no money for paper or paints and no friends to chat with through the night while they sipped on glasses of wine and smoked low-quality cigarettes. The days moved ploddingly, like a record player that slowed down the melody of a song—with a sense of her normal life but made almost unrecognizable at this laggardly pace.

With nothing else to do, she worried. She worried that Samual had been tricked—there was no Terezin, no building project. Perhaps he had been sent east—that terrifying but unspecific fate. Or they had just lined him up and shot him outside of the city. Or maybe, he went to Terezin but would be unable to send for her. She would be sent east, never to reunite with him again and never able to say goodbye.

But finally, she received notice at the apartment. She was to pack one bag of possessions, turn in her identification papers and rations cards, and report to the train station on a Tuesday morning. She was going to be part of the first residents of the new Jewish city, once known as Terezin, but renamed by the Germans, Theresienstadt.

It was hard to keep down her feelings of worry as she packed up the few things she was allowed to bring. If this place was going to be so wonderful, why did she have to give up her identification papers? She felt like she was losing her freedom by handing them over to the Nazis. Without identification, she could never leave Terezin. She could not walk around Prague, take a train to visit her family, or leave the country. Was this a new city or a prison? But she trusted Samual, and he had written to her trying to calm her nerves. He was working with the others in the building commando to make Terezin beautiful and welcoming for the Jews of Prague and all of Czechoslovakia.

The day before leaving Prague—maybe for good—came quickly. Hanna found herself hesitating in front of the pile of belongings that the Germans would take from the apartment she had shared with Samual. Those things were going to her people, she'd been told. The Germans were to pack up these small possessions and send them to Terezin to be shared among the community—the small oil lamp she used to see during blackouts, scattered art supplies, a few books, and the quilt they used to burrow under at night. It was not much, but no one seemed to have much these days.

She still had her ring—the ring Samual clumsily gave her in front of Old Town Hall. She smiled remembering how he had dropped it with nervous fingers. She still had that, and it still took her breath away.

She gave up her pastels and paintbrushes easily. They were nothing but remnants of a once-prized collection. She did not hesitate to give up her quilt either, though it had been a warm, safe haven for her and Samual on many cold nights.

Giving up her ring, though, that did not feel like a sacrifice for the greater good. Her community would never ask such a thing of her. If she handed over her engagement ring, it was not for her people, it was for the Germans. And that, she could not bring herself to do.

In just one more day, she would see Samual. A dark cloud seemed to lift when she thought of it. But even when she had him in her arms again, she still needed the ring. The ring was physical proof of his love for her. Yes, she knew Samual loved her. She could hear the love in his words. She felt it when she lay in his arms and when he nuzzled the soft skin below her ears. She saw his love when he looked at her with pride and, her favorite, bewilderment when she continued to surprise him.

But the ring was different. It was something she could see and hold and touch. Love was like the wind. She knew it was out there. She could feel it blow across her face as she walked the streets of Prague. She could smell it in the musty dirt scent when the wind blew down from the Ore Mountains. But it wasn't the same as seeing true proof of the wind with her eyes—the way it ripped through trees on a stormy night, tossing branches about. Samual's love, like the wind, was powerful, but she felt it most when looking at her ring.

The Nazis' instructions had been clear. All money and jewelry was to be handed over. In fact, it should have been handed over weeks ago as restrictions for Jews got tighter and tighter. But Hanna held on to the engagement ring. She had sold many things to help heat the small apartment and to sporadically treat herself to bread or a bit of meat. The ring, though, she had always safeguarded. In defiance, she continued to wear it, usually with the diamond turned toward her palm. The visible silver band was thin and not noticeable, she hoped.

She was not sure what the Nazis would do if they found her

ring—take it, obviously, but she wouldn't be surprised if there was some sort of punishment. Surely, Hanna's common sense told her, they couldn't arrest her for keeping her own engagement ring. But, in the last few months, she had seen enough of their senseless cruelty to know that might not be true. So she had to plot the best way to hide the diamond.

With little room in her small suitcase, she had to be strategic about what clothes she wore on her trip into Terezin. She chose her sturdiest remaining dress—a thick brown one with no style but strong fabric and short sleeves. She had a black sweater with frays at the wrist, which she did not possess the mending skills to fix, but it was her nicest and warmest sweater left. She put it on top of her dress. She considered herself lucky to still have a wool winter coat when she knew many people were walking in the cold without. Hers was in good condition, with a tall neck to shield her against the sharp wind and a long matching belt, so she could tie it tight against her shrinking frame. She had no stockings left and only one pair of wearable shoes—black Oxfords with a short, thick heel.

Her wool coat had big pockets in the front, but she did not trust putting the ring into them. It could easily fall out. She thought about sewing it into the pocket or lining, as she heard many people were doing with their treasured jewelry, but she reasoned that if even one woman was found smuggling jewels in that way, they would all be thoroughly searched. She feared hiding the ring in her suitcase. She may be separated from the bag, the Nazis were sure to open it and rummage through everything, or she could mistake it for someone else's luggage.

She decided the best place was in her mouth. The soldiers had no reason to make her open her mouth for inspection upon entering Terezin. She could easily hide it under her tongue if they did. While packing that night, she practiced keeping the ring in her mouth but discovered it was not an easy task. She found she could not speak clearly, and she would never be able to chew or swallow without choking on the diamond. She had no idea how long she would have to sit at the train station. Since she was allowed to bring a small amount of food in her suitcase, she had to assume she would be traveling at least long enough to eat a meal. But she wouldn't be able to eat without bringing notice to her hidden treasure.

She paced around the apartment that she was being forced to leave, walking the same path that she had watched Samual and David use in many nights of frustration. She touched the walls of the small kitchen, the bedroom, and sitting room—remembering the cozy nights with Samual, where they would whisper in the dark of curfew and blackout. There was no longer any coal for the stove, but in her dress, sweater, coat, and socks, she still felt warm. She relished the feeling, hoping that there would be many warm nights with a fire and the comfort of Samual's arms when she arrived in Terezin. She regretted again her lack of stockings. She did not look forward to standing on the chilly train station platform with her legs bared and her feet only covered by the thin leather of her Oxfords. With that thought, she finalized a plan for her ring.

♦

The walk from the small apartment to the train station was not an easy one. She pulled the door to the apartment shut tightly behind her but did not bother locking it, nor taking the keys. She had no hope that anything inside, nor the place itself, would be waiting for her and Samual if this war ever ended. She held her head up high as she took one last look at the home they had shared.

She walked the streets of Prague slowly, taking in every sight. Despite the city's beauty, it no longer held much for her.

She carried the burden of her suitcase through the streets, walking carefully. She had placed the diamond engagement ring around her second toe, deliberately positioning the diamond so it would not cut into her skin. But as she struggled the many blocks from the apartment to Prague's main station, the ring turned and started to rub its sharp edge against her third toe. As she walked through the slush and snow in her black leather shoes, the nuisance of the ring turned into a blister and then a sharp pain. Her mind was forced away from the pastels of the city, which were looking dirty with disrepair and winter weather, toward keeping her face straight and her walk steady despite the pain in her foot.

She was relieved to finally make it to the station. Her thoughts had been so full of the tasks leading up to her getting there that she did not think about what it would mean to be back at the place of David's arrest. Her steps and her breath stuttered when she walked onto the platform. She stood where she had held Samual's hand and watched David disappear from their view, into the mass of people around him. Today, the station was eerily empty of happy travelers and eager families waiting to reunite with loved ones. Today, it was only fellow Jews boarding the train to Terezin and the Nazis tasked with keeping the refugees in line.

She found a place on a bench, rested her suitcase in front of her, and prepared to wait patiently for her turn for inspection by the soldiers. She could not stop her eyes from traveling to the spot where she had seen Greta nervously fiddling with her gloves, where she had beckoned David toward her and the waiting soldiers. She resolved not to look at that darkened corner, not to remember the sight of the soldiers emerging from around Greta, ready to grab David out of the crowd. Hanna pressed her foot down, pressing the ring deeper into her flesh, letting the pain wipe that memory from her mind. She focused her thoughts on Samual.

When he had left for Terezin, she had let him talk her into saying goodbye at the apartment. It had been an early, gray morning when he left for the last time. "Please stay in bed," he had told her, though she followed him around the apartment in her nightdress, wrapped in their quilt. At the door, he kissed her and said, "I promise we'll see each other soon."

Sitting at the train station, looking anywhere but that dark corner, Hanna imagined Samual's last minutes in Prague, sitting on this same bench. She honed her mind in on the thoughts he must have held, the torture of being in the same place where they'd said goodbye to David before the arrest. Focusing on her guilt for letting Samual endure those tragic thoughts was preferable to looking behind her to that spot where Greta had stood frozen as David was captured.

The gruff bark of a soldier brought Hanna back to the present day. There were Nazis flooding the station from all entrances, yelling and herding the people into a line—first to be inspected and then to be loaded into a waiting train car. Hanna picked up her suitcase and walked gingerly to her place in line, trying to inconspicuously place pressure only on the heel of her throbbing foot.

She stood behind a woman holding the hand of a small girl. Since Hanna had not seen her nieces and nephews in many years, she had trouble placing the girl's age. She guessed about five or six years old. Her dark brown eyes were open wide, taking in all that was going on around her. The mother was also difficult to age. Based on the streaks of silver showing through her dark hair and the dark circles under her eyes, Hanna estimated she was around forty. But the woman's large pregnant belly suggested she was younger. The woman kept one hand tightly holding the girl and the other on her belly, as if to reassure the unborn baby inside of her that all would be well.

Hanna had her own doubts as to whether things were really going to be well in Terezin. A city all for the Jews seemed too good to be true, and in Hanna's small dealings with the Nazis, she knew them to be too vicious to be trusted. As she watched the line of people in front of her walk up, one by one, to the Nazi inspection, the feeling of worry that had settled in her stomach only grew stronger.

The soldiers had done this before. Every action was methodical, rehearsed, done as though it was second nature. First, the suitcase was taken and searched recklessly. Women's undergarments, cherished photographs, anything of value was tossed onto the ground, inspected, and possibly returned to the suitcase. Jewels and money were pocketed by the soldiers. Hanna watched three suitcases searched this way before a soldier came upon a food item tucked into the corner of a fourth suitcase, wrapped up in a clean white handkerchief. Hanna could see the *trdelnik* roll out of the handkerchief from her place a dozen people away.

Her mouth watered at the sight of the round pastry. She hadn't seen one since Prague Kofe was destroyed. It had been even longer since she enjoyed the cinnamon sugar cake herself. She could only imagine the price paid for this treat. The soldier laughed when he discovered this treasure. Before a word of protest could be made, he took a huge bite, chewing with his mouth open, laughing and making exaggerated sounds of enjoyment. The small woman who owned the suitcase said nothing, just stooped down slowly to gather up the rest of her belongings.

The soldiers turned their attention to the next in line—a family with two teenage daughters. Both of the girls clutched an arm of their mother and were staring, wide-eyed, as the soldiers searched through their belongings. The father had positioned himself in front of his family, forcing the Nazis to speak with him only. They found nothing of interest in the four suitcases, but one of the girls caught a soldier's eye. He beckoned her forward with a wave of his hand. She clutched her mother's arm even tighter. Hanna could not hear the words, but the girl's pleas were plain enough. The soldier grabbed her arm and pulled her to him. Hanna watched him ask the girl questions over and over as she frantically shook her head no. She realized he was asking if the girl was hiding anything. The malicious grin on his face told Hanna he had no intention of finding anything, but that did not stop him from putting his hands all over the girl, searching anyways.

When he reached the teenage girl's small breasts, he waggled his eyebrows at the father before groping her. He did not get far before the father shouted and tried to lunge at the soldier. The surrounding Nazis quickly pushed him back, then methodically took turns punching him until he crumpled to the ground. All the while, the soldier continued to molest the girl, the mother wailed, and Hanna had to force her small breakfast to stay in her stomach. No one else in the crowd made a move to help either the daughter or father.

Finally, the soldiers let the family go. It took all three of the women to help their patriarch to his feet and into the train. After that, several more attractive girls in line were searched for hidden items on their person, sometimes over the surface of their dresses, but sometimes not. No one again attempted to interfere.

Hanna slowly moved forward in line, waiting silently as the Nazis inspected the people in front of her. As she neared her turn, she became more and more nauseous, thinking of those beasts placing their hands on her, going through the meager possessions that she deemed worth keeping. Her breath quickened every time she felt the diamond cut into her foot. Thus far, the soldiers had not found anything of real value hidden on those they had searched. But Hanna knew she couldn't be the only person trying to smuggle a treasure into the promised land of Terezin.

As fear threatened to take over her body, she put her focus on the young girl in front of her. The child's mother kept pulling the girl to her, gently forcing the girl's head into her side, trying to shield her eyes from the horror of the soldiers, but the girl did not seem to want protection. She remained completely silent, but her eyes took in everything. She looked around, seeing the people in front of and behind her, all terrified. Many children older than this girl—and even adults—were shaking with fear or crying at the injustice of it all. But this little girl remained quiet and dry-eyed. Hanna was not sure if it was trauma or courage that gave this girl such solemn repose, but she decided to emulate it. If this child could be brave, so could she.

A woman with long, dark hair who stood directly in front of the pregnant mother and little girl took her turn with the Nazis. A subtle movement she made just moments earlier had caught Hanna's eye, and by the tug the little girl gave on her mother's hand, Hanna assumed the child had seen it too—the woman had brought a clenched fist to her face, as if scratching her nose or rubbing at her lips. At a glance, the action seemed natural, but as someone who had thought through this plan previously, Hanna saw it for what it was. She was almost certain the woman had slipped something into her mouth.

This woman reminded Hanna of her mother. They looked to be about the same age, and Hanna remembered her mother wearing the same style of dress—dropped waist, calf-length, probably at least a decade out of style. But this woman's dress was well made and well kept. She held her head high as she stepped up to the inspecting Nazis. One hand clutched her suitcase, gripping it so tightly that Hanna could see the knuckles were white. Her left hand resumed its position balled into a fist, but now clutching the fabric of the dress's skirt, probably to stop from shaking, Hanna guessed—her own hands trembled as she neared the front of the line.

The soldier did not grope the woman as he looked for hidden contraband—she not being of his taste, Hanna thought scornfully. Like with the others, though, the Nazis rummaged through the small suitcase, dropping unwanted items onto the dirty train platform and pocketing anything of worth for themselves. Going through the pockets of the woman's spare dress, a soldier found a small locket. He held it up and let the silver dance in the sunshine.

"No!" the woman said, on reflex more than anything else, Hanna assumed.

The soldier with the necklace cocked his head. "No?" he questioned. In watching him, Hanna did not think he spoke much Czech, but "no" was a word easily translated across borders. Hanna could only guess the number of times he had heard it from the people of Prague, and for what reasons.

The woman looked to her shoes, knowing she had made a terrible mistake.

The Nazi took one monstrous step and was standing in front of her. "No?" he questioned again. He lifted her chin with one black gloved finger. "No?" he said with more force.

The woman tried to remove her chin from his grasp, but that only caused him to grip it with his entire hand. The more she squirmed, the tighter he squeezed. From behind her, Hanna could not see the woman's face, but she watched the soldier. The Nazis behind him were barely paying the scene any attention, but rather seemed almost impatient to move on to the next person. But the soldier holding the woman's face was getting pleasure out of her terror. Hanna could tell. It was the same expression the soldiers had while kicking the white terrier. She wondered for a minute if it was the same man, but she realized the masks of cruelty blended one Nazi's face into another's.

Hanna watched the soldier as his face clenched in sync with his hand. The woman started to moan. And then the Nazi's eyes widened, first with surprise and then with triumph. He abruptly let go of the woman's jaw. She doubled over in sobs, but before she could fall to her knees, the soldier grabbed her by the hair and jerked her upright. She cried out. He laughed and said something to his neighboring soldier, beckoning him over with his free hand. Hanna could guess what made the soldier so happy—he'd discovered the woman's secret. His friend quickly pried the woman's mouth open, fishing for the jewel she had hidden in there earlier. With one soldier holding her head back by her hair and a second digging roughly inside her mouth, she had no chance to hide the evidence.

Within seconds, the second soldier had pulled a ring out from the side of the woman's cheek and was holding it up for all the soldiers around to see. Some of them cheered. The first soldier held open his free hand, gesturing for his prize. The soldier dropped it into his palm and gave him a hearty pat on the back. The Nazi never let go of the woman's hair. He yanked her toward him, shoved her face near his hand, showing off the ring, then whispered something into her ear.

The woman was sobbing and pleading, but without ever letting go, the soldier began to drag her out of the train station. Hanna took a step forward, and the quick movement made her own hidden contraband dig into her toes again. The pain brought her back to her present situation—she might be well on her way to the same fate this woman had just suffered.

The pregnant mother looked over her shoulder at Hanna and shook her head, just once. In that brief moment, their eyes connected—they were powerless to do anything. Their eyes could speak that for them. The little girl next to her had watched the entire exchange with silent composure.

By the time it was Hanna's turn to stand in front of the soldiers, her dress showed two blooming flowers of wrinkles from where her hands had gripped the fabric tightly. She felt sweat roll slowly down her back, but she forced her breathing to remain regular, knowing she had no hope of controlling her frantic heartbeat. The mother and her daughter had escaped without much harassment—Hanna assumed whatever beasts these men may be, perhaps they had no taste for such an obviously pregnant woman. She was sure she would have no such luck.

As she stepped in front of the soldier who had dug the ring out from the woman's mouth, Hanna focused on her breathing. The man leered at her with a carnivorous appetite. She knew he would not let her go through untouched. Her best hope was that they would not discover the precious ring that Samual had given her.

Samual. She focused her thoughts away from him as the soldier began looking through her suitcase, but by the way he hurriedly searched, she knew he was eager to do more. She would not think of Samual as this man felt her over. She knew if she allowed herself even a moment of comparison between how Samual's hands would caress her body, searching for the right places to touch her, and this man's attack, she may never be able to feel Samual's loving embrace in the same way again. The Nazis continued to take so much from her; she would never allow them to take Samual away.

The soldier ran his fingers through her hair, roughly pulling the pins out so he could feel the soft curls in his hands. She thought of her home, sitting with her parents and siblings at the large wooden table nestled snugly into the corner of the kitchen. During the holidays, there were usually many people visiting, between her brothers and sisters and neighbors stopping in. They would pull the table out of the corner so people could sit on all four sides. The soldier held her head between his hands, brushing his calloused thumbs against her lips. Her brothers would have to bring in chairs from all over the house—the desk chair from her mother's small office, the three wooden chairs from the front porch, the small stool from Hanna's vanity—so no one would have to stand. The soldier moved his hands down to her neck, for an instant gripping both hands around her throat and squeezing just tight enough that she knew that he held all the power. The table would be full of plates and cups and wine glasses and platters of food. The smell would permeate through the whole house, reaching up into the attic where the littlest ones would go to play among the old clothes and outdated hats. He ran his hands over her breasts, cupping them, trying to rouse her nipple from beneath the fabric of her dress and brassiere. While Hanna loved the warm smells and the full table, her favorite was seeing it empty, witnessing its scratches and dents and burns. The soldier moved down her sides, feeling hip bones jutting out from her frame, then cupping her buttocks in both hands, squeezing. One of the burns was the size of a dessert plate. Hanna's brother had once held the basket of rolls over a candle flame, distracted while telling a story about a classmate and an escaped goat. The soldier lingered on her thighs, moving his hands back and forth between her legs and her most sensitive parts, rubbing and moaning slightly in the back of his throat. Her brother did not notice when the towel keeping the rolls warm started smoking. Only when her father stood up violently did her brother drop the rolls and towel, now afire. The Nazi finally moved down her legs, rubbing each calf roughly as he looked up at her with a sadistic grin. The burning towel charred into the wooden surface while Hanna's siblings laughed and her mother shrieked about burning the kitchen down. Her brother never did finish his story about the goat.

It was the man's hands around her ankles that brought her back to her present-day horror. He was bent all the way down over her feet, obviously more focused on looking up her skirt than searching for hidden jewels. She stood frozen, staring at the top of the man's head. At some point in the day, he had discarded his uniform-issued hat. His hair was blond and greasy. Hanna stared at it with intensity, feeling that if she broke her gaze, she would break down completely. The Nazi looped his index finger into the top of her woolen sock, swiping around her ankle quickly and grinning up at her again. He moved his hands all the way up her leg again, under her skirt, before stepping away from her. She realized she had stopped breathing. She gasped. The soldier winked at her.

"Next!" he called. With one last lewd look, he added, "Unless you want more of that."

Hanna squared her shoulders, lifted her chin to look above the man into the cloudy sky of Prague, and walked on without a word.

Chapter 21

RACHAEL

Her eyes opened a few minutes before the guards started their cruel wake-up call. She valued these brief moments of peace. Chaya's head lay on Rachael's chest, the child's slow, heavy breath warming the skin over her heart. The summer warmth had come and gone quickly, and the weather was quickly deteriorating into yet another winter in Auschwitz. Even with Chaya's shared body heat and a relatively comfortable blanket recently stolen from *kanada*, Rachael still felt the night's cold settle into her toes and fingertips. Even during the day, the pale November sun didn't offer much more warmth than the moon.

Rachael lifted a hand to rub the sleep from her eyes. She tried to move slowly to not disturb Chaya, who would sleep even after the wake-up call if she were allowed. For a child with so much energy, she slept like the dead. Her vision cleared, Rachael saw her hand. The palm was covered in dark red dried blood. She quickly squeezed her fist shut, hoping to hide the telltale sign. Blood on her hands from the coughs that wracked her body in her sleep was like the black mark of death itself. She was a doomed woman. She felt it in her gut, her abdominal muscles sore from the strain of the cough. She felt it in her chest, which was burning from the inside. She felt it in her throat, so raw that it took an hour some mornings before she could speak intelligibly.

She kept her hand hidden from Chaya until she could get through the line to the half-frozen water bucket to wash. The confused look from Chaya and the looks of pity from her bunkmates told her that there was no hiding it. She must have blood on her face, giving away her secret. She washed the fatal mark away as best she could and swallowed a few gulps of watery coffee, though her stomach felt no need for anything anymore. Chaya continued to look at Rachael with worry but jabbered on about her wild dreams as though nothing was amiss. As always, Rachael was happy for the distraction.

She could tell it was going to be a long morning roll call. Her legs felt like they could not support her for more than a few minutes, so she knew, from her usual luck, that it meant she would be out there for at least an hour in the freezing cold. Plus, she could read the eyes of the guards like she used to read the morning newspaper with Alexey next to her sipping tea. This morning, they all carried the gleam of boredom and cruelty—one of the most dangerous and painful combinations in this place.

Chaya was a bundle of energy. Even at such early hours and in such cold, she bobbed slightly, rocking from her toes to her heels, as they stood in line surrounded by complete silence. Rachael kept her eyes forward, boring holes into the back of the woman's head directly in line ahead of her. But she was aware of her surroundings. She could feel the nervous energy vibrating off of Chaya. Rachael knew better than to try to calm the girl's fidgeting until it was absolutely necessary, so she used her peripheral vision to scan constantly for any guard walking nearby. If one came close enough to notice Chaya's movements, Rachael would gently touch Chaya's arm. It was enough to still the child until the guard passed on, still looking for an excuse to abuse one or more prisoners.

On this chilly morning, before the sun rose over the gray horizon, the guards paced the lines silently. They did not call out offenders for ridicule or beatings. They did not read through the list of numbers associated with the women before them. They did not even congregate at the front of the queue, smoking, joking, and trading camp gossip like normal women out for a morning stroll. Rachael was sure they were waiting for something. Everything inside Rachael hurt that morning—her legs, her arms, her abdomen, her chest, her head. She felt herself start to sway and widened her stance just a bit to help her balance. Chaya had made up a game of slight movements—forward and back on her toes and heels four times, a slight wiggle from side to side of her hips, a wiggle of the fingers on her left hand, a wiggle of the fingers on her right hand, a tiny shake of the head left and right, and a slow exhale of warm breath to make the air around her fog. Then the girl did it all over again. Over and over she made her small movements. Rachael counted them to keep herself standing upright. While the guards did not seem to be actively searching for a person to torment, they would never pass up the chance to beat a woman who collapsed during roll call.

Still trying to stare straight ahead, Rachael noticed a guard from one of the other camps approach two of the guards near the front of the women's queue. There was a short discussion. Then, whatever the guards had been waiting for seemed to have come to pass. They started moving quicker and with real purpose through the long lines of suffering, yet silent women.

The selection had already rounded up half a dozen women before Rachael realized what was happening. In this prison, Rachael knew it wasn't unusual to have a selection whenever the Nazis very well pleased, and roll call was no exception. The guard, though, pointing to women as she walked down a long row, seemed to have no discernable pattern to whom she sentenced to death. Rachael was used to seeing sick women, weak women, women who had finally lost their minds chosen for the gas chambers. They were of no use to the Third Reich any longer. Women who could stand for hours during roll call were mostly left alone, as long as they did not find themselves labeled as troublemakers.

That was why Rachael worried so endlessly about Chaya. She was a scrawny child who was good for nothing—in the Nazis' minds. Not only did she do nothing to serve the Fatherland, she took up space and air and food that could be used for another productive prisoner before she made her inevitable way to the gas chambers.

This selection, though, took no account for physical capabilities, it seemed. The guard in the front was not the only one pointing and condemning women. She saw guards all around the yard filling a quota that must have been run to them by the soldier who arrived last. Rachael found it hard to breathe as she watched women—some she recognized after many days of passing them in a queue or listening to them breathe softly in her barracks—hang their heads in silent despair as a soldier pointed to them, then to the end of the yard, where an uncovered truck bed waited to take them to the showers. One of the selected women trudged to *kanada* every day with Rachael. Another served the morning coffee and could easily be bribed for a second watery cupful if Rachael had anything sweet to offer in return. Another was a musician, a wonderful soprano, Rachael had heard. She would put on makeshift concerts for the commanders and their wives sometimes. She should have been sheltered from such a selection.

In just a few minutes, they had already filled a truck, by Rachael's estimations. And still the guards continued to walk through the lines and point. Rachael found that it was not only difficult for her to breathe, but her legs were shaking—noticeably shaking. Such a sign of weakness would get her sent to the gas chamber for sure. Chaya had noticed, too, what was happening around her. The girl's only tell of fear was her silence and lack of motion. She stood perfectly still, staring at the ground, not fidgeting. Rachael reached out her pinky finger to touch Chaya's arm ever so slightly, hoping it could express the encouragement that she was unable to voice.

She calculated that two trucks had been filled with soon-to-be-dead bodies when a guard finally started down her row. She reached out to graze Chaya's arm once more, not daring any further motion with the guard nearing them. At Rachael's loving graze, Chaya turned her head toward her. They both dared one look at each other. Chaya's eyes had the same look as when Rachael found her sobbing in their bunk the day they believed they had lost one another—utter fear and sadness. Knowing it was the most dishonest action of her entire life, she forced the corners of her mouth up in a small smile and gave the girl a nod. *All will be well,* she wanted to convey with those miniscule movements. *We will be all right; I will take care of you.* Whether Chaya could read those words in her half-hearted smile, Rachael would never know. The guard was now only a few people away from where they stood.

She knew it was over before the guard even reached her. She wanted to cry, to beg, to say she could not leave Chaya, but her mind was muddled. She couldn't breathe. The sadness kept her from thinking straight. The cough and blood in her lungs kept her from breathing. The edges of her vision became hazy, like trying to peer through the morning fog. She could not even register the guard's point of the finger in her direction.

But that was because it did not come. The Nazi slowly walked past her, looking her up and down, apparently finding more strength and life left in that body than she knew she had. Rachael felt her shoulders sag slightly in relief. Air came back to her sore lungs and her vision cleared. The fog lifted just long enough for her to see the guard point her long, plump finger at the child standing next to her.

She had no words. Or rather, she had too many words ricocheting around her brain. She could not pick a single one: *no, not her, take me, I love you, I'll protect you, I'll be with you, I'll make this right.* Her body was frozen for an instant, but her mind never stopped. Chaya, too, seemed as a statue. She had cocked her head, as a puppy does at a command it does not understand. Her brow furrowed. When she took a step to follow the guard to her much too early death, Rachael finally felt her limbs again.

She reached out and grabbed Chaya's arm, pulling her back in line. She only had an instant to convey everything she had planned to say to Chaya for the rest of their lives; she only had one touch—this grip on the girl's arm—to fill up her small heart with all the love the child would need to help her survive a hopefully long life alone and afraid. She wanted to tell the child that more than anything, she wished they had had more time together, that she would have surely died long ago and been nothing more than a cloud of smoke in the dark sky if it hadn't been for this girl, that this girl was everything that was right in the world—love and hope and sunshine and play and smiles—that she needed to stay who she was no matter what happened, or when it happened; she may only have a few more days of life, but Rachael would die over and over again to give her just a little more time, a little more chance for a real life; she wanted to tell Chaya how to survive, to hide and not trust anyone, to stay quiet and out of the way until the camp was liberated, to find a way out of this place to their home by the sea, to finally find her own family, to make her own family if she needed.

She wanted to give Chaya the ring, to tell her that as long as she held on to it, she would remember the beautiful life that was out there, and maybe she would also remember the surrogate mother she found in the death camp, and remember the stories Rachael told her—of real life and love and Rachael's family that had all been lost, because if someone remembered them, then they would live on. She—this small girl—carried them with her, and that was what saved Rachael. That was why she would gladly trade places with this child; that was why her last touch on the girl's arm was to pull her back in line while she herself advanced to walk behind the guard to the truck full of other condemned prisoners, to her death in the gas chambers.

But there was no time for any of those words.

The guard, who was already moving on with impatience, was expecting a prisoner to follow closely on her heels—silently and willingly—to that prisoner's own death. Rachael knew that, in the chaos of signing so many women's death warrants in such a short time, the guard only needed a number. In the second after pointing to Chaya, the Nazi had forgotten entirely about the small child she had just condemned. By moving quickly, Rachael took Chaya's place. In an instant, she had moved Chaya back to her rightful spot in the queue and took a step in front of the child, starting to follow the guard.

She pulled the ring from her pocket. No matter what might happen to either of them, Rachael would never let the Germans have the satisfaction of possessing this ring. It had been hers, and now it was Chaya's. She wanted to press the ring into the girl's hand—leaving an indentation for all time, the outline of the solid band and sparkling diamond pressed like a constellation on her skin to remind Chaya of how much she was loved. But Chaya was dazed by the sudden movements of being pointed toward death and then pulled back to life. As Rachael stepped past Chaya, she tried to pass her the ring, but Chaya did not open her hand to it, so it fell to the frozen earth at the girl's feet, bringing a little shine to the frozen mud.

Chaya's wide eyes met with Rachael's, then traveled to see the ring lying at her feet. Rachael took another step away from the girl. In her desperation to give Chaya all the hope she would need to survive, Rachael said what she hoped would convey all the words she had in her heart:

"I'll always be with you."

Chapter 22

HANNA

There were no Nazis in Terezin—at least not directly; no Nazis marching with terrifying clips down the streets; no Nazis to kick and beat and torture the defenseless and downtrodden. There were no black uniforms to blame for the misery and fear that permeated the ghetto, but the essence of the Germans was everywhere surrounding Hanna. It was in the forced German name of Theresienstadt. It was in the rules and hardships, the cramped conditions and meager food supply. The threat of the Nazis hung overhead like a gray cloud forewarning a downpour. Hanna begrudgingly gave the Nazis credit. Without even stepping foot inside the gates of Terezin, they still reigned supreme with fear and cruelty.

She had known the trick that was being played on the Jews from the very beginning. The treatment of her people at the train station forced her to acknowledge it. On the short train ride from Prague to Terezin, many people still believed the lies. Then the Germans gruffly ushered everyone off the train and forced them to carry their luggage almost two and a half kilometers. For Hanna, a young woman used to walking this distance on a daily basis, it was still a struggle. She fought with her luggage and had difficulty breathing as Nazi soldiers leered at her during the entire journey. She could only imagine how the elderly and the sick were managing. Only once did she see the pregnant mother with her wide-eyed daughter. The little girl was still silent but limping as her poorly fitting shoes slid on and off as she walked the far distance.

Hanna got her last sight of Nazis as she entered Terezin—just as the soldiers stole every last possession she and her people had. Without any lies or excuses, the Germans snatched her suitcase out of her hand and pulled on the collar of her coat until she freed her arms of the sleeves. She lost the bag that she had packed with so much care and purpose. She no longer had extra clothes, blankets, a jacket to bear the winter temperatures. But she still had her ring. Not without effort, she walked the two and a half kilometers with it slowly rotating around her toe, the diamond cutting into any area of skin it could reach. But the pain, instead of making her cry out, spurred her on. She would endure it if only to win this small victory over the Nazis.

She could not bring herself to regret coming to this place—even though she had just been robbed of every possession she had ever owned besides the dress and sweater she was wearing, the socks that would soon fill up with her own blood, and the ring that stabbed into her skin with every step she took. Even though she faced the terrifying prospect of enduring the winter without warmth or security, and even though she had left the city that she viewed as a lifeblood more than a home, she knew she would have walked this distance and more just to be with Samual.

He found her quickly after she arrived to her new home, which was a thin mat in one of the women's dormitories.

Hanna held on to Samual tightly, as if he was a life raft saving her from the storming waves threatening to drag her under.

"I just want to be with you," she said as she clung to him. "Please, God, just let us stay together." She didn't know if there were any gods still listening.

"Soon, my Hanna," he said, stroking her hair.

But it was not to be. They were separated far too soon, as he stayed in a dormitory at the other end of the ghetto.

As days turned to weeks and then to months, she recognized Terezin for what it really was—not a luxurious escape for the most elite of the Jews, as advertised, nor a safe haven for them to ride out the war, yet also not a prison, as many viewed it. She saw it was a cage: a cage meant to gather and contain the Jews until the Nazis found a more permanent solution. It was a constant source of irony to Hanna that Terezin was the place chosen for this cage. It had once been a military fort, with stone walls measuring almost four meters high. It had been built two hundred years ago to protect Prague from, of all people, the Germans. Hanna wanted to snort with laughter at the backwardness of it all: the walls had been built to keep the Germans out; now the Germans were using the walls to keep the Jews in.

When she voiced these fears to Samual in hurried whispers during their designated meeting time the next day on the street, he kissed her nose and replied with the mantra she was coming to despise:

"They can't kill us all."

"I don't think survival is what the Nazis have in mind for us," she argued with him. Their moments together were precious to her, but she also knew not another soul in Terezin. She had to release all her fears and worries on Samual or she felt like she would burst. "At every turn, they devise a way to kill, or rather, leave us for dead—starting with living conditions and ending in starvation," she said.

The small job Samual helped Hanna secure at the ghetto's hospital was repulsive and mind-numbing. She spent most of her time trying to block out all that she was seeing—the patients who came in with empty but bloated stomachs, the dry cough that wracked already frail bodies like an earthquake, the diseases and infections and injuries that could have been easily treated anywhere else with simple medications, but proved to be torturous and fatal in Terezin.

As hideous as she found work at the hospital, it was work. She saw many of the people of Terezin walking the cracked sidewalks with looks of desperation that mirrored the look on Samual's face the week before David was executed. It was the look of uprooted souls. It was the look of an unmoored life without meaning.

Hanna always stopped herself from complaining. She would remind herself that there were no beastly soldiers torturing people without provocation; there were no beatings in the street; there were no hateful people to spit on her; there were no executions of her friends. She and Samual managed, in a few months, to carve out a life for themselves. She would not go so far as to say a happy life, but a life, which was more than they had in their last few weeks in Prague.

After months of only seeing Samual on the street, he was able to use his connections with the building commando to find a private place for them. It was only for a few hours every third night, but it was precious time alone. The place was an unused attic over a one-bedroom apartment shared between two families. The fathers of both families were in the commando with Samual. They allowed Samual and Hanna, as well as two other young couples, to use the space in rotation.

The attic was long enough for Samual to lie down and stretch his legs, but not tall enough for either of them to sit up. Hanna did not mind. After months with nothing more than Samual caressing her cheek with his gloved hand as they parted, she preferred that they were as snug together as possible.

Those few hours were paradise, a paradise she never thought they would have again after David's arrest and Samual losing his job. If she closed her eyes, shutting out the sight of the attic rafters, and ignored the pain of the hard wooden floor on her back and the chill of the wind blowing through the cracks in the walls, she was able to pretend they were back in Prague, before Heydrich was in control and their lives took a turn for the worse. She could pretend that she was waking up in the early morning, lounging in bed before her shift at

Prague Kofe, that Samual was going to meet her at dusk for a walk over the Charles Bridge to feed the swans and pick lilies of the valley in the park.

Ignoring the cold, which was unrelenting despite Samual's arms around her, Hanna tried to picture their future—a life outside of the ghetto walls. "When we get married, we should have both of our families take the train into Prague to celebrate with us."

Neither of them mentioned that they had no idea where their families were or if they were even alive.

Samual simply agreed. "My family has never been to Prague. I can show my father the buildings I've worked on. Maybe by that time, I'll be back to designing and we can look at the new buildings I'm helping to construct."

"And I can paint a portrait of my parents," Hanna said. She closed her eyes to imagine her parents seated in their front parlor, which she would convert into an art studio because of its abundance of natural light.

"They'll love that," Samual whispered into her ear.

Hanna knew these stolen moments, these whispered conversations, were nothing more than wild fantasies, but she would never say those words aloud. The more she saw of Terezin and the state of the people, the more surely she knew the Nazis had no intention of letting the Jews leave this place alive. Their only intention in its design was to kill as many Jews as possible without firing a single gun. Thus far, from the condition of the people on the streets and in the hospital, Hanna would say they were quite successful.

Still, Samual found small ways to make her smile, to try to make her forget the world around them.

"I have a gift for you," he said. His breath moved the few pieces of hair that had fallen from her chignon to frame her face.

"You couldn't possibly," she said. These days, the most precious gift would be an extra piece of stale bread. She dared not dream of even a fresh piece.

Samual untangled his arms from around her body, and she felt an instant chill from the loss of them. He reached into his coat, which had been tossed down by their feet. He handed her a single slip of paper, folded up many times to fit into the breast pocket.

Hanna's heart dropped a bit. The only paper she had seen since coming to Terezin were usually orders to move—move to another barrack, move jobs, or the most dreaded, take the next train to move east. *Don't go east,* Hanna heard in her head, at the sight of that paper.

She rolled onto her side, facing Samual, and slowly unfolded the paper. He was grinning like a boy who had picked the first flower of the season for his schoolroom crush. She could not help smiling at his eagerness, though she still worried nothing good could come of such a paper.

She unfolded it completely, then turned it over to look at the back. She was confused; meanwhile, Samual continued to light up the dark attic with his smile. The paper was blank. Both sides were perfectly white, with the only blemishes coming from the creases where Samual neatly folded it to fit into his pocket.

Hanna still could not fight her smile as she said, "I don't understand. It's blank."

He nodded with enthusiasm. "Yes! It's a blank piece of paper."

Hanna laughed. "Thank you?"

Her confused answer did not diminish his excitement at all. He took the paper gently out of her fingers, handling it as if it was the most delicate china. "It's blank. It can be anything you want. You can create it into anything!"

Understanding dawned over Hanna. It truly was the best gift Samual could have presented to her. Her mind was already racing through all the things she could create with this blank canvas. When she lived in Prague, she was never at a loss for inspiration. She would make colorful pictures depicting the diverse people of the city, or the way the sunlight would reflect on the mosaic tiles of the synagogue, or the way the lilies of the valley would bend and turn as the children ran past them. But in Terezin, she had seen nothing of beauty. Nothing, she thought, except her ring.

Her mind was already imagining the picture: pencil lines sharpened to the finest point for the scrollwork around the sides, a blue like the middle of the ocean for the sapphires on the corners, just a hint of a rainbow on the bottom diamonds, showing how the light bent, reflecting and changing when it met the stones. She never got a chance to make a painting of it like she had wanted to right after Samual first proposed. Maybe this clean piece of paper was her chance.

"There's more!" he said, practically bouncing next to her. "I got this because I was asked to appropriate a space for a children's art class. We were given art supplies by the Nazis. Really more like remnants of art supplies and scraps of papers. I had to dig to find this one that was completely clean. But starting next week, children of the town are going to gather twice a week for art lessons."

"Art lessons," Hanna said wistfully. "The Nazis care about art lessons? Or children?"

"It seems that way," Samual said. "Though I doubt it's with pure motives. Nevertheless, there will be art lessons with art supplies. And you are going to be one of the teachers."

Chapter 23

CHAYA

She was not sure of many things in life; actually, most things confused her. But this she knew: Rachael would come back.

After all, she had made many promises about never leaving and keeping her safe and loving her and that pretty cottage they would have by the sea with the birds that sang while flying over the water and the little white seashells that she could line up along her windowsills.

She did not know exactly what a windowsill was, but she wanted one—especially one filled with seashells that sang the ocean's song to her. Some of the seashells did that, Rachael had said. She had described the shape of the inside of those types of shells, calling it a "spiral"—Chaya could see it if she closed her eyes.

These were the things Rachael had promised, so Chaya knew them to be true.

It was confusing though.

Chaya knew standing in line every day—twice a day—was not playtime. Rachael had told her that many times, when it was just the two of them. And during those times of standing in line in the morning and evening, Rachael would nudge her gently or barely whisper for her to hold still. It was so hard to hold still, but Chaya had seen the guards hit people if they moved too much. So she learned to hold still, at least when the guards were looking her way. It was a game of "freeze." If no one was watching her, Chaya could bounce on the balls of her feet or swing her arms back and forth. If someone looked her way she had to stop, even if it meant freezing in midair. She wouldn't even breathe. She always won.

But still, she knew it was serious. It was even more serious when the guards took someone out of line. Many days, they took lots of some-ones out of line. They would make them sit in the big truck. It was like the truck that Chaya rode in when she left the farmhouse cellar to come here, except her truck had a big canvas roof on top and canvas walls that blew in and out, like when she sucked air into her cheeks and pushed it back out with big puffs. She wished her truck hadn't had the canvas. It would have been more fun to ride that long way with the wind playing with her hair and the sun shining on her face and warming her arms. Though she wished to ride in a truck like that, she knew not to ride in this truck at the camp. It didn't go anywhere fun. She knew that because the women often cried when they climbed into the back, and because Rachael was very scared that Chaya had ridden in one already. She cried and cried and cried the day Chaya had told her about how she rode in the truck with the canvas sides.

Where exactly those trucks went with lots of crying women was just another thing in the long list of things she did not know. The truck did not come back though, at least not with any of its riders. Chaya did not want to take any rides, even one as fun as a truck with no roof or sides, unless she was with Rachael.

She understood that Rachael went on that truck for her, to save her from having to go with those other women, all crying and staring ahead without seeing the sky or clouds or sunshine around them. Most people in this place cried or stared ahead without seeing. Rachael was like that before she started to let Chaya snuggle and sleep in her bed.

"You brought me back to life," Rachael told her once.

"Like a ghost?" she asked, both excited and a little scared at the idea of Rachael as a ghost.

"Kind of," she said. "But just my heart. My heart had died. Then I met you, and it was alive again."

Chaya knew little about dead people and even less about dead hearts. When she asked Rachael, she said, "Dead people live up in the sky, with the stars and the sun."

"That doesn't seem like such a bad place to live," Chaya said. "People in the sky are free. There are no cellar walls and fences in the sky."

"I suppose that's true," Rachael said.

"So the people could fly from happy place to happy place, visiting the people they loved," Chaya said, liking this idea more and more. "Maybe they can even come back here?"

At that, Rachael just smiled without showing her teeth and gave Chaya a kiss on her dirty hair.

Chaya knew a lot more about people who had left, who were simply gone—the parents she must have had but did not remember, the family from the farmhouse, many of the women in the beds next to hers. They never came back—that she knew. With that knowledge, she started to doubt her belief that Rachael would return. It had never happened before, but she had also never had anyone like Rachael before.

The night when Rachael came back, after Chaya thought she had been lost, they hugged. Rachael held her so tight that it hurt her neck and made it hard to breathe. But she liked it. She could smell Rachael and feel how cold her arms were. It gave her goosebumps all over. She could hear Rachael's heartbeat because she was pressed so hard against her chest. Chaya had never felt anything like that moment. How alone she had been, without a family! But now she finally had something she had heard so much about—a mother who loved her.

Rachael would ask about her family. She would ask so many questions that Chaya didn't know how to answer. She wasn't sure how old she was. She did not remember how she came to live in the farmhouse cellar or what her parents looked like. She would close her eyes sometimes, squeezing them shut so tightly that she would see spinning circles behind her eyelids. She would push harder and harder on her eyeballs until tears would start to come out from the corner of her eyes, trying to see an image of her mother or father. When she finally gave up and opened her eyes, she only saw Rachael. Even the people from the farmhouse—who she knew were not her family—were hard to see now, no matter how hard she tried. But Rachael was right there when she tried to picture her.

She had lived at the farmhouse from as far back as she could remember. Actually, she did not live in the farmhouse but in the cellar under the kitchen floor, with her bed tucked behind shelves of canned cabbage and sugar beets. Her only company was the pile of potatoes in the corner. They became her friends and family. Each potato had a name, and she would pull them out of the pile one by one. She taught them how to play, so that they wouldn't be bored either.

The family that lived above the cellar, in the few rooms of the farmhouse, mostly ignored her. There were two girls, both older than Chaya, a boy who was even older and spent most days working with his father, and the parents. She saw what a family was through the cracks between the floorboards of the kitchen. The mother taught the girls how to bake bread and finish their schoolwork on the large wooden table in the middle of the floor. The father leaned back in his chair, smoking a cigarette, talking about the many chores needing to be done in the morning and congratulating the son on a job well done in the evening. These things never included her, so she knew she was not part of this family. The children received hugs and kisses on the forehead. There was teasing and encouragement. Sometimes, there was yelling, but Chaya could tell that even those harsh words were said with love. How she had longed to be up there, scolded alongside the other children.

There were prayers said together while holding hands every night, and sometimes, there was cake and singing. Chaya loved those nights best of all because the sweet smells of the cake would waft down to the cellar, filling the space around her with a happy aroma. Sometimes, if it was the mother whom they sang to, Chaya would even get a small slice of cake. That was the best thing in the world.

Most days, she lined up the potatoes or other cans of vegetables to play games. The little potato was her, and there were brother and sister potatoes. She was careful to be quiet, as they had told her to be. She lay on her cot, listening to the normal bustle of life above her. She knew that Ingrid struggled with something called long division and that Ilse begged for a new dress and shoes—within days, she could hear those shoes clicking on the floorboards above her. Their floor was her ceiling. That thought always made her smile. It was like she lived in an upside-down house.

She listened to Erich tell his father about where the cattle best liked to graze and which pig should be taken to the market. She had never seen these things—long division, shoes that click as you walk, cows or pigs. But she lived life alongside the family, like a picture hanging on the wall—seeing all, hearing all, but no one ever glancing her way. Of course, they all knew she was there. The parents often fought about her—the father wanting to get rid of her, the mother crying it was their "Christian duty" to continue to help her. Chaya did not know what either meant except that the mother wanted her to stay—invisible as she was—and the father did not.

Never did Erich acknowledge her. He did not bring her food, did not say her name in conversation, did not, as far as Chaya could see from the cellar, even glance down at the floorboards beneath his feet that were her sky. Ingrid never tried speaking to her, but when she was alone with her mother, she asked endless questions about the strange girl who lived in their cellar. Chaya loved those whispered conversations, though it was hard for her to hear much more than sharp reprimands that they did not speak of Chaya. Chaya had the same questions as Ingrid—she would have accepted any small answers.

Ilse never showed much interest. She sometimes delivered the plate of food, always without looking in Chaya's direction. She was still Chaya's favorite, because once she slipped papers through the cracks in the floorboards. Chaya ignored the scraps that rained down on her head one afternoon, fluttering back and forth through the damp cellar air. The sight of their descent was one of the most entertaining afternoons in Chaya's memory. It wasn't until a day later that Chaya realized Ilse was not coming down for the scraps, that—maybe—she had floated them down to Chaya on purpose, that—just maybe—they were for her. When she found the courage to pick them up and look at them, she found the paper was not scraps at all, but cutouts of beautiful girls wearing only their underthings. There were three girls—two with yellow hair like the glimpses Chaya saw of Ingrid's and Ilse's, and one with long, dark curly hair like her own. The rest of the scraps were paper cutouts of clothes—long dresses that flowed outward and reached the girls' toes, skirts with stripes and matching jackets, wool overcoats with smart gloves and hats. She placed the paper clothes on top of the paper dolls, dressing them up countless times in a day. Besides food and a dress that was a size bigger than her current one, it was really the only thing she had ever been given. And it was the most glorious thing.

Life went on day after day. Twice a day, Mama—that was what the family called her, so Chaya thought of her as such too—would bring a small plate of food to the top of the steps of the cellar. She looked forward to those moments more than anything else in her day. Rarely did Mama say anything. Chaya knew from some of Papa's harsh words that her entire existence had to be a secret. So Mama would most often leave the plate of food and little metal cup of warm milk on the stair without a sound. Yet, every time, she would look down into the cellar, searching until she locked eyes with the little girl; then she would smile. As the years went on, that smile became smaller and smaller, but still, it gave Chaya unbelievable joy. Some days, when she was feeling especially lonely, maybe because the whole family was outdoors all day so she could not take part in their fun from below, she would wait on the bottom step of the cellar. She would sit there all day, patiently waiting, expecting that smile from Mama that was both happy and sad at the same time.

As if she knew which days were hardest for Chaya, sometimes Mama would surprise her with the greatest treat of her life. Later in the night, after the house was dark and silent, with the father and the children asleep, Mama would creep back down to the cellar. She would tiptoe so quietly down the stairs that Chaya would not wake at the sound. Mama would gently shake her shoulder and motion her to stay quiet as soon as Chaya opened her eyes. She would take Chaya's hand and lead her silently up the stairs, through the darkened kitchen, out the rickety door, down the three steps, and onto the damp grass.

To Chaya, whose eyes were only used to the muted darkness of the cellar and the little light that seeped through the floorboards and around the cellar door, the night sky was the brightest and most brilliant thing she had ever seen. She knew she would never tire of seeing it. The stars twinkled and glowed like pure magic. The blackness was like a blanket falling softly over her head and shoulders and body, not suffocating her like the worn wool one she had in the cellar, but tucking her in softly and making her feel safe. The stars winked at her—friendly and with good humor.

On nights like these, Chaya wanted to ask Mama so many questions. She would answer some—the easy ones, like what a cow looks like. But the question that burned brightest in Chaya's mind—*Can you be my mama?*—she was never able to ask. Chaya thought those nights were like a spell. If she spoke too loudly or too much, if she moved too quickly, the magic would break and she would not only be sent back to the cellar but would never be allowed to leave again. And small as she was, she seemed to know the answer to that burning question. Mama was kind with her smiles and nighttime trips to see the stars, but she never kissed her or hugged her tight as she did Ingrid and Ilse. Chaya knew that only mothers did that, so this woman must not be her mother, nor wanted to be. Mama was a good mama to her children; Chaya simply was not one of them.

The night sky full of stars spreading as far as the eye could see was the one image Chaya could conjure back up as she lay behind the shelves of canned vegetables. Though she gleaned some information about the outside world from catches of conversation through the floorboards, the night sky was something that she had witnessed. She could close her eyes and see it clearly—the black and the bright—a mystery and puzzle to her.

As much as she loved the sun, the night sky with stars would always be her favorite. Before sharing the top bunk with Rachael, Chaya often tiptoed out of her bed at night to pop her head out of the glassless windows in the barrack. The blanket of the sky did not stretch as far and the pinprick lights did not burn as bright in Auschwitz as they did in the yard of the farmhouse; there were distractions of guard tower spotlights, burning lamps around each of the barrack walls, and distant city glows far in the distance. Yet, she could still see those friendly stars right above her head, still winking at her.

Chaya could not hate Auschwitz as much as Rachael did. To her, it was not all bad. She was allowed to move around and not stay hidden all day and all night; Rachael and sometimes other people spoke to her and let her speak back; she had freedom to play and jump and put her hands into the dirt or mud. And there was sunshine. The sunshine was a marvel to her. It was bright and hurt her eyes so much in the beginning, though she got used to it quickly. It warmed her skin like nothing she had ever felt before. She did not remember being cold in the cellar, but she had never felt the heat of the sun's rays. She was sure after soaking it in, when she walked back into the barracks, she would burn a golden yellow like the sun itself. She was always disappointed when her skin looked completely normal.

She would go back to the cellar though, if it would bring Rachael back. This place, even with the room to walk and explore and play in the sunshine, it was nothing compared to having Rachael with her. Chaya was not really sure where Rachael had gone. She had left the ring behind, so Chaya knew it was serious. But had she left the ring because she was coming back for it? Rachael had just been taken; she had dropped the ring and walked away. If she walked away, couldn't she walk back?

Rachael feared death over anything, though Chaya feared going back to the dark cellar by herself much more than this mystery called death. Rachael talked about a pain-free, beautiful life after this life. It sounded pretty good. Rachael's children—Radek and Catarina and the little baby—were in that place. Rachael said they were happy there, maybe even watching from the stars in the sky. Chaya would give anything to live in the stars, so she did not understand why Rachael had so many tears in her eyes when she talked about her children being up there.

Rachael told her once that people who were taken out of line and put on the truck with no roof were dead. That confused Chaya. She had seen death. It was a loud bang, sometimes a crack, and then there was lots of red. Rachael said the red was blood. Chaya knew all about blood.

It happened during the day. Mama and the girls were in the kitchen. The box that played pretty music had been gone for a long time, but the girls still remembered many of the songs. They were taking turns singing different words while Mama showed them how to take the vegetables from the big baskets on the floor and portion them into the small jars lining the wooden table. Chaya loved the days when the whole family stayed in the kitchen, with the interesting voices and noises they made and the smells that made her stomach grumble as they baked and chopped and stewed.

The kitchen door swung open so hard that it banged against the wall, rattling the dishes on the shelves above the sink. Erich entered first, followed by Papa. Then she heard the loud stomp of three pairs of black, heavy boots. It was difficult for Chaya to see faces through the thin cracks in her cellar ceiling, but she could tell each family member by sound—their voice, the fall of their footstep. These boots with their heavy footsteps and the harsh voices were new. The family never had visitors, not in the many summers and winters that she had lived in the cellar.

She saw shadows and slivers of the action in the kitchen. She was fixated by what was happening, though not really understanding most of it. The men in black boots—Chaya learned later they were German soldiers—pushed Erich and Papa to the far end of the kitchen. Both girls started crying—Ingrid in large, gulping sobs that Chaya thought might choke her, Ilse in quiet sniffles. Mama quickly moved the girls to the far side of the kitchen too, pushing them behind her. Their feet were all huddled close together, the sisters hugging and holding each other as close as Chaya had ever seen.

Papa moved in front of this family. His steps were slow, slower than ever. His heel touched the floor softly, then the middle of his foot, then his toes. He moved like that, soundlessly, a few steps toward the soldiers. He spoke in the same soft voice he used when it was late at night and most of the house was sleeping and only he and Mama were sitting in the kitchen.

"There is no need for this," Papa said. "No need to threaten my family. We are happy to help you with whatever you need. We are good citizens of the Fatherland. Like you."

One of the soldiers spit. His saliva landed right between two floorboards and dripped onto the dirt floor of the cellar. Chaya found this—more than the family's fear or the surprise at these intruders—most startling. She mimicked Papa's slow and deliberate footsteps, moving away from the spot where the spit oozed down.

"You're nothing like us," the soldier said. "You sit here in your safe farmhouse, with your full dinner table and your pretty girls." Chaya saw Mama's feet move closer to Ingrid and Ilse. "We are out there—fighting and dying for the Fatherland." The soldier spit again, in the same spot. "Don't say you are good citizens like we are."

"Of course," Papa said softly. Had his words not been directly straight at the floor, Chaya would have never heard him. "Of course. We are so appreciative of your sacrifice. What we have on our dinner table is yours. It's an honor to share it with you."

"Ha!" a different soldier laughed, though it was not the same laugh the family used when Ingrid tried to tell jokes or when Mama served dinner with flour still on her cheeks or in her hair. It was like no laugh Chaya had ever heard—really no laugh at all. "You cannot share what is not yours."

"What?" Erich tried to move in front of his mother, but Papa stopped him.

"This house, this farm, everything belongs to the Fuhrer. So it belongs to us."

Again, Papa's soft voice seemed to be aimed right to Chaya. "Of course. We live to serve him and our country."

"Do you?" It was a third voice. It didn't sound as scary. "Do you live to serve the Fuhrer and the Fatherland?"

"Of course."

"Hmm." The boots started to walk around the kitchen. They paused by the table where just a minute ago Mama, Ingrid, and Ilse had been readying the garden vegetables for the canning jars meant for the cellar. He walked toward the family huddled in the corner. Chaya heard Ilse draw in a quick breath. Ingrid sobbed even louder. After he circled the room, he repeated, "Do you?"

No one spoke. Papa did not answer. Only Ingrid's cries could be heard.

"That's not what has been reported to us," the third soldier said softly.

There was complete silence in the kitchen, in the house, in the entire world, Chaya thought. Ingrid had stopped crying, and even the regular sounds of the house and the farm—the creak of wind on the shutters, the soft brays from the cows in the barn, the bubbling or frying from the stovetop—fell silent as death. Chaya found herself following suit, holding her breath, though she did not understand why.

"Well?" the third soldier asked, his one word breaking through the perfect silence.

"I don't know what you mean," Papa said. Chaya had never heard his voice like that, like Ingrid's when she came home from school with a bad grade or Ilse when she burned the bread.

"I thought you would say as much." The third soldier snapped his fingers at the others.

"No!" Chaya heard Mama's cry. It was high pitched. For the first time, Chaya felt something grip her stomach, felt her insides go liquid. This was fear. She felt it throughout her entire body.

Both girls started crying. One of the soldiers was separating them. Chaya could not tell whose feet were whose when they were huddled together, and now, she saw one set of girls' shoes was being dragged through the kitchen, toward the door. Mama was trying to hold on to her daughter, but another soldier barred her path. Papa seemed frozen in place, his feet rooted to the floorboards. It was mayhem above her—the sobs of the sisters, the cries of despair from their mother, the silence that seemed louder than everything else from their father.

"Don't touch my sister!" Erich shouted. "You pig! You—"

A loud stomp from the third soldier's black boot interrupted Erich mid threat. Everything else stopped.

"What was that, my son?" The third soldier sounded like he was smiling.

"I'll tell you everything. Just let my sister go," Erich said. He was moving toward the kitchen door, moving toward his sister. Based on the stifled sob still coming from the corner, Chaya guessed it was Ilse who had been separated from the family.

"Tell me what?"

"Everything."

"Erich . . ." Papa started. His voice took on a tone of warning, but Erich continued to move through the kitchen.

"We have," Erich started. He took a deep breath. "We have a Jew hidden here."

There was a loud bang. It made Chaya's ears pound in protest. She had heard the breaking of glass and the clang of dropped pots before, and she had just heard that loud stomp of the black boots that rained down dirt from the floorboards. But never had she heard something so loud as that bang. Never had she heard something as terrifying as Erich's body falling to the floor. And never had she heard anything like the animal wail that came from Mama.

There was a click. She heard it distinctly, even over the cries of the women in the kitchen. The third soldier stood with his feet directly in front of Mama, blocking her path to her son. "Where?"

"Where? I don't . . . My son . . . He . . ." Mama was unable to speak, to breathe.

"Where?" The soft tone was leaving the soldier's voice.

Mama was silent.

Another bang. The shock of the sound in the midst of the quiet was as terrible as the crash of Mama as she fell to the floor.

Chaya did not understand these sounds, but the screams of Ilse and Ingrid after their mother fell to the floor, no longer moving, she was able to interpret. Something terrible was happening upstairs to this family she had watched for years. This mama was trying to protect Chaya with her silence. These soldiers, with their heavy boots and all their many questions and their loud bangs, were looking for her.

"Clearly," the third soldier said, "we know you have hidden a Jewish family."

Papa started to protest, the first words or movements he made since warning Erich from trying to save his sister.

"No!" The soldier raised his voice for the first time. "We know you have a Jewish family hidden here. Denying it, trying to hide it . . .

Clearly . . ." Chaya saw his arm sweep across the kitchen floor where Mama and Erich lay, starting to leak a thick, red liquid. "Clearly, it will not help you."

"Down!" Ingrid screamed. "She's down there. She's been down there the whole time!" She was hysterical, pushing against one of the soldiers that held her in the corner.

The third soldier walked slowly and softly toward Ingrid. He stepped over Mama's fallen body. The red had spilled onto the floor and was now dripping through the floorboards. Chaya felt it drip on her arm. It was hot, burning her skin. She saw on the other side of her, Erich's blood had also seeped through the cracks, creating a steady drip of red onto the dirt floor. It pooled in a puddle next to her feet.

"Excellent," the soldier said. He was close to Ingrid, kneeling in front of her. "She is down there? Besides her, how many do you have hidden?" He spoke sweetly, calming the erratic breathing of the scared girl.

Ingrid shook her head. "Just the little girl. Just the little . . ." She could not finish. Her words were swallowed by her fear as the soldier reached for her.

"Very good, little one," he said. He patted her head. Ingrid made a sound that reminded Chaya of a small kitten that had lived briefly in the warm kitchen, a soft mewling sound. "You!" The soldier's authoritative voice was back, startling Chaya and everyone in the kitchen. "And you." Chaya struggled to see what the soldier was doing, but the thin cracks showed very little of his movements. "Take care of the family."

Chaya had trouble remembering the details of what happened after that. The cellar door opened. The sun shone in from the open kitchen door as the soldiers marched Papa, Ingrid, and Ilse outside, Papa still silent. The sun was so bright that Chaya never saw the features of the man who dragged her out of the cellar.

She did not fight him. She knew this man was bad. She knew all the soldiers, especially the soft-spoken one with the bangs, were bad. But she had never been out of the cellar during the daytime, while the sun shone so brightly it hurt her eyes. That was good. The truck she rode in seemed good too. There were three more bangs and a lot more red coming from the remaining family members; she knew that was bad, very bad.

On that day, she learned about death and killing. She already knew about "gone" and decided she much preferred it. "Gone" meant they were coming back. Her parents were gone. So they could return. Papa and Mama and Erich and Ingrid and Ilse were dead. They were not coming back.

Rachael was not like that family, though. Yes, she was gone, but she had told Chaya many times that she would never leave.

So Rachael was coming back. She had to be coming back. At least, that's what Chaya told herself as she huddled in their bunk, stroking the rough edges of the diamond ring until she finally fell asleep.

Chapter 24

HANNA

It was unlike any classroom Hanna had ever seen. In any other world, in any other place, the space would never have counted as a classroom. There were no desks, no chalkboards, no cubbies with sack lunches and bookbags, no colorful handprint paintings adorning the walls. Back when Terezin was still a fort housing only a couple thousand military personnel, this may have been a spacious office for some high-ranking official. Today, it was stripped of all furniture and decorations. It held only a rusty iron stove in the far corner of the room. But without firewood, it sat useless and empty, and the room was as cold as the frigid temperatures outside. Though the room was meant to be an art studio for the children, it held no easels, pencils, paintbrushes, or blank canvases. But there were smiling children, and that, Hanna supposed, was all that was needed these days to make this bare and cold area a classroom.

The children were sitting cross-legged on the floor, many wrapped in home-knitted afghans against the late winter chill. A few lucky ones had hats and gloves, but most looked like they were better dressed for the warm days of summer with their threadbare dresses and shirts, jackets full of holes. Most bounced in their seats with visible excitement. Over the last few weeks, the Council of Elders had tried to get a handle on the rising population of children in the ghetto. Children and elderly made up most of Terezin, though it was not a place for either. Normalcy was the mission of the Council—normal routines, normal jobs, normal lives. That included education for the children. Unlike the children she'd seen in classes elsewhere, these kids seemed excited. Hanna pushed herself into the back of the room, her back pressed against the cold plaster wall, waiting—like the children—for the class to start.

Just as the children started to get restless and Hanna thought she might need to take control, a woman rushed into the room. She slammed the door behind her, causing the children jump. One small girl in the middle of the room started to cry. The woman laughed apologetically.

"Children!" she said. Her voice rang out like clear church bells. Hanna, along with the gathered children, could not help but relax. "Children!" she sang out again. "I am so happy you are here!" She spoke German, which to Hanna always seemed like a rough language. But this woman's words had a melodic cadence to them. The children seemed to hear it too, as they sat entranced rather than frightened. Hanna was learning that her fellow residents of Terezin were largely from Germany, sent here by their own people. Perhaps the children found in this woman's language a sense of comfort.

The woman had very dark hair, pulled into a tight bun with no stray wisps falling loose. Her eyes were dark and round, so large that Hanna thought her face could hardly hold them. Though the people in Terezin walked around with dead eyes, this woman's still shined with excitement.

She brought with her a suitcase into the room, carefully lifting it with both hands over the heads of the children sitting on the floor. The children looked curiously at this woman, then to the suitcase she was hauling through the room, then back to the woman.

When she reached what Hanna assumed was the head of the classroom, the woman smiled brightly again. "I'm just so happy you are all here!" Hanna saw some of the children warm to the woman's good cheer. Their nervous faces broke into small smiles. Even Hanna felt her shoulders relax a little. She did not realize they had been tense.

"I'm Frau Friedl Brandeis," she stage-whispered conspiratorially to the children. "But you can call me just Frau Friedl." She paused, looking expectantly at the children. They continued to stare wide-eyed, but more and more were smiling.

"Good day, Frau Friedl," Hanna said, hoping to encourage the children. A few mumbled it back.

The lackluster response did not seem to dim Frau Freidl's enthusiasm. She continued to beam and went on. "I bet you're wondering what is in my suitcase." She wiggled her thin eyebrows at the children. "Who's curious to see what's inside?"

Hanna took a step away from the wall, looking at the children. No one moved. She raised her hand. "I am, Frau Friedl." She pantomimed the desired response. "I want to see what's inside."

A few children started to raise their hands as well. Frau Friedl waited patiently, looking at the room. A few more hands went up.

"That's all?" she asked. "Maybe just me and . . ." She looked at Hanna questioningly.

"Fraulein Hanna," she prompted.

"Maybe only Fraulein Hanna and myself will see what's inside." Frau Friedl set the suitcase on the ground. Kneeling in front of it, she dramatically opened the left clasp, then the right. She looked around the room again. "Anyone else?"

"I do!" A little boy stood up abruptly. "I want to see what's inside!"

The boy next to him, obviously a little brother, jumped up alongside him. "Me too! Can I see inside?"

The dam broke. The curious children couldn't contain themselves any longer. Many raised their hands, some jumped up and down with curiosity, while others looked like they would hurt themselves craning for a look.

Frau Friedl laughed. "Very well!" she yelled over the commotion. "Very well! You shall all see what I have brought you all the way from Vienna!"

She slowly and dramatically opened the suitcase lid, little by little. The children craned their necks harder, eager for a first look. Frau Friedl hunched her shoulders over the case to keep the contents concealed. Even Hanna found herself on tiptoe trying to see over the top of the case. Finally, when the children's anticipation seemed about to explode, Frau Friedl pulled out the first item with flair—like a magician pulling a rabbit from a top hat. It was half a sheet of paper.

Hanna grinned, knowing the trouble Frau Friedl must have gone through to get even that much paper, and she smiled at the children who looked questioningly at the paper, then back at Frau Friedl with even more wonder. She handed the half page to the child sitting closest to the suitcase. She dramatically produced another paper, this time a fairly crumpled piece of wrapping paper, though large enough to cover a shoebox. She, again, handed it to a child sitting nearby.

Frau Friedl continued to pull out bits of paper—scraps, pieces of cardboard, more used wrapping paper—from the suitcase. Hanna quietly walked around the room so she could see inside. The case was filled with only that—any piece of paper Frau Friedl could get her hands on. There was enough for every child. They lined up, quietly and respectfully, one by one, to receive their piece of paper. Most even said thank you, though Hanna could tell from their confused faces that they did not understand the importance of what they had been given, or the sacrifices Frau Friedl must have endured to get it for them. Hanna knew, though. She already knew what it was like to be without even the most basic art supplies, and while the children may not have understood or appreciated it now, this day could change many of their lives.

One little girl came up quietly for her slip of paper. She had been watching the entire scene in silence, her wide eyes taking in every bit of action. Hanna recognized her as the same small girl from the train platform on the way to Terezin. It had been months since that day, but Hanna knew immediately it was the same child. She was dirtier than she had been that day on the platform, and much thinner. This was no surprise, as Hanna knew herself to have grown much dirtier and thinner too. The girl did not seem to notice Hanna, or rather, did not recognize her, as she waited her turn for a scrap of paper. Hanna smiled with affection and relief that among this place of strangers, she saw a face she knew. After the girl received her paper, a jaggedly cut piece of wrapping paper, clearly the leftover bits from a previous wrapping of birthday gifts, the girl looked straight at Hanna. Their eyes met. She did not smile or nod, as most would upon seeing a friendly face, but Hanna knew, nevertheless, that the girl did recognize her. This girl was one who missed nothing.

As Hanna continued to watch Frau Friedl hand out tiny scrap after tiny scrap, she felt a wave of guilt wash over her. Many of the children said thank you for even the smallest bit of paper—a shop receipt or a page from an old romance novel. She still had the page from Samual in her possession, a perfectly white piece of paper, though it was starting to dirty at the creases as she carried it around with her. She did not trust something as precious as this in her boarding room. She thought about carrying it in her shoe, joined by the engagement ring that she still wore around her toe. Her foot was now callused and toughened by the many months of rubbing against the diamond's sharp edge, but she knew the paper would not be so durable. So she had the blank page folded up and tucked into her brassier. Nights when she waited in the small attic for Samual to join her, she would take both treasures from their hiding places and admire them.

Now she could envision the picture that belonged on that piece of paper—this scene unfolding in front of her. She would make it black and white, using only charcoal smudges to show the shadows and dirt on the children's faces. It would be a challenge to capture the eagerness and curiosity in the children's eyes as they peered around the suitcase, hoping to uncover the riches hidden inside. But like a convalescing patient who needed to stretch his legs and expand his lungs, she needed a challenge. She could already see the picture focusing around the eyes—both the eyes of Frau Friedl and the eyes of the little girl from the train station. Frau Friedl's would be large, with sharp lines around the corners to show the hard life that she had lived, but also the joy that she was receiving by giving this small gift to the children. She would shade a little underneath, giving the eyes depth and the look of exhaustion. The little girl's eyes would be equally large, but there would be no joy, really no emotion in them at all. They would be flat—curiously so, for the viewer of this picture. *Flat, yet full of understanding,* Hanna thought. They would be eyes that would haunt viewers after they have walked away. Eyes that would linger in a person's mind.

Hanna's plans for her future picture were interrupted as Frau Friedl gave paper to the last child waiting. The children had started to talk to one another as they waited, and the room was humming with the sounds of high-pitched, eager voices. It was the sound of children, and though there were many in Terezin, Hanna realized this was the first time she had heard their chatter inside of the city walls. It was the sound of innocence and joy. Frau Friedl, still smiling, snapped the suitcase shut and stood up in front of the children.

"I think we are ready. Yes?" she asked. The group nodded expectantly.

For the next hour, the children were in silent awe of Frau Friedl. The basics of art that she taught were probably nothing new to them, but the way she treated them was something novel and exciting. She looked them in the eye. She listened to them completely when one asked a question or another told a long story about his home in the countryside with pigs and a barn. She asked them to look out the small window of the office.

"Tell me what you see," she asked them.

The children said nothing for a moment. Hanna realized that for many of them, this was the first time they'd been invited to think and speak with so much equality. Most of them were too young to remember their own school days, or even their days before the war. They had only known cruelty at the hands of the Germans and fear or impatience at the hands of their tormented parents. Seeing how they responded to Frau Friedl's encouragement, Hanna realized that these children were starved in more than just the physical sense. She was the first one to break the silence.

"I see people in lines," she said without looking out the window. Queues were the defining feature of Terezin.

A boy nearest to the window stood up and looked out on tiptoes. "I see the people in lines! And some of them have food, but just a little."

A little girl nudged her way to the window. "I see the building where my papa sleeps!"

"I see a tree!"

"The road."

"The sidewalk . . . but no one is allowed to walk on it."

"More buildings."

"The gray sky."

More and more children chimed in, some from memory like Hanna, without even nearing the window, some after popping their head in the small square and gazing out at the familiar surroundings of Terezin.

"Good!" "Yes!" "What else?" Frau Friedl kept encouraging them. She let them go on and on, never interrupting, until the last child spoke and it was again quiet.

"Those are wonderful observations!" she gushed. Hanna, along with the students, could not help but beam with pride. "But now," she said with sudden seriousness, "how does it make you feel?" She let the silence fill the room, taking over every bit of excitement from the children's earlier shouts. As Hanna felt the silence press in on her and all of them in that cold, empty room, Frau Friedl broke it one last time. "Now draw it."

Chapter 25

CHAYA

The next morning, she woke up with the ring clutched in her hand. She expected Rachael to be next to her. That one terrible night when she thought she had lost Rachael, she had been woken up by Rachael's return. They had both cried and hugged. Chaya learned that gone is better than dead, but returned is best of all. Rachael was not next to her in the small bed when she woke to the shouts of the guards, and there was no time to ask or have someone explain where Rachael had gone or when she was coming back. Chaya did not know what to do with the ring. Rachael always kept it in her dress pocket, but Chaya did not have any pockets. She did have the warm slippers Rachael had given her, so she slipped it quietly into the slipper of her left foot.

As she walked outside into the cold morning for roll call, the ring slid further down her slipper until it tucked under her heel. Chaya found it a little painful to walk on the firm, round band of the ring. And she worried that she might break the pretty stone with her weight, so she limped to the line, walking only on the toes of her left foot.

It was while in line that she felt the overwhelming urge to tug on Rachael's skirt and whisper to her, as she had many times before. Looking around the grounds, she was certain she was seeing a miracle.

The air was chilly in the prison yard, but the sun was starting to rise over the horizon, shining brightly. The ground inside the fence was brown and muddy and bare as usual, but outside the fence was a sight Chaya had only heard of in stories. Mama and Papa would read stories some days, and Chaya would listen from the cellar below. Most days, the family was too busy to sit still and read, but every few days, they would spend a whole morning reading stories from a large book. Chaya never saw the book, but she would hear Ingrid lift it from a shelf with a grunt and let it fall hard on the kitchen table. Then Papa would read.

Usually he read stories about a man who could perform miracles, like feeding hungry people. Chaya did not know about this man. She was always hungry, her stomach always made noise, and she never had enough to eat. Yet, this man never fed her. He brought people back to life, but the people that she knew who died always stayed dead.

So she preferred the old stories. She did not remember hearing them before, but when the family read the old ones, it gave her a sense of familiarity. These were the stories where kings reigned and bugs ate everything in sight and angels killed the men who were bad. Chaya had never seen these things happen either, but she still preferred when Papa read these pages. Her favorite story was about bread growing from the ground overnight. She could not remember a time when her stomach did not make funny noises to tell her it was still hungry, so the thought of food appearing like magic with the morning sunrise was something she had thought of often.

Across the prison yard, past the electrical fence, far off in the field, Chaya could see the bread. At least, she could see the mist that would burn off in the sunlight to reveal the magical food. The ground around her was its normal dirt and shallow puddles, but on the other side of the gate, there were little patches of mist clinging to the tall grass. It looked like clouds had descended from heaven to bring Chaya and Rachael the food they needed to stay awake and alive.

She was seeing a miracle, and she wanted to point it out to someone. She wanted to tell Rachael, but Rachael was nowhere to be found. All of her life, Chaya never had a person to tell things to, to point out the pretties of the world, to ask questions. Since she came to this place—this prison she knew Rachael and everyone else hated—she had someone. She had Rachael. But where was she? She knew, from hearing about families and seeing how the farmhouse family acted, that they were supposed to stay together no matter what. And wasn't Rachael her family now?

To the people around her, it was as if Rachael had never existed. After roll call, the women went off to their jobs, like it was any other day.

Maybe, Chaya thought, Rachael had returned late last night and did not want to wake her by climbing into their shared top bunk. Maybe she was now heading off to work as usual. Chaya hurried her legs to move faster than the line of women trudging off to *kanada*. She stood by the barbed wire gate so she could study the face of each woman as she filed past.

She tugged on the sleeve of the first woman who looked her way. "Have you seen Rachael?" she asked. The woman just shrugged her shoulders.

A few more women walked through the gate. "Where's Rachael?" she asked another. "Is she with you?"

This woman patted her head. "I don't know who Rachael is, child. Your mother?"

"She's Rachael," Chaya insisted. The woman shook her head and kept walking.

She stayed until the last woman, an old grandmother, limped by slowly, with a guard pushing her forward with a rough shove.

Chaya stayed even longer, hoping that Rachael was straggling behind—that she was still on her way. She stayed until a guard inside one of the tall towers yelled something at her and made his gun do a big bang near her feet. She understood his message and went back to the barracks.

She preferred to be outside, but Rachael had told her over and over that being in the barrack was the best place for her—the safest place. Chaya hated being trapped inside, but the barracks were better than the cellar. Light came through the big windows, as well as through the chinks in the walls, which reminded her of the cracks between the floorboards at the farmhouse. There was much more space to move in the barrack. She could run from wall to wall. She could zigzag between the bunks. She could even climb up and down. In the last few weeks, she had less energy for those things, but she felt better knowing she could play if she wanted. There was company in the barrack, too. Not great company, like Rachael, but much better than the potatoes in the lonely cellar. There were always women still sleeping, though some of them Chaya knew to stay away from.

"If they don't move," Rachael had warned, "it's because they have a virus inside them. That's like a little tiny bug that lives inside you."

Chaya shuddered at the thought.

"Keep your distance," Rachael said.

The next day, they would always be gone. There were rats and lice and lots of other bugs, especially when it was warm out, which was why Rachael said she was safe in the barracks. The guards did not like all the crawly things—Chaya didn't mind—so they stayed out of the barracks as much as they could. Also, she knew without anyone telling her, the guards did not like the smell. She barely even noticed it anymore. It was with her from the time she woke up until the time she went to sleep. She knew it must be bad though, because the soldiers would cover their noses with white handkerchiefs and make terrible noises when they had to get close to the bunks.

So she spent her long days while Rachael was gone in the barracks, or sometimes exploring the camp. She knew from the beginning to stay out of sight. In her first months here, when she still had the bit of padding from the farmhouse meal scraps, she could run quicker than the guards when they spotted her and threatened her with a whipping or worse. She would not dare try to outrun them these days. The extra food Rachael brought helped keep her upright, but she no longer had the energy for a footrace.

She also learned to stay away from the dark barrack full of sick people. The people lay all day in bed, never moving to relieve themselves but doing it right there on the bare mattress. And the sounds—it was like nothing she had ever heard. She had spent one sleepless night in the cellar long ago, listening to the tortured cries of one of the family's milking cows. She heard Papa and Erich talk in the kitchen about the pain the cow was in, trying to give birth to a calf. She thought she would never sleep again after hearing those moans of pain. But the cow's suffering seemed small compared to the people in that smelly barrack. "That's the hospital," Rachael told her later, "where sick people go. Stay away—you don't want to get sick yourself."

Chaya knew, though, that no one was cured in such a place. She avoided it at all costs.

Chaya wanted to walk from building to building to look for Rachael, even the smelly hospital one. But how upset Rachael would be if she was discovered by a guard and punished for wandering the camp! It was better to wait in the barrack like she did most days. She didn't mind. She would catalog all the things she did and all the things she saw carefully in her head to share with Rachael when she returned that evening. Since she had not seen Rachael since the morning before, her list of things to tell Rachael was getting very long. She occupied herself by repeating it over and over so she would remember every detail.

She ran out to the gate as the sun was setting behind the horizon and shadows turned to darkness. Chaya hoped that maybe Rachael had somehow joined the other women at *kanada* later in the day. Or maybe she had been there all along. The trucks that had taken her out of the camp gates had not come back, but this didn't mean anything. If Rachael was smart enough to trick them by taking her place on the truck, she could have easily snuck away. By the time Chaya made the lonely walk to the gates to wait for the returning workers, she had convinced herself that it must be so.

Rachael would be tired and hungry when she returned to the camp, since she had missed a full day of meals and a night of sleeping in their bunk. Chaya would be extra quiet tonight. She could save the many things she had been remembering for tomorrow. She would try extra hard to be good and just be happy that she was near Rachael, and to not give the woman any reasons to close her eyes and sigh as she sometimes did.

Chaya was so eager to see Rachael that she skipped back and forth by the gate. She kept her distance from the electric fence, though, remembering the warning shot from the guard towers earlier that morning. When the gates finally opened and the tired workers trudged back in, Chaya waited impatiently, bouncing on the balls of her feet. The next one through the gate had to be Rachael.

Person after person came through, but not Rachael. The woman who had patted her head in the morning gave her a small smile. Still Chaya waited; Rachael had to be next. Or she would be last, bringing up the end of the line because she was so tired. Chaya tried to calm her nervous energy, knowing that it could exasperate Rachael sometimes.

The last person through the gate was a guard that Chaya knew well. She carried a bullwhip everywhere she went, looped through the back of her belt. Chaya was terrified and fascinated by the whip. She had seen other guards use such a thing, but never this woman. The guard was talking roughly to a worker trudging behind the others with hair shaved and baggy pants tied up with an old rope. Chaya could not tell if it was a man or a woman. But as this was the women's camp, she decided it was a woman who did not look like she had the strength to make it through another workday. What Chaya did know is that the last worker was not Rachael.

Even after the longest day, Rachael had a different look about her than the others. She held her head up higher, not looking at her feet, but usually looking around the camp yard, searching for Chaya. She kept her face and dress and what little hair she was able to grow in the camp as clean as possible. She insisted that she and Chaya wash every morning. Chaya had not been used to such fuss. She was given a damp cloth and a small bit of soap once a week when she lived in the cellar, but rarely did she have the luxury of splashing an entire handful of water onto her face. It was a sensation that she did not think she would ever get used to. But, as Rachael had told her, it kept them healthy. Even this morning, without Rachael there, Chaya was careful to wash her face and hair in the pail of water, sticking her tongue out to catch the almost frozen droplets as they rolled down her face.

All of these workers coming back from *kanada* were sad—staring at their feet, their hands and hair and faces dark with dirt and ash and hopelessness.

None of them were Rachael.

The guard with the whip grabbed Chaya's upper arm as she walked past her.

"Are you trying to get yourself shot?" she asked. Her face looked angry, but her words were not unkind. "Or electrocuted?"

Chaya shook her head. As the guard pulled her along, Chaya looked back toward the gate entrance. "Rachael?" she asked.

"Is that your mother?" The guard whispered the words in her ear.

"I don't think so," she said.

The guard nodded, as if she understood.

"She's not coming back," she said, still holding on to Chaya's arm.

Chaya did not want to hear that. She wanted to run away from this guard, even though she was acting almost nice. Chaya was trained to run away from the guards. She knew Rachael would be so upset if she saw Chaya in this soldier's grips. Not only that, but Chaya did not want to be around anyone who would say such terrible things about Rachael.

"She is coming back," Chaya said. She stopped moving her feet so abruptly that the guard was forced to stop too. "She promised. She's not like the others. She won't be gone."

The guard shook her head. She looked sad.

"No!" Chaya yelled. She had never yelled at anyone before. She stared only at the whip, waiting for the guard to use it on her. "Rachael is not gone. And she is not dead! She told me she wouldn't!" The guard let go of Chaya's arm. Whether she reached for her whip or not, Chaya didn't wait around to see. She sprinted away, running toward the barracks and the bed she shared with Rachael.

Her lungs were burning and her legs felt like they could not go another step, but she ran without looking back at the guard or the gate. She didn't stop until she reached the barracks. She pushed past a few women who were painfully making their way toward the supper queue with their bowls and metal spoons. She scampered, like a frightened squirrel, up the lower bunks and into hers. When she finally stopped, she could not breathe. She also could not think about anything but getting air into her lungs. *In and out,* she thought. She breathed in and out. Rachael had taught her this on the only other night they had been separated. Chaya had cried so much that she was gasping for air. Rachael held her tight and whispered, "In and out. Breathe. In and out."

She lay huddled in a small circle, hugging her knees to her chest, trying to make herself as small as possible. She planned to stay in the bed until Rachael came back. She would live right here. She would not get up to eat or to use the bathroom. She would not wash her face or her hair. She would lay here, just like this, breathing in and out, until Rachael came back. If Rachael knew she was like this, she would come back right away. And all the other women and guards in the camp would see her like this. They would feel so terrible that they would find Rachael, they would tell her, and then Rachael would come back.

She reached into her shoe and pulled out the ring. She put in on her middle finger and repeated these thoughts to herself, spinning it round and round. With the ring in her grasp, Chaya felt sure all would be okay.

Chapter 26

HANNA

Her life seemed to abide by a routine. She refused to call it normalcy, because how could living in a cage, starving, and facing death on a daily basis ever be normal? But she had regularity. She woke up, itching and sore from sleeping on a lice-infested straw mattress in a room with far too many other women. She drank tea made from lukewarm water and tree bark to trick her body into thinking she had the sustenance to keep moving. She worked for ten hours at the hospital, always cleaning after the dead and dying—it was a never-ending job. She sneaked minutes with Samual, either on the street or in their private, little alcove. And she spent hours with the children and Frau Friedl.

Those last two things sustained her more than the inadequate rations ever could. Every time she saw Samual or when she saw a child hold up a drawing with pride in his eyes, she was able to smile. As long as she could find a reason to smile every day, she would survive.

Her stomach seemed to be less bothersome, maybe even fuller, on days like these—the days she was in the small classroom.

"Did you see my picture?" A small boy with a shaved head bounded up to Hanna, excitement radiating off of him. He started to hand her his picture—blue and pink crayon on a bit of browned cardboard—when he noticed Frau Friedl looking over her shoulder with a small smile. Shyness started to overcome his earlier excitement.

"I saw you working hard on it," Hanna encouraged. "Is it a butterfly?"

One bit of praise was all it took for him to turn the picture around, displaying it proudly to both his teachers. His face, grown sallow and thin, lit up.

"Look at mine next," another boy said, trying to elbow his way in front of Hanna and Frau Friedl. "It's a poem. Is that all right?"

"Is that all right?" Frau Friedl sang. "It is *more* than all right. Shall I read it aloud?"

Hanna loved those interactions, but more than that, she loved working with the silent girl with big eyes from the train station. She knew it was against any code of teachers to have a favored pupil, but she couldn't help herself. Catarina was not one with many words or smiles, but Hanna felt when the girl offered either, they were well-earned.

Hanna imagined that even before coming to Terezin, Catarina was a reserved child—serious, responsible, observant. Those were all traits Hanna saw of her, both briefly on the train platform and nowadays in art class. She was slow and precise in her drawing, taking twice as long as the children around her.

Catarina's works were often worth the wait. The child would gather up the scraps of the scraps—the insignificant pieces of paper that the other children overlooked in favor of something bigger, the leftovers from her classmates' works of art, even bits of garbage from the street that she found walking to class. She used these tiniest pieces, these unwanted traces of paper, to create something bigger. After tearing and cutting for almost an hour, using what little color there was and much meticulous placing, Catarina finally showed Hanna the artwork she had created.

Today, her masterpiece made Hanna's eyes fill with tears. It was a mosaic. Each remnant of paper was used to create a group of people—people wearing brown and white and tan clothes, people with long black hair and cropped blond hair, people with blue eyes and brown eyes and one with golden eyes, people holding hands.

"It's us," the girl said quietly in Hanna's ear.

"The art class?" Hanna asked.

Catarina shook her head. "No. Us. All of us. Here and in the world."

"It's everyone? Everyone in the whole world?"

She nodded.

Hanna could do nothing but agree and try to blink away the tears. But the emotion that overtook her seemed to please Catarina, because the girl awarded Hanna with a smile like she had never seen.

With a catch in her throat, Hanna called, "Frau Friedl, have you seen Catarina's piece?"

As expected, the little woman gushed over the picture until Catarina's cheeks flushed red. Catarina left the mosaic with her teachers and returned to her small workspace on the floor. Hanna watched Frau Friedl carefully fold the picture in half and slip it into her pocket. The action was not unusual, as Hanna had seen her do it over and over with the children's work, but after every class, Hanna forgot to ask the teacher what she did with the artwork. They did not hang in the classroom, and the children rarely asked to take them home. There seemed to be an unspoken agreement that the beautiful things belonged in this room and this room only, or with Frau Friedl and Frau Friedl only.

But even with precious moments like this in art class, it got harder and harder for Hanna to find a reason to smile, to keep waking up every day. That's all she wanted from life. But her reasons kept disappearing. More accurately, the people around her kept disappearing. There were more people needing care in the hospital, but none of them seemed to leave to rejoin their loved ones in the land of the living. There were so many dead from sickness and starvation that the cemetery overflowed. The hospital long ago stopped burying the lost souls in coffins. Those who left the world these days did so in the comfort of mass graves or cardboard boxes. Rabbis gave services once a day for those who died the day before. Only family members would attend, for if one attended all the funerals of friends and close acquaintances, there would be no time for anything else.

Handling the daily disappearances was much easier when Hanna was working at the hospital. It was no mystery where these people went. And it was not one by one, but rather people dying by the dozens.

Hanna knew the answers to all the questions—questions such as, why? Why were so many people dying? Because there was no food to sustain their bodies, no warm rooms or clothing to protect from the harsh weather, no medicine to treat even the most common of illnesses, and no care from those in the outside world to change these conditions. The bigger question on the people's minds was, what happened to those who were gone? For the ones Hanna saw losing their fight in the hospital, it was an easy answer. Their souls—those poor, tortured souls on earth—were in a much better place in the heavens. Their bodies—those emaciated remains of what was once a human life—were discarded in any way possible. It was not humane, but life in Terezin was anything but humane. It was survival.

The ones who disappeared but did not die were harder to understand. Why were they gone? Where had they gone? Were they still of this earth or buried in a shallow grave just paces outside of the city walls? There were multitudes of rumors, but no answers.

Oftentimes, the people disappeared in the night. One day they were in the queue for their daily slice of stale bread, and the next, their small cot was assigned to new arrival. As Hanna had yet to see a set of Nazi boots inside the cage of Terezin, she often wondered about how these disappearances took place. Though she hated to talk of these real-life horrors when she escaped reality in Samual's arms, she had to ask.

He shook his head sadly. "The orders come from the Judenrat."

"I thought those leaders were meant to make our lives better," she said. "Didn't the Judenrat set up the children's art classes? And the music lessons? And the small garden on the south side of town?"

Samual nodded. "It's complicated."

Hanna felt blood rush to her cheeks. She found her temper rose very easily since coming to this place. "I do not see how it is," she said, angrier than she intended. She missed her old, easygoing nature like she missed seeing the pastels of her beloved Prague. But as with both, nothing was to be done about it. "Stealing people out of their homes, sending them who knows where, is the opposite of helping us. The Nazis are not here, but those men let them continue to rule over us."

Samual sat up on his elbows, his head barely grazing the slope of the attic roof. "They are not here visibly, but the Nazis are everywhere. They put the Judenrat in an impossible situation. 'Give us one hundred names,' they say. 'Give us one hundred names, or we'll shoot two hundred people.' So the Judenrat gives them one hundred to save another one hundred." He paused and lay back down, sighing heavily. "But save another one hundred for what? None of us seem to know."

"To live," Hanna said. "Right?"

Samual gave her a half smile. "Right. They can't kill us all." Hanna smiled at his words, because they were just a joke between them at this point. She was no longer sure even Samual still believed that.

That was exactly what the rumors said though—that, in fact, the Nazis were killing all of the Jews. It was known that those families who disappeared were told to pack their belongings, as they were headed east.

East. David's last words still rang clearly in Hanna's head. *"Don't go east."* Those words, paired with Samual's, were a chorus running through her mind—never changing, always looping. *"Don't go east." "They can't kill us all."* A harmony of contradictions. The refrain of those words did not change, but the song seemed never-ending.

People were loaded onto trains like cattle, taken to the middle of a field, and shot in the head.

Families were forced to dig their own graves before being cut down by machine gun fire.

There were camps set up for Jews in the East.

Camps better than Terezin.

Camps far worse than Terezin.

Camps where families were reunited.

Camps that made Terezin look like Eden in God's own image.

People were burned alive.

Men were forced to fight the Allied soldiers on the side of the Germans.

Women became slaves to the depraved desires of the Nazis.

Over and over and over. The rumors were never-ending, always changing.

The only thing Hanna knew for certain was that people were one day here and the next day gone. Their only trace might be a small pink slip of paper that held their orders to pack up and be ready for the next train out of Terezin.

It seemed the Nazis were intent on killing every part of the Jewish people, without even setting foot inside the walls of this caged city. Hunger preyed on their bodies. Unanswered questions feasted on their minds. And the loss of all joy and hope destroyed their souls.

That was how Hanna felt as she walked to the small office that had become a safe haven of art, creativity, and freedom for her and the children. On that day, though, a member of the Jewish Council was standing in front of the door. His eyes were sad, but his body barred the way into the classroom with determination.

"Art class is no longer allowed," he said simply.

"By whose order?" Hanna demanded.

"It is no longer allowed."

"We were given permission by the Judenrat," Hanna continued to argue. "And they were given permission by the Nazis, as we know they decide nothing for themselves." She stared coldly at the man.

He sighed—Hanna sensed regret behind it—but, then, he straightened back up, arms crossing over his chest. "Art class is no longer allowed."

The children were starting to crowd around Hanna, trying to get a glimpse of the confrontation, trying to understand why they were no longer allowed this one place of brightness and security.

Hanna knew she should stop. She knew no good could come of this argument, but her blood pressure was rising, and her heart was breaking, not just for the children, but for her own peace of mind. She could not hear the confused chatter of the children around her anymore, only her own hot blood pulsing in her ears.

She leaned close to the man, hoping only he would hear her snarled insults. "You sniveling, cowardly, poor excuse—"

"Hanna!" Frau Freidl called her name with the same ring she would use to amicably ask for the children's attention. "Hanna!" she said again with a smile of false cheer. "Is there a problem?" She nodded respectfully to the man as she took her place beside Hanna, linking their arms. She smiled kindly at the man from the Jewish Council. "I'm Frau Friedl Brandeis. I teach this art class. How may I help you?"

The man nodded curtly at Frau Freidl, obviously not trusting her show of good spirit. "The art class is no longer allowed."

Hanna took a menacing step toward the man. "If you repeat yourself again, I'm going to scream," she said. Frau Friedl continued to smile at him, while pulling Hanna back to her side.

"This is by order of the Judenrat?" she asked. Hanna was surprised she was able to keep the accusation out of her question.

"It is."

"Of course." She gave the man a slight bow. "We understand." She turned, still holding Hanna's arm tightly, and faced the children. "There is no more art class, children." Her voice still held its normal, bright tone. The children looked crestfallen, and Hanna would have released her rage on the man behind her if Frau Friedl were not still holding on to her. But the art teacher gave the children a big smile. "Not to worry, little ones. Not to worry. Now, off to your homes."

With that, she led Hanna away from the heartbroken children and the office that had been their classroom.

"Why did you just let that man dismiss our class?" Hanna asked. "You just walked away. You *smiled*." She tried to keep the accusation out of her voice but did not think she accomplished it well.

Frau Friedl, still smiling that serene smile, squeezed her arm. "Shhh," she whispered.

With nothing but trust to hold on to, Hanna followed Frau Friedl through Terezin.

They finally stopped in front of the small, fenced-off garden in the center of the city. Hanna had stopped walking past this place months ago. It was torturous for her to see a sweet little escape inside the caged walls and not be allowed to enter. They did not go in, but stood together, enjoying the view of green—a small patch of grass, lilies of the valley growing wildly to the side like ground cover.

"I would never give up on the children," Frau Friedl said. Her voice was sterner than Hanna even though possible.

"Of course, Frau. I never thought . . ."

"You did. For a minute." Frau Friedl looked at Hanna and relented with a small smile. "But if I fooled you, I certainly fooled the Judenrat." Her smile grew. "And then they will fool the Nazis."

Hanna let out a breath of relief. Knowing Frau Friedl would fight back was a tremendous comfort to her. "What do we do now?"

"Teach the children, of course," she said, "as we have always done. They cannot stop us."

With that, Hanna and Frau Freidl plotted to continue their lessons and to continue giving as much solace to the children as possible through art and free expression. Their work was too important, and Frau Freidl, Hanna soon learned, was not someone to back down from doing what was right. She simply put on her same serene smile and continued moving forward.

With so many families leaving Terezin alive or otherwise, it was not difficult to find an empty room. They set up a new classroom in a vacated two-bedroom apartment in the same building where Frau

Friedl lived. The new space seemed like a luxury. It was much larger than the old classroom, and it had three windows, letting in the sunshine of the season. With more space and, sadly, fewer students, the children were able to spread out and stretch their cramped limbs while working on their masterpieces.

Since Frau Friedl did not want anyone to suspect the class was still in session, she never kept a schedule. She would walk the streets on the morning of a class until she found a student. Then, like a giant game of telephone, the children would pass the message one by one until class began in the afternoon. Spreading word of the upcoming lesson came to be the children's favorite part. She also noticed that their faces were brighter, stronger, maybe even happier with the idea that they were deceiving the Germans. They were breaking the rules. They were resisting.

The joy of fighting back continued to give Hanna just one more reason to smile throughout the day. She would hold back a smug grin as she walked to class on those appointed afternoons, but her smile quickly faded when she entered the classroom and found one less child had arrived, as seemed to happen every time.

She was happy she had never used that precious piece of paper from Samual to draw the children in the art classroom. She knew if she had, each day she would have to erase one face, two faces, three faces from the picture. It was just a matter of time until there would be no more faces left. Or she would not be around to do the erasing. Every day, there were more and more pink slips being brought into the classroom to be used as scraps, and every day there were more and more children disappearing from the ghetto.

Once Hanna said something to a child who brought in such a slip of paper. She thought it disrespectful to use it for art. But the child, a small boy of about twelve, saw it differently.

"I shouldn't use the paper?" he asked. Instead of being hardened by this life, he was being whittled down like a piece of black poplar.

"How do you think your friend would feel?" she asked him.

He smiled at this. "Like he's a part of my art forever."

She could not argue with that.

No one in the room spoke of their diminishing numbers. If there was an unfinished work of art, another child would pick it up and continue the work, knowing how their friend intended it to end. Hanna remembered back to her girlhood years, when she loved to set out small scraps for the stray cats. After a few weeks, though, she noticed that the bowl was overflowing with food, as the cats no longer came around to feast. Soon, Hanna thought, there would be enough art supplies for all the children.

She said a small prayer of thanks every time Catarina arrived for class. Hanna felt relief, but also guilt, overwhelm her each time she opened the door of the apartment that doubled as their art studio and saw Catarina there with her round eyes, watching the other children, waiting with her small hands folded in her lap. The girl still did not say much, but Hanna would find a reason to be near her before the end of class. Each time, Hanna would sneak her a small portion of her rationed food or some small treat Samual had managed to smuggle into the ghetto. The girl would never speak her thanks, but her eyes expressed more gratitude than her words ever could.

Hanna wanted to walk the child home. She wanted to meet her mother, maybe even meet the baby, who was surely born by now. She wanted to hold the girl's hand and fill up those big eyes with hugs and love and words of encouragement. But Hanna knew the dangers of getting attached. Day after day, there were fewer children to teach and to love. So she held her feelings in but could not help but pray that someday, she would teach an art class with both Catarina and her baby sibling. What a sad world it was where this was the measure of her happiness—staying alive in Terezin just to see this girl and her family grow up.

Hanna realized her hubris as soon as she saw the paper. She had watched people at the hospital die and families all around her disappear.

She worried constantly over the fates of those who left without explanation, but she rarely worried for herself. As she walked to her small cot in the women's dormitory, the feeling that overcame her when she saw the pink slip of paper was not terror, but amusement. She laughed loud enough for the other women in the room to look at her with concern. And they should be concerned for her, Hanna thought, for she had just received her orders to go east.

Chapter 27

CHAYA

She stayed in bed for a full day. In the beginning, her mind never stopped and she could not lie still. Her fingers played as if they were in charge of her body; her legs kicked without her willing them to. She wanted to stay in a tight ball until Rachael came for her, but her arms hurt from hugging her knees too tight and her back cramped from curving around her legs for long hours. But by the time she missed the second day's dinner queue, she found it easier to lie still, close her eyes, and think of nothing. All desire to play flew out her head like the birds Rachael said soared over the sea. She wanted to make everyone sorry. *Everyone.* Rachael for not coming back yet, the other women in the camp for letting Rachael go, the guards for taking her away. But as time went on, she found it hard to keep her eyes open. Had her eyelids ever felt so heavy? Had it ever felt so nice to let them close and let the darkness come in? Maybe she would never get up. From how tired her entire body felt, she didn't think she would have the strength to.

She was the middle of a thick darkness—more than sleep—when she felt a gentle shaking of her shoulder.

"Rachael . . ." she whispered. She did not have the energy to open her eyes, but the corners of her mouth turned upwards—an involuntary smile.

The hand shook her again. She used all her strength to open her eyes for a moment. A woman was standing on the lower bunk, looking into her face and shaking her awake.

"Rachael," she said again.

"No, dear," a familiar voice said. "No, not Rachael."

Chaya closed her eyes again. She only wanted her missing Rachael.

"Child. Chaya," the voice tried again. She recognized it now as Irene, the woman whom Rachael always scowled at, but Chaya liked. "You must wake up and eat something. When is the last time you ate?"

She tried to roll away from Irene but found she did not have the power. Irene shook her harder.

This time, she opened her eyes. Irene held up a bowl with a spoon.

"Eat, my dear. You need to eat something."

Chaya shook her head. "I'm waiting for Rachael," she whispered.

Irene started to rub Chaya's shoulder and arm, just as Rachael did each night before falling asleep. "You can't wait for Rachael like this. You need to eat. You need to be strong. It's what she wanted for you."

She closed her eyes again. She could almost hear Rachael telling her to eat. She never smiled so prettily as when Chaya ate, especially when she ate from Rachael's bowl. But not eating would really show her—nothing would upset Rachael more. If she knew how weak and sad Chaya was, she would never stay away.

She tried to roll over again, but only had the strength to turn her face away.

Irene shook Chaya once, roughly, like a guard would. "Eat." She sounded angry. Chaya looked at her again. It was not often people were angry with her. "Rachael gave everything she had for you. This is not how you repay her."

That made sense. Rachael *had* given everything she had, even the ring, before she was marched off by the Nazis. The ring was everything.

Did Rachael want her to stay strong to protect it so she could give it back when she returned?

Chaya got out of bed and ate the bowl of soup.

She woke up the next morning and attended roll call.

She ate the food given to her. She met a nice woman who scooped the ladle into the pot of soup and then into Chaya's bowl. When she saw Chaya, she would smile, put her finger to her lips as if she was telling a great secret, and give Chaya an extra spoonful.

Chaya rarely played in the barracks but spent most of her days wandering the camp, sneaking into corners to avoid the guards. As much as she wanted to punish everyone for keeping Rachael away, she did not know how to mope or pout. Her body wanted to live even if she did not. Her heart wanted to keep beating even though there was nothing worth it beating for.

She noticed life in the camp was changing, and not just for her. It reminded her of the endings of the bedtime stories Rachael used to tell. Chaya could sense when the story was nearing the end. She would get excited, with a nervous energy, wanting Rachael to talk faster, speed it up, so she could know how it ended. But she would also feel sad. This story was ending. Would the next one be as good? Would there even be a next one? That's how the camp felt to her these weeks and months without Rachael.

Some of the prisoners seemed to be looking for the ending of the story, too. Chaya saw many of them look up to the sky and whisper to one another. "The guards can't hurt us anymore," they said. "They are more scared of us than we are of them."

Chaya asked the soup lady what was in the sky, because when she looked up, she didn't see anything. "Hope," the woman responded. "Keep watching. There's hope up there."

She was not the only one who couldn't see this hope in the clouds. Other prisoners whispered, "If the Allies get any closer, they'll kill all of us just to take out the Nazis."

Chaya did not know what the Allies were. She guessed that they must have been the ones in the sky with the hope.

It was the guards who seemed most changed. If this was one of Rachael's stories, they would have been under some sort of magical spell. Some of them walked through the camp like they were still asleep. Some were openly kind. The guard with the bullwhip, whom Chaya saw more and more often, started offering small bits of food to prisoners.

One afternoon, that guard found Chaya stretching between two barracks. She was lying on her back, toes pointed and arms above her head, trying to cover the ground between the two buildings like a bridge. She didn't notice the guard until she was blocking Chaya's view of the sky and the still unseen Allies' hope. Chaya sat up quickly, preparing to run away, but the guard placed her hand on the girl's shoulder.

"I brought you something, child," she said. It was strange to hear nice words coming from this gruff woman. It was as if an evil queen had the voice of a small field mouse. Chaya smiled at the thought. "Yes, little one," the guard said. "A treat. Isn't that nice?"

Chaya nodded and accepted the small brown square that the guard handed her.

"Chocolate," she explained. "I bet it's been a long time since you had chocolate."

Chaya remembered the name of the treat but could not think if she ever had a piece of her own. She took a nibble and smiled.

"Yes," the guard smiled and nodded. "I'm Elke," she said. "What's your name?"

"Chaya."

"Lovely. Chaya, remember, I'm Elke. Remember what a nice treat this is."

Not all the guards acted like Elke. Some seemed to have gotten even meaner. Instead of treats for the prisoners, they only had the quick pull of the trigger. More and more people died and disappeared. One night, an entire barrack full of people was gone. Chaya heard the other prisoners talk about the gas chambers. She knew such places were true. She saw the smokestacks puff out black clouds for three full days after those people were gone.

Chaya just waited. She waited for Rachael to come back. She waited for someone to tell her what to do or where to go. She could see the story of Auschwitz was ending, but she did not know what that meant. Would she be gone or dead like so many others? Would she be free? That was another word that was thrown around the camp more and more. She had no idea what it meant.

She still walked to the gates every morning to watch the workers trudge out to their assignments and every evening to see if Rachael was finally in the long line of those returning. The guards in the towers no longer paid her any attention. She could get close enough to the fence to hear it humming with electricity. The fence, though, even seemed to have lost its energy to continue on as before. More and more often, it had no song for her.

Chaya wanted to tell Rachael everything—the games she played, the places in which she hid, the whispers she overheard. She created a new game to help her remember the growing list of things for when Rachael came back. Chaya could now fit two fingers inside the ring. She would twist it with every memory she recalled in her mind.

Some prisoners escaped from the fence but were brought back and beaten to death in the prison yard. Twist.

The pretty lady in the supper queue gave her three bites of real meat the other day. She told her that she used to be an art teacher. Twist.

The barrack two buildings down from their own was emptied and all the people still inside loaded into those big trucks. Twist.

This is what had her distracted on the day her own barrack was cleared and she experienced her second ride in the truck—trying to twist and remember everything she needed to tell Rachael.

It happened so fast that she did not have time to be frightened. She was sitting in the far corner, on the dirt floor. The soft moans and coughs of the women still in bed even though the sun was high in the sky had become background noise. She barely heard them anymore. She was imagining the conversation she would have with Rachael when she returned, smiling at the thought of staying up all night whispering with their faces so close they were almost touching. She twisted the ring around her two fingers. It was no longer the sparkling treasure that Rachael had dropped at her feet months ago. Chaya's fingers had left bits of dirt in the fancy design on the sides. Instead of sparkling silver, the sides of the ring reminded her of the bare, tangled branches of the small bushes at the edges of the fence. When Rachael had the ring, everything about it—the diamond, the blue stones on the corners, the little gems lining the edges—was like bright springtime. Under Chaya's care, the ring looked like cold winter.

She felt the air change in the barracks before she heard the shouts of the guards. The door swung open and the breeze blew in, followed by the soldiers. She had nowhere to run and nowhere to hide. She had played enough games to know when she had lost, or when the game had fizzled to an end. Instead of trying to duck under the closest bunk, she tucked the ring back into her oversized slipper, letting it slide down her ankle and settle beneath her heel, and walked to the soldier by the door.

Her second ride in the truck was not very different from her first. Just like when she was driven away from the farmhouse, she finally saw the place where she had lived but never truly seen. The day she left the farmhouse in the Nazis' truck was the first time she had seen the land in all its glory. She kept the picture of the pretty little farmhouse with its matching barn in her mind all this time. She saw the green of the cow pastures and the yard in front of the house where Ilse and Ingrid picked tomatoes. It was as beautiful as she had imagined, except for the figures of Ilse, Ingrid, and their papa lying in the grass leaking red. Just like during that ride, Chaya knew something bad was happening. When she left the farmhouse, she knew the family was dead, but she was going somewhere new. And that new place turned out to be somewhere she did not have to hide in the dark among the jars and vegetables. She felt the wind on her face and moving her hair for the first time, and she breathed in fresh air. Was this happiness?

She had the same jumbled feeling as she rode on this truck, watching the camp where she had been held a prisoner get further away. She knew they were headed to the furnaces and the chimneys that blew dark, choking smoke into the sky. She knew that people went there to die. But it was where Rachael had gone, where Rachael still might be, and she had the wind in her face and ruffling her hair. There was no fresh air to be had, as it became thicker and thicker as they neared those smokestacks, but the sun was shining, and she was free from the barbed wire fence. Was this happiness again?

Until she moved her gaze from the prison camp, which was now blocked by other buildings, she did not even notice the other women. They didn't seem to feel the way she did about riding in the truck. Many were crying, but without sound, except for a few who sniffled. Their faces reminded her of the floor of the cellar, striped with daylight, as the tears cleaned a path down their cheeks.

The truck stopped outside a short building with no windows. It looked like it would be much warmer inside a building like that but not as fun to play. The sun had no big spaces to peek through. This place, despite its lack of windows, looked more inviting than most places Chaya had been to before. Trees and small shrubs surrounded the building and dotted the grounds. It was the middle of winter, so there were no leaves, but the branches reached out to her, the wind tangling their skinny limbs—she could stare at the bare trees for hours, getting lost in their maze. But there was no time for that. The people in the truck were quickly herded from the open bed into the building's enclosed walls.

"The death block . . ." the woman next to Chaya whispered. Then the woman's breaths became fast, and her legs seemed to stop working. Chaya jumped down from the truck, but the woman did not move. A soldier gave her a shove that sent her flying from the back of the truck, landing hard on her face. When two other guards lifted her up by the arms, the gray snow beneath her had turned a dark red. Chaya kept walking, following the train of people into the windowless building.

She had heard all the things people said about this place. When she was in the barracks, she was invisible to most people, so it was easy to hear their whisperings. She usually did not understand what she heard, but Rachael would explain what she could later in the night. Chaya knew this short, little building was not a good place to be. She felt it when she set foot into the room lined with cots. She was always hesitant about any place where the daylight could not shine through, but it was more than the darkness. There was a sadness in this place. Chaya knew the smell of blood. She also knew the smell of sadness. It was thick and wet—like the tears that ran down her face at night when she wished for Rachael to come back.

She found the bed in the farthest corner. She huddled herself into a ball, hugging her knees tightly to her chest, and waited for the long night to end. She tried to sleep, but her thoughts kept returning to Rachael, as they usually did. Did Rachael come here? Did she sleep in this same bed, waiting for the morning light and thinking about Chaya? Was she as scared? The longer the night wore on, the darker it got, the more Chaya was sure she knew the answers to those questions. Yes. Yes, Rachael had been here. But where was she now?

Chaya was relieved when, hours later, two guards opened the door, letting the morning light in, turning the black of the small room into dim gray. Unlike the guards during morning roll call, these used gentler voices.

"Everyone up," the first guard called. He clapped his hands twice. "Up. Wake up."

His calls were not needed. Chaya didn't think anyone had slept. The room was quiet, besides the noises from the guards. No one seemed to have any tears left.

"Into the shower room," the guard said. "That's it. Stay in line."

Maybe she still knew nothing of the world, but she was not fooled by this game of pretend the Nazis were playing. She knew what was in that room. It was the room of gone and dead, but it was nice to have the guards speak kindly. They spoke softly, even gently. Chaya had never seen soldiers act like this—friendly almost. For the first time since she saw the Nazis through the cracks in the cellar ceiling, she realized that inside each brown uniform was a real person. Did this soldier have three children like Ingrid, Ilse, and Erich? Did that soldier have a pretty wife at home waiting with a warm supper every night like Mama did when Papa came in from the fields at dusk?

As each person filed out of the barrack, a guard stood on either side of the door. They handed each prisoner a small piece of soap and a towel. The soap in Chaya's hand was dry. The soap given to her at the farmhouse was always soft. She loved to squeeze it in her hand and see it squish out of her fist. This soap did not slip or squish but flaked into her palm when she squeezed it. This soap had not been used in ages.

Chaya followed the line of prisoners out of the building, past the guards, across a small path to the showers. She only had a moment to glance up from the shoes in front of her to see the growth of the small shrubs lining the buildings. She sighed with disappointment; she would have loved to see the bushes all green instead of this twiggy brown of winter. She was ushered into a small room with benches in the middle of the floor. The men in their group had been separated to another room.

The small room in which Chaya found herself was white—white walls, white floors, white lights. The wooden benches in the middle looked more comfortable than the barrack bunk she had shared with Rachael. There were hooks—also painted white—all around the walls. On the far end of the room was another door. It was cracked open.

As was her habit, Chaya moved deep into the room, into the corner farthest from the entrance. She wanted to push herself into the corner until she blended into the wall. She wanted to feel the two cold walls press against her shoulders to know she was sheltered by these solid structures. But she was unable to camouflage herself in this room. The dirty gray of her dress stood out against the clean brightness of the walls. No one could disappear in this room.

After the women filed into the small room—some sitting on the benches with their backs perfectly straight, most standing against the wall—two soldiers commanded them to undress.

"Clothes off," the first one said, continuing his calm instructions. "Hang your clothes on these hooks." He gestured to them. "Then you can get them when you come out of the shower."

Chaya was not fooled, nor did she think anyone else was. They would not be returning to this room.

From her corner, she continued to try to melt into the walls around her. She watched the other women slowly disrobe. The younger women, those who still had some brightness in their eyes, tried to cover their nakedness from the soldiers who were pacing the room. The older women, those who seemed already dead or gone, had no shyness. They undressed and stood like statues awaiting the next order. From her corner, Chaya could see into the other room, where the next order would lead them.

Chaya had only ever showered one other time in her life—upon arriving at Auschwitz. She was so new to the world and to life in the prison camp back then that she did not even know to be terrified of what might come out of the silver contraption overhead. That time, it was water, not poisonous gas. The water was so cold though that it felt like fire. And just like a fire, the freezing water left red marks all over her skin where it hit her. In her shock, Chaya froze. It earned her the first slap in the face that she would receive in Auschwitz. That, too, confused her. What was this place where cold burned like fire and little girls were hit for standing still?

The second soldier came right up to her.

"Undress!" he said. He glared at her, his eyes threatening.

She slowly started to undress, still looking into the shower room. She could see the silver faucets where water was to come out, and there were drains scattered around the floor. It looked cold to Chaya—cold tile, cold water. As she peered closer, she noticed that while the walls were clean, there were scratches on the tile throughout the shower room. Chaya shuddered. It looked as if a monster had tried to claw its way out. Or that a monster had been let in with the people.

The soldier nudged Chaya was his gun again. He dug it into her ribs. "Move," he told her.

She leaned into the corner of the dressing room and lifted her left foot up. She started to take off the shoe. She felt the ring shift under her heel, still held firmly in place by the large slipper Rachael had given her months ago. The Nazis had not bothered to search the prisoners before sending them to the death block. Chaya was happy the Germans did not yet have this ring, but she realized she had no one to pass it on to.

In that instant, she understood everything Rachael had done for her, but also everything that Rachael had hoped for her. Rachael had wanted Chaya to live. She had wanted Chaya to remember her, to remember all the things she taught her, the recipes she recited to her, the stories of her family. If Chaya lived, then Rachael would always live. And not only Rachael, but those she loved—Alexey, Radek, Catarina, and the little baby. If Chaya lived, when she held the ring Rachael left to her, she would remember everything, and Rachael would always be with her, just like she promised.

Chaya also knew in that moment that she was going to die. She placed her hands over her ears and closed her eyes. She could see what was going to happen: the guards were going to herd her and everyone else into that shower room. They were going to close the door, lock it. The people were going to become monsters as thick, white gas was pumped in through the showerheads. They were going to scream and wail and push each other and scratch like animals at the door and walls, trying to escape. There would be no escape. The gas would fill the room, then fill their lungs. Chaya would gasp and gasp for air but only gulp down more and more poison, until her eyes popped out and her lungs burst.

She had felt loneliness—loneliness probably more than any other feeling in her life. She had also felt fear and worry. Knowing, right now, that she was going to die was a whole new feeling. She was sad for herself. She still wanted to see the sea. She wanted to see the green leaves and colorful blossoms on the trees outside. And if she died in that shower room, burned in the furnaces next door, no one would ever know that she had lived, that Rachael had lived, that her family had ever lived.

But she was ready for the gas, too. She was not strong enough to do what Rachael had wanted. She could not win this game and was ready to give up. She pushed herself out of the tight corner of the dressing room and took her first step toward the door of the shower room. In the moment that she did so, the floor lurched under her feet and threw her back to the wall. Noise ripped through the dressing room. Crashes and explosions and wrenching metal and screams of terror rang all around her. The building shook, the lights flickered. Then it went dark.

Chapter 28

HANNA

When the truth of that paper finally registered, she panicked. She had always hoped when the time of crisis came, she would face it with courage and grace. That little scrap of paper showed her the true make-up of her character, and she was ashamed. Stricken by panic, she grabbed the orders of her departure in two days' time and ran from the building.

She was just learning what it meant to fight back. While her work with Frau Friedl and the children may not have been the same as killing Germans on the front lines, she knew it was important and unfinished. She needed to stay in Terezin—not just for her own survival, but for the fight, for the art classes, for the idea of standing up for what one believes in. These were her thoughts as she ran through the streets, searching for something she was sure she wouldn't find—safety.

She was out of breath and her legs burned from the exertion. Months and months of near starvation did not allow for the energy Hanna needed to escape her fear. Her short run took her to the small park—gated and closed off from the people of the ghetto. She leaned against the waist-high fence, catching her breath and letting the tears of frustration and fear wash down her face. In Prague, a garden like this, with its flowers and sculptures, would have soothed her troubled soul. But the Nazis had taken even that appreciation for beauty from her. She wanted to rage—to scream and cry and hit something. Did she have nothing left?

Of course she did. She was ashamed to have not thought of it immediately. Even prior to coming to Terezin, her safety and security were rarely found in a place, but with a person. She needed Samual. He would be able to help her.

Hanna invoked the children's telephone system to help her find him. He often spent time with the children of the ghetto, talking with them, encouraging them, helping out in the small homes as the building commando was allowed. With his ties to the leadership of the ghetto, Hanna was sure he would be able to help. Samual would be able to lean on a contact in the Judenrat to get her removed from the deportation list.

She was pacing the street outside of her dormitory when he approached. She had crumpled the pink slip of paper so much, the words were barely legible. He said nothing but grasped her shoulders to stop her from walking further. He crushed her into his chest, wrapping his arms around her. She was surprised by his strength. Though he held her during their stolen nights in the attic, it had been a long time since she felt his arms hold her with power. Where nourishment had failed him, it seemed his passion and concern strengthened him. The embrace took the breath out of her, yet she felt like she could breathe for the first time since seeing the deportation order. They stood in the street, as one, for many minutes.

"I can fix this," he whispered into her ear. Hanna tried to shake her head in doubt, but her whole body was still crushed into Samual's. He must have felt her effort because he repeated his words. "I can. I can fix this."

With those words, Hanna felt hope enter her, buoying her as she was drowning in despair. It was enough to bring her out of the rolling waves of sadness. She believed him.

"I'm so sorry, love, but I need your ring."

Hanna gasped. Her impulse was to pull away and say no. The engagement ring he gave her—it felt like centuries ago now—was her only tie to their former life. Samual told her once that it reminded him of Prague. She had loved him even more for saying that. The ring reminded her of everything before Terezin. It was long walks around the city, looking at the architecture for the thousandth time, but seeing something new in it; it was the old familiar customers at Prague Kofe; it was evenings in Samual's apartment with David and Werner and Greta, all of them smoking cheap cigarettes. It was hope and life and beauty.

The impulse to protect it was gone in a minute. She was not the same girl who had been given this ring. Now she was a woman who could not afford sentimentality and vanity. She understood that he needed bargaining power. Though his position with the building commando may be one of prestige, when all was said and done, everyone answered to the Nazis. He could use the ring to bribe someone to get her off the list. Or they would use the ring to bribe a more powerful someone. She wordlessly nodded her assent into Samual's shoulder.

Samual held her even tighter for a moment before releasing her. He steadied her as she took off her shoe and removed the ring from under her sole. Her socks had long ago worn too thin to keep wearing, and they were never replaced. Even her toes had lost the plumpness to hold the ring in place as she walked, so it would roll around as she walked to the ration line, to art class, and to the small attic to meet Samual.

He kissed her forehead and walked away without a word, taking with him her little relief of hope. It left her body as she exhaled and watched his back disappear down the street.

♦

It hurt Samual a little that she gave the ring up so easily. They both knew it was the practical thing to do, but he had turned into a man who believed in symbols. This ring was a symbol of everything. He was appalled at first when she showed him she still had it—that she had taken such a huge risk in smuggling a diamond ring into a place like this, where it was of no value to her. Not only was it of no value, but having it was extremely dangerous. Every day that she kept it in her shoe was another day she could be caught. But as things got worse and worse in Terezin—the place became more and more crowded with Jews, the people went longer and longer without food—Samual became proud of Hanna and her small act of defiance. She would not let the Nazis take this one thing from her, this one thing that Samual had given to her to prove his love. Yet today, she handed it over to him wordlessly. He knew it was silly to be saddened by her practicality, but all he wanted to do was hand the ring back to her. It was hers. It was theirs. It was not the Germans'.

He had intended to bribe an official with the ring. He knew it was a risk. They could both end up on the next train east just for being in possession of such a thing. At first thought, though, it seemed like his only option. As he continued to think about it, getting past the initial shock of Hanna's pink slip of paper, he knew he could come up with a better way.

Samual was never one for surprises or grand gestures. It seemed like a lifetime ago that he planned the perfect moment to present Hanna with this diamond engagement ring. Although she said yes and was wearing the ring by the end of the night, he couldn't say that his plan had been a success. It was funny to remember how he had needed everything to be perfect—the restaurant, the words, the motions. He was a different man now. He didn't need perfection; he just needed the diamond ring back on Hanna's finger and her by his side.

He took his idea to Rabbi Leo, the head of the Judenrat and a man he had come to respect during their time at Terezin. Samual received a degree of protection, being part of the building commando. The Nazis had broken many of the promises they made to the men who first came to Terezin to build it up for the rest of the people, but thus far, the majority of them had remained safe from deportation. *They, and their families,* Samual noted. From the moment Samual had seen his future in the facets of the diamond ring outside the shop window on Celetna Street, he knew Hanna was his family. She was more than that. She was the family he had chosen. It was time to make it so in the presence of God, their people, and their persecutors.

He would marry her. Tonight.

Samual expected a small wedding—he, Hanna, and Rabbi Leo. No more was needed to make it official. If they said the vows and signed the marriage certificate tonight, Rabbi Leo would be able to present it to the Germans tomorrow, with plenty of time to remove Hanna's name from the deportation list. But Rabbi Leo insisted on more.

"It should be a true celebration—a wedding between two people who love each other. Love," Rabbi Leo said, "is life. And the people of Terezin need life."

That's how Samual found himself planning the biggest surprise and grandest gesture of his life. The irony struck him immediately: in a place where survival was everyone's biggest, and often only, concern, he was attempting to surprise Hanna with a romantic wedding. He enlisted the remaining children in Terezin. The children knew Hanna from the art lessons, and Samual had been working with many of them since the beginning. They trusted him and loved Hanna. Getting them to help was the easy part.

By nightfall, Samual had a wedding ceremony ready for his unsuspecting bride. There was a small gathering behind the bakery—a scarce yard that was often used as a secret synagogue. Many of the children had gathered with what remained of their families. Rabbi Leo had informed some of Samual's fellow building commando friends, and Frau Freidl stood near the front. She had worked with a few other artists in town to create a quick *chuppah*.

In another life, he and Hanna would have laughed over the sorry-looking chuppah—the blessed item that was to represent the new home they were creating with this marriage. It should have been a freestanding structure adorned with lilies of the valley and white roses, like Samual knew Hanna would have preferred. Instead, it comprised four mismatched poles. Two, Samual was sure, were broken off of an old wooden chair. The people who were tasked with holding those corners would have to keep their arms stretched over their heads so the fabric on top would clear the couple's heights. The front two corners of the chuppah were united with a thin cloth—maybe an old curtain, Samual guessed. Frau Friedl and her artist friends had quickly painted a scene on the sheer fabric—stars, a moon, whisps of wind. It reminded Samual of the night sky painting by Van Gogh in Hanna's art books. The cloth was not large enough to drape over the four poles, so to complete the chuppah, Frau Friedl had hung two dark blue overcoats on the remaining poles. When Samual looked questioningly at the unconventional canopy, she smiled and shrugged.

"I thought Hanna would appreciate the effort to at least match the colors," she said.

"I have no doubt Hanna will appreciate all of it," Samual said. He did not know how to express his gratitude, but the woman with large brown eyes seemed to understand.

Other than the chuppah and the small crowd gathered in the makeshift, outdoor synagogue, there was little to show that this was a wedding ceremony. But Samual did not mind. There were people, many strangers, with joyful smiles, and some even with tears in their eyes. And soon, Hanna would be there. Some of the students from the art class offered to bring her to the space behind the bakery. Samual wished he could have surprised her with so much more than this—a clean dress, perhaps, or even fragrant flowers to carry down the aisle. None of those things were to be had, but he still had the diamond and sapphire ring in his pocket. Soon it would be back on Hanna's finger, and she would be by his side, not on her way to the terrifying, unknown East.

Hanna arrived as the sun began to set behind the squat buildings of Terezin. Its bright summer shine had transitioned into a warm glow of orange and red. It softened the brown of the dirt beneath their feet and shadowed Rabbi Leo standing underneath the chuppah.

As Samual expected, the surprise of the wedding was given away when the excited children found Hanna. She had run the whole way to the bakery with four children trailing her like the wedding train she would never wear. She arrived breathless and grinning. A few curls had worked their way loose of the knot she wore, framing her smile. The curls were not the glossy ones that Samual had first noted at Prague Kofe, but the smile was the same. It was a smile of complete happiness that he hadn't seen since their carefree days in the city.

She paused at the beginning of the small aisle that was formed simply by the group of attendees parting like the Red Sea. If Samual hadn't started walking toward her, he thought she would have run down the aisle to him instead of taking her time with the traditional wedding march to the chuppah.

He pulled her to the back wall of the bakery and the nearby people looked away, giving them some semblance of privacy.

"Perhaps I should have asked you," he said with a grin. Hanna was still smiling that true smile he used to know so well. Tears were in her eyes. "Will you marry me?"

"I believe you already asked," she said playfully. "And I believe I already said yes."

Samual nodded in agreement. "True. Then let me phrase it this way: will you marry me today?"

"I would have married you yesterday," she said.

It was Samual's turn to feel his eyes prickle with tears. "I have to tell you," he said, whispering now, dropping all teasing tones, "this isn't because of your deportation. Well, it is. Our marriage will make you ineligible for deportation because you'll be the wife of a building commando member. But it's not just that."

"I know, love," she said softly, placing her hand on Samual's arm.

"You probably do know, but I have to say it," he continued. "I want to marry you because I love you more than life itself. And because you're the most beautiful"—she scoffed at this, but he continued—"woman I've ever known. And because you're kind and brave and . . ."

She stopped him with a kiss. "I know, love."

"Then let's get married."

"Finally."

Samual could not imagine a more beautiful bride as they began the marriage ceremony. Hanna looked as she had since coming to Terezin—exhausted with dark circles under her eyes; hair limp and dull, falling out of what used to be a perfectly coiffed bun at the nape of her neck; clothes threadbare and patched, hanging loosely on her starved frame. She was unable to change into anything resembling a wedding dress, though some of the children had snuck bits of greenery and flowers from the forbidden garden in the center of the fort. Frau Freidl placed tiny white buds into Hanna's hair and gave her a small bouquet of the lilies of the valley that grew wild and un-manicured in the garden. Samual felt it a shame to place a veil over her face for even a few moments. The signs of hard life were slowly melting away under the warm glow of her happiness, and he did not want to shade it for even a second. So when he was handed a thin lace handkerchief someone had scavenged to work as a veil, he handed it back with a polite thank you.

"I will not hide your beautiful face from my view," he whispered to Hanna. Instead of veiling her as tradition demanded, he kissed her softly on the cheek and walked to his place under the chuppah.

Hanna made the slow procession down the aisle. One of the guests—a stranger to both Hanna and Samual—brought out a fiddle and played a slow and soft wedding march on the strings. Hanna matched her steps to the notes, making the short walk last longer than Samual thought he could bear. After all those years of waiting to make Hanna his wife, he did not know if he could wait a minute longer. When she finally joined him under the makeshift chuppah, he could feel his own face glowing with happiness.

Tradition said the chuppah was symbolic of the home they would create from their marriage. Samual thought it was appropriate. It did not cover them, nor would they have a roof over their heads here in Terezin—not a roof that was their own, anyways. But they would find a way to live, just as their friends found a way to put this wedding and chuppah together.

While the four poles with the makeshift canopy did not allow for a lot of room underneath, Samual still felt the emptiness for a moment. This was the place where his family should stand. He should have walked down the aisle with his mother and father. Hanna should have been escorted by her own parents. But it was just the two of them. There was no way to even get word to their families about this wedding, nor had they heard anything from their loved ones in years. *Ironic, again,* Samual thought. He was marrying a woman his mother and grandmother would have approved of wholeheartedly, in the traditional Jewish ceremony that they'd always wanted for him, but they could not be here with him to see it. He refused to let their absence mar the day though. Even under German rule, he and Hanna were together. And that was all he needed.

Samual loved seeing the surprise on Hanna's face when Rabbi Leo continued with the exchange of rings. Just as he had originally planned, Hanna thought her diamond ring, with the corner sapphires and intricate scrollwork, had been used to pay off Nazi officials. Her eyes grew wide when Samual pulled it out of his trouser pocket. To her delight and his embarrassment, his hands shook as much as the day he first proposed. Once again, he dropped the ring. The guests chuckled softly at his clumsiness, but Hanna laughed out loud, a beautiful sound that reminded Samual of the chimes in Maisel Synagogue. She picked up the ring for him and pressed it firmly into his hand.

"After this," she said, "I'm not giving it back."

"And I'll never ask for it back," he promised with all sincerity. He placed the ring on her right index finger, in the Jewish tradition, and kissed her lips softly. Loudly, for everyone in Terezin to hear, Samual declared, "I am my beloved's and my beloved is mine."

♦

Hanna always thought that men were like paintings. When seen for the first time from afar, she was often mesmerized, breathless, and completely infatuated. But as she got closer, as she really studied the artwork, she started to see the flaws—where the colors bled together because of time or moisture, where the shadow was not quite conducive to the angle of light, how the artist didn't capture perfectly the crinkle of a smile or the gleam of an eye. Perhaps she was too critical. She expected too much; she wanted perfection. Men, too, often let her down when she got close enough to see their shortcomings.

She knew, standing under the oddest, yet most beautiful, chuppah she had ever seen, Samual was not perfect. He was not without flaws, but she had seen him up close and knew the painting for what it was. And she did not think she could ever love anything—or anyone—more.

This was certainly not the wedding that she had dreamt of as a little girl. She had no dress or veil. No tiered cake or flowers. No family to give her away. Her parents and siblings were most likely dead or sent east. But she was saying her vows to the man she would love long after death separated them. And she had a new family to celebrate this marriage with—the people they had met in Terezin, the children from class, and Frau Friedl, who stood next to Hanna with tears in her big, dark eyes, her arms shaking from holding the pole of the chuppah above her head.

Hanna felt no sadness or regret for what should have been if the Nazis had not upended their lives. She only felt love and happiness as Rabbi Leo read the first of the Seven Blessings. "May your journey together be filled with generosity and forgiveness," he read, his voice catching on the last word. "May you be committed to the paths of courage and hope. Blessed is the Source of Generosity who created such good, remarkable people!"

Samual squeezed Hanna's hands tighter, as she tried not to imagine the things in their future that would require courage and forgiveness.

The blessings continued to be read by their loved ones. Samual's friend from the building commando, with whom they shared the small attic, said, "Wherever you travel, wherever life may take you, may the love of your family and friends always echo in your hearts." He paused, taking a steadying breath. "Even across great distances and time. Blessed is the Source of Love who supports the edifice of love."

Though she had heard these blessings many times, she never realized how they would apply to her life during this global war.

Frau Friedl's voice filled the backyard synagogue next. "With the strength of your relationship, may you help transform the world in big ways and small ways. May your love for each other be a source of warmth and inspiration for your people."

Hanna felt the weight of what Frau Friedl was asking them to do—and on their wedding day, no less. Hanna knew that it was only because Frau Friedl believed their resistance, their fight against the Germans, was so important that it needed to be a part of their sacred oath.

Rabbi Leo finished the blessings with Hanna's favorite part. "May you always find refuge tucked within your love," he said. "May you find a place to hide out, a place to reflect. Blessed is the Source of Safety, who brings joy to this couple."

With those last words, there was not a dry eye in the place. Even in this celebration of love, the threat of the Germans rang strong. But all the wedding attendees rejoiced in the few things the Nazis would never be able to take away—love, hope, and the will to keep living and keep fighting.

There was no celebration after the simple ceremony, with there being rules against dancing and music and no meal to share with their friends. But all congratulated the newlyweds, though Hanna had never met many of them before. She did not begrudge them taking any opportunity to bask in another's glow of happiness and hope. She would not release Samual's hand, even as one or another guest pulled her into a friendly embrace. It wasn't until Frau Friedl, one of the last people to leave, engulfed Hanna in a hug did she release her husband and place both arms around her friend. They stood there for many minutes, until Frau Friedl finally broke away.

"You have been given a second chance," she told Hanna. "Marrying this dashing young man was a great step in making it count." Hanna grinned in agreement. "Make it count," Frau Friedl repeated. "I know you can."

When the last guests had left, Hanna and Samual made their way to their new home. The building commando was able to move them into the house beneath their solitary attic, though Hanna had come to love their bed in the cozy alcove they had made for themselves over the last few years. She had no mementos of this day, except for the contraband lilies of the valley she still carried in her hand. With his arm around her, Samual sheepishly apologized for not giving her the wedding of her dreams.

"When all this is over, we can redo it, with our families. We can have a real celebration."

Hanna shrugged. "Maybe we can do something, but this was practically perfect in every way."

Samual nodded slowly in agreement.

"Only," Hanna said, voicing her only regret, "I was sad to see Catarina missed it. I would have loved it if she were there."

Samual opened his hands for her flowers. "I'll prepare your bridal suite. You can try to find her. The children's messaging system probably did not reach her."

Hanna kissed Samual's cheek. "I'll be home quickly," she promised. "But I think I'll take these flowers to share with her."

It did not take long for Hanna to cross Terezin to the small apartment Catarina shared with her mother and two other families. She had walked the girl home many times from art class and stood on the street making sure she arrived safely. But the families were not to be found inside. Instead, nailed to the door of the apartment, Hanna found a pink slip of paper.

Chapter 29

CHAYA

She didn't know what being dead felt like. Maybe this was it. Cold. Hard. Hurt. She was lying on the floor. She could only see black, and there was a noise in her ears like the buzzing of a thousand bees. Past this hum, she heard soft cries and faint words. Her head hurt. Rachael never talked much about death and what exactly happened after this life, but she was very clear that there would be no pain—no pain, no hunger, no fear, no cold. She felt all of those things, so this must not be death.

She blinked several times, clearing the darkness from her sight and quieting the ringing in her ears. She was still in the dressing room. The room with the showers was empty. None of the people in the dressing room seemed to have entered it. Many were on the floor like Chaya. Most were crying, though some were smiling as tears ran down their faces. Chaya had never seen someone smile and cry at the same time. She did not know such a thing was possible.

The soldiers seemed as confused as the people—confused and maybe even a little frightened. They all had their guns at the ready, swiveling them around the room, pointing from person to person, but unable to settle on who was the true enemy. Chaya heard the soldiers and prisoners alike whisper the words: "Resistance." "Explosion." "Uprising." "Invasion."

She didn't know what these words meant. She could tell though, by the way they were said by the prisoners, that they were good. Soon, the door to the dressing room burst open. A large group of soldiers tried to enter the already-full room. They smashed into still-dazed prisoners with their shoulders and guns until they reached the back wall. Then they shouted in their harsh language for everyone to leave the dressing room. With warning shots fired into the air, the people were rushed back to the death barrack to see what was in store for them next.

They stayed in the death barrack for two nights. They were not fed, and the bucket of water they were given each morning was only enough for a few drops per person. Though she had never felt hunger and thirst as she did in those two days, she felt better than she had in months.

Chaya listened from her corner as people whispered rumors with eyes glowing like little suns. "They blew up the crematoriums," one said. "Took out two, maybe three of them."

"Who did?"

"A resistance group inside the camp," another said.

Chaya still did not understand exactly what the Resistance was, but after listening to more people talk about it with wonder in their voice, she decided it was a group of magical heroes, like the brave princes who rescued princesses from dragons and tall towers with their swords of steel.

"Now what?" someone asked. "Clearly the Germans defeated the Resistance, or we wouldn't still be in here."

This, also, did not make sense to Chaya. In the fairy tales, the heroes always won. But these people were not sad. They had cheated death once and now lived off the hope that they could do it again.

"It doesn't matter," many said. "It's beginning. People are fighting back. The end is beginning."

To Chaya, though, endings were not always good. And if these magical heroes of the Resistance could be defeated, the engine of death in Auschwitz was not to be stopped.

Yet Chaya found another hero, though she would never call her such. It was late in the second night in the death barracks. Many of the prisoners were asleep, but Chaya could only close her eyes for a few minutes at a time.

She needed to keep remembering all the things she would have told Rachael had they been together again. Now, with no one to tell, what would happen to those memories? Maybe they would float out of her body when she died, like white fluffy clouds drifting into the sky. Maybe the wind would carry those cloud memories out of Auschwitz, out of the dark countryside surrounding the prison, up over the blue sea that she was meant to live by, overhead to another girl her same age. Maybe that cloud would pour down the memories, like a warm summer rain. The girl would look up, and she would receive all those memories. She would know Chaya's name, Catarina's quiet eyes, the small baby's thin cheeks, the stories Rachael had shared, the ring that Rachael had cleaned every night and that Chaya had played with in the small squares of sunshine. Maybe she would tell her friends or parents or children someday, and they, too, would know of these people whom everybody else had forgotten, these people who had been filled with poison and turned into black ashes. It was a nice thought, and Chaya played it to herself over and over. She started to believe it. So, she would not sleep, because only by remembering over and over and over again could she keep everyone alive.

When the woman guard with the bullwhip—Elke, Chaya remembered—opened the door of the death barracks just wide enough so she could slip in, Chaya was awake. She saw the shadow of the guard. She did not see her face, and she did not hear the quiet steps, but she knew who it was because she could see the bullwhip's faint outline in her shadowed silhouette. She found Chaya quickly, as if she knew she would be hiding in the far back corner. She also seemed to know that Chaya was not asleep, because she did not lay a hand on her to wake her.

She whispered so quietly that it was more of a breeze against Chaya's face than real words: "Come with me, little one."

Chaya was usually afraid of the guards, even this one who had given her chocolate and other treats, but at that moment in the death barrack, Chaya had nothing left to fear. She was to die in the gas chambers. She had been preparing her memory cloud for two days. She wished she had more time to be sure that it worked, but she really was not one to complain. She sat up on the cot, placed her feet on the floor, feeling the ring still safely embedded in her heel, and rose to follow the guard.

Elke said no other words. She still did not try to touch Chaya. She placed her hand on the bullwhip, preventing it from swaying as she walked swiftly but silently past the other cots. She did not slow her pace as they made the long walk from the barracks, through two camps Chaya had never seen before, to end up at the old women's prison yard that Chaya knew so well. The guard cracked open a second door—this one to a barrack not far from the emptied one Chaya had lived in with Rachael—and motioned for the girl to enter. Then she closed it soundly behind her.

Chaya did not know why Elke saved her. For many days, she did not even realize she had been saved. The death barracks were emptied into the crematorium that next morning. The furnaces ran steadily for another few weeks, but Chaya stayed as far away from the billowing clouds as she could. Her old barrack was empty, and she could not find Irene. The only person she recognized in the prison was the woman from the soup line.

"I did not see you in the queue the last few days," she whispered to Chaya. "I was saving good bits of potato for you." She winked.

Chaya only nodded and took her bowl to sit by herself. She spoke to no one, and no one spoke to her, especially not the guard. Elke never even looked her way whenever they happened to cross paths.

After the explosion in the crematorium, it did not take long for the Germans to lose control of the camp. It seemed that every morning, Chaya woke up to less and less order; even the morning roll call was skipped one day. There were only a few guards left. She never saw them leave but knew they were now gone. After the guards started disappearing, the meal queue ended. Her new friend who dished out the soup had no food to give one morning.

The gates were still locked—they were still captive—but they had no one to guard them. Is one still a prisoner without guards and chains?

She had never lived without order. At the farmhouse, there was a strict routine. The rooster woke everyone up before the sun, and the smells of breakfast brought the whole family to the kitchen. Chaya would receive her small breakfast when Papa and the children went out to the barn to start their work. She would spend the day listening for signs of life outside of the house and observing from below as Mama worked in the kitchen, cooking, cleaning, mending, and teaching the girls. The night would end with a cheerful dinner above her head, the family chattering and laughing. Then, darkness would fall, and she would resume her spot on the cot, burrowing under the blankets. A surprise bit of food or trip outside to see the stars were the only things to disrupt this pattern.

In the camp, it was the same every day—a harsh wake-up call, a splash of cold water or a mug of something lukewarm, the long roll call, an even longer day of occupying herself while staying away from danger and the Germans, then a miserable and lonely evening of waiting to see Rachael walk home from work detail—and trying not to cry in disappointment when she never did.

All that regularity was gone now. She found comfort in schedule and routine, so she tried to keep it. She woke in the morning and lined up outside her barrack, waiting for the roll call that never came. She hoped that maybe someone would see her and tell her what to do next. But day after day, that did not happen. So she would stand at attention for as long as her legs would hold her still, which, with the soup queue gone, was not long anymore.

She was standing at roll call, alone, with no one to call out the numbers in lieu of names, on what felt like the coldest day of the year, maybe the coldest day in all of history. A few flakes of snow blew in the icy wind. She shook everywhere: her legs from weakness as much as from the cold, her toes inside the slippers and the hard wooden clogs, her fingers like icicles on the edge of a roof—stiff and ready to fall off.

On this coldest day, the gates of Auschwitz finally opened. Chaya stood at attention, watching a new army, new soldiers, new men with guns enter the camp. Her untrained eye could barely tell the difference between one captor and the next. These soldiers looked the same to her, except they did not have the fine creases in their soldier pants or the shiny black boots that the Germans wore. These soldiers, instead, wore a look of exhaustion and hunger that Chaya knew well. They had red on their shoulders—such a brilliant, bright color Chaya had never seen on clothing before. She had only seen brown and gray and green her whole life. She wanted to reach out and touch the red stripes on these new soldiers, but she was afraid—red to her meant blood, and blood meant death. Instead, she left the unattended roll call and hid in her favorite corner in the barrack she had shared with Rachael—a barrack that had long ago been emptied.

It was in this corner that Elke with the bullwhip found Chaya. Most of the guards had left a few days before—some taking prisoners with them, many taking food and treasures from *kanada*. Those few who stayed tried to help the prisoners—the sick ones left behind in the hospital, the starving ones unable to move from their cots, and the terrified ones, like Chaya, hiding in corners. Elke came to Chaya with slow steps. She held her hands out in front of her, showing the girl that she meant no harm. As Chaya watched her curiously, Elke dropped the bullwhip.

When she was close enough to touch the child, she knelt down in front of her and gently placed her hands on Chaya's knees.

"It's time for you to come with me," she said softly.

Chaya said nothing. This woman confused her. She knew the guard saved her from the gas chamber, but she was still a Nazi. She had still rounded up Rachael and marched her off and away. She still kept all these women prisoners in this camp.

The guard searched for Chaya's hand, hidden in the folds of her dress, and pulled her to her feet.

"I'm not going to hurt you," she said. "I'm your friend, remember? I helped you. I helped your mother once. I'm your friend." She moved Chaya toward the door. "Friend," she said again. "Remember that."

Elke led Chaya through the camp, past prisoners crowding around the new army and through fences that separated the camps, until she stopped in front of a new soldier. This one had red on a round hat that lay perfectly straight on the man's head. He had red on the tips of his collar. Elke brought Chaya so close to this man, she thought if only she was taller, she could touch those red triangles.

"This child," Elke said, "she's starving. Her mother was killed. Her father was killed. I saved her from the gas chamber." Elke looked down and patted Chaya's shoulder fondly. The sudden movement made her jump. The soldier's eyebrows twitched up at this. "I saved her. I'm her friend. She needs food. She needs a home. I want to take her home and care for her." His eyebrows twitched up even further. "I'm her friend."

Chaya said nothing. Elke without the bullwhip looked at her expectantly. She smiled, but the smile did not make Chaya feel good or safe. It was the same smile many of the Nazis used right before they swung their fist hard into a prisoner's stomach, right before Chaya would hear a cracking sound of ribs. She took a small step away from Elke.

"Your friend?" the new soldier asked. He spoke German but his accent was so heavy, Chaya struggled to understand him. He talked as if he had something rolling around in his mouth. Chaya wanted a closer look to see what was in there. He looked down at her. "She is your friend?"

Chaya gave the slightest shake of her head. She didn't think she meant to do it. It was a reflex, but this woman—though she may have walked her out of the death barracks—was not her friend. She was not her hero. Those were words that could only be used for Rachael. This woman took Rachael away. Because of this woman, Rachael was gone. Dead.

The soldier with red made a funny noise from the side of his mouth. Instantly two more soldiers were upon them. They grabbed the Nazi roughly, holding tight to her upper arms, the way Chaya had seen many a guard grab and drag away a prisoner.

"You ungrateful brat!" Elke screamed. Spit flew from her mouth in a spray of rage. "I saved you! You would be nothing but ash and bone if it weren't for me!" She continued to yell curses at Chaya, but the red soldiers were already pulling her away.

The new soldier knelt down on the frozen ground so he was eye to eye with her. "The Nazis are friend to no one. She was a liar." Chaya could not tell if the last sentence was a question or a statement, but she nodded in agreement. He nodded back and started to search the many pockets in his uniform. After a few seconds, he seemed to find what he was looking for. It was a small piece of something pink, the color of a person's tongue. "Doctor says I cannot give you food yet. He says it will make you sick. But, here, try this." He handed the small piece to her.

She took the pink thing between her fingers and pinched it. It was soft and firm at the same time. She felt a smile start to form on her face.

"It's chewing gum," the red soldier said. "You chew it. No swallow. Just chew."

Chaya did not understand chewing without swallowing, but she did understand chewing to make a thing last. The man mimed popping the gum in his mouth and chewing with exaggerated movements of his jaw. Chaya followed suit.

Since the doctors would not let the prisoners eat much, chewing gum from the new soldiers—Chaya eventually learned they were Russians—became her new favorite pastime. Many of the prisoners were terrified of the new soldiers, but she gravitated toward them. They were cruel to the Nazis, which Chaya did not find disturbing, and they were kind to her, always ready with a small bit of food or a piece of chewing gum. She hid less and less.

The ground started to thaw and the fields around the barbed wire fence started to show shades of green. She stood at the entrance to the prison yard. The gate was open and the grass on the other side called to her. The young woman from the soup line stood next to her.

"You can go out there," she said.

Chaya nodded but did not take a step toward the gate.

The woman placed her hand on Chaya's shoulder. "What do you see?"

Chaya looked up at her and smiled. "Green."

The woman nodded as if she understood all that the word meant. "If you look very closely, you can see all different colors in the grass. Shades of green. Maybe a little yellow. Brown. If I had paints, I would make the grass a rainbow of greens."

Chaya started to walk toward this rainbow. No one stopped her. The woman stood inside the gate, smiling. She waved once and went back into the prison yard.

Even though it was still cold, Chaya took off her wooden shoes and her wooly slippers, the left one now with a sizable hole in its heel where the ring had worn through the fabric. She marveled in the feel of the pokey grass tips and the slimy mud between her toes. She took the ring out of the slipper and fitted it on her finger. It did not look right, so she fit it over several blades of grass. She loved the colors of the blue sapphire against the green blades. After knowing that feeling of freedom for her feet, she could only be induced to sleep inside the fence on the coldest nights when she needed the barrack walls to block the wind.

Eventually, the American soldiers came. These were the heroes the camp prisoners had whispered about for months. Chaya immediately understood. While the Russians were kind to her, the Americans were fun. They always slipped pieces of chocolate into her hand and put their fingers to their lips, telling her it was a secret. They taught her to throw a small white ball. They gently tapped her on the shoulder and took off running, motioning for her to follow. With the added food from the soldiers and the sunshine and freedom of the fields, Chaya found the strength to run farther and farther. She did not understand the language these American soldiers spoke, but their smiles were easily understood.

It was the bluest day Chaya could ever remember when she and her friend from the soup line joined the Americans and most of the remaining prisoners to walk, one final time, out of the gates of Auschwitz. She did not understand where she was to go next, but she knew she couldn't stay there any longer. She was ready to leave. She wanted to start the journey that would end at the small house by the sea, like she and Rachael had always talked of.

Before the column of soldiers and freed prisoners departed, Chaya ran off alone to the field outside of the gates. She took off her shoes and socks—both new from an American soldier—and felt her toes in the dirt one last time. This was the land where hundreds, thousands, millions of people were resting. Their souls were in the sky, but their ashes had rained down and stayed in this field. This was where Rachael was. Chaya took out the ring and moved it around in the sun's rays. She had wondered for a long time what to do with it. Chaya knew that Rachael had given her the ring because she wanted Chaya to remember her, to remember her family. She wanted them to all live on. But Chaya did not need the ring to do that. Rachael and her family—even though Chaya had never met them—were inside her.

The ring was Rachael's, and it belonged with her. Using her hands, Chaya dug a small hole. She placed the ring in there and gently covered it with the dark soil. She watered the buried treasure with a few tears. But when Chaya stood and saw the march to freedom had started, she smiled wide. She ran to catch up with her new friend from the soup line.

"Can you tell me more about the different colors of green?" Chaya asked as they walked through the field, toward the trees.

"Of course," she said. "Is that your favorite color?"

"I think so," Chaya said.

"Green is a good one," she agreed. "My favorite color is white."

"White!" Chaya laughed. "That's not a color!"

The woman gasped in anger, but Chaya could see she was joking. "White is all the colors," she said. "It's where all the colors start. And," she leaned in close to Chaya's ear, "it's the color of new beginnings."

"White?" Chaya said. "Maybe that's my favorite color, too." The woman smiled and held out her hand. Chaya took it.

Chapter 30

HANNA

She stared at the white paper. It was no longer as pristine and perfect as the day Samual gave it to her—opening up a world that she thought was long closed in Terezin. It had been folded over and over with the creases making their own design in the paper. The edges were bent and starting to tear. It was no longer a clean white, but it was still empty.

She had never been able to bring herself to transform the blank canvas into something alive. She had so many ideas for it—the oasis that she and Samual had created in their little attic; the little office that was the original art room, full of children creating and learning; Frau Friedl's lively eyes as she showed the children how to express with just paper and pencil the joys and terrors they felt; Catarina's solemn and silent face that saw and understood everything around her. But now, most of those things were gone.

Hanna pushed the paper away from her, as she sat on the small bed she shared with Samual. She did not want to add the water stains from her tears to the other imperfections that had creeped onto her page.

Besides the attic room in which she was sitting, all her other inspirations were gone.

After the wedding, Catarina was gone—just another name on the long list of those who had disappeared without a trace. Samual spent the night comforting Hanna and trying to relieve the guilt that threatened to overwhelm her. On that night, she still did not know the extent of her guilt and grief. Had she known, she might have placed herself on that train heading east as she was intended. While she cried over the lost little girl, Frau Friedl, too, boarded the train, never to be heard of again. It was days before Hanna learned about her friend.

"I think she knew," Samual said gently. "I think her final words to you were meant to keep you going. To keep you hopeful. And defiant. Just as she always is."

Hanna appreciated that in her grief, Samual referred to Frau Friedl in the present tense, though they both knew that she was gone. Past tense. No more.

"Someone had to fill my number," Hanna cried. "Because I am here, she is gone."

"No, my love," Samual reasoned. "If she knew at the wedding, she received her slip days ago. She did not replace you. You were supposed to join her. Yet, she was so happy you were not."

How was she to ever know if that was the truth? Was Catarina on that train to fill the quota? Was Frau Friedl? If Hanna had obeyed orders, instead of skirting around them with a quick wedding to a respected building commando, would the two of them still be here? Those questions tortured her.

When she finally roused herself out of the attic, she went straight to the new art classroom near Frau Friedl's apartment. She wanted the comforting hum of children working on pictures and poems. She wanted the reassuring words and embrace of her friend. But the apartment was empty. The small scraps of paper usually left behind after a successful class were cleaned up completely. The errant marks of pen and paint on the floor and walls had been scrubbed clean. Any trace that this apartment had been a thriving community of young artists had vanished, just like its teacher.

Finding the door cracked open, Hanna searched her friend's former apartment for clues, but she did not need to find the slip of paper to tell her where Frau Friedl had gone. And she did not find it. Maybe Frau Friedl knew that bit of paper would finally break Hanna, when it seemed nothing else could. She did find two suitcases—the same one and another identical to the case she had first brought to the children filled with all kinds of makeshift canvases. The cases were locked, and there was a note asking that they be delivered to a woman Hanna had never met.

With her eyes so full of tears that she could barely walk straight, she carried them as directed. The suitcases were a light and easy burden. Hanna would never disrespect Frau Friedl's wishes by trying to look inside the locked cases. But she knew the cargo she carried. She had watched the teacher hide away every treasured artwork the children made since the beginning of their classes. Though many would think these works insignificant, Frau Freidl knew the importance of what the children had created. When Hanna found the right apartment, the woman nodded to her as if she had been expecting her and her strange packages. She took the suitcases and closed the door in Hanna's face.

Maybe she could use her blank canvas to draw the suitcases—worn from their journey from Austria to Czechoslovakia to Terezin, carrying what Frau Friedl deemed most prized: an outlet for the fear and horror and sadness the Jewish people experienced at the hands of the Germans. She could draw Frau Friedl holding the suitcases, shoulders slumped with the burden she carried. It could be a portrait of Frau Freidl from the back, walking away from this place. Then she could imagine her friend in a better place, a happier one, and she would not have to face those eyes—eyes that would never accuse Hanna, but were, nonetheless, impossible to face.

It was not just the guilt that Frau Friedl might have taken Hanna's place on the train, but that Hanna had not been able to transform the world, with big changes or even little ones, as she had been charged. Frau Friedl trusted her to continue this fight, and she had failed completely. Only a week after the wedding, Terezin was cleared of children. They received deportation slips, separate from their families. Hanna knew that some much braver adults tried to fight for them, and when that failed, insisted on joining the children. Hanna was not among them. She only watched in horror as her promising art students boarded a train heading east, heading to only God knew what terrors.

She held the stubby remains of a charcoal pencil, hand shaking slightly, over the paper. She did not know where to start and was scared to begin. This could be her last drawing.

She heard Samual hurry up the ladder into their small attic. His head appeared from the floor hatch.

"You're a commissioned artist!" he said proudly.

Hanna slowly lowered her pencil before looking at Samual.

He repeated his words.

Hanna just shook her head in disbelief and confusion.

"You've been commissioned, with a few other artists in Terezin, to make drawings, paintings, whatever, of Terezin," he explained.

"Commissioned by who?"

"The Judenrat," he said.

She frowned at him.

"The Nazis," he admitted. "They want artists to depict life in Terezin for the world to see."

"They certainly do not," she said with a bitter laugh. The Nazis, above all else, wanted the world to know nothing of the plight of the Jews. To say they would kill to keep their secret was an understatement.

Samual shrugged. "That is what Rabbi Leo told me. That, and that he recommended you specifically."

Hanna turned to the small porthole that served as their window. "I want nothing to do with anything the Germans have planned."

Samual crawled across the attic to sit by her. He put his arms around her and whispered into her ear. "Even if it means you'll have access to all the art supplies you could need?"

Hanna couldn't stay away from art any more than she could stay away from Samual. It was a part of her, and despite her distrust of the Nazis, she found herself part of a group of talented artists trying to find beauty in the place that had tormented them, starved them, murdered them for years.

It was a little easier to find such beauty as the Germans were actively making Terezin more livable. Samual learned that officials from the Red Cross were due to visit, and the Fuhrer wanted to show the world what a model community he had created for the Jewish people. Whether or not these changes would be permanent, no one knew. Hanna had her guesses, but she decided to take comfort in the improved living conditions while they lasted.

The improvements seemed to be vast. The trash was cleared from the streets, flowers were planted, buildings were repainted. The smell of death seemed to waft away between the cleaning of the remains and the fragrance of the newly planted landscapes. Fresh bread and green vegetables were distributed with the rations. Poetry readings and small drama productions that had been held in secret were openly encouraged to continue. People smiled more. The deportations seemed to have slowed, and the astounding death toll at the hospital eased. Between the full diets and sudden access to medicine, the hospital was not such a hopeless place for Hanna to spend her days. Best of all, the artists were supplied with all the materials and tools they needed, just as Samual promised. They were commissioned to portray Terezin, so that not only the Red Cross workers would be witness to Hitler's Gift to the Jews, but the entire world could admire the city.

Hanna was charged to paint the garden. In preparation for the Red

Cross visit, the park bench had been repainted, the path covered with small pebbles, the weeds pulled, and the grass cut short enough to invite a picnic blanket or a barefoot stroll. The lilies of the valley had been pruned and cultivated so that they looked like they had been planted with purpose by the Germans—hiding the truth that they were native to this land and grew in defiance of the Nazis' decree.

She had been given an easel, more colors than she'd seen for many months in Terezin, and a canvas that was larger than anything she would have dared to purchase even during her best days in Prague. Though the artists she had met through the project were renowned and some of the most talented in Europe, she felt little pressure. She was promised more canvases and paints to correct or restart the picture, until perfection was achieved. Of course, it was not her idea of perfection that mattered, but the Germans'. She had decided to paint the park at dusk, as the sun was setting behind the horizon. The pollen in the air glowed like fairy dust in the sun's parting rays. The white lilies of the valley took on tinges of purple and blue, like a bruise just starting to surface. The bench cast a long shadow over the grass, and the place was peaceful.

People had been encouraged in the last few weeks to visit the park, to treat it as a true public place. The Germans were smart and sly. They knew the newly pebbled path needed to look trodden. The grass needed indentations of picnic blankets and lounging forms.

But with the children gone, what was the point of a park anymore? The people could pretend to enjoy the flowers and the warmth of the sun, but all true warmth was gone from the ghetto when they shipped the last child off like a piece of excess cargo cluttering up a warehouse. The instructions from the Nazis were clear: the artists were to depict Terezin as it looked now, as the Red Cross hoped it would look, as the Germans wanted it to look. The outside world was not to know about the starvation and cruelty and neglect and torture and deportations and murders.

Even in her anger, Hanna could appreciate the quiet beauty of the park, though she was reluctant to admit it. In frustration, she looked hard at the garden, absentmindedly spinning the ring on her finger that she dared to wear openly since the wedding. She found that it didn't move as easily. Their improved diet was working wonders and plumping her up slightly—another falsehood that the Nazis were spouting in preparation for the Red Cross visit.

She moved her easel from one spot to another, trying to catch an authentic view of the garden—maybe some small clue that would reveal what it truly was to the people of Terezin: another cruelty. It was a place of refuge that they had been denied. But the labor crews had done their work. There were no imperfections, no remnants of truth.

Art was about truth; it was about showing life and people and places as they were, in their essence. She saw art not only as a way to portray beauty, but also to cut through the surface and show the realness underneath.

After she left the garden that first night with a still blank canvas, she expressed her frustrations to Samual. "It goes against everything as an artist to do this. I can't paint a lie." He nodded in understanding. "And if I play into the Nazis' hands, how am I helping our people? If we all act out this lie that Terezin is a Jewish paradise, the Red Cross will never know the truth, never help us."

Hanna was sitting cross-legged in front of the little attic window, looking out on the dark, empty street. It was a better sight than it had been just weeks before, but she knew those improvements, too, were artificial. Samual sat behind her, softly running his fingers up and down her back. Despite the anger and sadness and guilt, whenever Samual comforted her like this, she could purr like a contented kitten.

He kissed the nape of her neck gently. "Let's be clear about one thing—the Red Cross is not here to help us."

Hanna was surprised at his words—such stern and cynical words said with such a gentle touch. She looked away from the window and into his face.

"They want to see this lie as much as the Germans want to show it to them," he continued. "If they see the truth, they would have to step in. They don't want to step in. They are going to look at the surface, see what they want, and leave."

"And then everything will go back to the way it was?" Hanna didn't need to pose it as a question; she knew it all along. But it felt much more final, more depressing, hearing it from Samual.

"Just like it was before," he confirmed, again kissing her neck. "So it won't matter what you show the Red Cross. It won't make a difference."

Hanna rested her head against the cool windowpane in defeat. "But someone needs to know. Someone needs to know the truth of what the Nazis are doing. Even if they kill all of us—"

"They can't kill all of us," Samual interrupted. They both chuckled softly at his mantra. Hanna was sure he had long ago stopped believing it.

"Even if they do kill all of us," she insisted, "someone needs to know what they've done. Our people deserve that much. They deserve a history."

"Agreed," Samual whispered. "So, what are you going to do about it?"

Hanna went back to the park the next day at dusk. She painted the last strokes of the picture not long after the sun set completely and a sliver of moon was visible in the distance. It was a lovely picture, of an elderly couple sitting close on the bench and lilies of the valley creeping along the side of the canvas. It portrayed the false garden as Hanna saw it. Her fellow artists complimented her perfunctorily, but she did not take offense. She knew the picture was adequate but not moving. It had no heart.

She saved the true feeling for the blank page Samual had given her. She could have nicked an extra canvas and plenty of paints, but she decided to use the worn page instead. The medium alone told much more of the truth of life in Terezin than her entire painting of the park. With the creased page and a new charcoal pencil set, courtesy of the Nazis, Hanna drew what she really saw when she looked at the garden, even now with all its fresh makeover.

It was the garden of the last few years, growing wild—lush but overgrown flowers in some areas, sparse and burnt grass in others. The park bench was without paint or occupants and was lopsided from disrepair. The garden itself was a sorry sight, but the viewers' eyes were drawn to the small faces looking in from behind the locked gate. It was the faces of several of her art students, including Catarina with her deep, serious eyes. As sad as the park was, those faces and their wistful expressions were heartbreaking.

This artwork was just for Hanna and Samual. But she felt immensely better having completed it.

She was not the only artist who used the coveted supplies to create true masterpieces—works of art that told the real story of Terezin. This was the story the Germans would do anything to keep secret, including eliminating all the artists who had worked on the Red Cross project.

Unlike most of her new artist friends, Hanna was spared the terror of being pulled from her bed at night and dragged into the unknown, or as she assumed, into a vacant field where she was executed with a single gunshot to the head. Instead, she simply found a second deportation order.

There was no miracle this time. Hanna knew that. Her deportation orders were personal. She was no longer a number to the Germans, one more Jew to fill a quota. She was a name, a threat, a liability. She knew too much about the truth of Terezin, about the lie to the Red Cross; she had proven herself an unreliable secret-keeper of the Third Reich. But still, Samual took the pink slip of paper from her, kissed her forehead, and went to Rabbi Leo once again. Hanna held out no hope, but let her husband relieve his guilt by doing everything he could for her.

She did not panic this time. She was ready. When she set down her charcoal pencil after perfecting the last line of her drawing, she knew this—or something like this—was to come. One did not fight the Germans without consequence. She knew this when she thought of David, of Frau Friedl, even of the children they'd encouraged to put their feelings on the page. She only had one final thing to do.

She remembered the path she had walked, in a daze, to deliver Frau Friedl's suitcases according to her last wishes. Though Hanna was not usually good with street names or landmarks, it was almost as if she knew she would need to follow this path again. Her feet took her in the direction of the mysterious woman's apartment. She knocked only once, and again, the woman opened the door, like she knew Hanna was coming.

She held out the folded piece of paper—her opus—to the woman. "I have another piece to be included with Frau Friedl's artwork."

The woman looked at the page still in Hanna's hand and shook her head. "I cannot include it."

Hanna pressed it toward the woman. "You must," she said. "It must be seen."

"So show it," the woman said. Hanna was struck at this woman's coldness. She kept her hand with the paper extended. Finally, the woman sighed and pushed Hanna's hand away gently. "I cannot include it because I no longer have the suitcases. But that does not mean you can't show people the truth."

Hanna felt the fight that had kept her calm depart her all at once. She felt herself teetering on the edge of hysteria, like a paintbrush balanced precariously on a pallet, soon to tumble into the abyss. "How?" she said in a small whisper.

The woman looked apologetic for the first time. "I do not know. But people need to see it—whatever it is. If it shows the truth, then it must be seen. That is how we will go on after this."

With shaking hands, Hanna unfolded the page and held it up for the woman's inspection. Hanna did not know if this stranger was an artist, but this felt like the most important critique she had ever faced in her career. The woman looked at the drawing for a long moment, bringing her face closer to the black and white lines.

"Thank you," she said softly. "Thank you for showing me."

Samual came back that afternoon looking triumphant. In his left hand, he carried her pink notice of death. In his other, he carried his matching orders.

What does one do when facing death? She had never truly asked herself that question. Perhaps she should have, since life these last few years had been barely a notch above survival. She had kept herself going with Samual's love and strength, with her small reasons to smile, with a persistent hope that she would somehow keep escaping death. Though she laughed or even rolled her eyes when Samual said it, she still believed that the Nazis couldn't kill all of them. How could they kill an entire race of people without anyone stopping them? So while she still thought it may be true—the Nazis couldn't kill all of them—she knew now that they could certainly kill her. And Samual.

She refused to let her last hours of life be full of self-pity. She and Samual held each other for a long time in their attic oasis when he came home with their twin deportation orders. They kneeled on the hard boards, arms around each other, their heads barely touching the sharp incline of the roof. Hanna matched her breaths to Samual's soft exhale that moved the stray hairs on her neck, and buried her face deeper into his chest. She thought she could spend the last days of her life exactly like this and feel no regrets.

As the sun set and darkness fell on their last night in Terezin, Samual roused them from their numbness and led Hanna by the hand outside. She thought to protest, to say something about curfew and rules and what would happen if they were caught, but stopped herself. What would happen if they were caught? Nothing worse than they were already facing in the morning. So they stole through the darkened streets, savoring a few final memories of their life together.

Samual took her to the park—the same one that she had depicted in her drawing. It was only days since the Red Cross had completed their visit, but the park was already resorting to its original neglect. The paint was holding on the bench, but the grass had quickly outgrown its trim.

Weeds were popping up again, and the lilies of the valley were creeping past their manicured edges. Samual led her to the middle of the lawn and pulled her down so they were staring past the few trees, into the night sky.

As they looked up at the stars, she felt the pressure of the moment. These stolen minutes could be some of their last together. She needed to make them special enough to last her a lifetime. This memory had to get her through whatever lay ahead of them to the east. Torture? Starvation? Separation? Death? She needed to fill this time with Samual with enough love to sustain her for days, weeks, months, years to come.

She knew he felt the same because the contented silence that they usually enjoyed felt pressurized. It was growing with tension. She felt tears start to burn her eyes, not with the thoughts of tomorrow but with the fear that she was ruining this last moment with Samual. She wanted to say everything in her heart—how her life was complete only with him in it; that he was her rock and comfort and best friend and lover; how she would have given up and died long ago but the thought of him and of their life together gave her hope and determination; that she would hold on to that hope and love no matter what came next. But neither of them were much good at sentimental speeches. Hanna knew how to tease him with her words and love him with her touches. Many of their most moving exchanges had taken place in silence, with her lying in his arms and matching her breath to his.

But touches fade. Only seconds after his hand released hers, Hanna would lose the feel of his heat. She needed words to recite back to herself during the most trying times to come. She needed a mantra to repeat when the sound and tone of his voice had faded from memory. Words would sustain her in the future, but in the present, they were failing her.

So she spoke of something that they'd always had a common love for—beauty.

She nudged his shoulder lightly and pointed up to the night sky. "Do you see that star?"

His eyes followed her finger, squinting with the effort to find the correct star.

"I need more instruction than that," he whispered.

"There's a small cluster of stars here," she pointed again. She spoke of a small patch of sky pinpricked with faint lights. This cluster didn't shine brightly like so many other visible stars in the sky, clear and intense as the burning of a candle. The ones she pointed to were more like the muted glow of coals slowly burning out.

"I see the cluster," Samual said.

"Do you see the blue star?"

"Blue star? In the cluster?" He continued to look.

"It reminds me of my ring," she said.

"The blue star . . ." He was still searching.

"That cluster of stars is just like my ring . . . White diamond shining from the farthest reaches of the heavens, but with blue mixed in. My ring is the only one like it in the world. And you can search this entire sky and find no other blue stars." She pointed again. "That star is special."

"I can't believe you still have that ring," he said.

"It has not been without trying," she teased. They continued to look at the special cluster of stars. "But I'm not worried about losing it," she whispered. "I don't see how I'll be able to keep it from the Nazis tomorrow." She felt the tears coming again. "But I'm not worried, because I have that blue star. No matter where we are, the stars in the sky are the same. So I'll be able to find my blue star, and I'll see my ring."

Samual fiercely wrapped his arms around her, crushing her face into his chest. She let him hold her for a minute before she gently pulled away, freeing her face to speak again.

"So let those Nazis take my ring."

♦

The crowd of people with matching pink orders—slipped under the doors, set atop mattresses, hand delivered by a shame-faced member of the Judenrat—stood silent at the train station outside of Terezin the morning of their deportation. Hanna looked at the many people and the few Nazis. It was the first time she had seen a Nazi since entering Terezin. They had grown in her imagination into beasts that barely resembled men—razor sharp teeth, grunts and roars rather than speech, tall and muscular like the ogres in children's stories. But in the gray morning light, they were none of those things. If they had not been holding machine guns and wearing looks of pure hatred, she would have thought them just boys. If the people around her had just a shred of fight left in them, just a glimmer of hope, they could charge these boys playing war and win their own freedom. Hanna saw the revolt in her mind, but knew it was useless. There was no fight or hope left.

And how could the people feel anything but fear? The Nazis herded the people into the train cars like they were no better than pigs being led to slaughter. The crowd was quiet and clearly compliant, but the Nazis still fired their guns into the air, shoved those unlucky ones on the edges of the crowd, and used the butts of their rifles to beat down any person they thought was moving too slow. The train car was metal with a sprinkling of straw on the ground. At first Hanna thought it was meant to act as bedding, but as the soldiers pushed more and more people into one car, she realized they had no intention of letting them rest on this trip. Samual held firm to Hanna's hand, gripping it so tightly she was sure there would be bruises. The ring cut into the bones of her fingers, but like when she walked from the train station into Terezin, the pain kept her present in the moment. He tried to shield her from the mass of people pressing in all around them. She had never been afraid of tight spaces, but after this trip, she was sure that would be changed for the rest of her life. She kept her face flattened into Samual's chest. She focused on just his arms around her bony shoulders, trying to ignore the feel of strangers against all sides of her body. Her nose pushed so tightly into him that she had problems breathing deeply.

She had never known cold before that train journey. She had never known hunger. She had never known exhaustion. She had never known despair or fear and complete hopelessness. The train never stopped. The air that had been an early winter chill in Terezin became a constant freezing wind that pierced through the slats of the train car. The Nazis did not give out food, nor did any resident of Terezin ever dream of having enough to bring any with them. There was a bucket of water in the corner of the car, but it was emptied quickly. Hanna was sure the Nazis were just going to take them east until the train drove off the edge of the world or they all died of starvation and cold. She was unsure which she wished for.

There were times when she tried to sleep—briefly when she and Samual were allowed a few minutes of rest on the floor of the train, but mainly while standing on her feet with her lungs inhaling the scent and feel of Samual. Other times, Samual would whisper to her, bringing up their favorite attic oasis conversations—plans for the future, fond memories of their happier days, long and detailed accounts of his favorite architecture in Prague. He would ask her about works of art—pictures she had created, ideas that festered in her brain still unfulfilled. He had her rework her final masterpiece over and over—the picture of the garden in Terezin as she had seen it every day for years. That picture now hung by a nail in their cozy space where she had managed to find a sliver of happiness in Terezin. Only once did she cry. Though she was surrounded by sobs and wails of grief and terror, she only let her shoulders shake silently with her own overwhelming doubts once, and only when she was sure Samual was safely in the land of slumber where he could not worry about her.

Finally, the train started to slow down. Hanna and Samual had been standing, his back against the cold metal of the train car, his arms wrapped around her, for what seemed like days, or weeks, or even years. The system of human consideration had broken down ages ago, so Hanna and Samual were not allowed their turn to sit. With people pushing against them on all sides, though, it did not take much energy for Hanna to stay on her feet. Her legs could have given out completely and she would still have been upright in Samual's arms. As the train slowed even more, Hanna saw an elderly woman Samual had helped into the train car. She was slumped in the corner, her head rolling around with every jerk and sway of the train. In fact, every part of the woman's body moved with the motion of the car, as if she had lost all support from her muscles. Hanna buried her face back into Samual's shoulder as she realized the woman must have died recently.

The train stopped. She was out of time. She pushed her head even further into his shoulder, hoping to shut out the cruel world around them. Into his collarbone, she whispered, "I'm sorry, Samual."

Though they stood among an unbelievable number of people, with the eerie silence and her eyes closed, Hanna could imagine they were alone. Samual's grip around her tightened just slightly. "What do you have to be sorry for, my love? I'm not sorry for anything."

She turned her head into his neck. "This is all my fault . . . If I hadn't worked with the other artists . . . If we hadn't made those paintings . . ."

"Then we wouldn't be here?" Samual finished. He squeezed her again. "We would have ended up here anyways. That was always their plan for us."

"But maybe it wouldn't have been now," she insisted. These were the words she wanted to say to him the night in the park, but she had been too terrified that he would blame her like she blamed herself. Now she knew she could not part from him, possibly forever, without admitting her guilt. "Maybe we would have had more time."

"Maybe," Samual agreed. "But if they hadn't caught you, it would have been me."

Hanna tilted her head back so she could look Samual in the eyes. "You?"

He gave her a hint of a smile and kissed her nose. "For an artist, you are extremely unobservant," he teased, giving her a taste of their old banter. "I was smuggling food into the ghetto since we arrived. But everyone was getting desperate and sloppy. If they hadn't caught you, they would have soon caught me."

"You? You were smuggling food?" She was shocked, not just at Samual's activities but because she'd been so lost in her own fight that she never realized what he was up to.

"So, I must also apologize." Samual's eyes begged her for understanding. "I just could not stand by anymore. I couldn't—"

"I know," she said. "I know. Me too."

"We would have ended up here anyways. It's not your fault," he said.

"Nor yours."

"Nor mine."

The train jerked suddenly, pushing the people against her back. Samual grunted as the crush pushed him harder against the metal train wall. They started to hear shouts from outside.

Samual squeezed her suddenly, forcing the breath out of her lungs. "You'll make it through this," he whispered frantically in her ear. "You'll survive. I know it. I can feel it."

"You too," she started.

"You will make it." This time his words were more of a command than an encouragement. "You will survive. They can't kill all of us."

The train door opened, and Nazis started pulling people out of the car. The first few were so surprised that they crashed to the ground outside. The Nazis kicked at the fallen ones and continued to pull people from the train. What had been deathly silence just moments ago erupted into a living nightmare.

"They can't kill all of us," Samual repeated. "You will survive."

Hanna tried to tell him that she loved him, that they would be together at the end of the war, that he, too, would survive this. She wanted to repeat his words: "They can't kill all of us." She wanted to tell him goodbye, but she couldn't bring her mouth to form the words. She knew this goodbye could mean forever. Their words were drowned out by the sound of machine guns fired into the air. The mass of people moved them from their quiet corner of the train car into the madness of Nazis shouting, dogs snarling, and people shrieking in terror.

Hanna had often heard of the end of days, when beasts would devour the people of the earth, when fire and brimstone would rain upon the land, when humanity would be lost to all the powers of evil, when the sun and moon and stars would no longer shine. She had read those words. As she was pulled from the train car onto the ground, she knew she was living them.

Soldiers with guns and dogs were dragging people from the trains and pushing them into lines. Those who fell were stampeded by their own people, or beaten by the soldiers, or left to be devoured by starving dogs. There were screams and cries and brutal German words filling her ears. She wanted to cover them to block out the pandemonium, but she would never let go of Samual's hand. She gripped it as her only lifeline.

In front of her, a young man limped along, hurried by the soldiers. He tripped and tumbled face down into the dirt. Hanna went to help him up, but Samual jerked her forward. As she turned to see him, he was kicked in the back by a Nazi. He cried out but did not move to get up. The soldier kicked him again, this time in the back of the head. The boy did not cry out a second time but remained motionless. Samual continued to pull her forward with the mass of people, and she lost sight of him.

Ahead, Hanna could see the people being separated—men to the left and women to the right. She saw an older couple refusing to be pulled apart, but three soldiers unleashed their bullets on them, making the lovers convulse and their bodies ooze rivers of blood. They collapsed together, their limbs and blood mixing into one lifeless pile. Hanna held on to Samual's hand with both of hers.

The line was moving too fast for her to say anything. Tears were pouring from her eyes, and her stomach was trying to heave up all the food she had not eaten in the last few days. She was unable to breathe.

Her thoughts were blank. She knew she should say something to him, look into his face one last time, feel his arms around her or his lips on her, but he was gone. One second she was clutching his hand with all of her might, and the next second she was holding nothing. She did not possess the strength to keep him with her. She was pushed into the crowd being herded to the right. With hundreds of people panicking and running in terror, she did not even get one last glimpse of him.

It was at that point that she was sure she had died. While her legs continued to move her forward with the crush of people, her mind marveled at how painless it was. She didn't feel the shot or hit or bite that ended it all, she thought. All this time running away from death, but it was nothing to be afraid of. It was nothing at all. That's what she felt: nothing. She shuffled with the others, not feeling their bodies press on her, nor hearing their wails of fear and despair. She just continued to move forward, wondering if Samual, too, was dead. She hoped he was so they would be together.

Ahead of her, the mass of women straightened into a line. It was not the organized, tidy queue that characterized life in Terezin, but it had some semblance of order, with the Nazi soldiers barking and shoving people into place. Hanna remained dazed as she moved closer and closer to a table, where an older, almost kindly looking German sat. She watched the man—not far from her grandfather in age, she imagined—calmly inspect each woman as she stood weeping and pleading in front of him. He motioned each soul to the left or to the right.

Feeling started to return to her. Her heart still felt like nothing more than a void, but she realized she was anything but dead. The instinct to remain anything but dead gripped her, though she tried to fight it. The first sensation that her body registered was the soft mud under her. Her shoes sank into the ground as she trudged closer to the man sitting in judgment. Logic would have told her that the earth was wet from recent rain, but in her muddled state, she was sure it was saturated with the tears and blood streaming from the people around her.

Screams of pain jolted her back to this life. About a dozen women in front of her, two soldiers were holding tightly to the arms of a gray-haired Jewess. She was trying to scream, but it came out a gurgled and muffled cry. One of the soldiers had a metal tool in the woman's mouth. With a strong tug and a laugh, along with the woman's long moan, the tool—a pair of rusty pliers—pulled out a gold tooth. Hanna heaved at the sight of blood spurting from the woman's mouth and the soldier hoisting the gold piece, still in the grip of the pliers, over his head like a trophy.

It was then that she remembered her ring. Brazenly, she still wore it on her finger. In the madness of loading onto and off of the train, no Nazi had yet noticed. But, as Hanna glanced at the older German still studying and judging the line of women one by one, she knew her luck had run out. Just as she did the night before in the garden with Samual, she felt a surge of pride in her ability to trick the Nazis this long. They had tried to take everything from her, but they had failed. And though she had no hope of holding on to the ring any longer, they would still fail.

For a moment, she imagined her beautiful ring on the finger of some Nazi sweetheart or being tossed into the pile of other precious items stolen from the Jews—later to be sold or melted down to supply the Nazis with more bullets or guns or bombs to annihilate her people. She could not bear it.

With her eyes never leaving the German dealing out life and death, she slid the ring off her finger and popped it in her mouth. She would swallow it and keep it with her, deep inside her, for all time. But dehydration and fear made it impossible for her to swallow anything. She continued to move up the line. The man ushered two more women to the right—sisters, Hanna thought, by the look of them. They bowed their heads slightly in gratitude for being kept together. Together in life or death, though, Hanna did not know. Discreetly, Hanna brought her hand to her mouth and released the ring into it.

She closed the diamond in her fist, giving it the final squeeze that she had been unable to give to Samual. She felt the cold metal kiss her sweaty palm. She wanted to grip it so tightly that it would leave a lasting impression, cut her skin, forever scar her. But she hadn't the strength. She did not even have the time to give her ring one final memorizing look, as the crush of women continued to press her forward toward a set of metal gates that read: "Work Sets You Free."

Hanna knelt quickly and placed the ring on the ground. As she straightened up, she placed her left foot overtop the ring, sinking it into the soft earth. Her ring—the token of love Samual had given her. Her ring—his gift to her, representing the thing he had loved most before Hanna, Prague, their home. Her ring—her symbol of light and hope against the Nazis.

The cries and screams of chaos became muted around her. She felt herself surrounded by an eerie silence. The women in front of her continued to move down the line, sorted right or left. Life or death. Death this way or death that way. Hanna pressed her foot deeper into the mud, letting the filth rise around her shoe and leak into the holes of her well-worn and poorly patched leather pump. The thought of where Samual was now paralyzed her, choked her, devastated her. So instead she focused on her ring, still connected to her by the sole of her foot. She saw in her mind the cut of the stones and the shine it gave off, even in these darkest times and under the grayest of skies. The she pressed her foot down harder, imagining the mud turning her shining diamond and sapphires dark, the miniscule particles of dirt blending into the complex scrollwork until the entire ring was one piece of hardened earth and stone.

She felt the numbness of utter loss when she thought of Samual. But as she lifted her foot out of the mire and took a step away from the ring, she felt victorious. The ring was buried deep from the Nazis' grasp. No matter what lay ahead of her, she had won in this small matter. They had not taken the ring from her. And, she thought as she neared the front of the line, if she could beat them in this, she could beat them again.

EPILOGUE

With the sun high in the cloudless blue sky, it was difficult to imagine the horrors that this place once held. Katherine kept glancing up to the sky to remind herself that beauty still existed in the world. During this trip with her mother and grandmother, it was easy to forget her now seemingly carefree days at university. And yes, she could admit it to herself, she was afraid to enter the gates.

"Work Sets You Free," it said.

But it was a lie. Work never set her grandmother free. Though Grandma rarely talked about her time in Auschwitz, Katherine knew from her own research that the Russians set her free. Work almost killed her. That and starvation, depression, and of course, for many, the gas chambers. Katherine admired her grandmother as she easily walked through those gates, with the black and white traffic arm permanently propped open. She leaned heavily on the arm of Katherine's mother, but her head was held high.

And here Katherine stood, outside the gates, afraid to go in. She admonished herself. Her grandmother had lived through a year of this hell, and Katherine was too terrified to even set one foot inside. She had grown up with the knowledge that her grandmother was one of the few to survive the Holocaust. And she knew the woman she called Auntie was in Auschwitz with her grandmother, but walking into this place made it too real for her. She would just wait outside in the sunshine and grass.

It was impossible for her to imagine her grandmother and aunt in this place—shorn hair, lice-ridden, little more than skeletons in rags. Actually, it wasn't impossible for her to imagine. She had done enough research in her history classes to see it perfectly. Rather, she did not want to imagine it. Her grandmother—who always armored herself in the best clothes and shiny red lipstick, even at her current age of eighty-six—she never belonged in a place like this.

Grandma rarely talked about her experiences during the war, and especially about her time in Auschwitz. Katherine was almost a teenager before her mother told her that her aunt was not an aunt by blood, but by love, as her family put it. It wasn't until her grandfather passed away a few years ago that more family secrets were revealed. Grandma casually mentioned one day that she had been married before. That first love of hers had died in the gas chambers of Auschwitz. Katherine assumed that she did not speak of this first marriage out of respect for her loving husband who provided for her for almost fifty years and with whom she had three healthy children. When he passed though, she slowly started to open up about the life she lived before this one that included Katherine.

That brought them here. They traveled across Europe to visit these places that Grandma once knew—some that she loved and some that haunted her nightmares. She had walked them through the different quarters of Prague, pointing out buildings and statues that had aged better than herself. They even took a guided tour of Terezin, the ghetto in which Grandma lived for years. It wasn't until after they walked out of the former fort that she quietly told them she had been married in a small patch of grass behind an old bakery.

Today, though, was the hardest. Katherine knew her mother had mixed feelings about reliving this with Grandma. It was difficult to hear about a life before the family she recognized. Maybe her mother was even a little jealous. Was Grandma happier before the war, with this mystery man who breathed his last in Auschwitz? No doubt, her life would have been drastically different if both of them had emerged from this hellhole alive.

Late last night, after Katherine's mother went off to bed, she posed these questions to her grandmother. Was it the role of grandmother that made her so wise? Or maybe it was all the experiences she had lived through.

"I regret nothing of my life," she told Katherine, patting her hand gently. "Everything made me who I am today. I don't let myself think much of what might have been. What is the use? What might have been? Who knows? All I know is what is. The concentration camp brought me your aunt. Then, we had a wonderful life after the war. I found a man I loved very much. I had children. And now I have grandchildren. This is a life I could never have imagined for myself when I was in the concentration camp. Yet, I lived it. What more could I ask for?"

"Do you miss him, though?" Katherine persisted. "Your first husband?"

Grandma's eyes were misty. "Every day." She was silent for a long while. Katherine thought the conversation had ended, when she spoke again. "But he also made me part of who I am. And thinking about him, though I miss him and it makes me sad, it also makes me smile. And when you have something in your life that makes you smile, you never regret it."

Perhaps Grandma did not regret the short time she had with her first husband, or even her time in the ghetto and concentration camp, but Katherine regretted it for her. It was especially difficult to help her grandmother place flowers on the mass grave outside of the Auschwitz gates. Katherine's mother had spent the better part of the morning searching the nearby town for just the right flowers. Grandma insisted she did not need assistance, though. She asked them to stay behind as she finally got a chance to properly say goodbye.

Watching her walk away with the bundle of flowers in her arms, Katherine thought her grandmother looked twenty years younger.

Her spine was straight, she walked with no limp from the arthritis in her knees. She carried the flowers like a bride walking down the aisle to a grinning groom. But when she reached her destination, she dropped roughly to her knees. Katherine made a move to go to her grandmother, but her mother's arm stopped her.

"She needs this time alone."

They watched quietly and from afar as Grandma spoke softly to the grass where she could only pretend the remains of her first love lay, because really, no one knew. Katherine imagined that her grandmother filled this man in on her life—the job she worked at for years, the husband who took her to the ocean every summer, the children who made her proud, the grandchildren who made her laugh. She imagined that Grandma told him how much she loved and missed him every day. Then, Katherine watched as her grandmother kissed the tips of the flower petals before laying the bundle of lilies of the valley in the grass. When she walked back to Katherine and her mother, she looked twenty years older, with a tear-stained face.

And that was the crux of the matter—Katherine could not bear to see her grandmother look so defeated again. So she stayed outside of the walls of Auschwitz, admiring the sun and the grass as the other women in her life moved to the barracks inside the gate. Katherine moved off the path leading to the gates proclaiming the way to freedom. She did not want to stray far, but she let her feet pull her into the lush greenery. She wondered how the land around such an awful place continued to grow and be fertile. She expected the horror and depression and death to seep into the ground, poisoning it like salt, making it inhospitable to any life. But the land had bounced back—like her grandmother, Katherine supposed.

Her mind was full of her grandmother when she noticed the sun's light reflecting off a stone in the ground. She walked past it but had to admire how the stone struggled to reach out from the shadows of the surrounding grass and to bounce back the sunshine through the black dirt of the ground. She bent down to see this defiant stone, daring to shine in a world of shade, only to find it was more than a stone. It was a dazzling ring—still glimmering despite the obvious years of living in the soil. She used the hem of her shirt to clean the grime from the crevices around the stones and the scrollwork on the sides. As she admired it, she heard her mother and grandmother coming toward her.

Her mother held Grandma's hand tightly as she said, "I'll never understand how you survived in such a hellhole."

Her grandmother answered, "I don't think I ever will either. All I knew was they could not kill all of us."

AUTHOR'S NOTE

(This contains spoilers)

Diamonds in Auschwitz is a work of fiction, but like all my favorite books, grounded in much fact. The idea for the story came like a strike of lightning. I read about a woman who had held on to her engagement ring throughout her time under Nazi rule and while living in the Jewish ghettos. As she entered the gates of Auschwitz, she could not bear to let the Nazis have it. So she pushed it deep into the mud before going through the selection line.

That image of a beautiful, valuable ring in the mud outside the worst place on earth stuck with me for a long time. I started to think about what it must have taken to hold on to something so precious—the ingenuity, the determination, the bravery. Then I thought about how finding a treasure like that could change someone's life. Of course, the ring had no monetary value to a prisoner in Auschwitz—she couldn't eat it or barter its true worth. But in my mind, there's always a value to beauty and art.

This story is about that: how something beautiful could keep hope alive in a place so ugly.

That was the story that came to me as one big lightbulb. Then I started researching, and the rest of it came bit by bit.

I started backward with Auschwitz. I learned about the people who populated it, the awful conditions in which they lived, and where they'd originally come from. That took me to Prague.

Prague. Wow. After learning about that city—its history, its architecture, its position during World War II—I wanted to make that place its own character in the book. In a book about beauty, I could not have stumbled upon a more perfect setting than Prague, the City of a Hundred Spires.

The city was mostly spared from the horrors of war, compared to other occupied cities, in the beginning. But when Reinhard Heydrich came into power, things deteriorated quickly for the Jews of Prague. He worked hard to sow seeds of discord between the Jews and other residents of the city, by offering free lunches and pay increases to non-Jewish workers. This in no way justifies but helps to explain Werner's actions when he betrayed David. Also, fear can make people act in terrible ways.

Jews were often beaten by the Nazis, then denied medical treatment, as happened to Alexey. Young boys, falsely accused of a multitude of crimes, were rounded up, forced to write a final letter to their parents, and never heard of again. Rachael's torture of never knowing what truly happened to Radek was very real for many parents.

The descriptions of Prague and its architecture are the (much enjoyed) labor of research. If the story reads like I am in love with the St. Charles Bridge, the synagogues and churches, the parks along the Vltava River, then I have succeeded. I am, in fact, very much in love with all of Prague.

Prague led me to Terezin, the Jewish ghetto set up outside the city. (The Germans called the ghetto Theresienstadt. I chose to use the Czech name for authenticity to my characters . . . and because it's easier to pronounce.) It was mostly populated with artists, musicians, writers, and professors.

Once I started diving deep into my research of Terezin, I discovered the facts about art lessons for children in the ghetto. The lessons did happen, and displays of the children's art can be found in museums around the world, including the US Holocaust Memorial Museum in Washington, DC. I actually based Catarina's work off pieces in the book *I Never Saw Another Butterfly*, a collection of drawings and poems from the children in Terezin. Friedl Dicker-Brandeis did smuggle in scraps of paper, lead the art classes, and then make sure the works were smuggled out of Terezin when she was deported to Birkenau. Of the 15,000 children deported from Terezin to Auschwitz, only 100 survived.

Before their deportment, many of the children helped smuggle food into the ghetto, as Samual said. They placed the packs of food on their backs, often looking like hunchbacked children.

The Red Cross visit was also based in fact. The Nazis worked hard to make Terezin look like a model community for the Jews, replanting the park, increasing food rations, and commissioning artists to create fake pictures of life in the ghetto. Sadly, life didn't just go back to normal after the visit; it got considerably worse.

The acts of the Germans on the train platforms, both going to Terezin and to Auschwitz, were based in fact as well, including Hanna's assault and the fate of Rachael's unnamed baby.

Last, Chaya's saving grace when facing the gas chambers did, in fact, happen. Near the end of the war, resistance workers within Auschwitz succeeded in blowing up one of the crematoriums. While the revolt was quickly stamped out, it gave me a chance to show the inside of the gas chamber and the real fear of the people facing it, while still saving Chaya.

I hope these places and characters—both fact and fiction—show you as much beauty, hope, and resilience as they have shown me. I hope you find inspiration in these diamonds in Auschwitz.

ACKNOWLEDGMENTS

I always thought writing was a lonely business, but when I reflect on the people who helped me get here, I'm not lonely at all.

First and foremost, thank you to my family, Phil and Luci. Phil—my high school sweetheart—you support me in every way possible, from appointing yourself as my own personal CFO to giving me many, many pep talks when I thought this dream was one I can never accomplish. I love you and couldn't do any part of this life without you. To Luci—my girl—you are the artist that inspired this book. You are the Chaya (which is Hebrew for "life") in all my stories and in my world.

Thank you to my first readers: Cassie, my number one reader and friend, who may have read this book more times than I have; my mother, who called me halfway through the book worried about David (I told her if she's worried about David's fate, she may not want to finish the book . . .); my wonderful friends from book club (Allison Slabaugh, Olivia Critchlow, Peg Dalton, and Stephanie Cerney) who gave me the confidence and encouragement to be vulnerable with my writing; and Paula Neidlinger, for her mentorship, guidance, and tireless work to make me (and my website) look amazing.

Thank you to the many others who have supported me just by being my friends (and family). Just asking about the progress of my book kept me going during some of the lonelier moments of writing: my father,

Michael Anderson, Rachel Mundell (my Rachael namesake), Lisa Boyle, Brandi Smith, Hannah Nichols (Hanna's namesake), Rachel and Josh Stewart (also my professional medical advisors), Dale Hamand, Scott and Jan Heeren, Jean Ann Tenney, Shari Lewis, Suzy Elliott, and Cindy Hamand (my champagne toast buddy).

    Now on to the list of people who turned words on the page into a real book. I'm so grateful to the team at Greenleaf Book Group for taking a chance on a debut writer. Thank you especially to Ava Coibion, Benito Salazar, Erin Brown, and Tenyia Lee.

    Last but certainly not least, much heartfelt thanks to you, the reader. Thank you for reading this book out of the countless amazing books out there. Thank you for spending time with Rachael, Hanna, Samual, and Chaya. Thank you for turning these few words on a page into a story.

ABOUT THE AUTHOR

Meg Hamand has had a heart for storytelling since her first poem was published in an anthology in elementary school. Since then, she graduated with a degree in English and creative writing from Indiana State University. She's been published in multiple print and online publications and recognized in the "Michiana 40 under 40" by the South Bend Chamber of Commerce. She lives in Northern Indiana with her high school sweetheart, daughter, and miniature dachshund, Nixon (named after Captain Nixon from *Band of Brothers*, not after the president).

www.ingramcontent.com/pod-product-compliance
Lightning Source LLC
LaVergne TN
LVHW041620060526
838200LV00040B/1360